THE DAY AFTER NEVER

ISBN-13: 978-0989475549

ISBN-10: 9780989475556

Cover Design by Damonza.com

Author photo by Jennie Thunell Photography
www.jenniethunell.com

Skylighter Press, St. Petersburg 33704
Printed in The United States of America
First Edition 2016

Subscribe to series updates at:
www.nathanvancoops.com

Books By Nathan Van Coops

In Times Like These

The Chronothon

The Day After Never

THE DAY AFTER NEVER

NATHAN VAN COOPS

Skylighter
Press

St. Petersburg, Florida

The Master Speed

No speed of wind or water rushing by, but you have speed far greater. You can climb back up a stream of radiance to the sky, and back through history up the stream of time. And you were given this swiftness, not for haste, nor chiefly that you may go where you will, but in the rush of everything to waste, that you may have the power of standing still-off any still or moving thing you say. Two such as you with such a master speed, cannot be parted nor be swept away from one another once you are agreed, that life is only life forevermore, together wing to wing and oar to oar.

— Robert Frost

"Time is a dangerous ocean, and we are all adrift. Each of us will reach a moment when we find ourselves on the wrong side of time from those we love. Whether by a day or a decade, the current shows no mercy. But I believe time is an ocean with borders like any other. One day we will all come ashore together."-Journal of Dr. Harold Quickly, 1992

CHAPTER 1

The Neverwhere

I once wished for a painless death.

I regret that wish. A stab of suffering would have marked the transition—a final fierce debate with the darkness, my body still screaming live! live! live! right to the very end. A torment's end would have at least brought closure, some sense of passing. Instead, I'm left wondering if this haze around the edges of my mind is really what's next or if I am merely witnessing my final failing synapses in a particularly leisurely fashion.

If I'm not dead, I damn well should be.

I'm a time traveler who broke the rules.

In order to continue one's existence, the laws of the universe dictate basic prerequisites like having mass and occupying space. They demand in no uncertain terms that you obey physical laws such as gravity, momentum, and thermodynamics. The real stickler, of course, is that one stay confined in time. Causes must precede effects, and under no circumstances should one shirk the bonds of time entirely.

That's the rule that got me into trouble.

I don't know where I am exactly. I should say, rather, that I don't know *when* I am. Where is familiar enough. This is the room where I died.

The St. Petersburg Temporal Studies Society has a very academic feel to it. Old bricks meet louvered windowpanes along one side of the room. There is a chalkboard. The tables and sinks around the room are speckled with the residue of unwatched experiments bubbled over and hastily wiped up. Aprons dangle in a row near the cupboards and plastic face shields hang on hooks near the eyewash station. It's missing a few elements from when I was here last—primarily the bloodstains and the party guests.

I died in a particularly public and festive environment, full of champagne glasses, cocktail dresses, and passed hors d'oeuvres. I was suspended in midair at the time. I'm not now. My sneakers are resting comfortably on the laminate floor.

I find the fact that I have sneakers on simultaneously comforting and disconcerting. Familiarity suggests comfort, but the presumption that I ought to be dead makes me nervous. I hadn't thought they would let me into Heaven in worn Adidas and a T-shirt from *The Gremlins*. Perhaps the guardians of the Pearly Gates have lower standards than I suspected. That or I have found myself somewhere else. The thought of the common alternative makes me less than enthusiastic. Could Hell come with multi-colored chalk and safety glasses?

I check my wrist.

No chronometer.

There will be no blinking out of this place again. Not that I imagined that would be possible.

I pull out my pockets. All empty.

It's not how I recall them being when I died. Exactly the opposite in fact. This place has not received everything I took with me, it seems.

Wherever I am, no one is here to welcome me. It's eerily quiet. Dead silence would be an appropriate term. Silent as a tomb? Also accurate and equally depressing.

I take a step.

I don't feel especially dead. I'm not having trouble breathing or hearing from what I can tell. My mind is definitely foggy, though. Actually, everything is foggy, especially through the windows. Hazy. Dreamlike even. Can't see much of anything out there. Seems odd for Florida. It's rare to get dense fog here. I wander into the hallway. I've been here before, too, on a tour.

My first visit to the St. Petersburg Temporal Studies Society is burned rather vividly into my brain, my friends and I hoping to meet the father of time travel, Doctor Harold Quickly. We were desperate then, trying to find a way home. We didn't meet him that day, however. Doesn't look like I'll be finding him today either. Every room I poke my head into is vacant. There is a fish tank in the lobby producing bubbles but no sign of fish. If this is the last-minute flashback of my life just prior to my death, I got the low budget version. I'll have to have a few choice words with the director. I push my way out the front door.

The glistening fog outside is even denser than I saw from the lab. A few cars line the sidewalk beyond the wooden sign for the building, but beyond that is just nothing. The fog is more colorful than I'm used to. If it's refracting light from somewhere, I have no idea how. There is a hint of blue above me, but even that seems vague. No sun.

A few yards into the fog on the street I'm forced to stop. I can't see a darned thing. Looking back at the lab I can still make out the building's details. I have to admit that's strange. Directional fog. I take a few steps back toward the building. Curiosity and nervousness are losing ground in my mind to regret and unease. I don't know what's out there in the fog, but I can tell it's not going to be what I want to find. The only thing still keeping the fear of the unknown at bay is the memory of why I'm here.

I came here for a reason.

I came here for her.

St. Petersburg, Florida- 2009

They say you can't love a machine.

I respectfully disagree.

I think we all get one. One seemingly inanimate creation of steel and glass and shiny chrome that transcends its physical limitations to connect with our soul. One machine that understands us.

Or maybe I just really like this motorcycle.

The object of my affection is beautiful but flawed. Even in its current state it makes more sense than most of my life. I fiddle with the ignition wires and run my fingertips under the fuel tank. With the seat up, the tank pops loose easy enough. I tilt it forward and peek underneath. Somewhere in all this bundled electrical wiring, I've got a short.

The motorcycle is older than I am, though she doesn't look it. In her heyday in the early '70s, the 450cc Honda was the coolest bike on the road. This particular bike didn't get to experience much of that time. Someone bundled her away into a garage with less than 2,000 miles on the odometer and she sat collecting dust for the next few decades. Lying abandoned among other forgotten treasures, she waited while her contemporaries cruised America's blue highways. By the time someone's son—who didn't have a motorcycle license, but did have a Craigslist account—found the bike, the glory days of the '70s Honda were gone.

She's still gorgeous. Needed spark plugs, battery, and a new dose of fluids, but once I got her home and wiped the dust off, her chrome was still shiny. She's a fresh-faced beauty half a century from her own era. That's where I can relate. She's out of touch with time, and just a little bit broken. I run my hand gently across her rear fender.

"Should I be jealous?"

I look up to find Mym leaning on the doorframe of the open garage door. She's smiling and lovely. Her blonde hair is curled away from her face and she's regarding me with crinkles at the corners of her radiant blue eyes.

"Just tinkering. It's good riding weather."

Mym surveys my oily hands and dirtied cargo shorts. "You almost ready to go?"

"Is it five already?" I snatch up a rag and begin to wipe my hands.

"You need a few more minutes?"

"Yeah, just a few. Gimme fifteen and I'll be good."

Mym smiles and pulls the chronometer pendant from the neckline of her dress. "Okay. I'll be back." She moves a step away and presses her hand to the garden fence. Then she vanishes.

I stare at the empty space she's vacated. Even after all my prior adventures, the sight of someone time traveling still leaves me in reverent awe. Maybe it's because it reminds me that it wasn't all some illogical but convincing dream.

I drop my tools back into their respective drawers in my toolbox and close the garage door. I trot up the stairs to my apartment above, and cruise through to the bathroom, shedding clothes as I go. The summer breeze is humid and blowing through the open windows. I don't bother to let the water warm up—I just let the cool stream douse me. When I emerge a few minutes later, wrapped in a towel, I find Mym leaning on the edge of my bed and browsing through novels on my bookshelf.

"That was fifteen minutes?"

Mym raises an eyebrow and double-checks the clock on the wall. "Twenty. I was being generous. Someone's not as efficient as he thinks he is."

"I'll have to talk to Abe about slowing down your chronometer." I toss the towel at her and walk into the closet. It takes me a while to find anything decent to wear because my wardrobe options seem depleted. I vow to make time for laundry soon, and when I come back out I'm dressed in jeans and a button-down shirt. I finish fastening the top two buttons in front of the mirror. "Where are we going again?"

Mym sets *The Neverending Story* back on the shelf and looks me over. "We were going to check out the 1996 US women's gymnastics team at the Olympics, remember? I wanted you to see Kerri Strug land that vault. The energy of that moment was just amazing in person."

"Oh, right. That sounds awesome. I think I'm ready. Do we need tickets or anything?"

"We'll pick some up on the way back. You can find a ton after the event is over. We'll recycle a couple." Mym winks at me. "Since we can't get to 1996 on one jump, I thought we might swing by and see Phelps win his gold in Beijing on the way." She rummages through her bag and extracts an anchor for us to use. "Round out the Olympics-themed date night." She tosses the anchor to me. I'm surprised to find that it's an actual bronze medal.

"This is real?"

"Amazing what people will sell on eBay." Mym pulls a degravitizer from her bag and starts degravitizing a different anchor that is much more mundane—a four-pronged steel fork. Using the metallic, Mag-lite shaped degravitizer, she removes the gravitite particles inside the fork so it will be ready for use as an anchor. Since only things with gravitites in them can time travel, the fork will stay behind where we left it, and we'll arrive at another time in its life in the same relative location.

When the green light on the device finally illuminates, Mym references a photo of the fork on a table so we can orient ourselves for landing. It looks as though we'll be arriving in an area where a bunch of tables have been arranged with place settings.

"We're getting dinner first?"

"Yep. Dinner in 2005, entertainment in 2002 and 1996, and home in time for bed. Don't you love dating me?"

I lean over and kiss her. "I like the final destination especially."

I clasp my fingers through hers and feel something rigid on her finger. Holding it up, I inspect the silver ring on her right hand. "Someone buying you jewelry? Who's my competition?"

"I've had this one for a while. Gift from my dad when I turned sixteen. Hardly competition."

I almost say that she just needs a ring for the other hand, but hold myself back. "I know. Dad's little girl, right? No competing with that."

She smiles and strokes my cheek once before turning back to her task with the anchor. She arranges it on my writing desk at a height where it will match our destination table and we touch our fingertips to the fork. I dial the concentric rings on my wrist-mounted chronometer and Mym uses her own pendant chronometer. She counts off for us as we get ready to press the activation pins. "Three, two, one."

Time traveling is instant. Just a blink and we arrive on a shaded outdoor patio next to a table set for two. The table is in a quiet back corner of an otherwise busy restaurant. Diners are being served seafood entrees and chatting loudly over a background of blues music. I spot a security camera on the roof and wonder if that is how Mym got the photo of this anchor location. My attention is brought back to the present by Mym's snort of laughter. Her hand is over her mouth, trying to contain her mirth.

"You forget something, Ben?"

I follow her gaze down to my chest, which has suddenly become bare. "What the—"

A few other restaurant patrons have turned their attention to our back table now, following Mym's laughter to the sight of my half-naked form. They stare at me in curiosity, leaning toward one another. A few fingers point in my direction, guiding more eyes to my current embarrassment.

"Damn it." I try to recall which shirt I had put on. Whichever it was, it clearly didn't have any gravitites in it and is still lying on the floor in 2009 where we made our jump. I look back to Mym who is smiling and shaking her head. I frown. "I'm sorry, babe. I didn't realize I put on the wrong shirt. I really need to get my wardrobe up to time traveler standards."

"It's okay. I kind of like this look on you." Mym smiles and brushes her fingertips across my chest before stepping past me and leading the way toward the exit. "Come on, we'll sort it out." I follow her through a wooden gate at the side of the patio and onto the sidewalk, away from the lingering stares of restaurant patrons.

The warm streets of Atlanta are busy with pedestrian traffic. Mym starts thumbing through images on her MFD. The multi-function-device is about the size of a phone but contains many of her time traveling apps, including a photo collection of available free-standing anchors in different years and timestreams. She holds one image up for my inspection. "There's a lamppost over on Peachtree Street that we can use to get to a year where Dad has a stash of other anchors. He might even have a shirt you can borrow. Shouldn't take long."

I nod at a pair of ladies in sun hats who cast sideways glances at me as they pass. One mutters behind her hand and the other woman laughs once they are past. As they breeze by me, my mind suddenly goes fuzzy. My vision dims slightly and I teeter, trying to keep my equilibrium. *Oh God, not this again.* Out of the corners of my eyes the world around me is getting . . . foggy—a shimmery sort of haze. I concentrate on Mym, still rummaging through her phone in front of me. I reach for her shoulder, a way to ground myself to this reality and keep my balance simultaneously. Mym looks up.

"You okay?"

Looking into her eyes, the dizziness passes.

"Yeah, I'm good." I let my arm drop back to my side. "Hey. Do you mind if we just head home? I know you wanted to show me the Olympic highlights and I think it's a super-great date idea, but I could use a night off. Ever since I got back from the chronothon, we've been going somewhere fancy every night or seeing amazing events in history and—I'm not saying I don't love that—but I could use a break, too."

Mym lowers her MFD. "It hasn't all been fancy. The Olympics are pretty casual, actually. Fancy would be Queen Elizabeth II's coronation, or—"

"You know what I mean though, right? Maybe we can just put in a movie or something. Hang out on the couch?"

Mym considers this and nods. "Sure. We can do that." She smiles. "I could bring my database over. I have the Twenty-Second Century Academy Award Collection on Immersion 4D—"

"Or . . . maybe I could just pop in a DVD?" I grin at her.

"Or that," Mym says. "That sounds fun, too." She lays a hand on my arm. "Ben, I'm sorry. I forget sometimes that this is all new to you. I'm not trying to overwhelm you."

"You're not. These last couple weeks have been great. So great. I really appreciate you showing me all these amazing events. I just . . . kind of need a little bit of my own life mixed in, too, you know?"

"I totally get that. Come on. I'll find another anchor we can use and we'll go back to your place. From here on out we'll do some things you want to do. I'll get to see a normal day in the life of Ben Travers. It'll be fun."

"Thanks. I promise it's not as boring as it sounds."

"I do get you shirtless on a couch, right?" Mym smiles and leans toward me. "I can get excited about that."

I lean over and kiss her. "Deal. We'll make the couch a clothing optional space."

Mym laughs and leads the way onward. "Race you there."

"Time travel may offer a way to skip birthdays or revisit favorite years, but there is no escape from getting older. At the end of every day, no matter what era you are residing in, your life is passing into memory. Memory is our greatest treasure and I've found it's the only one worth hoarding. Luckily it's worth even more when shared." -Journal of Dr. Harold Quickly, 2013

CHAPTER 2

The Neverwhere

There are voices in the fog. I heard a shout. It was muffled, but could have been someone arguing. It's gone now. I thought the silence was more unnerving, but now I'm not sure. As much as occupying this strange space alone is disorienting, there was a sense of security when I thought I was the only one here. I might be dead, but it's hard to be scared of yourself. Other dead people? That's a different story. Especially if I can't see them.

I've attempted three laps around the Temporal Studies Society building now. I can't make it all the way around. I can see three sides of the building but the fog on the one end is so thick I can't even see my own hand in front of me when I try to move forward. I've given up trying. Growing up near the water, I've been pretty familiar with fog, but this stuff is beyond any level of humidity I've ever encountered. The thing is, it's not even wet. It's just nothing. Vaguely colorful nothing.

I concentrate my efforts on the side of the building where I can see the best: the front. Outside the front door of the Temporal Studies Society, I can see grass, cars, even road signs. One end of the street is dense fog, the other is clear. I stare down the clearer route. I've come that way enough times. I know that end of the street pretty well. Turning to the west I see only a wall of fog and mystery.

I finally decide to move east and stay in the center of the road. If I follow this far enough I can make it to my neighborhood. The idea of home is the only comfort I can find in this place. I may not be in Heaven, but I'm in St. Petersburg, and that's close enough. I know people here. Or at least I did. Whoever is making noise out there in the fog may not be a personal friend, but I don't have any reason to suspect that they're some demonic imp or harpy, so that's something.

The houses around me vary in clarity. At some points the fog is thicker than in others, mostly in the center of blocks. Intersections seem to stay a little clearer and the main streets like Ninth and Fourth are clear as can be. I trot up the steps of the Tropical Smoothie at the intersection of Twelfth Avenue and look in the windows. It's all clear inside but no people. No cars driving up and down Fourth Street. Normally I would be taking my life in my hands jaywalking across Fourth Street, as it's a main thoroughfare. Today I just stand in the middle of the road and no one is there to notice.

I break into a jog heading east into my neighborhood. I pass homes with yards that ought to have dogs barking at me, but the locals are nowhere to be seen. As I near my apartment, the fog is nearly dissipated. Little wisps linger in backyards and under apartment stairwells, but the sky is blue above me now. The moon is even visible, a three-quarter view calmly traversing the daylight sky. I can't help but feel encouraged.

The spare key is hidden under the flowerpot where it always is. I trot up the stairs to my above-garage apartment and unlock the doorknob. It swings open freely and reveals the undisturbed interior. Home. I slide the deadbolt shut. Whatever is out there in the fog can stay out there. I don't need them. Here I will find some answers. I'm sure of it.

My garage apartment is typically sunlit and spacious. The perimeter of windows normally lets in plenty of light but is high enough for privacy from the street. One of my ex-girlfriends used to refer to it as "The Tree House." It's home turf, the site of innumerable gatherings of friends, parties, and activities. Now I scan the silent rooms looking for any sign of life at all. A few fish have co-habitated with me over the years, usually acquisitions from some carnival ring toss game or another, but my landlord hasn't allowed other pets. Right now the fishbowl in the corner of the kitchen countertop is only occupied by the trailing roots of my philodendron.

My fridge is bare. That seems pretty normal. There may not be much in the way of food inside but the freezer is still humming. Ice cubes in the trays. There is nothing out of place other than the sheer absence of other people.

I step back into the living room and spot my flip phone on the coffee table. The light on the corner is blinking. *Messages.* I lunge for the phone and open it, dialing my friend Francesca's number first. If anyone will believe me without question, it will be her. I wait for the ringtone, but nothing happens. I try again to no effect. I check the signal bar and try 911, waiting with shaking hands for someone's voice or even an automated menu. It doesn't come. I curse and throw the phone at the couch cushions. *You useless piece of shit.*

In the back of my mind, the logical part of me is berating my lack of sense. Dead people can't use phones. *Who are you going to call? Ghostbusters?*

I stare at the phone and fume. The light on the corner is still blinking. I ignore my own nagging logic and snatch the phone back up. Two voicemails from work. I hit the play button and wait impatiently for my boss's voice. I haven't been at work for a few days. She's probably furious. I've never been more excited to hear her voice.

The phone stays silent. I stare at the progress bar in frustration and tap the play button again. No sound. I curse at the phone and try another method. I dial my own phone number into the phone. *Come on, just someone's voice. Anyone.*

The phone is ringing.

Oh God, it's actually ringing! I clutch the receiver closer to my ear and hold my breath. *Come on. Work.*

The line picks up. Dull static fills the other end.

"Hello? Is there someone there?"

I get a chill up my spine and shiver. The phone line goes dead.

Come on. I was so close. I dial the number again.

Work. Please work.

The phone rings six times. Then static again.

I dial once more, stubbornly optimistic that something will prove this feeling wrong.

This time I get nothing. The phone gives me only silence in reply.

No.

I don't want to be dead.

I don't want to be dead.

Shit.

St. Petersburg- June, 2009

We've only made it fifteen minutes into the movie. On screen, Mikey and the rest of the Goonies have just discovered the treasure map in the attic. I'm more intent on Mym's bare legs draped over my lap and her hands grasping my T-shirt and dragging me closer to her horizontal position on the couch. I let my lips detour to her neck and ears before finally reaching her mouth. Her kisses are firm and warm, and her hand slips under the edge of my shirt to my back.

"This needs to come back off. It's so hot in here." She starts to tug at my T-shirt and I laugh.

I trace my fingertips over her legs to the edge of her dress that has ridden up her thighs. "Maybe we can both shed a few layers." I smile and start to remove my shirt, but stop when the phone starts ringing on the coffee table. I stare at it with annoyance, then stretch to try to reach it.

Mym frowns. "What are you doing?"

I kiss her and swing her legs off me. "I'll just turn this off so it doesn't keep bugging us." I lean over and snatch up the phone, pressing the volume button to silence the ringer. I glance at the screen and glimpse the number. "That's weird."

"What is it?"

I flip open the phone and hold it to my ear. "Hello?" The other end is just static. "Hello?" I wait a second longer, then close the phone again. "Huh. I've never had that happen before."

"Is someone calling you?"

"No. The phone number it showed was mine."

"Voicemail?"

"Maybe. I do have a couple I need to listen to. But I've never had my own phone call me before." I set the ringer to vibrate, put the phone back down, and lean toward Mym. "Where were we?"

Mym smiles and runs her hand up my arm. I lean in farther, angling toward her lips. I stop as the phone starts ringing again. "Damn it."

Mym's smile fades.

"Sorry. I swear I put this thing on silent." I grab the phone again and glance at the screen. It's still my own number calling. I let it ring in my hand a few more times before finally flipping it open.

"Hello?"

Static.

I slowly close the phone.

"Ben? What are you doing?"

"Sorry. Just trying to stop it from bothering us."

"It wasn't ringing."

"What?"

Mym is staring at me cautiously. "Your phone wasn't ringing."

I look from her to the phone and get a brief chill up my spine. I pop the battery out of the back and toss it onto the table. I set the phone down gently in front of me and watch it, half expecting it to ring again. I can still feel Mym staring at me.

I raise my eyes to the front door and the leather jacket hanging on the coat rack next to it.

His jacket.

On the TV, Mikey and his friends have tied Brand to the chair with his workout equipment and are escaping on their adventure to the sounds of Cyndi Lauper.

Mym sits up and props her hands on the edge of the couch cushion. "Talk to me. What's going on?"

"I'm sure it's nothing."

It doesn't feel like nothing. It feels like one of my dreams.

"He's still trying to talk to you, isn't he?"

"I don't know. Maybe I'm just tired."

Mym frowns at me. "Ben—"

"What? What am I supposed to do? He died. I don't have the foggiest idea how to deal with that. It's not like I can change anything. I can't undo the past. I get that he saved us but if I go back and undo that, I'll just ruin everything he died for in the first place. It's hard, but he's gone. It's not my fault that I made it out and he didn't. I shouldn't have to feel guilty about that."

Mym is studying my face. "I doubt he's trying to contact you just to make you feel guilty."

I put my hand back on Mym's leg. "Whatever his issue is, it's not like I have to deal with it right this second."

Mym frowns and moves my hand off her leg. She stands and straightens her dress, tugging the hem back down toward her knees. "I think we do need to deal with this. Do you think he'd ignore you if you were calling?"

"He's not really calling. I'm just imagining things. And yes. He's me, so whatever I do is probably exactly what—"

"I know you, Ben. "

"*I* know me. I *am* me. So if he's dead then he should just deal with that on his end. That's what I would do. I just finally got my life back here. I'm trying to get things back to normal, not turning my phone into the Psychic

Hotline. I just want a little bit of peace. Is that so much to ask?"

Mym crosses her arms. "So you're just going to do nothing? Let him take the fall for us and not try to help him?"

"No. I'll help. Eventually."

"When? When you feel like you've got nothing better to do?"

"We're time travelers. We have all the time in the world."

"You know that's not how it works."

"Look, I just want a little time to have my own life back. I want you, and I want a normal day where we can just hang out without some alternate version of me butting in."

"He's not butting in. He might really need your help. Sometimes when you get stuck out there on your own, you just really need someone to listen and to be there for you."

"That's fine, but he needs to wait till I've had a chance to get my life back the way it was."

"*Your* life. That's all that matters."

"No. That's not what I meant. Look, I don't get why you are so concerned about this other me out there. Is this version of me not good enough for you or something? Why can't you just not worry about it right this second? I get that he was the version of me that saved the world and everything, but I did my part too."

Mym glares at me. "If that's what you think, then you really don't get it." She snatches up her sunglasses and flings open the door, disappearing down the steps.

I sigh and follow. "Mym, wait up." She's halfway to the sidewalk by the time I catch her. I grab her elbow and spin her around. She has tears in her eyes. She yanks her arm out of my grip and smacks me in the chest.

"You can't abandon people just because it makes your life complicated, okay? If you think that I would want to be with someone who—" She flails at me again and I catch her wrist this time, finally realizing that this argument isn't just about the other me. I grab Mym around the shoulders and pull her to my chest. She struggles briefly, but then collapses into tears, suddenly sobbing against my shoulder. "It's not fair to do that to people. You don't know how it feels . . ." She chokes back her tears, her face buried in my chest.

We stay like that, still for a few seconds. A bit of pollen from the oak tree lands on Mym's hair and I brush it away, smoothing the strands behind her ear. Finally she speaks again, quietly this time. "Please don't be like that. Don't be like *her*."

"Who?"

Mym merely sniffs in response. I wrack my brain for what Mym has told me about her past. *Is she talking about some other version of her? What other woman is she . . .*

"Your mom?" I tilt my head to try to see Mym's face. She has a hand to her cheek, trying to stem the flow of tears. "What happened?"

Mym lifts her head and runs her hand across my chest, pausing on the wet spot she's made on my shirt. "I'm sorry."

"It's nothing. Tell me what happened."

Finally she raises her eyes to mine. "She made a decision. Just like everyone does. She just didn't choose us."

"You and your dad?"

She nods. Then shakes her head. "No . . . it's complicated. We got split up. She wanted to just hold onto life the way it was . . . and dad tried to go back for her, only . . . things had gotten twisted and we were already there. Another version of us."

"And there was only one of her . . ." I take hold of her hand. "How old were you?"

"I was a baby. Well, toddler, I guess. Not quite two."

"Do you remember her?"

Mym sniffs again and wipes at her eyes, trying to shake off the emotion. "Not from then. But I saw her again. Later." She looks up at me, considering my face, perhaps deciding whether to tell me the rest or not. Finally she continues the story. "I knew dad checked in with her, asked her advice. For a while they made decisions together about how he should raise me. Schools I should go to. Things like that. It was always hard to keep away though. I ran away once to go visit her and saw how she was with the other me. Dad hated that I did it, but I had to see her for myself. He told me not to—that it would just make it harder. And it did, but that didn't stop me."

"Did you talk to her? What did she say?"

"She said, 'The heart isn't meant to be split in two.' And she's right. She's always been right. It's too much. Taking me in would have meant either taking me away from my dad or having two husbands in her life. She made a hard choice, but she never should have had to. And that's why it's just been dad and me for so long, because he got that. He knew what it was like to lose the most important person in his life, and then—when he died—I wasn't supposed to go back, but I did. And you made it work, but I lost him anyway.

"It's not the same as it was. He has to divide his time now, too. And just for once—for once—I want someone to choose *me*. I want someone to choose me, and to stay."

"I *am* choosing to stay. That's what I want more than anything. I'm just trying to go back to a normal life."

"That's what I'm afraid of. What happens when *we* get complicated?" She shakes the tears from her hand and backs up a few steps, letting my fingers fall from hers. "What happens if being with me disrupts your normal? If you're not going to be able to handle this life, then you need to tell me right now. I can't do this again. I'm not going to get left on my own. Not again."

She stares at me with glistening blue eyes, tracks of tears down her cheeks.

"You're not going to lose me. I promise. I'm back. I'm not going anywhere." I let my hands rest on my hips. "It's not like we can't solve this issue with my—dreams. I'm sure I can get him to stop bothering us. I'll just figure out what he wants . . ."

Mym sighs and turns away. "He's you, Ben." She pulls her chronometer from her shirt and places a hand to the street sign next to the driveway. "So you need to figure out what *you* want."

The next moment she's gone.

I stare at the vacant space for a few seconds, my brain stubbornly refusing to process anything else.

"Son of a bitch. Why does time travel make everything so damn difficult?"

I kick a piece of bark back into the neighbor's yard. "Is it so hard to just meet a nice girl and be happy? No, you had to pick a time traveler. . . and then die. And *then* not stay dead. Stupid idiot." I tromp back up the stairs and slam the door.

I stare at my dismembered phone still lying on the coffee table. *Has it gotten so bad that I'm just imagining things?*

There is a knock on the door behind me. *That was fast. I guess she changed her mind.*

I swing the door open and find a young man standing on my porch surrounded by a mound of luggage. The man's freckled face is exuberant. He's wearing an outfit that involves pegged, acid-washed jeans, a flannel shirt tied around his waist, a neon green tank top and Velcro sneakers. One of his arms is glistening with what appear to be a few brand new tattoos, and he has made an attempt to grow a beard, though only a few reddish-brown patches have shown up for the job. He's trimmed the sides of his head short but grown his hair long on top and parted it in the middle, a style reminiscent of Jonathan Taylor Thomas circa 1994. He grins and drops the bag in his hand to reach out to me.

"Ben! I made it!"

"Tucket. What are you doing here, man?" I start to accept his handshake, but he switches to a fist-bump at the last minute, leaving us at an impasse momentarily while I sort out how to respond. Finally we bump fists and he laughs.

"You said I should come look you up when I graduated from the Academy. Two-thousand-nine! I'm so STOKED to be here!"

"Ah. I did say that, didn't I . . ." I open the door a little wider and survey his pile of bags. "Looks like you brought your . . . life, with you."

"I wasn't sure exactly what I might need so I thought I'd better bring it all, you know? I've been studying twentieth and twenty-first century culture, but I wanted to make sure to fit in."

I notice his left hand has a sparkling silver glove on it. "You're doing a great job so far." The last time I saw Tucket, he was assisting with my visit to the Academy of Temporal Sciences during the chronothon. Perhaps it was because he was working at the time, but I had not been subjected to his enthusiastic clothing choices. I check the street to see if any of my neighbors have noticed him and step aside so he can enter. "Let's get you indoors."

Tucket gathers up his assorted belongings and shuffles through the door. I take one of his bags that's in danger of springing loose and lead him to the second bedroom that I've turned into an office.

"I guess I can set you up in here temporarily. The futon is reasonably comfortable, you can use the closet for—"

"OH WOW!" Tucket drops a couple of his bags and starts playing with the light switch, flicking the overhead lamp and fan on and off rapidly. "This place is so great! Do you have a landline? I read about landlines. I really like rotary phones."

"Uh. I don't have a land—"

"Ooh! And these views aren't digital, are they?" Tucket bounces over to one of the windows and starts playing with the blinds.

"That string opens the—"

Tucket has moved on to the desk and is admiring my pens and pencils with exclamations of awe.

"Actually . . . why don't I just leave you alone in here for a bit to get settled. Make yourself at home."

"Oh, man. That would be baller," Tucket replies. He beams at me and starts poking a finger at my desktop computer monitor.

I back into the hallway and close the door. *Dear God. What have I done?*

I step into the bathroom and shut the door, one more barrier between me and this invasion of my privacy. I stare at the mirror and try to get my mind straight. "This day will get better." My reflection doesn't seem convinced. I open the medicine cabinet and reach for my toothbrush just so I'll have some excuse to linger in the bathroom a little longer. A droplet of water drips onto my finger from the brush. *That's weird. Did Mym use my toothbrush?* I consider the wet bristles, then shrug and run it under the faucet. *I guess we must be in a more serious relationship than I thought.*

When I run out of teeth to clean, I poke my head back out of the bathroom and look around. I find Tucket seated on the couch grinning at the television with the remote in his hand.

"Is this film an accurate depiction of your current culture?" He points to the scene of Chunk getting terrified by a frozen body in the Fratellis' freezer.

"Yes. That's exactly accurate." I take a seat on a stool near the couch. "So, Tucket, how long do you see yourself staying? Is this like a vacation for you? Do you have *other* people you are going to be staying with also?"

"Well, it's not only a vacation, though I am really excited to explore your timestream. The only way I could get a waiver to travel here was through the Academy Liaison Program. They gave me an assignment to do so I could get authorization."

"What sort of assignment?"

"I'm here to register you for the Grid. And your friends of course."

I sit up straighter. "Wait, what? What do you mean register us? ASCOTT wants you to do this?" While Tucket has always seemed harmless enough, my dealings with the Allied Scientific Coalition of Time Travelers have been rocky at best. They make for any entirely different brand of uninvited guest. "What do you mean by *my friends*, too?"

"Oh. Well, Francesca Castellanas, Blake Hitchings, Carson—"

"How do you know about them?"

Tucket looks surprised. "I did research. For the school. After I met you during the chronothon I was so excited about it that I decided to make my graduate topic 'Early time travelers of the twenty-first century.' I gathered all the information I could find. I had help though. My friend Cassandra in Academy Prep wrote a paper too and used it for her—"

"You're the reason they know about us at the academy." I put my hand to my head. "Dang it. How much did you publish?"

"Just what I could find, it wasn't a lot of information on you as individuals, but I also tried to show how twentieth century music and culture, like the Beatles, created big influences on time travel culture. You know how much I like the Beatles and their—"

"Why does ASCOTT want us registered with the Grid? Are they trying to track us?"

Tucket blinks as he tries to process this. "You don't *want* to be registered? Why would you not want to be on the Grid? The safety benefits alone are—"

"How much do you know about what happened in the chronothon, Tucket?"

"I know you won. There was some sort of confusion about the ending but they said they awarded you first place. It was a big success, right?"

"I definitely wouldn't say I won. No one really won that fiasco." I run a hand through my hair and stand up. "Look, I'm not sure how much I can help you with this registration assignment. What's it going to involve?"

"I'm supposed to get all of your friends together and go over ASCOTT's expanded rules for safe time travel. They gave me a procedure to use. It even has visual aids."

"Rules. Okay, like for all time travelers or just us?"

"They are the same for everybody in the central streams, but there are a few specific ones for your timestream. The liaison office says there has been an increase in time travelers going missing lately, and there have been some unusual robberies, so they want to keep everyone safe. They put out some special protocols for the November Prime. That's here where you live."

"I do know that much." I step over to the coffee table and pick up the pieces of my phone. "I'll call the others and see what they say. I guess we may as well hear it all together."

Tucket watches me snap the battery back into place in the phone. "Wow, do you have to do that every time you make a call? Is that because your power technology is so primitive that you can't leave it on?"

I hold up a finger to silence Tucket and hit the speed dial button for Blake. He picks up on the second ring. "Hey, Ben. What's up?"

"Hey, man. We need to round up the crew. We've got a bit of a situation over at my place."

"Oh shit. More of those chronothon thugs?"

"No. Not quite like that." I watch Tucket get off my couch and start poking around my laundry closet. He laughs with glee at the sight of my box of laundry detergent and starts taking pictures of it with a camera shaped like a Ping-Pong ball. I return my attention to the phone. "Just come over. I don't think any explanation I can give you will do this justice."

"Okay, I'll grab Mallory and we'll head your way."

"Thanks, Blake. And do me a favor. Make it soon."

"They say necessity is the mother of invention. I've found that a lack of time is usually the mother of necessity. Whatever begot our lack of time is a branch of the family tree I'd just rather not associate with." -Journal of Dr. Harold Quickly, 2009

CHAPTER 3

The Neverwhere

I'm a ghost.

That has to be it. I died, and now I'm caught in some sort of ethereal plane between worlds. That is the only conclusion that strikes some chord of logical truth in my mind.

The problem is, I don't believe in ghosts.

I should have known this would happen. Nothing is ever as simple as it seems. When I did this to myself—making a jump through time without an anchor—I didn't have a lot of time to think things through. I did what I had to in order to keep my friends safe, but I didn't plan for anything beyond that point.

This is a particularly shitty dilemma. If I'm right, I'm a ghost. If I'm wrong . . . then what the hell else could I be?

The problem with not believing in ghosts is that I now feel very unprepared to be one. I should have spent more of my life watching scary movies. I could've stored up some type of functional knowledge. As it is, my frame of reference involves characters with names like Casper and Moaning Myrtle. Hardly role model material.

Oh. And Patrick Swayze. I guess he was pretty cool.

Staring at the interior of my vacant apartment, I'm at a loss for what to do with myself. If I am a ghost, shouldn't there be people for me to haunt? No one has shown up with any chains for me to rattle or ominous warnings to give to anyone. I'm certainly not occupying anyone's Christmas: past, present, or future. The idea of a Scrooge to chat with even sounds appealing.

I open the front door again and step onto the porch to listen. There was someone out there before. Noises in the fog. I'm not the only one in this mess. The big question is, am I better off alone or trying to get help? Who else lives here?

The fog is still lingering in the hollows of trees and little corners of my world, though most of the view from my porch is clear. The daytime sky still holds the three-quarter moon and I get the distinct feeling that it is in the same spot as it was before.

It's funny how you take for granted the constant motion of the universe. Heavenly bodies shouldn't ever be fixed. Life is movement—each moment of our existence a glimpse from a planet careening through the cosmos in a spinning whirlwind of a galaxy. We don't see the blur of speed, but we live it.

This scene is static and all wrong. That moon hanging in the sky is a lie.

Screw this place. I need answers.

I tromp down the stairs and out to the sidewalk, then stare up and down the street, trying to decide which way to go. The hesitation is all it takes for the doubt to sweep back in. I turn around and head for the garage. I find my softball bat leaning against the doorjamb where I left it. The feel of cushioned grip tape in my palms soothes my nerves a little as I walk back to the street. I don't know what good a few feet of aluminum and some decent bat speed are going to do me against whatever is out there, but if there is one thing I've learned of late, it's that there are few things more useless than a weapon you left at home.

I entered the neighborhood from the west, so I walk back that way, toward the streets where I heard the yelling. The fog thickens again and I rely more heavily on my other senses. They don't tell me much. No birdsong. Not so much as a buzz from an insect. The slow scuffing of my footsteps is my only company—until I hear the chanting.

I'm nearly to Fourth Street. This section of the road hosts a selection of restaurants, a surf shop, a bike shop, and half a dozen other businesses. It's a busy road and one I travel frequently, so when I turn the corner of the surf shop and stare down the street, I know what I should be looking at. I should be looking at a Tijuana Flats Mexican restaurant and a Starbucks coffee shop.

That is not what I'm seeing.

Somehow, merely by turning the corner, I've stepped into Oz. My head tilts back to take in the buildings that soar twenty stories high. I can see downtown from here and it has grown vertically by hundreds of feet. Bright, shiny buildings with glittering spires. Towers full of green plants form elaborate vertical gardens. Through a space between buildings I glimpse a winged structure spread out like fingers in the direction of the bay. It appears to be some sort of solar panel. It's still St. Pete. At least I feel it is, but this incarnation is centuries beyond my home time.

What brings my attention back to earth is the girl on the steps of the building near the corner. What used to be the Tijuana Flats Mexican restaurant is now a far bigger and more imposing stone building. A church perhaps. There are no stained glass windows or crosses, but something about the thick, rugged design exudes durability. A sense of history. I've never seen it before.

The girl on the front steps is perhaps eighteen. She's got her knees clenched to her chest, arms wrapped around them, with her head on her forearms. She's rocking herself and chanting in a sing-song rhythm. I can't make out the individual words, but she has a beautiful voice. Her hair is black and curly, tied loosely behind her head, and she's wearing a sort of frock but no shoes.

"Are you okay?" I call from a distance.

Her head pops up in alarm and she considers me. She climbs to her feet and wipes her face with her arm. She straightens her frock.

"Are you—" She stops herself and studies me. Her eyes linger on my softball bat. "Who are you?"

Not wishing to scare her, I let the bat dangle casually in my hand, the least threatening position I can manage. "I'm Ben. Are you okay?"

The girl nods. "Are you the one I'm supposed to meet? You don't look like . . . what I expected."

"I don't think anyone was expecting me," I reply. Looking at the building behind her, I can't help but voice my curiosity. A heavy gate stands open and leads into some sort of courtyard garden. "Where are you? I mean . . . when are we?"

She narrows her eyes. "You don't know? How did you—"

A boom of thunder rolls across the sky and cuts her off. Black clouds are now swirling overhead, a swelling thunderstorm. What's more significant, however, is that the top of the building has changed. The tall structures have instantly deteriorated. No stones fell or crashed around us. They simply aged. The top half of the buildings are suddenly in ruin, while the bottoms remain intact. But the ruin is creeping lower.

"Go. You shouldn't be here!" The girl shoos me away. "I'm supposed to recite the message to him by myself. I don't want him to see you. He's coming this way." She clambers back up the steps of the church.

"Who's com—"

"GO!" She sweeps her arms toward the far side of the building and I finally obey, dashing out of sight around the corner. As I move, the buildings around me continue to deteriorate. The destruction is creeping slowly lower, oozing down from the sky. No cracking, no sound, just the silent attack of age. I duck lower and lower, trying to not get caught in its grip. Walls turn from shiny and painted to weatherworn and broken. Windowpanes turn jagged. Other parts go missing entirely. As the storm overhead intensifies, the building right next to me transforms. I drop to all fours as the destruction descends around me. Finally I stop and lie prone on my stomach to make myself a lower target. I cover my head with my arms and wait.

The top of the church vanishes. Three of the four walls disappear, but reveal a smaller structure inside where I spotted the courtyard garden. There are no plants now. It's just a square room, with four arched doorways, one on each side. Inside the center chamber is a fire pit, lit and burning. It's raised up on multiple stone steps. Inside the arched structure, I see the girl who told me to hide. She's standing in the center of the room and I'm viewing her profile. She's shaking and talking nervously to herself. She takes one glance toward me, then fixes her eyes forward.

I'm lying prone in a narrow section of earth still untouched by the destruction. The ground is clear and clean of debris—a sidewalk of smooth concrete near an ornamental hedge. I feel as though I am lying in a shadow—a narrow sliver of different time untouched by the aging around me. Whatever has brought the destruction can't see me here. At least not yet.

The girl is standing rigidly at attention now, her eyes on someone or something approaching from the side of the building I can't see. She speaks softly, too softly for me to hear. Whoever she is speaking to is beyond one of the pillars of the square room. She bows and begins to chant her song. Her voice wavers only once in the beginning. It takes a few minutes to complete and then she falls silent. I hear the murmur of another voice, deep and masculine, but too far away to make out. Their conversation goes quickly. She recites something else, stares into the fire and lowers her head like a penitent attending confession. I don't see what the man she's speaking to does, but the girl goes suddenly rigid. Her hands fly to her head, grasping at her hair. Her mouth is open, screaming, but no sound escapes her lips. With eyes wide, she turns and looks at me.

I jolt to my feet, snatching up my softball bat.

I'm too late. The next moment she's gone, vanished as if she never existed.

The sight of her vanishing sends a cold chill through me. I don't know who is around that corner. I don't want to see.

I run.

I sprint away as fast as I can. I don't look back.

I don't know where I'm going. As soon as I turn the corner of the ruined building next door, I'm in the fog. Blind and staggering, I keep going, pressing my softball bat ahead of me as I flail forward.

The fog is whispering to me. Voices. Murmurs.

They all say the same thing.
Run.

St. Petersburg. June, 2009

Mallory Watson has never been great at hiding a stink eye. While the look she is giving Tucket from across my dining room table is not hostile, I can tell he has a long way to go before winning her over. She keeps opening her mouth to say something and then thinking better of it. Blake's fiancée is not the only one who looks skeptical of the young man's credibility. Francesca is seated on the other side of Blake and it's clear that she's likewise never seen anyone quite like Tucket. Neither girl will be impolite enough to say anything aloud, but I know their shared glances have conveyed plenty about their opinions of Tucket's attire.

I did try to tone him down. Getting rid of the sparkly glove was a small victory. I told him that no one would take his presentation seriously if we were distracted by his pop star stylings. It turns out his more professional attire was no less distracting. He chose a bow tie, suspenders, and glasses. He called it his hipster look, but landed a bit closer to Steve Urkel since the suspenders came in rainbow stripes. I gave up on fashion advice and simply sat down at the table with my friends. Thankfully, Carson showed up with beer.

Of my assembled friends, Mallory is the only one who is not a time traveler. Carson, Blake, and I are on the same softball team and we were together when an accident at the St. Petersburg Temporal Studies Society sent us back in time. Francesca had showed up that night to cheer us on, so she got zapped, too. We all ended up in the 1980s. It took the better part of a month to get home and we only managed that because of Mym and her dad.

Of the five of us seated around the table, Carson is the only other person still wearing a chronometer. I doubt Blake has considered jumping again in the short time he's been back with Mallory. He has his arm draped around her now as if not ready to let her out of reach. Francesca made a jump to the 1970s to help me celebrate surviving the chronothon, but I don't think she's been anywhere since.

Carson hasn't mentioned any side trips since I've been back, but time traveling has come pretty naturally to him so I wouldn't be surprised if he's blinked around the local timestream a bit. I'd swear his red hair looks longer than when I saw him a few days ago. Perched on the stool he's dragged over from the living room, he looks casual but curious.

Whatever Tucket has to say will be news to all of us. While I did run into a few ASCOTT officials in my prior adventures, I was always playing catch-up with the people around me. Since Doctor Quickly taught us the basics in the 1980s, we've been largely ungoverned. I had rather hoped to stay that way.

Tucket has set some sort of device on the floor between my dining room table and the rest of the kitchen. He seems proud of it, whatever it is. It looks a bit like a stereo, if stereos were the size of Tic-Tac containers. I nurse my beer and watch him putter around it while we wait for the show to start. He finally seems satisfied with his invisible preparations and a musical jingle precedes a holographic person that springs up in my kitchen.

"Congratulations, graduates. Your time at the Academy of Temporal Sciences has ended, but your true journey has just begun . . ."

"It's the only version I had," Tucket apologizes. "They said I could just use my copy since they don't really make tutorials for people like you. I mean, people in your circumstances—grandfathered into the system." Tucket moves out of the way so we can have an unobstructed view.

The man in the hologram introduces himself as Dean Alan Brockhurst, and the date he is speaking from is 2157. He proceeds to talk up the wonderful opportunities available to time travelers in the twenty-second century. He then reminds us of the limitations on approved timestreams to navigate and warns us against activities that will create unauthorized new ones. A timestream map behind him shows various sectors or zones. I notice our spot in 2009 falls under "Post millennial/Pre AOA." As best I can discern from reading other labels on the chart, AOA stands for "Age of Awareness." Through the dean's continued explanations, I learn that it refers to when the general public becomes aware of the possibility of time travel.

The dean reiterates the need to stay confined between the borders of the "Central Streams." These consist of branches of the Fractal Universe that have been created from the Central Primes. Mym's dad, Doctor Quickly, labeled the first fractures of time that he discovered after letters of the alphabet and the first twenty-six were labeled Primes. Each additional fracture of those streams added numbers and letters to differentiate them. A separate cluster of streams that seems to originate elsewhere carries the designation of "Negative Primes." That area of the chart is grayed out and apparently not approved for travel by ASCOTT.

Tucket is smiling at the dean and occasionally looks us over approvingly. When the dean gets done expounding on the joyous life we can expect by minding all the rules decreed by ASCOTT, and diligently adhering to the Grid protocols, he waves goodbye and vanishes back into his Tic-Tac box like a benevolent genie. Tucket claps.

The expressions on my friends' faces are hard to read. Blake's eyebrows seem locked into an arched position. Francesca and Mallory are still just staring at Tucket with mouths pressed shut, arms crossed, and bodies angled in the least receptive postures I've ever seen. I get up to grab another beer and Blake raises his finger to signal he's ready for another, too. Carson is the only one who seems eager to discuss the presentation.

"So when you graduate from the Academy, do they have any kind of job placement program? What kind of jobs do time travelers do in your century?" Carson leans forward with his elbows on his knees. "What are the best careers?"

Tucket seems pleased to be called upon. "Oh, there are great opportunities. Historians of course, and there are always jobs for researchers. The Academy recruits temporal scientists for the other science programs and we get plenty of students who opt for space travel."

"Space travel?" Blake asks. "What kind of space travel?"

I hand Blake his beer and pop the top off mine.

Tucket picks up his projector box and slips it into his pocket. "Long distance exploration or reconnaissance. There are spaceports with ships that start voyaging out to neighboring stars, looking for new life. There are a few authorized space gates, too. Those can get you into deeper space where you can find work. A lot of people head for Diamatra. It's a system humans are hoping to colonize for its great natural resources."

"Good luck with that one," I mutter.

"There are lots of jobs in law enforcement. Crime scene investigation is done by time travel. There are bounty hunters, too, of course. Those are mostly contracted. And some get recruited by major casino operations to police illegal time travel gambling."

"We've heard of them. Journeymen, right?" I say.

"Yes. Exactly. If you like travel, a more respected profession would be in one of the courier services. There are delivery services all over the central primes that carry messages and packages, since reaching family and friends in other timestreams can be so difficult. And we have special positions within ASCOTT itself. Lots of those are classified, but really important. They keep time travelers safe."

"Hey, Tucket, there's something I noticed," Blake says. "Why do the central timestreams on the chart he showed us only go up to 2600 or so? I think I might have seen only one branch that made it past then. What happens after that?"

Tucket crosses his arms and nods. "Okay, so that is the upper limit of the central streams because that is where ASCOTT stops governing."

"Does someone else start governing?" Blake asks.

"No. They just didn't feel it was necessary based on the reduced population density. There aren't many time travelers up in those streams."

"Why not?" Carson asks.

Tucket hugs himself a little tighter. "So, my girlfriend was a synth. I mean, she still is, but in the 2150s. I mean, she's still there and she's still a synth, but she's not my girlfriend anymore."

I recall the synthetic people I ran into during the chronothon. Tucket had explained that the term had become preferred since "artificial intelligence" denoted something inferior. The synths were treated as equals, or at least were becoming so. Tucket's breakup is news to me, however.

"She said that we just weren't very compatible if I was going to be a time traveler. She said that it was a good opportunity for us to explore options among our own peers." He fidgets a little and looks at the floor. "So it's kind of like that."

I don't see how his explanation clears up any of Blake's question, but no one seems eager to pry. Tucket continues to stare at his feet.

"She obviously doesn't know what she's letting go," Francesca says.

"Exactly," Mallory echoes. "You shouldn't worry about her. You are going to find someone else, or another . . . um, what did you call it?" She stalls out, but looks determined to stay supportive.

"You are going to like real girls, Tuck." I slap him on the back. Not having any experience with dating robots, I'm making an assumption, but I don't have much else to work with.

The girls get up from the table and gather closer to Tucket as well. "Definitely," Mallory says. She brushes a strand of her mousy brown hair behind her ear. "There are lots of girls who are going to love your, um . . . style. And you are from the future—which you might not want to tell anybody about—but I bet you are going to have so much to offer. Eventually."

"I do have a really great appreciation for twenty-first century culture," Tucket says. He's raising his chin now and enjoying the attention from the girls.

"There you go!" Francesca says. "Women are always looking for a man who's cultured. Mal and I were just talking about that the other day, weren't we?"

Mallory nods vigorously. "Absolutely. Culture. We're all about it."

Blake is smirking behind his beer. He doesn't seem to mind his fiancée doting on our new friend. "You girls should take him out. Introduce him around. I bet your friends will get a kick out of it. I mean, they'll love to be cultured by him."

Mallory gives him a withering glare, but goes back to smiling at Tucket. "They will. And we'll show you the sights in St. Pete."

"I've been working on my dance moves," Tucket says. "I was hoping to go clubbing some time. I hear that is a big part of your culture."

"Uh, maybe?" Francesca replies. "I guess we could take him to a club. You're twenty-one, right?"

"I made myself some local identification cards. I wasn't sure how many I'd need so I made a lot. Actually, if you think about it, I'm negative 128. I could have put *that* on them. HAHAHA. Cause I was born in—"

"We're with you, buddy." I clap Tucket on the back again and make for the fridge to search for more beer. They seem to be disappearing quickly tonight. As I set my empty in the sink and pop the top on my next one, the front door swings open. I look up in surprise. Mym has her hand lingering on the doorknob. She takes a glance around the room at my guests and lands on me and my freshly opened beer.

Mym doesn't seem inclined to come in so I walk over to the door to greet her. "Hey, where did you—"

Her voice is low enough for only me to hear as she searches my face. "We have our first fight and you use the rest of the night to have a party? Nice, Ben." She spins on her heel and disappears back out the door into the darkness.

I come unfrozen as my brain tries to catch up. "Shit." I set the beer on the coffee table and race after her. When I get down the stairs I scan the sidewalk. I walk to both corners of the block to make sure, but it's clear that she's vanished. I punch the stop sign and mutter curses to myself as I mount the stairs to my apartment again. My friends mute their conversations as I walk back inside.

"Is everything all right?" Francesca asks.

"Yeah. Just . . . having a few communication issues." I pick up my beer again. "Hey, Tucket, how do you usually go about finding someone if they're a time traveler? You said there are bounty hunters and such, but what are normal methods they use to locate other time travelers?"

"Oh, well most of those jobs involve time travelers looking for regular people who have committed crimes. That's pretty easy. Jobs like the Journeymen have, hunting down other time travelers, that gets really hard. If you don't know where someone has been, you can't find them very well. And there are laws about when you can locate someone for a crime. You can't convict someone of a crime before they commit it, even if you know they will. You have to wait and get them after."

"What about if they aren't criminals? How do you just find your friends and such? You said there is a courier system right? They deliver messages. How do they find people?"

"The Grid." Tucket grins. "That's in the next part of my presentation. Are you ready?"

I frown and move back toward my seat. "Yeah, we may as well hear it." Mym isn't registered with the Grid, so whatever he says won't help me find her, but I am curious about how it works. More specifically, I'm curious about the best ways to stay off it, since uninvited guests have not been working out well for me so far.

My friends take their seats and Tucket sets up his projector again. I settle in and take another sip of my beer. I'm determined to take this one slow. I have a feeling that I'm in for a long night.

When I've seen the last of my friends out the door at the end of the evening and get Tucket settled, I'm finally able to retreat to my bedroom. As I close the door behind me, I find Mym propped up on some pillows on my bed, reading a book.

"Hey." She lowers the book and gives me a faint smile.

"Hey."

"I'm really sorry." She follows my progress across the room. "About earlier. I didn't mean to be so . . . I can have a bit of a temper when—"

"It's okay."

"You just caught me off guard. I wasn't expecting you to have a bunch of people over."

"It wasn't a party."

"I figured that out later. I've been eavesdropping a little from in here. Who were the new people?"

"New? Oh. Well, Blake brought Mallory. She's in on the situation, though apparently she shouldn't be. The other guy is Tucket Morris. I met him at the Academy and he wanted to come visit. Apparently ASCOTT recruited him to try to get us registered with the Grid. I guess they've been losing track of some time travelers lately. They want to get everybody registered for safety reasons."

"Really? What did you tell him?"

"We listened to his presentation, but said we'd have to think about it. I can't speak for the others, but I don't think any of us want them tracking us. Safer or not."

"Interesting. Hey, speaking of safety, did you log your jumps from today?"

"The Atlanta trip? No. Not yet. I guess I figured that one hardly counted."

"They all count," she replies.

"Yeah, I suppose. I have a bunch of unlogged jumps from the race, though. I'm not super worried about logging every single one."

"Well, you should be. It's important. How many times do you plan on going back to those places?"

"Probably never."

"Uh huh. And how many times do you think you'll be jumping in and out of your own apartment?" She raises an eyebrow.

"Okay. I can see your point." I crawl onto the bed next to her and bury my face in the pillow. "I'll log them in the morning."

"Clearly I'll need to work on your organizational skills if I'm going to keep you alive. Oh, that reminds me. I got you a present." She slides off the bed and snatches up her bag from the floor. She extracts sets of something tubular and rigid and lays them on the bedspread. "We're going to solve your clothing issues."

I sit back up to examine the gift. "What is it?"

"Portable gravitizer. It's one of dad's. He has a few mobile ones for traveling and he said you could have this one." I examine the sheaves of tubing and bundles of wiring. Unlike previous gravitizers I've seen that looked like microwaves, this unit appears to have flexible dimensions. There is also a vial full of blue liquid that I recognize as condensed gravitites. Mym hands me a few loose pages of notes. I recognize Doctor Quickly's handwriting. "Some assembly required."

"Cool." I skim over the sketches and instructions. "I like it. Thanks, babe."

Mym smiles. "I figured you would." She leans over and kisses me. "Just don't zap yourself with it. Inanimate objects only."

"Got it." I bundle the equipment up and lean it next to the messenger bag I have hanging on my closet door. "I'll start getting my clothes treated so I can avoid more involuntary nudity."

Mym climbs back onto the bed. "There are worse things." She grins at me.

I slide back onto the bed beside her. "Speaking of nudity . . ."

Mym slips under the covers and wraps herself up. "You have a house guest, mister. That will have to be in your dreams."

I mutter a little and work myself under the covers as well. "Let's hope he's not here too long."

"Does he know I'm here?"

"He saw you come in earlier. His eyes got pretty big so I think he knows who you are. He likes researching this century. I'm betting you've been in his research."

Mym is quiet for a few minutes, possibly contemplating the implications of this new information, but then finally rolls over to face me. She speaks softly now, our faces only inches apart. "I didn't mean to get so emotional earlier. About my mom."

"It's okay."

"It's just that being here with you, this thing we're starting, I need to know it's going to work. I don't think I can handle having to lose someone else so soon. I almost lost you during the race and I tried not to show how scared I was of that but—"

"It's really okay."

"Wait, listen to me." She sits up a little and stares into my eyes. "I know these dreams you're having are bothering you, and I don't know what you need to do to fix them, but I'll help you, if you want me to. These things you keep seeing and hearing are significant enough that it's affecting your life, and I think you should figure it out. You want answers, so I want to find them, too."

"You don't think I'm delusional?"

"No. I think you're the guy who saved the world, and that had consequences. You saved me. You saved all of us. I know it cost you something, but you're a real life hero."

I frown. "That's the thing. I'm not. I might have been the guy who came home after, and sure, I did some of it, but the version of me that did most of the saving, he didn't make it back." I stretch out and stare at the ceiling. "He's the hero."

Mym props herself up on her elbow. "Then we help him."

I watch her eyes. "What does that mean for us? What if he wants something that is going to keep us from getting back to the way things were?"

"It'll be okay. We'll just have to find out together. Just don't think I'm letting you out of my sight again. And no more pretty mafia girls signing you up for chronothons." She smirks at me.

I wrap my arms around her and pull her closer. "Okay. I like this plan." I kiss her again and when our lips separate she retreats to the crook of my arm and lays her head on my chest. I address the ceiling. "Although it's not like I can go anywhere right this second anyway. Like you said—houseguest."

"His name's Tucket Morris?"

"Yep. Apparently he's my biggest fan."

Mym curls up tighter against me and mumbles into the bed sheets.

"Second biggest."

When I throw off the covers in the morning, Mym isn't there. I get dressed and wander out into the living area. Tucket is sitting across the table from Mym, cups of coffee in both of their hands.

"Ben!" Tucket grins at me. "Good morning! Guess what I did?"

"Oh God. What?"

"I made breakfast!" He points to the counter in the kitchen. Sure enough, a pan of scrambled eggs sits on the counter amid plates loaded with various fixings. There are also pancakes and buttered English muffins. "Mym took me to the store. I used paper money!"

I open the fridge and find it stocked with various juices and a selection of vegetables. I don't recognize any of the labels on the cartons. "Where did you guys go?"

"Colorado," Tucket blurts out. "I saw the Rocky Mountains with my own eyes. I'd seen them in the metaspace, but the view in real life is just as good."

I pour myself a glass of orange juice and look at Mym. "You have a gravitizer in a store out there?"

Mym nods. "Family friend owns a health food store I like. They have so many great brands. Best place to shop in this decade."

I consider the carton. "Says it doesn't expire till 2018. That's a perk. I love this place already."

"Expiry dates from the future have to be adjusted to local time," Tucket begins to explain.

I smile at him. "I know, Tuck. I was just joking."

Tucket stares at me for a moment, then starts laughing. "Oh, that's a good one. Haha. Because you already do that! I did see the ketchup you had expired in January and I was like, whoa is this guy CRAZY? But now it makes sense. You must have gone to the past to buy that, right?"

I look at my bottle of ketchup. *Damn. It did expire in January.* "Oh, you know it. So pancakes, huh?" I surreptitiously drop the ketchup into the trash and grab a plate. "Looks delicious."

After breakfast, Tucket is fascinated by the process of hand-washing dishes. I let him go to town in the soapsuds while I escape to the living room, snatching up my phone and finally pushing the button for the messages I have from work.

I have been bracing myself for the tirade from my boss, wondering where I'd been the past few days. To my surprise, the first message is actually one of my coworkers, Dave, calling from the office phone, reminding me to bring back the timing light I borrowed from him because he needs it to finish a job on the Evinrude motor he's working on. He playfully adds that I should also bring back the rest of the tools I've bummed off him since I've been there.

He follows this up with a joking complaint about his wife getting on him for never fixing anything at home and how he blames it all on me for having all his tools. During the call, someone else apparently tries to call the shop. Dave attempts to put the person on hold amid advice from Deb, the office manager and, being technologically inept, he messes it up. The second message is just a follow up by Dave from a few minutes later, apologizing for cutting the call short and attempting to blame the error on the phone system. I can hear Deb laughing at him in the background.

I hang up and stare at my phone, trying to wrap my brain around the situation. Dave's complaint is not a real problem. He easily has just as many of my tools riding around on his toolbox as I have of his. But the fact that no one seems to have mentioned my having disappeared for the better part of a week doesn't make a bit of sense. I had assumed the messages were going to involve me getting fired amid a slew of curses from my boss. I double-check to make sure there are no more messages I missed.

Nothing.

I pocket my phone and snatch my keys off the hook near the door. "Mym, do you mind keeping Tucket company for a few minutes? I need to shoot over to the marina and check on something."

Mym slides a plate into the drying rack. "You need any help?"

"No. I'm good. Shouldn't take long." I give her a quick kiss.

"Are you going driving?" Tucket asks. "Like a real human-operator vehicle?"

"Uh. It's a pick-up truck."

"Groovy." Tucket beams. "That must be so righteous. Do you get scared, knowing how dangerous it is?"

"Um. No. Look, I'll be right back. Don't wander off anywhere while I'm gone, okay? I really like my neighbors and they, um, appreciate privacy . . ."

"Oh no worries, bro." Tucket gives me another fist bump.

I trot down the stairs and scan the street. My old Toyota isn't in any of my usual spots despite there being plenty of available spaces. I check around the corner just in case I parked it there. I haven't used the truck much since I've been home, but can't imagine why I would have moved it. I go back upstairs and poke my head back inside. "Hey, Mym. You didn't by chance use my truck did you?"

"No. Is something wrong with it?"

"Hard to say. It's AWOL."

"Did one of your friends borrow it?"

"Not that I remember."

"They probably ask you in the future and then come back in time to borrow it," Tucket says, as if this is the most obvious solution. He continues dunking a saucepan in the sink.

"Okay. Just checking," I say, trying to puzzle out what could have happened to it. "I'll take the bike for now."

I head back downstairs and open the main garage door. It takes a few minutes to get the tank secured back on and roll it out of the garage. The turn signals are still shorted somewhere in the wiring, but I can live without them.

"Is that your hog?"

My heart jolts in my chest. Tucket has appeared right beside me. "God, Tucket. You scared the crap out of me. I thought you were staying upstairs to do dishes and hang out with Mym."

"I did. But then when it took you a little while to come back I decided that maybe I missed an opportunity to see how you drive, so I decided to check it out."

I can hear water running through the pipes from upstairs. "So the other you is still up there with Mym?" The edge of his Temprovibe is peeking out from under the sleeve of his shirt. *He's going to be harder to keep track of than I thought.*

"Yeah. We wash the dishes and Mym teaches me how to use the gas stove. That's really cool how you still plumb explosive gases into your homes and drive your own cars even though people could just swerve and kill you at any time they want. This place is like the Wild West. I love all the danger. Now you're going to ride this!" He puts his hands on his hips and admires the Honda. "I mean, this is REALLY dangerous."

I slide the key into the ignition and kick start the bike. It takes three tries, but then roars to life.

"How does the hog know where to go? Is there anywhere to program the route in?" Tucket leans over and scrutinizes the gauges.

"This motorcycle is from 1972, Tucket. A little before GPS."

I let the bike idle and go back into the garage for my helmet and gloves. Tucket's comments shouldn't be getting to me, but I cinch the helmet a little tighter than usual.

"So how do you get where you're going without a navigation system?"

"You just have to remember. And read road signs."

"Gnarly. Road signs. That's so millennial."

I get seated on the bike and rev the throttle a couple of times to warm it up faster.

"So if you get run off the road or hit by another car, do you want us to come get you? Do you have an emergency plan or maybe a way for the bike to alert us in an accident? How would you—"

"I'll be back before you know it, Tucket." I knock the kickstand back with my heel and get rolling. "Stay here."

"Okay. It was nice knowing you. I mean, just in case you die. I really like that you let me visit and meet your girlfriend." He shouts the rest as I ride out into the street and turn the corner. "I'll be sure to let the Academy know how nice you were!" I rev the throttle again and drown out the rest as I streak away.

"When arriving in a new place and time, you will displace the atmospheric gases around you naturally, but items with more mass, like raindrops and insects can still present a fusion hazard. Avoid precipitation at all costs and stay away from lamplight. Darkness is preferable. If you do get fused to a bug, no one wants to see that anyway." -Journal of Doctor Harold Quickly, 1907

CHAPTER 4

The Neverwhere

I am terrified. I would have thought that death would mean an end to being scared, but now the unknown is changing the rules. Whatever is going on in this place, I am certainly not resting in peace. I am running, and I am afraid.

I can't see much. I've gotten off the street and plunged down a foggy alley, still clutching my softball bat. I sprint past a few trash bins and out onto the street at the far end. I'm on the opposite side of Fourth Street from where I started—Sixth or Seventh Street now. Not sure why I headed this way. Just running. Fleeing the destruction behind me.

I'm back in St. Petersburg. My St. Petersburg from 2009. The vision of destruction I left behind is gone. It's a relief, but I don't stop.

A bigger clearing in the fog opens ahead and I recognize the apartment building where one of my ex-girlfriends used to live. I linger there, finally able to see a little farther in the glistening haze. There is something to this clarity. I am finding it easier to see near places I've spent a lot of time. My apartment, the smoothie shop, now here. Whatever clues there are to this place, I feel like that is one.

After the intensity of what I just saw—that girl vanishing into thin air— I'm ready for a taste of the familiar. Looking at the two story apartment building, I get the feeling that I'm not just looking at an old building. I'm looking at my past.

Kaylee was a fun girl, but too young. She had barely finished college when I met her. She waited tables at varying hours and felt like she could party the rest of the time. Her habit of showing up at my place at two or three in the morning made me late for work on multiple occasions. I tried to keep up at first, mostly since she was pretty enough and seductive enough to talk me into about anything, but I finally stopped seeing her after having to pick her up hammered at the police station at 5 a.m. on a Wednesday morning. She took the breakup in stride and would still text me on occasion as if she had forgotten it happened. *I wonder if she knows I'm dead.*

I walk around the side of the Spanish-style building to the back of her old place. Kaylee's is the apartment on the lower corner. A 4x4 cement step juts out into scraggly crabgrass doing its best to survive in the sandy, fire-ant-infested dirt between the back of the apartment building and the parking lot. I open the screen and peer through the window of the door. A crayon drawing of a cat holding an Easter basket is stuck to the fridge. I remember that. Kaylee's autistic nephew, Bryce, had drawn it for her because he didn't like rabbits and said he wanted an Easter cat.

I study the rest of the kitchen. The drying rack near the sink is cluttered with Kaylee's mishmash of USF Tervis Tumbler cups, just how I remember it. It shouldn't be. Kaylee moved out of here at least six months ago. Right now, I don't care. I just need a place to hide.

I try the doorknob and it opens.

I slip inside and lock the door behind me. The place is cold, over air-conditioned, the way Kaylee always kept it. It's a small apartment, but her novice landlord had made the mistake of including the electric bill in her rent, so she kept the pair of wall units running all the time. I pass through the hallway to the living room and check the lock on the front door. I don't know what good it is going to do against my unknown enemy, but I feel a little better once I've placed the chain across it.

I set the bat down on the coffee table and, after checking the security of the window latches, have a seat on Kaylee's cinnamon-colored couch to ponder my dilemma.

There are other people here. That much has been proven. Even if the young woman got yanked out of existence in front of me, there was no doubt that she was here. I need to see if there are more. I also need to know who did that to her.

Thunder rumbles overhead. Curious, I move to the front window. The sky above is still clear blue in sections to the west, but toward Fourth Street it has continued darkening. A towering grey thunderhead is lingering over the area where I've just come from.

The tops of the skyscrapers downtown are visible beyond the houses across the street. The buildings are in ruin, if they can even be called buildings, and there are far more of them. Whole floors have been torn out of the nearest tower perhaps a block distant. It stretches skyward at least a hundred stories, far taller than anything I have ever seen in St. Petersburg. Farther south, the clock is missing from the top of the Bank of America building. That building, one of the tallest in town during my time, is now dwarfed by skeletal spires of steel and concrete all around it. What was a healthy city now resembles a bombed-out warzone.

I crane my neck to see farther down the street. Other buildings are changing again in front of my eyes. The transformation is moving like a wave. Not dramatic. No tumbling roofs or falling walls. The houses simply transforming—colorful and whole one moment, burned out or vanished the next. What's more, the streets that were clean and dry are filling with water. No, not filling. That would involve some sort of action. When I look back to an area that was previously dry and find it under three feet of water, it's as though it had always been that way. It hurts my brain to even process it.

A rattling distracts me from the scene. Someone is attempting to turn the doorknob on the back door. I slide away from the window and duck into the single bathroom, closing the door behind me, but leaving just a crack to peer through. I realize too late that I left my bat on the coffee table. The doorknob rattling stops amid muffled curses. Someone is splashing through water at the side of the building. A moment later, a shadow falls on the blinds on the far side of the kitchen. The silhouette is of someone tall and I catch a momentary glimpse of a shaggy face attempting to peer through the space at the edge of the blinds. The window rattles and there is more cursing.

The would-be intruder makes his way around the front of the apartment and tries the front door. Another boom of thunder rolls across the sky and I hear a yelp from the man. The door is shaken furiously, but doesn't budge. The cursing abates as suddenly as it came and I am left in silence. The quiet is interrupted only seconds later by the pattering of rain on the roof. The patter quickens to a steady drumming and I edge back out of the bathroom. I stay low and dash across the living room to snatch up the bat. Outside is blackness now. I retreat again, this time to the bedroom. I close the door and turn the lock.

Kaylee's bedroom is not as I remember it. Despite being a free spirit elsewhere in life, her apartment was always tidy, the bedroom most of all. I recall her bed being constantly made up with a preponderance of frilly pillows to weigh it down. Not today. The room looks lived in. All but one of the pillows have been dumped on the floor and the comforter kicked to the end of the bed. Kaylee's little writing desk is in disarray as well, pens and pencils scattered about. A yellow legal pad is lying atop the desk with a few pages hastily torn off. The pad is bare, but has deep indents in the top page from someone pressing hard while they wrote. Curious, I pick up a pencil and brush it across the page the way detectives do in old movies. The word that appears means nothing to me, but was obviously important to someone. It's been repeated across the page no less than ten times in thick block letters.

ZURVAN.

I scribble a little more on the page and find a symbol drawn multiple times around the words. The symbol is a circle with blades or wings coming out of it and flames issuing from the circle. It resembles the sun or a star, but with a vaguely technological vibe. I stare at the page, trying to make sense of it. While I am pondering the sketches, the rain stops outside. I tear the top page off the tablet and stuff it into my pocket.

Sunlight and blue skies are back when I open the front door. The view of the city skyline is back to normal as well. Condo towers and office buildings from my time are reflecting sunlight from glistening windows. Despite the recent downpour, the ground around the apartment isn't wet. I creep out to the sidewalk and check the gutter. Not so much as a trickle. I scan the houses around me. All have returned to the way they were before. No ruins. No water damage.

I turn around and have started toward the apartment when I catch movement around the side of the building in the bushes. I freeze and lift my bat. Cautiously, I take a few steps toward the shrubbery. I'm still a dozen yards away when they shake violently and a man sprints from hiding behind them. I raise the bat to swing, but he bolts the other direction, shaggy hair trailing down his neck. He's barefoot and his pants are dirty at the bottoms of the pant legs. I glimpse only a ragged beard and wide, dark eyes before he dashes away, but there is something very familiar about him.

"Hey! Wait!" My yell goes unheeded as the man disappears around the corner of the garage next door. I run after him and turn the corner into the alley, but by the time I get there the man has vanished. I trot down the alley to see if I can spot where he went, but pick up no sign of him. Frustrated, I return to the apartment. If the man has been living here, perhaps there are more clues to who he is.

Once inside, I lock the front door behind me again and scan the apartment. I return to the bedroom to look for something else that might give me a clue to his identity. As I round the corner of the doorway, I stop in my tracks. The bedroom is changed. The bedspread is back over the bed and pillows are neatly stacked in order the way Kaylee always preferred. The writing desk is tidied up as well. No sign of the scattered pens and pencils. The notepad is gone. I open a few drawers and find it under a roll of stamps and some thank you cards with ducks on them. The pad looks wholly intact. No pages torn from the top. Baffled, I reach into my pocket and remove the sheet I folded up. I open it to find that all of my sketches are gone. I stare at the blank sheet, then rifle through the pages of the notepad. Blank. Blank. Blank. Six pages down I find the shredded edge of a page where one has been removed. I slip my page into the space and the edges match up perfectly. *What the hell?* I stare at my page a little longer then flip through the ones above again. No indents. No markings. Whatever clues my mystery visitor had left, he has managed to take them with him.

I rummage through the desk till I find my pencil again. I know what I saw. I draw the symbol of the flaming circle with wings, filling in as much detail as I can recall. Then I write out the word I read and underline it.

ZURVAN

I tuck the paper into my pocket and shut the drawer to the desk. I pause, reach back into my pocket and double-check my paper. This time my drawing is still there. I try it one more time just to be sure. Staring at the sketch of the winged sun, attempting to burn it into my memory, I can't help but hope I am onto something significant. I don't have much to go on, but anything is better than hiding in my apartment waiting to be attacked. Somewhere there is an answer to the riddle of this place. I am going to solve it.

St Petersburg-2009

A chain link fence surrounds the Saint Petersburg Southside Marina. The gravel drive features an electric gate with a keycard access to keep vehicles from pulling directly through. It's supposed to keep unauthorized persons from getting near the boats, but since the nearby pedestrian gate finally rusted off its hinges last summer, the effect of the fence has been mostly decorative. A "No Trespassing" sign lists to a slight angle near the gate and may keep the honest folk out, but otherwise the sidewalk is unimpeded and has become a favorite avenue for the army of neighborhood cats who scavenge through the high-and-dry for remnants of successful fishing trips.

The marina maintenance shop is a low building opposite the high-and-dry with three bays with electric doors. The area in front of the doors is typically cluttered with more boats than the crew of mechanics can ever actually fix in a day, but my bosses, especially Tammy in the office, are nothing if not optimistic when they make promises to customers. Larry, my usual shop supervisor, tries to keep Tammy in check, but boat owners are a demanding bunch and always eager to have their boats back in order, mostly so they can go back in the racks and not get used for another three months.

Today appears to be another hectic morning. I imagine it is even more so since I have been missing work all week. I don't know how Dave managed to not mention my absence in his message. Had Tammy been listening in? Was his voicemail about bringing back his tools some sort of code to tell me to be careful? If so, I missed the message. Dave is not really the type for codes anyway.

Since my gate card is in my missing pick-up truck, I park the bike in the visitor lot outside the fence and use the pedestrian gate. Rounding the tail end of a used Bayliner on a trailer, I spot my truck parked in my usual spot near the side of the high-and-dry. It gives me pause. I walk slower past the next pair of boats and keep them between me and the maintenance shop. *Something is definitely not right here.* My toolbox has been rolled into the shop work area near a motor-less Crownline cabin cruiser. In the next bay, Dave is puttering around the back of a center-console skiff. He laughs about something and makes a comment to someone. A moment later a man walks out of the parts room and strides over to my toolbox. He's me.

"Holy shit." I duck low behind the boat in front of me and backpedal a few feet, hoping no one has noticed me walking up. *What on earth is going on?*

I skirt around the front end of the trailer and squat low so I can see under the bow. From my vantage point I can just make out the other me fiddling with something on the top of my toolbox. Something about him looks a little off. It's odd to be looking at myself from a distance, but this is even stranger than that. The man in the shop isn't just me—he looks different. He looks older.

"Shit shit shit." I slink back behind the boat, not sure what to do. If anyone sees me, I could cause some sort of temporal paradox or at minimum cause some serious confusion for my coworkers. I mutter under my breath. "Who are you, and why are you doing my job?"

I try to process through my options. The man in the shop is definitely not a past version of me. It's hard to say how much older than me he is, but it has to be at least five years. Maybe more. Something about him just looks weathered. Ruling out the past, I need to figure out whether he could possibly be a future version of myself, or whether he is an alternate version of me—some other derivative or an imposter from a different timestream. *Just what I need. More of me to deal with.*

I do a mental run-through of the few encounters with other versions of myself I've had. It was always from a distance. The alternate version of me I glimpsed when I visited a wrong 2009 never saw me. I dealt with other versions of me from a distance during the chronothon, a nearly paradoxical issue that I resolved mostly by avoidance of direct contact. I've never had one this close to me before and definitely never had one attempting to commandeer my life.

I climb up into the boat on the trailer, keeping low and ducking into the cabin so I can get a better look from cover. I peer through the cabin's circular port window, trying to get a clear view of this imposter. He's not wearing a chronometer. That makes sense. Even if he wasn't elbow deep in boat motors all day, Dave would certainly have asked him about it. Dave is not one for subtlety or even privacy. I'm at a loss for what to do until the other me, obviously feeling the heat of the day, shoves the sleeves of his T-shirt up over his shoulders, trying to cool off in the stifling summer humidity of the shop. That simple motion gives me the info I need. It's not much, but it allows me a quick view of the inside bicep of his left arm. The skin is slightly less tanned and decidedly bare.

The inside of my own left arm now sports a tattoo, a recent acquisition from Bozzle, my friend and fellow competitor in the chronothon. The eight-pointed compass rose is my reminder of that event and also a way to keep track of my own history. The lack of a tattoo on the other me's arm tells me that whoever he is, he was never this version of me. That is enough to go on. Whatever happens next, at least I don't have to worry about a potential paradox. With that issue determined, I resolve to have a word with him.

There are different types of customers at the marina. There are the serious fishermen who get out all through the week, the weekend warriors who love taking their friends out for days of drinking and sun tanning, and the folks who like having a boat more for the sake of saying they have one. This last type rarely ever use them, especially during the week, and today that's what I'm looking for.

It takes me a few minutes to sneak around to the side door of the high-and-dry and into the stacks. Vern Bennett, wearing his usual camouflage hat and tank top, is working the forklift and I have to wait until he has shuttled a boat outside to the docks before attempting to scale the racks.

The high-and-dry is able to stack boats three high, and the one I want is on the top level. Doctor Herbert Longletter owns the now dusty cabin cruiser and the staff has a running bet on how long it will be till the boat touches water again. It's been in its spot for nearly ten years and, with the exception of occasional cleaning and tune-ups by the staff, it has not moved. The current odds favor it being there till Doctor Longletter is dead. For me, it will do perfectly.

Once Vern is out of sight, I scale the side of the racks nearest the Longletter boat. Until recently, a fear of heights would have kept me from attempting this stunt, but a lot of things have changed about me since becoming a time traveler and heights no longer get my heart rate up like they used to. It could be that time travel has presented so many new ways to die that heights just couldn't measure up. It's these dangers that I bring to mind as I ensconce myself in Doctor Longletter's cabin and set my chronometer.

Mym's dad, Doctor Quickly, seemed to take guilty pleasure in elucidating the variety of ways time travelers could snuff it. Involuntary fusion was high on the list—accidentally jumping to a space an object already occupies. I make sure to stand clear of the spartan furniture in Longletter's cabin to avoid that fate.

The floor is plastic and flat, a good surface to travel from, no soft carpet or cushioning that might retake its original shape during my absence and end up fused into my sneakers on my return. I decide to use the edge of the mini countertop as my anchor. The chronometers are designed to ground through the nearest object that doesn't contain gravitites. I didn't bring my degravitizer along to check whether Doctor Longletter is a closet time traveler and has somehow gravitized his boat. I let the thought go as highly improbable and work on the assumption that the boat will make a good anchor.

I press my fingertips firmly to the countertop as I dial my settings to arrive at 4:30 that afternoon. Failure to keep firm contact could cause me to ground through the floor, which in this case wouldn't be that bad. In other scenarios, not keeping contact with an anchor while jumping could be devastating, especially if that means you don't have firm contact with any anchor at all. I recall a brief image of the other me at the end of the chronothon, suspended in the lab at the St. Petersburg Temporal Studies Society.

My other self made the jump without an anchor, in order to rid the lab of blood samples that could be used against my friends. The sacrifice worked, but it was a one-way ticket to the Neverwhere. I linger on the memory of watching my other self disappear. *Does he know that I survived? Is he aware somehow of what happened after his death?* I try to imagine what that felt like, sacrificing everything. As many questions as I have about his fate, I have no illusions about how much I owe him. It's everything.

I shake away the memory and concentrate on the task at hand. I double-check my settings, mentally note the time, and press the pin on the side of the chronometer.

I've blinked across the day.

The sun now lights most of the floor of the high-and-dry. I move toward the door of the cabin and punt something into the wall. Looking down, I find the key to my motorcycle on the floor next to my foot and my cell phone in the corner where I kicked it. *Damn. That was lucky.* I mentally chastise myself for not emptying my pockets of non-gravitized objects before jumping. Luckily both bounced clear when I vanished. Had they landed under me, I could have arrived with them imbedded through my foot. Shaking my head at my own stupidity, I climb down the girders again and drop to the dirt.

"Hey there, Ben."

Shit. I turn around to find Vern standing five feet away over a dirty, red Igloo cooler. He's popped the top on a can of Miller Light. "Hey, Vern. Getting an early start?"

"It's five o'clock somewhere, right?" Vern chuckles. He shifts his gaze nervously and nods toward the stacks. "Whatchyou doin' up there?"

I glance up at the boats above me and try to think of a convincing lie. "Customer called and wanted me to look for his wife's camera. Thought she might have left it in the boat."

"No joy?"

"Nah. It's probably in one of their vacation houses somewhere. You know how doctors are. Would have been old and ratty if she left it here anyway. They haven't used the boat in years."

"You had me worried they might be taking it out. Got ten bucks on it making till at least 2015." Vern holds his beer low behind his leg as he gestures with his other hand, perhaps hoping I'll forget I've seen it. As much as I probably ought to be worried about our forklift driver drinking on the clock, the fact that he doesn't want to be caught means he owes me now, and he's not likely to mention this conversation.

"All right, Vern, I gotta get going. Catch you later."

Vern ducks out of my way, beer still low and out of sight. "Right on, man. See you tomorrow."

My truck is still here, meaning my other self ought to be too. I walk out the back side of the high-and-dry and skirt around the building to the employee parking spaces. My supervisor has already left for the day. Typical. Larry takes full advantage of being on salary whenever possible, usually lighting out by four every afternoon. The shop gets more relaxed once he's gone, especially Dave, who uses the opportunity to gab about whatever information he hasn't managed to spill in the course of the day.

I peer through the windshield from my hiding place behind my truck and watch the shop on the far side. True to form, Dave is leaning against my toolbox chitchatting while the other me cleans up his tools. Dave's Subaru is parked next to my pick-up and it's a guessing game as to which of the two will leave first. I have my hopes set on Dave clearing out, giving me a chance at catching my other self alone.

In a frustrating turn of events, the two men eventually walk out of the shop together. I mutter a few choice swearwords and start to look for another place to hide. Luckily, when the men are halfway to the vehicles, the other me stops and feels in his pockets, then has to turn around, apparently lacking his keys. He waves Dave on and the two part, Dave climbing into the Subaru and driving away while I hide on the opposite side of my truck.

I'm curious how my other self will react to my presence. My heart is beating faster, not sure what to expect. I lean on the back of the truck and wait.

The other me makes it about halfway across the lot before he looks up and sees me. His expression is not so much surprised as irritated. It's a bizarre feeling to be staring at myself. My face looks off, mostly because I am used to seeing myself in a mirror, not this opposite and asymmetrical version of me—the way I really look. Will look, anyway, in however long till I'm that age. My dark hair is still half-heartedly pushed away from my face, a few days of stubble darkening my jawline, familiar T-shirt and flip-flops. There are changes though also, a hardness in the eyes that I don't see now when I look in the mirror. This other me looks just a bit more worn.

"I wondered when you'd show up." He stops about twenty feet away, fiddling with my spare truck key in his fingers. "Figured you'd notice the truck going missing. Just a matter of time, I suppose."

"What are you doing here?"

"What does it look like? Working."

"You don't belong here."

The other me slowly crosses his arms and sighs. "Don't I? It's my life as much as yours."

"Not this one. Where'd you come from?"

The other me looks me over. "Look, I get that you got here first. I saw you'd come back to the apartment—saw you with *her*." He scowls a little. "I just want what's mine. I know we have a problem here, but we should be able to work something out. Learn to share."

"Share what? My life?"

"Hey. It's our life. I have just as much right to be here as you. If the Quicklys hadn't screwed us over, neither one of us would be in this mess, but we are, so we have to deal with it."

I try to figure out what he's talking about. "So what version of me—of us—are you? You met Quickly in 1985? What happened?"

"Elton Stenger happened."

I recall what Mym had once told me about her different attempts to save her father from Stenger, the killer from our time. It hadn't worked on the first attempt. She had made multiple tries before finding the combination of events that ultimately led to my success in getting rid of him. The failed attempts left loose ends.

"What happened to the others?" I ask. "Francesca and Blake. Carson."

The other me narrows his eyes. "They didn't make it back."

"So you came back on your own, and what? You just planned to go back to work?"

"There're worse plans, believe me. It took me a few years of doing, but this is the November Prime, where I belong." He stabs a finger toward the ground. "And before you get riled up and start saying that you were here first or whatever, just know that I've got just as much right to be here as you."

I consider what he's saying. It's true that my claim on this timestream is just as tenuous as his. There are multiple versions of us now that could call this place home. It complicates things.

"I haven't seen you near the apartment." I say. "How long have you been back?"

The other me walks over and leans against the truck. "A few days. I was steering clear till after we talked. Wasn't sure how you'd take it so I kept putting it off. I just pop in here or there when I need things. Change of clothes. Stuff I didn't think you'd miss."

"*That's* why my closet seemed so bare. I thought I'd just—wait, did you use my toothbrush yesterday?" I recall the soggy bristles. "Oh God, how often have you been coming in?"

"I snuck in to get cleaned up after work. I've been sleeping at Kaylee's, but she's a little weird about me keeping things there. I didn't want to shower over—"

"Kaylee? You got back together with Kaylee? What the hell, man? Isn't she a little young for you?"

The other me glowers back. "Hey, I might have taken a while to get back, but I'm not *that* old. Maybe thirty-two or three, if that."

"You don't know for sure?"

"No. Do you?"

The question takes me aback. I haven't done a great job of recording how many days I've been traveling. *Could the few months worth of traveling I've done have bumped me past a birthday?*

"Look, man," he says. "Whatever the situation is going to be, we can work it out. Maybe we can trade off weeks at work or something. Share costs. I don't know. Two is better than one, right? All I know is I'm back. I might be a little older than I should be for this date, but I don't care. This is where I'm from and I'm not going anywhere."

"Have you talked to anyone else?"

"No. Just Kaylee, and a couple of her friends. I almost went to see Francesca, but I couldn't bring myself to do it." He stares at the ground momentarily and I can't help but wonder what happened to my friends in his timestream. I decide I may not want to know.

I consider the maintenance shop. "You can actually keep the marina job. I was planning to quit anyway. Things are a bit different for me now." I look at his crossed arms. "Where's your chronometer?"

"Kaylee's place."

"Dude, you can't just leave it lying around. It's priceless. If one of Kaylee's stoner buddies came across it . . ."

"It's not lying around. I hid it. I'm not an idiot."

I contemplate the situation. Older Me just stares back at me. It must be just as strange for him to be looking at me, a slightly younger reflection.

Despite the weirdness of the situation, I'm comfortable around him. He somehow feels like family, already trustworthy regardless of our differing pasts. Finally, I sigh and put my hands in my pockets. "I'd feel better keeping the chronometer at my place. Why don't I follow you back to Kaylee's and grab it. You can keep the truck, and we'll figure something out about our stuff. I'm not sure what Mym is going to think about this . . ." The other me's face twitches a little. "What? What is it?"

"Nothing. Just haven't had to deal with her in a while. What's she doing here?"

"She's my girlfriend."

"Oh God. You're dating the girl who got us into this mess?"

"She also saved us."

"Saved you, maybe. Not how my story went."

I study his face, wondering if I even want to know what he's talking about. "Look, you're back, so let's just deal with that. I don't know what any other Myms did in other timestreams, but my Mym is cool and you'll have to get along with her. I mean, not too well or anything . . ."

He smirks. "No worries. I'm not going to try to steal your girl."

"I doubt she goes for old dudes anyway."

"Kaylee hasn't complained."

"Yeah, well, Kaylee is hardly the paradigm of good judgment."

The other me smiles. "I could think of a comeback, but any insults you make to me are really just insults about you, too, so I guess there's no need."

I smile back. "Fair point." I pull the motorcycle key out of my pocket. "My bike's out front. Where's Kaylee's place?"

It turns out that the apartment Kaylee moved to is near the marina, ensconced in the Old Southeast neighborhood. The brick streets and old trees resemble those in my own neighborhood, but this southern incarnation sports a few more houses in need of work and a few with overgrown yards. I turn into a dirt alley and park behind a 1920s home that has been converted to apartments. Kaylee lives in the downstairs of the blue-and-white, wood-sided house. The back porch is cluttered with cheap patio furniture and a full ashtray sits atop one of the tables.

"Who else lives here?" I point to the ashtray. "Kaylee didn't start smoking, did she?"

"She always has friends hanging out here. You remember how she was. Social butterfly."

Other Me leads the way into the back of the house. I get the lingering scent of pot mixed with something floral. We find the flowers a moment later when we enter the living room. A bouquet of roses has been delivered and is sitting on the coffee table.

"From you?" I ask.

"Shit no. Roses are tacky. Whoever got those doesn't know her very well."

"Yeah, I remember her being more the wildflower type. Looks like you have some competition anyway."

"Whatever," the other me scoffs, but his face has darkened slightly. "Come on. It's in here."

Kaylee's bedroom is decorated much the same as the apartment I remember. The bed is piled with pillows and everything is neat and tidy. The corners of her dresser and her writing desk host small potted plants. Other Me goes straight for the desk, pulling open the top drawer and, as he rummages for his chronometer's hiding place, tosses various items onto the top—a deck of cards, a container of buttons, a yellow legal pad.

My vision suddenly darkens and grows light again. My view of the top of the desk flashes back and forth from cluttered to mostly empty, and I'm somehow seeing Kaylee's old apartment, blinking between the two views as fast as someone flicking a light switch on and off. *What the hell?* I try to orient this strange set of visions. *What is he showing me now?* One scene has the older me rooting through the desk. In the other, the desk is bare with the exception of the yellow note pad. As the views shift back and forth, words and symbols keep appearing and disappearing on the page. *There.* Heavy-handed sketches and a repeated underlined word. Zurvan. I'm brought back to reality by the other me stepping in front of the legal pad.

"Whoa, man. You okay?" His arm finds mine as I teeter, and he steadies me on my feet.

"I'm—I'm good." The bed seems like a better option than falling over so I take a seat.

"You look like shit."

"That's what it felt like, too."

"You okay?"

I don't really know how to sum up the current circumstances my mind is dealing with. Despite the fact that this person I'm talking to is me, he's been living a different life for the past few years. Our similarities no doubt outnumber our differences, but that doesn't make the differences less significant.

I don't know how to begin explaining the version of me—version of us—that I saw go missing at the end of the chronothon. Explaining that this other version of me has been sending messages from beyond the grave is even farther beyond my abilities to put into words. I take the easy way out and simply nod. "I'm fine. Did you find the chronometer?"

He holds the chronometer up in his palm. I recognize it as the first one I ever used. Doctor Quickly has seen fit to get me some upgrades since. My current incarnation looks similar, but I've added a couple of parts and it's tuned to make farther jumps. The original version could only jump a year on its own, a bit farther plugged in. I have to respect that this other me found a way home from the 1980s using it. He may have taken some detours and taken years to do it, but he survived. That is no small feat in the time traveling business.

I'm curious about his story, but right now I just want to go home and unravel this mess in my mind. I hold out my palm for the chronometer. Other Me, to his credit, hesitates only briefly before placing it in my hand. I brush my thumb across the shiny concentric rings on top. "I'll take good care of it for you. It will be there if you need it."

"Good riddance as far as I'm concerned." He shoves the contents of the drawer back inside and slams it shut. "What now?"

I ease myself off the bed and back to my feet, making sure I'm steady. The mental displacement seems to have passed. I take one lingering glance at the desk drawer, but am not tempted to look at its contents again. I remember what I saw.

"I'm going to head home. I'll fill the others in on the situation so they aren't surprised."

"Blake and Francesca?"

"Yeah. And Mym."

"She going to be around a lot?" Other Me frowns.

"Some. And I actually have another houseguest at the moment, in case you run into him. Friend I met in the future. He's a little . . . well, you'll see. Hoping he's not staying for long."

"Full house."

"Yeah. Things are getting a little crowded."

"You ready for this?" He gestures back and forth between the two of us. "It's weird, right?"

"Not as weird as I would have thought." I consider him for a moment, then hold out a fist and he bumps it. "We'll figure it out." I head for the door. "Call me if you need me."

"Can't. You've got the phone."

I pause at the doorway. "We'll get another one. We'll see if the phone company has an option for that. The family or other selves plan. Whole new market for them."

The other me smiles. "See you around, Mr. Travers."

"Ditto."

As the door closes behind me, I pause to look at the chronometer in my palm. *This is going to be interesting.*

By the time I park the motorcycle back in my garage, the clock on the wall reads ten past six. I've missed most of the day. It's a solvable problem.

I hang my motorcycle key on a hook on the wall and remove my cell phone this time before I set my chronometer. I recall that Tucket had said I didn't come back right away in the morning so I dial my settings to more or less match the real time I have spent away, and use my toolbox as my anchor. When I blink back to the garage that morning, the place is quiet. I trot up the stairs.

"You lived!" Tucket grins immediately upon seeing me.

"Safe and sound."

Mym is in the kitchen, puttering around with something that smells of butter and garlic.

"More cooking lessons?" I ask.

"Figured it wouldn't hurt for you to have a few meals available in this place." Mym checks on something in the oven. "Especially since you have guests. Did you find out what you needed to?"

I retrieve my logbook from my bedroom and return to the kitchen table to jot down the times of my morning's worth of jumps. I lay the pen on top of the logbook and rest a hand on the table. "I actually have a few things to talk to you about. My morning got a little complicated. Tucket would you mind giving us a few minutes of privacy?"

"Fifteen? Twenty?" Tucket wipes his fingers off on the kitchen dish towel.

I look Mym in the eyes as I respond. "Let's go for a full hour."

"Okay, save my spot." Tucket taps out a sequence on his Temprovibe, then places a hand to the wall near the refrigerator. He adopts an Arnold Schwarzenegger accent for his parting comment. "Hasta la vista, baby." The next moment he's gone.

Mym glances at the spot where Tucket has vanished, then turns her eyes back to me. "Sounds like you have something serious to talk about."

I keep my eyes locked on hers. "I think it's time that you tell me what happened to the others."

Mym studies the logbook at my fingertips for a moment before responding. "Are you sure you want to know?"

"I have to know." I pull the other Ben's chronometer out of my pocket and hold it out to her. "They're starting to come home."

"A common misconception about throwing cocktail parties for time travelers is the expectation that guests will arrive on time. To the contrary, the first half hour of your event is often reserved for shooing away inebriated time travelers who have already enjoyed your party and are intent on reliving it." -Journal of Dr. Harold Quickly, 2130.

CHAPTER 5

The Neverwhere

It's time to experiment.

I might be a ghost, but that doesn't mean the laws of the universe have stopped working. Wherever I am, this place should have rules like any other. Sitting on Kaylee's front stoop, I've listed the things I know so far on the yellow sheet of paper, underneath the drawing of the winged sun.

1. There is less fog in places I've been frequently—no fog where I've lived.

2. Kaylee's apartment is decorated from six months ago, how I remember it, even though I know she moved.

3. There are other people here. One vanished. One did something to make her vanish. One ran away.

4. The scenery can change.

I stare at the meager list and try to come up with any logical deductions. The first two items are the most promising. There seems to be a connection between places I've been able to get to so far. I've only been able to navigate to places I've been before. *Easy enough to test.*

I get off the step, pick up my bat, and head for the fog that lingers in the intersection at the far side of the apartment. I consult the street sign. I usually approached Kaylee's apartment from my place, so this side of the neighborhood is not somewhere I spent much time. Sure enough, the fog in this direction is dense, clinging to the frames of houses and walling off the spaces between them. Looking back the other way I can see all the way to the end of the block. *Okay. What else do I remember in this direction?*

After a few moments I recall that Kaylee took piano lessons from a girl who lived on the other side of the alley, perhaps a block down. I had picked her up there once or twice. If my memory is correct, I should be able to cut through the yard of one of these places, hit the next road and make it there.

Walking up to the space between the nearest two houses, I test the fog with my bat, then take a cautious step forward. I've definitely never been this route before. The fog surrounds me as soon as I'm out of view from the street. I can see it vaguely behind me, but as I continue onward, the nothingness swallows me up. I keep my bat ahead of me, probing the fog. It's silent this time. No whispers. No voices. Making me wonder if I really heard them before at all.

It makes no significant difference if I keep my eyes open or shut. My options are darkness or iridescent nothing. I walk for what I imagine to be around fifty yards, then things start to clear. I make out vague shapes of roofs and some porches. I find the street. All the buildings are lacking definition, even the ones I'm close to. I walk right up to one, but can't make out any additional detail. I wonder if this is what it's like to be going blind—everything a hazy blur.

I head west toward the piano teacher's apartment building. It appears from the fog like a ship, a solitary figure in a barren sea. I can make out the top of the piano in an upstairs window.

It worked.

I can go places I remember.

I consult my list and put a checkmark next to item one.

The second item on the list seems like the next variable to figure out. Kaylee's apartment was decorated the way I remember it, not the way it would have looked when I died. Looking up at the piano teacher's apartment, I have to admit that it looks the same as I recall as well. I have no idea whether the piano teacher still lives there or not, so it's hard to say if my experience of the place is concurrent with reality. I need a different location to experiment on. I try to remember something in the area that shouldn't exist anymore. After a few minutes of contemplation, I head for my bank.

Fourth Street and all of downtown have been in a constant state of renewal since I've lived here. Restaurants changed hands or changed names. Bars and even the Cineplex have evolved. The closest change I can think of is the new Chase bank across the street from the Tijuana Flats. Until recently, it's been a weedy lot with an old oak tree. They chopped the tree down and hacked it into firewood. I have a memory of standing there watching the men cutting the tree up. I was sad to see it go. It had been a good-looking tree.

When I get to the corner of Ninth and Fourth Streets, I slow down. There is no sign of the destruction I saw before. No sign of the futuristic St. Petersburg or the ruined one. There is only a Starbucks on the corner in all of its generic glory. I pause before rounding the corner of the Starbucks and try to imagine what I'll see across the street. With the girl getting taken from the deteriorating church in front of my eyes, I didn't have time to notice the buildings around her. I concentrate on the visual of the old tree where it stood, and step around the corner.

It's there.

No bank.

I stare at the oak tree, its lofty branches reaching for the sky.

It shouldn't exist. I saw it chopped down. What does that mean for me? For one, this place isn't real. That much is certain. The thought gives me a queasy feeling of impermanence. If nothing around me is real, am I? I'm suspicious now and study my hands, one holding the softball bat, half-afraid that by simply acknowledging the fragility of my situation, I might blink out of existence. I certainly feel solid, but have I ever felt any other way?

I do a mental inventory of my body. I'm not hungry. Not especially thirsty or tired. Should I be? I place a pair of fingers to my wrist and feel for a pulse. At first I feel nothing, but after pressing harder, get the steady pumping against my fingertip. Does that prove anything? I've never not had a pulse. What would that feel like? My head swims with possibilities. Is this all some abstract dream?

The situation is beginning to stress me out. I walk over to one of the patio tables at the Tijuana Flats restaurant and sit down. If this experience I'm having is made up of only places I remember, what was that girl doing here? I know I've never met her. Certainly never met the storm guy either. I stare at my list again, running down to the last item.

Scenery can change.

I look up and stare at the old oak. Can I remember it another way? I close my eyes and concentrate, imagining the new bank building that replaced it, with its shiny blue logo on the sign. I get it firmly in my mind and open my eyes.

The scene is different.

True to my imagination, the bank building has appeared in the lot across the street. Unlike the reality I remember, however, the tree is still there too. Long elegant branches are still protruding from the top of the bank, swaying gently in a non-existent breeze.

Damn. What does that mean? I get out of my chair and walk into the street, taking a better look at this odd amalgamation of my memories. The trunk is protruding solidly from the roof of the building, casting shade onto the parking lot. Not how I remember things, but how it would look if the two different times overlapped. *Interesting.*

I'm still staring at the branches overhead when I feel something cold on my legs. I look down to find I'm standing in two feet of water. *What the hell? Where did this come from?* I look up to find the scene around me has changed again. No longer am I looking at the Saint Petersburg of 2009. The city is back in ruins—if it can even be called a city.

The bank has vanished, quicker than a thought, like everything I knew had never even been. All around me is the rubble and skeletal frames of once monstrous buildings. There is something stretched out across the sky like a sail. The remnants of the solar array. The landscape is scarred and ruined—a post apocalyptic war zone. My stubborn oak tree still rises from the water, but everything I recognized around it is gone.

The interior of the church is visible again, the small square room with four arched openings, one on each side, facing the cardinal directions. Through the nearest arch I can see the fire burning at the center of the single room.

Dark clouds are swirling overhead again. I feel the menacing certainty that it is the same storm as earlier, and the same fire I viewed in the flickering vision I had when the girl vanished, though I have no logical explanation for that assumption. The wind has picked up, making waves and lifting droplets of water from the surface. A spattering of salty mist hits me in the face. I am still trying to figure out what has caused the change when I hear it.

Something is splashing around the corner, a periodic sloshing that I recognize as a person wading through the flood. Terror of the unknown grips me and I move, sloshing myself now as I struggle to get out of sight. I just make the cover of a bit of ruined wall when the approaching figure reaches the corner. I crouch low in the murky water and peer into the street from the safety of cover.

This one is no teenager. And no one I've ever seen before. Foreigner does not begin to describe the man. He is certainly not a native of my time. Bearded and serious, his dark eyes bore into the surroundings with a fierce determination from under a dark turban. His soaked linen robes impede his progress through the flood. Once a desert tan, the bottoms of his garments have absorbed enough seawater to take on a deeper shade of brown. The man is not especially tall, but he appears to be strong. Leather bands wrap around the wrists of his muscular forearms. He was stepping doggedly through the floodwaters despite the resistance of his clothing, propelling himself through the murk at considerable speed with the aid of a metal-capped staff. Now he has stopped and is staring at the oak tree. My tree.

It takes me a moment to realize that the tree is out of place here. There is nothing growing anywhere else in sight. It's here because I am. The man finally detaches his gaze from the tree and scans the area. His expression, previously merely determined, has taken on a wary hostility. He shakes an arm loose from beneath his robes and brandishes a long, curved knife. He waits, perhaps for a sound that will reveal the presence of an intruder. I hold my breath and try to wish my oak tree out of existence again. Get rid of the evidence. I don't want to vanish. I fear this man, and I have an almost primal urge to avoid him at all costs. I dare not move, thinking that even the water must belong to him and could betray me.

The man raises both his arms, elevating his dripping sleeves from the water and closes his eyes. He is concentrating on something and he begins to hum. Softly at first, then louder. The humming builds to a peak before he lets out a shout that sounds like "Ha!"

Saint Petersburg vanishes. Everything except my tree.

I'm somewhere else entirely.

Desert.

Rocky, sandy hills are all around me, stretching out in every direction. My oak tree is the sole green invader. My ruined wall and the water I've been crouching in are both gone and I'm left exposed, blinking in the blazing sunlight. Just a few dozen yards of sparse dirt separate me from my companion. He appraises me with the same intensity he had shown the ruins of St. Pete. The corner of his mouth twitches and his fingers tighten around his knife. I realize that I'm holding my bat in front of me so I lower it to one side, holding my other hand up in what I hope is a gesture of peace.

He shouts something at me in a language I don't understand.

"I don't want a fight," I shout back. "I just want—" I don't know what I want. I want to not be here, for one, but that doesn't seem like the right thing to say. "I'm going to go my own way."

The man with the knife speaks again, this time in a Middle Eastern accent. "English. What are you?"

I don't know how to answer that.

"Who sent you?" the man barks.

"I'm—" I falter again. The story of how I got here hardly lends itself to brevity. "I'm from Saint Petersburg."

His brow furrows. "Another sacrifice?"

It's clear we're not on the same page. I have no idea what he's talking about. I don't want anyone thinking of me as sacrificial, no matter when they are from, so I'm quick to respond this time.

"No. Not a sacrifice." I cast a few more glances at our sandy surroundings. There is a scent of smoke in the air. "Just—visiting." I take a step away. "Where are we?"

The man slides his knife back into his robes. I relax a little.

"Enough of you." The man's hand flashes back out of his robes, stretching and somehow grabbing ahold of me even from a distance. I'm frozen in shock from the impact. I can see his hand, still yards away, but I can feel it on my face as if he was next to me, clamped on my forehead, fingers boring into my temples. I grunt from the surprise and the sudden pain, swinging the bat ineffectively in an attempt to dislodge his grip. Safely distant from my flailing, the man furrows his brow and squeezes harder.

"Gahhh!" I drop the bat and grasp at my head, trying to find his invisible hand and pry it off. There is nothing to grab. I get the horrifying sensation that the man is now *inside* my skull, wrenching at the roots of my mind, tearing my very soul out of me. The pressure is unbearable. *Get out. Get out get out get out.* I scream and scratch at my head, trying to hold onto myself. I can feel myself slipping, my consciousness dimming, a step away from oblivion.

My vision flickers.

Anger and my instinct to fight battles with my sheer terror. *I won't die again.* I shout at him to get out of my mind, but no sound escapes my lips. For all my rage I'm a flame being pressed between fingers, furious but fleeting—nearly snuffed out.

"NO!" The yell is in my voice, but I didn't scream it. A shape drops from the branches of my oak tree and lands in the dust near the trunk. The familiar figure is still barefoot and ragged, but he springs upright and goes rigid with intensity as he throws both of his hands out in front of himself. "Not him!"

The new man's arrival is enough of a surprise to momentarily distract my attacker. The pain in my head abates and is then stopped as a brick wall appears between us. The man from the tree and I are now in the interior of a building I recognize. The colorful felt banners hanging from the top of the wall give it away. It's the inside of my grade school gymnasium. The tree is still with us. It's growing up from the wooden floor and clean through a set of aluminum bleachers. My savior looks at the tree and then hisses at me. "Get rid of that thing. He'll remember it too."

I falter for words. There is just too much to process. I collapse to the waxed hardwood of the basketball court. My mind is still recovering from its near extinction and I haven't any clue how I've gotten here, let alone how to banish my imagined but persistent tree. The other factor that is causing my mind to reel is that the other man is clearly recognizable now, despite his tattered appearance and overgrown facial hair. The hazel eyes staring at me with intensity are plenty familiar.

He's another me.

The ragged me squats down next to my position on the floor and places his hand on my shoulder. "The tree. Concentrate. Remember that it doesn't belong here and it will go." He points to the oak, as if I could have failed to recall where it was. The top branches are growing through the roof. He then points to the window of the door near the bleachers. "Hurry!" The view outside is still sand dunes and sun. He grips my shoulder tighter, fear in his voice. "You are still binding us to him. Remember this place as it was."

I struggle to concentrate on the scene around me, climbing to my elbow and picturing moments from grade school. Pep rallies. Basketball games. I get one image in my mind of Meghan Daniels addressing the auditorium in a vivid green dress as she ran for class president of the sixth grade—the day my years long crush on her started. I'm distracted by sand blowing through the crack under the door. The door is rattling on its hinges. I close my eyes and remember. Green dress. White barrettes. Remember.

The rattling stops.

When I open my eyes, the tree is gone. The sand is gone. We are still in the gymnasium, but the view out the window has changed. The other me moves to the door to look. He pushes open the double doors and nods. The blazing clear sky of the desert has been replaced with dotted cumulus clouds. Beyond him is the green grass of our school's soccer field. The streets of my hometown in Oregon lie beyond the chain link fence at the end. I lie back on the floor and stare at the fluorescent overhead lights buzzing behind the cages meant to protect them from errant dodge balls.

The other me comes back to interrupt my view. He looms over me now, the ragged man from a tree. Another puzzle to solve.

"What is this place?" My voice comes out scratchy.

The ragged me glances around the gymnasium then looks back down. "The past." He extends a hand to help me up. "The past we remember, anyway."

I grip his hand and let him pull me to my feet. "This place is all memories?"

He nods.

"Who was that then?" I point toward the door. "The sand man. I don't remember meeting him before."

Ragged Me twitches a little. "No. This place is memories, but we aren't the only ones here. Some people remember worse things." He gestures toward the door. "Come on. Let's go home."

I stagger after him, still aching somehow from the attack on my mind. *I feel like he bruised my soul.* I pause as we near the door, cautious. "He can't find us here?"

"I don't think so." He considers the view outside. "Unless he has been here before. Have you ever taken anything from Oregon to Iraq, or maybe Iran? Have you ever left anything there?"

I shake my head, confused. "No. When would I have done that? I've never been to Iran."

"Yes you have. We were just there. So was your tree."

"Well, I've never left anything—" I look down at my empty hands. "Oh shit. I left my softball bat there."

"It's okay. We bought that in St. Pete. It won't connect to here. Come on. We should be safe for now, but we'll be careful." He strides into the daylight.

I follow him out the door, still mystified by this place, but happy to have an ally. I pause and pull my scrap of yellow paper from my pocket and scribble another line on my list.

5. *This place is the past we remember.*

I watch the figure of the other me striding barefoot across the soccer field. His ragged jeans are scraping the tops of the grass. His presence means that I'm not the only time traveling version of myself who's had trouble staying on the right side of reality. If he's here too...

I scribble one more line.

Someone has killed me at least twice. I need to warn the others.

St. Petersburg, 2009

"That makes four of me that you know of." I'm sitting across the kitchen table from Mym trying to process all that she's told me.

"The ones from here anyway." She's fiddling with her empty coffee cup. "There could be more alternates later on, or if someone else split your timestream. They wouldn't necessarily be time travelers though."

"Good. This is already confusing enough. Some versions of me better be staying where they belong." I fidget with my now updated logbook. "I can see why ASCOTT puts so much emphasis on the Grid. I knew running into other selves was a thing for time travelers, but I wasn't expecting to have to share a medicine cabinet." *Or my dreams.*

Mym's attempts to save her dad in the 1980s apparently yielded its share of duplicates. From what she knows, there is at least one more of me unaccounted for somewhere and a few of her as well.

"This other you from the marina—he said he had a place to stay?" She tucks a stray strand of hair behind her ear.

"He's staying with a friend." I pick up his chronometer and study it. "Doesn't seem like he has any plans to leave."

"Okay. At least that's one less variable to deal with. Who is the friend he's staying with?"

"Kaylee. She's—an old friend."

Mym eyes me skeptically. "Uh-huh. How old?"

"Well, I guess she's not so much old, as . . . irrelevant?"

"What makes her—"

Mym's MFD erupts on the table. Loud, persistent sirens accompany a buzzing vibration. Mym grabs for it immediately, giving me a respite from the conversation.

"Damn." Her eyes scan frenetically across the screen.

"What is it?"

"I've got to go. We've had a security breach at one of dad's labs." She abandons her seat and rummages through her bag on the kitchen counter. "I need to make sure he's all right."

"I'll come with you," I say. "Is everything okay?"

Mym pulls a deck of playing cards out of the bag and starts degravitizing it on the countertop. "Stay and wait for Tucket. He's due back any minute. I'll send word as soon as I figure out what's going on." She pauses and then hands me her MFD. "Actually, take this. I have another one where I'm headed. I'll message you."

I accept the multi-function-device and watch as she finishes degravitizing the cards. "Which lab is it?"

"Valencia. 2017." She grabs a handful of my shirt and kisses me quickly.

"I'll be right back." The next moment she has spun the dials on her pendant chronometer and disappeared.

I pick up the deck of cards she left behind, then set it back down carefully, not sure whether she intends to return via the same anchor. I back away from the countertop and consult her MFD. The device is not unlike a mobile phone, flat-screened and compact. Various icons glow on the screen. One in particular is getting new alerts or messages repeatedly because it keeps hopping around the screen to attract attention. I tap on it and watch as the screen becomes a video monitor.

The scene displayed is the interior of an industrial loft. It's a space I've never been to, but it resembles others of Doctor Quickly's labs—clean, comfortable spaces full of as many armchairs and books as there are scientific tools. The drastic difference here is that the place has been ransacked. The screen cycles through various angles of the loft shot from security cameras. Furniture has been knocked over and drawers dumped out. A wastebasket is on fire. The shot that arrests my attention, however, is a ground level view of an interior wall. A framed piece of art has been flung to the floor and the wall has been spray painted with a symbol—a flaming circle with wings. *There it is again.*

The screen view shifts before I can get a better look and I struggle to stop the flow of images. I've only managed to freeze the next shot of a ripped up armchair when Tucket reappears next to the refrigerator.

"What up!" He grins and immediately looks around for Mym. "What happened to—"

Before I even have time to respond, the front door bursts open and three people pile through. Mym is trailing her father, Doctor Quickly, and his long-time friend and chronometer-maker, Abraham Manembo. Both of the men are in deep conversation with each other and seem to be paying little attention to their surroundings. A fourth member of the group follows Mym in. Muscular and bearded, the man smiles when he sees me.

"Cowboy Bob!" I set the MFD on the counter and head for my suddenly crowded living room. Bob crushes my hand with his and smiles as he shakes it. His dark eyes and sun-seasoned face seem near the same as I saw him last, though it's hard to tell with time travelers.

"I hear this is where all the high rollers hang out." Bob claps me on the shoulder. "Chronothon champion now, eh?"

I shake my head and smile. "Oh, you know it. Living the life of luxury as you can tell."

Bob looks around my cramped apartment, then nods toward Tucket. "This must be your butler."

"I'm actually Tucket Morris," Tucket replies, offering a hand to Cowboy Bob. "I've never had any training as a butler. I don't think the Academy offered that. I studied pre-millennium culture and the influences of twentieth-century music on the time travel community."

"U2? Nirvana? Who's your poison?" Bob asks gravely. His eyes twinkle with amusement.

"Well my favorite band has always been Avocado Problems, but when it comes to twentieth century bands it really all starts with The Beatles."

"You play at all?" Bob asks, picking at an imaginary guitar. "We should jam sometime."

Tucket lights up at this suggestion and starts into a conversation on his favorite guitars. I leave him to Bob and make my way to Mym. She reaches for me.

"Hey, sorry to just invade like this." She keeps her voice low. "Seemed like the safest plan at the moment, get everybody together and see what to do."

"I saw some of the footage on your MFD. Someone ransacked the lab?"

"Yeah. We don't know exactly why, but dad has a few ideas." Mym angles us toward her father and Abraham. Abraham looks serious, no sign of the brilliant smile that usually contrasts sharply with his dark black skin.

Doctor Quickly inclines his head toward me also. "Ben, sorry for the short notice, but we thought we'd better rally the troops as soon as possible. Is your friend here reliable?" He glances toward Tucket. Bob has skillfully maneuvered Tucket into the kitchen and out of earshot.

"He's all right. Technically he got sent here by ASCOTT, but I trust him."

"ASCOTT may be the least of our problems right now," Doctor Quickly replies. "Where can we talk?"

I steer our group into my bedroom and shut the door behind Abraham once we're inside. He pats me on the shoulder and, when he speaks, his voice is full of concern. "It's good to see you, Ben. How have you been sleeping?"

"I wish sleep was my only issue. The dreams have been coming on when I'm awake now." I turn to Doctor Quickly. "Which I actually need to talk to you about. I saw a symbol on the wall of your lab in the security footage. A sort of flaming circle?"

"It's one of the clues we're working with," Quickly replies. "One of the few we have. As you know, this isn't the first time one of my facilities has been attacked. I've faced my share of hostilities over the years, but this group seems new."

"You saw them?"

"Indeed. They waited till they knew I was there and attempted to gas the place. A rather nasty nerve toxin meant to incapacitate me. I have protocols in place for that eventuality, so I was able to get out, but just barely."

"Who were they?"

"Kidnappers," Mym interjects. "The toxin wouldn't have killed him. The lab security system identified it as a knockout gas. They tossed the place, and vandalized it, but we're guessing the vandalism is just a cover for the abduction attempt or possibly a robbery. We won't know till we can have a closer look. And we don't know why they're targeting dad."

Abraham crosses his arms. "It would be a simpler question with anyone else. Harry here would be useful for any number of schemes. Suggesting someone wants to make use of his knowledge or equipment doesn't narrow things down very well. We need more information on this group and what they're after."

"I hate to say it," Quickly replies. "But I've made enough public appearances in my life that it's likely that a persistent kidnapper could find me elsewhere and succeed. They can find another version of me. Kidnap me somewhere easier, if that is what they're after."

"That's assuming they are time travelers." Mym says. "They could have been linear."

"Too hard to say," Doctor Quickly replies. "Too many variables. We need more information. What is this you were saying about the symbol? You've seen it before?"

"Just recently," I reply. "The last ... vision . . . I had earlier—well, actually *later* today—that symbol was in it. It was on a notepad."

"Where was this?" Doctor Quickly asks.

I scratch my head. "It was in the apartment of one of my ex-girlfriends."

"What were you doing there?" Doctor Quickly asks. Mym is watching me intently, obviously wondering the same thing, if with a slightly different level of curiosity.

"There's another me in town. He's staying there for the time being. We were working a few things out."

"And this former girlfriend of yours knows the origin of this symbol?" Abraham asks.

"No. I only saw it in the vision. The notebook here was blank. If it's showing up in my dreams that means it's coming from the *other* other me." I gesture vaguely toward the ceiling. "Departed Ben, or whatever we want to call him."

"What did the dream feel like?" Abraham asks. "Was there a particular emotion affiliated with this symbol? Any other clues to its origin?"

"I don't know about any emotions. I was so busy trying not to black out that I didn't get much of a feel for that. There *was* something else though. A word or name that was written with the symbol. Zurvan? It was underlined like it was important."

"Zurvan?" Abraham asks. "The Zoroastrian deity?"

"Is that a person we know?" I ask.

"A person history knows, to be sure," Abraham replies. "Zoroaster was an ancient holy man. Before most of history as we know it. He even preceded my namesake, Abraham, though many of his teachings were said to have influenced the Judeo-Christian traditions that followed. The concepts of a single God, Heaven and Hell, even the idea of a Devil have their roots in Zoroastrianism. Zurvan is the name of a god whose origins also grew from Zoroastrianism. Though I believe that Zurvanism conflicted a bit with orthodox Zoroastrian teachings."

"You think the attack has something to do with religion?" I ask.

Doctor Quickly responds. "That seems unlikely, but I suppose it's possible. From what I know of religious history, despite being a dominant force in antiquity, Zoroastrians are one of the smallest religions in the world these days. Mostly in India, I believe."

"Did you piss any off recently?" I ask.

Doctor Quickly allows himself a smile. "I wish I could say with certainty that I haven't, but as you are discovering lately, it's hard to say what influence your life might be having in the world, especially if you are not the only version of you living it.

"If there is a connection between the attack on me and the Zoroastrians, I would be more inclined to believe we are dealing with time travelers," Doctor Quickly continues. "Could be some fringe sect. I have a hard time suspecting modern day Zoroastrians are out to get me. From what I know of their religion, it's rather peaceful."

"We are dealing largely in conjecture, Harry," Abraham says. "How do you want to proceed?"

Doctor Quickly looks at me. "With all the help we can get. We'll need to cover a lot of ground, temporally speaking, to find some solid evidence and see who is behind this. I would suggest we steer clear of the other labs for a while. I need to check up on the other versions of myself that I know of, to make sure none of them have been attacked. Then we can start to narrow down our leads about what they are really after."

"I want to get into the Valencia lab before the police do," Mym says, fiddling with the ring on her finger. "I think we need to start there."

"It could be dangerous," Doctor Quickly says. "I don't want you going in there alone. Benjamin, would you be willing to assist in the investigation?"

"Of course. Whatever you guys need." I look to Mym. "As long as I'm on Mym's team."

Doctor Quickly smiles. "I doubt she'd have it any other way. I want you two to be careful though. We still don't know who we're dealing with. We've arranged with Bob to have a contact point set up at his ranch in Montana. You're familiar with the place, I believe. A meeting there should be secluded enough to keep us off the radar of our mystery attackers, but let's be sure to keep a wary eye out anyway. In the meantime, perhaps you can research the symbol connection as well. During these dreams of yours, does it seem like you have any way to communicate with your departed self? Is the information one way or could you get him a message?"

"I've never really tried deliberately communicating with him. Hasn't really felt like an option. I can try it next time, I guess."

"I'm just curious what your other self knows that we don't. He sounds like someone we may want on our side. If possible, getting in touch with him should be a priority."

Mym slides off the edge of the bed where she's been leaning. "When we find these guys who attacked you, what do you want us to do with them?"

"Good question," Doctor Quickly replies. "We need to discourage them from any more attacks, for sure. Let's cross that bridge when we come to it. Right now we need to find them before they find some other unsuspecting version of me and get whatever they're hunting for."

I notice the bag hanging from my closet doorknob that has the portable gravitizer in it. "Hey, sort of a side topic, but since you are here, I have an idea I'd like to run by you. Sort of a science project that I thought of earlier."

"Something that will help us out?" Doctor Quickly asks.

"I'll show you and let you tell me."

My idea has required a jump into the near future to arrive at a time after my earlier self got home from the marina. Doctor Quickly and I aim for about seven. The sun is still shining through the western windows. I lay out the portable gravitizer pieces on the floor of the garage as Doctor Quickly studies the motorcycle. He strokes his chin and paces the length of the bike. "So you want to gravitize the whole thing?"

"You said we'll need to cover a lot of ground. I thought it might come in handy."

"Indeed it would." Quickly holds his arms wide to try to measure. "I've never tried gravitizing a whole vehicle using a portable before. Probably need to take the wheels off to make it fit inside the perimeter of this unit. Of course we could always do them separately." I can see he is intrigued by the idea. "I suppose the utilitarian issue would be having a way to gravitize the fuel when you fill up. Otherwise you would leave it behind. Perhaps some sort of gravitite injection system . . .

"And you will need a way to anchor the bike to a temporal ground during a jump. The tires won't make very good conductors," Doctor Quickly adds. "I assume you'll want to be able to make jumps while moving. Not that I recommend it, but it would certainly be useful."

We are able to arrange the portable gravitizer into a shape that will fit the frame of the bike. We have to do a bit of wrenching to prop the bike up without its wheels, but without them it just fits inside the clear insulated sheeting. The power dims a little as we apply the solution of gravitites via a stream of electricity. The test works. After running Mym's degravitizer test light across all the areas of the bike, the light glows a steady red, indicating that all of the items are gravitized.

Bob and Abraham are eager to join in the project and even Tucket tries to help. He seems in awe of Doctor Quickly and is uncharacteristically calm in his presence.

I notice Tucket has acquired a new leather bracelet on his wrist with some metal studs on it.

"Cowboy Bob gave it to me!" Tucket exclaims. "He says he got it straight from Bono at a U2 concert. Says it will make me look more rock and roll." He clenches his fist and holds up the bracelet, then proceeds to play some air guitar. "Me and him are going to jam sometime."

Bob is the one who actually comes up with the solution for the jump device in one of his casual comments. "There are plenty of benefits to time machines that can travel. You should just use my trick. Throw out a trailing line to the ground, then use the ground as a local anchor. Easy." I recall my previous trip to Bob's ranch and our flight aboard his hot air balloon. He would suspend a cable from the balloon and make time jumps via anchors on the ground. He could even trail degravitized anchors and jump to other places if he wanted.

"If you have some wiring, I'd bet Abraham could find a way to plug your chronometer into the bike's electrical system. You'll be able to do longer jumps that way. Can probably keep your chronometer charged up, too."

Abraham chimes in. "Actually, I've got another addition that will make this process even easier. Have I showed you my timer delayed chronometers yet, Ben?"

"No. Is it cooler than my current system?"

"Not sure about cooler, but it will let you keep both of your hands on the handlebars while you jump."

Abraham disappears to his workshop and comes back with some additional parts for my chronometer. The extra toggle and timer lets me select an increment of time, like ten seconds, press the pin, but not have the action happen until the timer ticks down.

"Just make sure you've got your hand on your anchor by the time it hits zero," Abe says. "Bit of a safety hazard if you don't."

I adjust the dial to the off position. "Got it. We've had enough unplanned trips to the Neverwhere as it is."

The mechanical detour to the garage doesn't seem to have bothered anyone. If anything, having the project to work on seems to be a good distraction from the attack. Doctor Quickly, Abraham, and Bob all pitch in at various times in troubleshooting and testing the modifications to the bike. We work on it for a couple of hours, but we end up doing a lot of the wiring and parts construction in Abe's tool shop. Jumping back and forth between locations lets us use up less "real time" in my garage, and between the four of us, the modifications come together pretty fast. It's only after a late dinner upstairs when Tucket asks me if I am planning a road trip that I remember he still doesn't know anything about my new plans.

"I'm just going to be doing some traveling." I lean against my bookshelf and try to sound casual. "Helping the Quicklys out."

"Can I come?" Tucket's eyes light up. "I've been wanting to see more of this timestream. Are you going to paint your fuel tank like an American flag and cruise around like Peter Fonda in *Easy Rider*?"

I shake my head. "Actually I've only got room for two and I think Mym already has dibs on the back." I'm hoping desperately that Tucket is picking up on my hint. "But it's been great having you visit. Maybe you can spend a little time on your own traveling around, or . . ."

Tucket looks up wide-eyed. "Wait! I have it!" His hands flash to his Temprovibe and suddenly he's vanished.

"Oh shit," I mutter.

Mym joins me from the kitchen. "What happened?"

"I lost Tucket again."

Mym touches my arm, then shakes her head and walks away.

My apartment has become decidedly crowded. Even with Tucket absent there is a shortage on privacy. Post motorcycle project, Doctor Quickly and Abraham have taken over my kitchen table and are poring over a bunch of timestream charts. Mym has commandeered the couch and has hot-wired my TV to display the contents of her MFD. She's navigating the internet at speeds that make my brain hurt, downloading data on Zoroastrianism, Zurvan, and any symbols that look like they could resemble a flaming circle with wings. Cowboy Bob has circumnavigated the apartment at least ten times now, but with his casual ease and polite banter, it took me half a dozen laps before I realized his repeated glances out the windows throughout the day were anything more than curiosity at the view. It finally dawns on me that he has been taking guard duty, keeping an eye out for trouble. I also now notice the bulge at the back of his shirt concealing a handgun. That more than anything else lets me know that, however casual he may seem, he's taking the situation seriously.

It's Bob who alerts us to new arrivals, though of the friendly variety. Carson and Francesca show up independently from one another. My cell phone had spent most of the day in the cabin of the Longletter boat so I missed both of their calls. Carson was apparently just enquiring as to whether I was playing softball this week and decided to swing by. Francesca was convinced after a half dozen calls that something was clearly wrong and I was in danger or dead. Her concern turns to elation when she finds the apartment full of the Quicklys and Cowboy Bob.

She and Bob have an enthusiastic reunion near the front door. I introduce Carson to Bob and Abraham and, in what I take as a ringing endorsement of trust, Doctor Quickly fills them in on the attack on the labs and our plan to look for the attackers.

The information has differing effects on Carson and Francesca. Carson is immediately ready to join in the hunt and is full of questions. Francesca adopts a plan of defensive paranoia and it's not long before she is doing laps around the house with Bob, fretting about shapes in the darkness and casting withering glances at neighbors out walking their dogs.

I finally hunker down on the couch with Mym. She seems to sense my mood. "How are you holding up?"

"All right, I guess." I repress a yawn. "Although when I said I wanted to show you a day in the life of Ben Travers, this wasn't exactly what I meant."

Mym puts a hand on my leg sympathetically. "I'm sorry. We sort of took over your life."

"It's okay." I gesture toward the TV-turned-computer. "Find anything good?"

Mym drags some notes onto the screen, seemingly from nowhere. "Not much on the symbol, but tons on Zoroaster. The guy really had a following. Funny thing though, for being so famous, historians have had a hard time nailing down when he actually lived. Some are saying twelve hundred BCE, others say six hundred. A few old texts place him at six *thousand* BCE. It's all over the place."

"It's strange that I've never heard of him."

"You've probably heard of his followers. They were big into astronomy and science. People thought they were magicians—called them Magi."

"Magi? Like 'We Three Kings of Orient Are,' Magi?"

"Yeah, probably the same ones. It was a whole class of astronomers slash priests. Zoroaster was from Mesopotamia in any case. Modern day Iraq and Iran. It was the cradle of civilization back then."

"I've heard about some of that. Didn't the wheel first get invented there?"

"That's definitely one of the places. It's also where they first started writing."

"Anything else specifically about Zurvan?"

"One interesting thing. Zoroastrians worship a god known as Ahura Mazda, an all powerful creation spirit, very similar to the Judeo-Christian God. But a fringe sect also believed in a god named Zurvan. He's believed to be the god of infinite space and time.

"Zurvanites credit Zurvan's influence on tons of myths and legends. There were quite a few about the prophet Zoroaster too, like where he got killed by the stars in a rain of fire for trying to restrain them. Some of the stories get a little crazy."

"Wow. God of time. That doesn't exactly seem like a coincidence." I watch her browse through a few more sites. "No luck on the symbol?"

"Not yet. A few Egyptian hieroglyphics popped up as possible matches and a couple of etchings in the catacombs of Rome, but nothing recent. Nothing to show why it would be spray-painted on Dad's wall. I want to go do a sweep of the lab now that I know what we're looking for. I feel like maybe I'm missing something."

"So how do we tie it together? I'm guessing we need more to—"

"Hey, Ben," Bob interrupts. "You expecting a delivery?"

"Not that I know of." I get up and follow Bob to the front window. He points down to the street. A flatbed truck has pulled up in front of the apartment and is offloading something covered in a tarp onto the sidewalk. Bob walks downstairs with me to meet the driver who intercepts us in the driveway.

"One of you Benjamin Travers?" The man has a belly that precedes him by a foot and the rest of his proportions are equally oversized. When I show interest, he shoves the clipboard and a pen into my hands. "Promised a guy I could have this here and offloaded by nine-thirty. Made a real big deal about it. You tell him traffic was shit, but I made it." The driver consults his watch. "Couple minutes to spare."

"Who did you—"

The man walks over to the unwanted delivery and yanks the tarp away. Sitting on the pallet is a rocket-shaped contraption with a single wheel protruding from the side. A dusty windshield partially blocks the view of a leather seat in the opening of the pod. The vehicle is set at a slight angle to one side and both Bob's and my heads tilt sideways to take it in.

"Would you look at that," Bob says. "

"Good enough?" The truck driver asks, jerking his clipboard back from me. "Didn't put no dings on it or nothin'. Looked like that when I loaded it up."

I lift Bob's arm from his side so I can consult his wristwatch. The second hand is ticking upward toward 9:30. "What was he thinking?" I let go of Bob's arm and observe the empty seat of the sidecar. There is a pregnant pause as the truck driver stares at us, waiting for his okay to leave, but I don't take my eyes off the sidecar. Sure enough, the space is spontaneously filled by a squatting man in vintage motorcycle goggles. He laughs out loud as he spots us in the driveway. The truck driver stumbles backward in shock.

"I knew it would work!" Tucket exclaims. He slaps the sides of the cockpit with both hands. " I had it shipped all the way from the seventies! What do you think, Ben?"

I can't help but laugh as I take it all in. The truck driver turns on his heel and makes for his truck as fast as he can waddle. He doesn't look back as he slams the door and fires up the engine. The truck lurches into gear and lumbers down the street at high RPM, still trailing straps behind it.

I smile back at the grinning young man in the sidecar. "I guess you did it, Tuck. Welcome to the team."

"Time travel and parenting are both difficult enough on their own. Combining them . . . ? Let's just say that when your six-year-old daughter discovers that every day really could be her birthday party, your cupcake and piñata budget is going to need to be revised."- Journal of Dr. Harold Quickly, 1992

CHAPTER 6

The Neverwhere

"You can call me Benny." The ragged other me is standing near the gate of 355 Maple Drive, my childhood home. "I know it might get confusing with both of us being here."

"I never liked being called Benny," I reply. "Except maybe by Mom. She got away with it."

"You remember the hideout under the house?" Benny asks. He unlatches the wooden gate and lets us into the yard. There is an eagerness to his movements, like he's excited to show me this memory.

"I spent a lot of time under there."

"Yeah, we did," Benny replies, prying at the lattice work that blocked the crawl space under the house.

When I was around eight, I discovered the hole and built the hideout. At first it had only been cardboard boxes scrounged from local dumpsters laid flat on the dry dirt. I borrowed my dad's flashlight and mom's feather duster and started cleaning up the boards and pipes around my space. I had a hard time finding motivation to clean my bedroom, but for some reason my hideout got lots of attention. I layered some old rugs over the cardboard and found a way to stack books on the plumbing pipes that dangled from the floor beams. I hid and read, or drew imagined treasure maps on the boards until the batteries would die on the flashlight. I switched to Dad's electric camping lantern but, when that proved unreliable, I finally had to run an extension cord under the house. That was what gave me away. That and my dog, Brisco.

The mostly retriever mutt was still young and inquisitive then and he sniffed me out and started barking. I tried to shush him through the lattice, but he was convinced I was trapped and needed rescuing. When Brisco wouldn't stop barking I dragged him into the hideout with me. This was infinitely preferable for the dog and, after a few licks to my face, he was content to investigate the hideout in silence. It was too late. Mom had ears like a wild animal, tuned to the merest hint of danger. I was trapped, a victim of my burgeoning desire for independence and mystery, and my mom's drive to protect me from black widows and all the creepy-crawly terrors that haunt a mother's dreams. Even though I held Brisco tight and kept him from bounding to her call, she found me. The traitorous extension cord led her right to me.

Standing outside the memory of this house, almost twenty years later, I get a pleasant sense of nostalgia. I kick a few leaves around the flowerbed and uncover my ineptly hidden extension cord. Benny smiles and nods in appreciation. "You're remembering that day."

I squat and peer through the wooden lattice guarding the crawl space. "So how does it work? We see whatever we happen to remember at the time?"

"No. It's more than that." Benny studies the walls. "This is the real place. We can only see it how we remember it, but other people can remember the same place differently, like you just did."

"You mean I changed it?"

"Yes. The extension cord wasn't there for me until you remembered it. Of course I remember it now, so even if you stopped, I might still see it. It's part of my memory too."

"Who are you? I mean, what version of me—us, are you?"

"Time enough for that later. You want to see if Brisco is here?"

"What?" I recoil at the thought of my dog being in this place. "How would—"

Benny senses my concern. "No. Not here. But you can see him sometimes. See others, too. Come on. I'll show you." Without further explanation he heads for the front porch and enters the house.

It's an oddly surreal experience seeing my childhood home this way. The interior is familiar, but slightly off. It takes me a few moments to process through the fact that various rooms are displayed in slightly different eras from one another. In some cases I'm seeing the most current incarnations of drapes and wall colors, but in other rooms I'm seeing furniture or fixtures that no longer exist. I know for a fact that my parents got rid of the portable dishwasher when they remodeled the kitchen a few summers ago, but having only been there to visit a few times, I couldn't tell you what they bought. The prevailing memory of the kitchen contains the outdated countertops and the refrigerator from my youth. I wouldn't be at all surprised to open the door and find a rack full of colorful freezer pops. I stare at the floor where two shiny silver pet bowls share a rubber spill mat.

"This is all an illusion, right?" I question my companion. "Brisco is dead, but he's not here, is he?" I was home from college the weekend the old dog died. We buried him in the backyard. A sad day, to be sure, but a natural one. No sign of time travel involved.

"He's not here with us, but he's on the other side."

Benny has the eager expression on his face again. Something about him seems foreign. I want to ask him how old he is and how he came to be in this place. He's another me, but there is more than the scraggly beard and unkempt clothing that separates the two of us. Something in his eyes is different too.

"You have to cross over." He crouches low, staring into the space near the dog bowls. "We're already in the right place. You just need to find the time . . ." He furrows his eyebrows in concentration. To my surprise, the air where he is looking begins to shimmer. For a moment, the space he's looking at takes on the multicolored hazy quality of the fog outside. The next thing to happen totally surprises me. I hear my mom.

Enraptured by this whole chain of events, I squat next to Benny and peer into the space near the fridge. Benny has created a sort of window into the kitchen. Roughly two feet square at first, it expands slowly as we stare into it.

"Good, good! Having you here helps," Benny exclaims. "Keep concentrating, it's almost big enough." He has his hands held in front of him as if he can push the shimmering window higher.

The interior of the hole looks the same as the kitchen we are standing in, but there are distinct noises coming out of it. A screen door slams and then someone walks right through us from back to front, swishing into the kitchen in Capri pants and a lavender apron. She heads for the cupboard and swings it open.

"Oh my God! Mom!" I stare incredulously at the image of my mother looking younger by almost two decades. Her blonde hair is long over her shoulders and she is humming something. She plucks a can of dog food from the cupboard and sets it on the countertop. "Can she—can she see us?"

"No. She won't hear us either. But wait. It gets better." Benny smiles. The view of the kitchen has expanded now beyond the limits of the room, old memories building on one another and filling in the last of the gaps.

My mom scrounges through the drawer and extracts a can opener. The puncturing of the can cues a new sound, claws on the linoleum at high speed. A blur of fur comes hurtling around the corner and skids to a stop near the refrigerator. Brisco is full of life and wriggling. His hindquarters can barely contain themselves as he whips his tail back and forth. He's young, somewhere close to the age he discovered me under the house, but it's hard to tell.

"He looks so good." The scene in front of me hits me all at once and I have a hard time even looking at it. I choke down the urge to cry.

I don't want to be dead anymore. I don't want Brisco to be dead, I want to be back there, back alive where I can grab hold of my mom and tell her I love her, feel Brisco's tail thwacking back and forth against my legs as he squirms in glee at being petted.

Benny looks at me sympathetically. "It was that way for me the first time, too. It gets easier though. Look." Benny points to the dog.

Brisco has stopped wriggling under my mother and is staring intently in our direction. My mom steps past him and sets his now full food bowl down. Brisco takes a step toward it instinctively, but looks toward us again and freezes.

"Go ahead," Benny says. "Call to him."

"What do you mean?" I ask.

"Just do it."

I squat a little closer to the dog, not much more than an arm's length away now. "Brisco? Can you hear me, boy?"

The dog's tail starts wagging again, but I can tell he's conflicted—so many competing urges showing in his body language.

My mom has finished pitching the empty can into the trash and is now standing over the dog. "Come on, Brisco. Eat your food."

The dog wags his tail harder and looks from the bowl to her face and then back in my direction again. My mom nudges the bowl with her toe. "Eat, you silly dog."

I can't help but smile at the dog's curious but exuberant expression.

"You're a good boy, Brisco," I say. "It's okay. Eat your food."

The dog barks once at me, a quick greeting, then gives in to his desire for the food. He plunges his face into the bowl, but his head pops up again between bites, chomping down the Alpo while still trying to keep an eye on me.

"Can he see us?" I still find the situation unbelievable.

"I don't know what he sees," Benny replies. "But he knows we're here. He can sense us somehow."

"Smart dog," I say. Brisco's tail wags a little faster, even as he continues his lapping assault on the crevices of the dog bowl. My mom straightens a few things in the kitchen before hanging her apron on a hook and retrieving her car keys. She takes one lingering glance around the room and, for a moment I wonder if she feels something different, like she senses us too, but then she opens the side door and departs, locking it behind her. I watch her silhouette vanish with a fresh pang of loss.

I look back to the dog. "I feel like I remember that about Brisco. I always thought he was seeing things we weren't."

"He was. I know he's seen me plenty of times."

"How often have you done this—visited the past?"

Benny straightens up and brushes at his pants. The room goes back to vacant again. I consider the empty silver pet bowls. They seem even more abandoned now.

"It's all I've had really. Trying to keep myself—trying to stay. . ."

"Sane?" I offer. "I can see how a place like this could get to you."

Benny nods. "It does. It's . . . lonely." He glances around the room and finally settles back to me. "You can see why I was surprised to see *you* here."

"Yeah, I can imagine." I ponder the circumstances of his appearance from the tree and my subsequent rescue. "The others here—that guy in the robes. What are they all about?"

"You need to stay away from him. He's bad news." Benny twitches a little. "All darkness and storms, that one. Cities in ruins, deserts that catch on fire. His memories are all that way. Dead or dying places."

"Why is he here? What is he doing?"

"I don't know how he got here, but I know what he does. He's a collector."

I frown. "Collecting what?" I can't remember any items in any of the places I've seen him that had any value.

Benny let's his eyes wander to the window as he replies.

"Souls. He collects people's souls."

◇◇◇

St. Petersburg-2009

It's after eleven when Doctor Quickly has finished laying out his plan. Despite his explanations, It takes me a bit to wrap my mind around all of it. The basic problem seems to be that there are a variety of places and times where the attackers who invaded his lab might reattempt to acquire him—if that was their goal. Assuming they are time travelers, they also might go after a different version of him in other timestreams, or try to attack him at a younger age.

Some of the other versions of Doctor Quickly are in contact with one another and will be able to call for help in the event they are in distress. Others won't and will need to be located and warned in person. I don't really understand the logistics of how Doctor Quickly has managed to keep his various selves from interacting and messing up each others' lives, but I make a note to ask him later for his system. I get the feeling it may be a useful skill to have.

Mym, Tucket, and I have been tasked with checking up on a couple of the lab spaces in the not-too-distant future of the November Prime, starting with the scene of the first attack. I'm also supposed to search out any way of getting in touch with my departed self and find out what he knows about the mysterious symbol I've seen.

Francesca is going to be a contact at home while Cowboy Bob visits a few other timestreams near 2009. Doctor Quickly and Carson will investigate locations in the early part of the twentieth century. Tucket seems disappointed to not be tasked with that excursion, since it's his favorite century, but he's feeling too proud of being a part of the process to consider defecting from his assignment.

It took a little bit of time to get Tucket up to speed on the situation, but once he understood that Doctor Quickly was in danger, he committed whole-heartedly to the team. We are supposed to send reports from our various missions to Abraham, who will man the tachyon pulse transmitter back at Bob's ranch, and keep us all informed of developments.

Doctor Quickly volunteers to help me gravitize the sidecar and turns down an offer of assistance by Tucket. When the two of us are alone in the garage, it's clear that getting the motorcycle ready to go is child's play for him. There is something more on his mind. He leans against my workbench and studies me as I fiddle with the bike.

"I want you to know, Ben, that Mym speaks very highly of you. It's been wonderful seeing her so happy. Truly."

"Thanks. I'm definitely glad to have your approval. It means a lot to me."

Doctor Quickly nods, then runs his hand over the bike's handlebars.

"That being said, there are a few things you should be aware of. I'm always trying to do what's best for her, protect her as much as a father can in these circumstances."

I pause in my wrenching of the sidecar attachment bolts. "I'm a careful driver. I've actually been riding motorcycles a long time—"

"No, no. That's not what I meant. Though that is certainly good to know." He scratches at his head as if unsure of how to continue. "Mym is . . . well, special, as you already know. Raising a daughter who could time travel on her own from the time she was a teenager had its challenges. Not least of which was trying to define some sense of boundaries. It's hard to put limits on a girl who can be anywhere, anytime."

I smile. "I can imagine. Seems like you did a pretty great job though. She turned out well."

"Indeed, but I need to level with you, Ben. As a father, I've had to keep some things from her. She's a grown woman now, able to make all of her own decisions—and she has—but even so, there is a lot of her mother in her.

"It would be unjust to saddle her entire gender with this characteristic, but in my experience, at least the women in her family all have a natural predisposition for worrying. Perhaps it's a side-effect of how caring they are. But worry can be a plague. It can cripple you if you let it. It eats away at your freedom. I didn't want that for Mym. I wanted her to be able to enjoy herself in this world, see it in all its wonder."

"I think she does," I reply. "She's certainly shown me plenty already."

Doctor Quickly smiles. "I'm glad for that. You two have been good for each other." He paces around to the other side of the motorcycle. "You've had quite a bit of adventure yourself, and you've seen in your travels that not all time travelers share the values we do. Your experiences in the chronothon exposed you to some of the nastier elements of this world." He trails off and I'm not sure if there was meant to be a question in there somewhere.

"Are you saying we're going to run into more of that this trip?"

Doctor Quickly puts his hands in his pockets and nods. "I know the time has come when I can't keep these aspects of my life away from her much longer. Danger is a real part of the path I've chosen and, as much as I would wish it away if I could, the danger still falls on the people I love."

I finish mounting the attachment bolts and roll my wrenches up in their travel case. "If it makes you feel any better, she's pretty tough. I've seen her in action. If anyone is likely to protect anybody, it will probably be her saving me." I note the seriousness of Doctor Quickly's face and add, "But I'm definitely going to look out for her in every way I know how."

"I know you will. It's possible that we may be dealing with a completely new threat here. I take security very seriously when it comes to my labs. I keep them completely secret whenever possible. The fact that this group located and attacked one of them does not bode well for us."

"Who else knows about your labs?"

"The people in this house are the only time travelers I've trusted with that information. Bob and Abraham have been my confidants for decades. My assistant Malcolm watches over a few places for me in linear time and I've enlisted a few other assistants over the years, but, individually, none of them know more than a few locations. In fact, I don't know that any one person in the group knows the locations of every lab with the exception of other versions of myself."

"Even Mym?"

"Mym has seen the majority of them," he replies. "But, true to my wishes, her travels have kept to the neighborhood, temporally speaking. When she met up with you in the twenty-fourth century, I believe that was the farthest she had ever traveled in time. You have gone farther into the past via the time gates in the chronothon than even I have traveled. I hear you saw ancient Egypt?"

"Briefly. The race didn't leave much time for sightseeing."

"Still. Must have been fascinating."

I nod, but don't reply. That part of the chronothon seems like a different lifetime—some crazy dream I woke up from.

Doctor Quickly continues. "Mym is a young woman now, and for all I know, she may have seen far more of the Fractal Universe than I'm aware of, but there are places—limits to this world—that I don't suspect she's seen. There is some knowledge that changes you, and you can never be the same once you've seen it. With Mym, I think I would know."

"I'll do my best to keep us out of trouble, but I'm new at this myself still, so I don't know how much good I'll be."

Doctor Quickly hands me the last few tools to put away. "You have the smarts, Ben. You never would have made it home if you didn't. And I know you have courage. The chronothon proved that. Just promise me that if the day comes when you find yourself up against something you know you can't handle, you'll keep her out of the fight. Make sure you bring her home."

I nod slowly. "I will. I promise."

Doctor Quickly keeps his eyes locked on mine for just a second longer, then drops them to the bike, his tone back to the task at hand. "Well then. Looks like you're ready to roll."

I lift the garage door and survey the shadowy streets. "I think I'll take it for a spin real quick. See if I can get the hang of this sidecar before I take on passengers." Doctor Quickly helps me guide the bike out into the driveway and closes the garage door for me as I get it started.

"Abraham and I will be heading out," Doctor Quickly says. "I'll be back in the morning for Carson."

"You have somewhere safe to stay?"

"Abe has a few tricks up his sleeve. We'll be fine." Doctor Quickly waits till I pull out into the street, then waves and heads back inside.

I take it slow at first, getting a feel for the turns and enjoying the quiet streets. The sidecar is an odd sensation to get used to. I can't lean into the curves, which throws off my sense of balance. My first few turns are sloppy, the extra wheel of the sidecar coming off the ground and causing me to weave all over. I'm happy to be testing the new rig alone and not with Mym on the back. My promises about being a good rider would seem pretty hollow.

The stars are out and the air has cooled. I ride along the bay and through downtown, then make my way south on some of the side streets. I decide to try out the time travel functions of the bike, setting my chronometer for a one-second jump, then setting my timer to tick down from ten. I extend the grounding wire and let the timer count down. I jump as expected, skipping over the required second. I try it a couple of times, wondering what I must look like to anyone who might be poking their head out of their curtains, an old bike vanishing and reappearing in spurts down the street.

After a few successful jumps, I stow the jump cable and go back to cruising. I end up in the Old Southeast neighborhood without much thought, but since I'm here I decide to check up on my alternate life.

Lights are still on at Kaylee's house. I park the bike and approach the porch cautiously. I don't really know the protocol for calling on another self's life, especially late at night.

Through the window I can see Kaylee on the couch. Other Ben is standing on a stool replacing a light bulb in the living room ceiling fan. I can't really think of a reasonable way to get to him without alerting her so I simply wait till he's done and knock. It's Kaylee who answers the door.

I've had the experience of seeing different versions of the same person before and I know the strange feeling it causes as your brain tries to process through it. It's much more amusing watching it register on someone else's face.

Kaylee is a pretty girl. More so when she has her mouth closed. Currently she's staring slack-jawed from the doorway and does a double-take of the other Ben in the living room. He shakes his head at me from beyond the coffee table. I notice the bouquet of roses has disappeared.

"Not very subtle, are you?" He steps around the table to join Kaylee.

"Oh. My. God. Are you serious right now?" Kaylee has regained her composure and is scanning both of us rapidly. "Benji, you didn't tell me you had a brother!"

Benji? I note the sour expression on the other me's face. I wonder if he really is the Benji I know—the old man I met in the desert when all this started. He certainly seems to be developing the grouchy attitude.

"You never mentioned me, Benji?" I chide.

My other self flips me off. I just smile. I'm pretty sure Kaylee knew the basics of my family tree when we dated, but retention of facts was not always her strongest trait. She grabs my hand and drags me indoors. "Oh, wow. You guys look so similar. It's like you could have been twins. How much younger are you?"

I glance at Benji, but he just shakes his head.

"I think we are going to have to tell her anyway," I say. "She may as well know the secret."

"Secret? What secret?" Kaylee's eyes are wide, but she seems oddly energized by the suggestion. She's literally bouncing on her toes at the sight of the two of us together and whatever mystery it might entail. The effect on her ample bosom is hard to ignore. The top she has on is not doing the best job of containing her exuberance.

Benji notes my drifting gaze. "Let's talk outside." He brushes Kaylee's arm. "Kayls, I need a minute with my *brother*, okay?" Benji points toward the porch and I back out the doorway, holding the screen door open for him. Kaylee starts to say something in the way of an objection as Benji steps outside, but he simply shuts the door as if he hadn't heard.

"You look like you're having fun." I put my hands in my pockets and lean against the porch railing.

"She's not the issue. Don't worry about my situation. What are you doing here?"

I study his face. He looks annoyed.

"I thought I'd let you know that I'm going to be doing a bit of traveling. Figured you could use the apartment if you needed to. And our other stuff." I hold my phone out to him. "Temporarily anyway."

Benji reaches for the phone and inspects it briefly. "All right."

"And I put a bunch of money in the checking account. I won some money recently and set myself up with the bank to just automatically pay all my bills. I actually bought the apartment the other day. Seemed easier."

"You bought the apartment?"

"Well, I had to buy the house next door too because they're on the same property, but yeah, basically. Saves me from having to ever pay rent. Thought that might be useful since, you know, I'm traveling a lot."

"Just can't sit still, can you?" He sinks into a patio chair.

"Lots of world to see," I reply.

He shoves the ashtray away and rests his arm on the table. "Just because the universe rings the doorbell, doesn't mean you have to answer. Sometimes a simple life is enough."

"I'm . . . managing. What happened to you, man? It's like a couple years away and all of a sudden you're ready to pack it in. You want me to dial you up a nice senior living center, reserve you a rocking chair and a sponge bath?"

Benji shakes his head. "I know you think the Quicklys are where it's at. I won't burst your bubble, but they know the universe isn't half as rosy as you seem to think it is. They've seen their share of the shit out there. Probably caused some of it."

"I've seen my share of shit, too. I raced a chronothon. That wasn't a summer picnic. Doesn't mean I want to crawl into a hole and hide."

"Yeah, well, wait a little. This time travel mess? It gets to the point where you can't even remember what normal life was, and you couldn't get it back if you tried. I know you have your time traveler girlfriend and you think you've got it all under control. You think you can handle it. I won't try to stop you. Just know that the grass doesn't really get greener out there. It gets dark. Really dark."

"Noted." I straighten up. "Well, if this little sunshine session is over, I guess I'll get going. Glad you and Kaylee can play house or whatever. I'll bring you over some crocheted doilies next time so you can keep your furniture pretty. Maybe a case of Ensure." I step off the porch and head for the bike.

"Ben."

I pause and appraise my older self. He's standing now, one hand on the porch railing. I wonder if he's about to wish me safe travels, repentant for being such a downer.

"I think it's best if we keep our lives separate. I don't want you telling Kaylee about time travel."

I turn around, gravel and sand crunching under my sneakers as I take a few steps back toward him. "You're going to try to pull this brothers act off with our friends? Kaylee is one thing, but it's not like other people aren't going to notice the difference."

"I'll keep an eye on things while you're gone. Then, when you get back, we'll divide things up somehow. Keep it fair."

I glare at him, at once angry and hurt. I feel like I'm getting broken up with. Ditched by someone I never wanted around anyway. "Listen, man. I'll do what I want. You can pack up and go whenever you feel like—"

"When you come back." His response cuts me short. He just stares at me, his eyes unrelenting.

"Whatever, man." I spin on my heel and head for the bike. I snatch up my helmet and start strapping it on. "Make sure you call Mom next week for her birthday. And don't be a dick."

"You're going to see, Ben. It's not what you—"

I drown him out with the roar of the engine as I start the bike. I rev the throttle a few more times just for emphasis, but Benji doesn't attempt to speak again. He just watches from the porch. I make more noise than necessary as I peel out of the driveway. I sneak one look in the side mirror as I roll away, but Benji is already headed back inside. I shift gears and launch north toward home.

What's with everybody tonight? First Doctor Quickly, now this? I try not to wonder what Benji knows about the Quicklys that he would consider "dark." I attempt to write him off as simply jealous of the life I've found, but even the thought rings false. I know him. I know me. Whatever he's talking about is more than just the stuff of petty rivalry.

Moths dance around street lamps as I navigate the way home. I blaze by in a fury of noise and leave them to their fruitless worship of the light. I follow my own solitary beam through my neighborhood and up the driveway to my garage. The living room windows have gone dark.

The door to Tucket's room is closed, but light is still illuminating the floorboards. I find Mym in my bedroom.

"Hey, you." She looks up from her novel and smiles. Something about the image of her sitting there triggers a feeling of déjà vu. I pause, but then shake off the sensation, too weary to deal with any more temporal confusion.

I flop onto the bed next to her and rest an arm across her lap. "I just want to sleep this evening out of existence."

"What happened?"

"Other self problems."

When she keeps waiting for an explanation, I give her an abbreviated account of my talk with Benji. I leave out the conversation with her dad.

"He thinks we're bad for you or something?" Mym's brow is crinkled in concern.

"I don't know what he thinks. Somebody clearly pissed in his cornflakes somewhere along the line because he's being a tool."

Mym frowns. "This is another you we're talking about."

"I don't care. I'm not going to end up like him. Freaking bitter old man."

"He's not that much older than you," Mym replies.

"Yeah well, he's older. So old man is what he gets. Especially if he just wants to pack his life away and call it a day." I roll onto my stomach and bury my face in the pillow, my extended hours finally catching up with me.

Mym nestles down at my side. "I don't know. You're the one who wanted a relaxing day at home." I can hear the smile in her voice.

"Well, I was wrong," I mumble into the pillowcase. I lift my head and find Mym's intense blue eyes only a few inches from mine, studying me. I kiss her softly before stuffing my face back into the pillow. "Tomorrow, we go time traveling."

"As a child I had hoped to be an astronaut. When I learned I did not meet the requirements for NASA, I was initially heartbroken. Fortunately, the qualifications to be a time traveler were yet to be written. Truly new frontiers merely require the vision to find them."-Journal of Dr. Harold Quickly, 1969

CHAPTER 7

The Neverwhere

There is a concrete barrier on the curve of San Joaquin Boulevard just before it heads downhill. The concrete is scuffed and marked from the occasions when it performed its function of keeping inept drivers and stumbling pedestrians from inadvertently hurling themselves down the rocky grade beyond. Besides being a deterrent to wayward travelers, the flat concrete blocks make a sturdy outpost for viewing the vista beyond.

Benny and I are seated on the barricade with our feet dangling, facing the sprawling view of our childhood town. Oregon was a peaceful part of my life, an era of bike riding and tree forts. My friends and I ran in the wooded hills till sundown, coming home with clothes stained from weeds and fingers darkened by blackberries. The nighttime meant hide-and-seek in the neighborhood, lying prone in neighbors' flowerbeds, then dodging street lights and racing for home base, breathless and exuberant.

The view of town is quiet now, though lights do still illuminate the twilight. I can't be sure if it's my own memory or Benny's populating our surroundings. Studying the houses below I spot details of homes that I wouldn't have known I remembered. Benny is quiet beside me, musing at the scenery. It seems a familiar routine.

"How long have you been here?" I ask.

Benny wrinkles his nose as if the question itself is distasteful. "No time here. Too hard to say. I think . . . I think sometimes that maybe I've always been here."

I try to ascertain if he's trying to be metaphorical. "But how did you . . ." I trail off, not sure how to approach the subject gently.

"Die?" he asks. He turns toward me just slightly, studying me with one eye. Then he looks away. "Everybody wants to know that."

Staring at the vacant city streets I try to guess who "Everybody" could mean. I wait him out, just watching the fog shimmer at the edges of the woods and in the gaps between memories.

He finally speaks. "They all lie, you know? They tell you that you're going to Heaven. That you'll see all your loved ones on the other side. Nobody talks about this." He waves a hand angrily at the air.

I ponder his words for a bit before responding. "This place is something, though. Something real enough to interact with. Definitely not Heaven, true. But do you have any idea where we are?"

"No. This place is nothing. It's a glitch. The space between spaces." He chucks a broken fragment of concrete down the hill. "At first, I thought there had to be a way on from here. Like maybe this was Purgatory, and God was just making me wait. Wait, wait, wait. Like if I was good enough, He'd open a door, let me in to where everyone else is."

"No door?"

"No." He studies another fragment in his hands, turning it over in his fingertips. "I don't know what that means. I'm not good enough? There is no God? I don't know." He chucks that fragment too. "I don't know where the others went, but they sure aren't here."

"What others?"

"The other ones. The dead people we know. Grandpa, Uncle Tom, Mrs. Donovan's kid—all of 'em. They should've been here, right? If this was where you go when you die, where is everybody?"

He cups his hands and yells down the hill. "COME OUT, COME OUT, WHEREVER YOU ARE!" The yell echoes off the houses around us. His hands drop to his lap and he stares.

I gaze with him into the dim twilight. No children spring from flowerbeds. No one races for home base.

"What do we do then? Just hang out? Remembering things?"

Benny shakes his head. "No. We can't even remember what we want to. If I go there . . ."

I wait for the rest to come, but it doesn't.

"The guy in the desert. The one you saved me from. Does he know something about this place? Like maybe a way on?"

Benny narrows his eyes. "Zurvan. He's not going on. I've watched him. He's definitely not looking for any door to Heaven. He's going back."

"Back? What do you mean? Like back to being alive?"

"He's preparing. Making plans. He talks to people. Sends messages."

"To who?"

"I don't know, but they listen. They send messages to him, too."

I recall the man's deep voice and brooding expression. My mind objects to the thought, still sore from the attack, but I can see his eyes boring into mine, his hand stretched out to crush me.

"No. Don't." Benny grabs my arm. I look down to my clenched fist and notice that the top of the concrete barrier where my hand is resting is now dusted with coarse brown sand. Benny brushes it off rapidly and gets to his feet, dragging me up after him. "Never bring him here. Never." He jumps off the barricade, leaving me behind as he strides down the barren street. He stops and holds his hands out. The air shimmers ahead of him. The opening appears again, tiny at first, but then larger. Through the shimmering portal I recognize the outside of my apartment in St. Pete. The three-quarter moon still hangs in the sky above it. Benny steps through the portal and gestures for me to follow.

As soon as I'm through, I turn around, but it's as if our detour to Oregon never happened. I'm looking down Oak Street again, bathed in the humid Florida night air. Benny has his arms crossed and seems to be shivering despite the warmth. He doesn't make any move toward the apartment, giving me the hint that this stop was for me, not him.

"You're leaving?" I don't mean to sound worried, but it comes out that way.

"Have some things to do. Can't stay."

He's avoiding eye contact. I don't press the issue. Instead, I take a new tack. "I need you to teach me."

Benny finally meets my gaze, but his eyes narrow. "Teach you what?"

"This." I gesture to the air behind me that we just appeared through. "I need to know how to get around the way you do. Change places. See the past."

Benny shakes his head and his shoulders sway back and forth with it, almost as if he's rocking himself. "Too much to learn. No time."

I frown at him. "I know there's no time. That's why I'm asking. If Zurvan comes back—"

"Shhhhh. Don't talk about him!" Benny glances about as if expecting the turbaned man to spring from the bushes. "Not here." He backs away from me and turns toward the corner.

"Benny, wait." I try to follow.

"Tomorrow. Not tonight. I'll teach you tomorrow." Benny gives another shiver and bobs his head up and down. "Tomorrow will be better."

I stay where I am and let him retreat from me. "Okay. Tomorrow then."

Benny nods once more and turns away, breaking into a sprint and disappearing around the corner of the neighbor's house.

I watch the corner for a few more moments, then let my gaze drift upward to the partial moon still hanging above the fog. *How do you know when it's tomorrow in a place with no time?* I lower my head and stare at my apartment, realizing that I may have just been duped. *Shit.*

I shrug off the annoyance at the situation and climb the stairs to my apartment. It's vacant and quiet—not that I expected different. I check each room just to be sure, and then plop down on the couch. Benny's shivering form runs off again in my mind. *Fine. Ditch me. I'll teach myself.*

I sit up straight on the couch and try to determine how to start. Somehow sitting feels wrong so I stand back up. *What am I supposed to look at?* I survey the living room, then settle on the open space between that and the kitchen. I fixate on the space the way Benny did, holding my hands out in front of me to open up the window to the past. Nothing happens. I concentrate harder, but I'm not sure what I'm hoping to see. Frustrated, I move a few steps closer to the kitchen. *Come on, Ben. Concentrate.* I screw my face up and stare hard into the open space between me and the kitchen counter. I pry at the air with my fingers as if I could break it open by hand. I keep at it for what seems like at least ten minutes without any success.

I mutter curses at my stubborn apartment and try one more time, calming my mind and trying to get specific. *I want to see my apartment in 2009. I want to see the time I left. June, 2009. June, 2009. Come on . . .*

The air shimmers with color.

Elated, I raise my hands above me and shout, "Yes!"

My concentration is broken. The shimmer vanishes.

Sonofabitch.

My success was short-lived, but my spirit is buoyed. *It's possible.*

The space in front of me is back to normal, but I catch a whiff of a peculiar scent that my experiment has left behind. It's lingering around me. I take a longer sniff and try to place the smell. Sweet. Familiar. I wrack my memory to try to place it. *It smells like . . . warm maple syrup.*

Curious, I gather myself up to try again. I place my hands out in front of me and squint. *Ben Travers, master of time. Here we go.*

St. Petersburg-June, 2009

Mym is some sort of breakfast wizard. I would have sworn she was only out of bed five minutes ahead of me, but when I stumble into the kitchen, there are waffles. More reasons I love dating a time traveler.

I am not the only one who gets waffles. Our sendoff ends up including a visit from most of my friends. Blake and Mallory, Carson, Francesca, and Tucket all get servings. Mym even makes a plate for a surprise guest, Other Me. When Benji walks in the door, he looks every bit as surprised to find all of us in attendance as my friends are about seeing him. I do some hasty explaining of the situation and how Benji is going to stand in for me in my absence. To their credit, my friends don't freak out at all to his face. Even Mallory, who has yet to witness the level of strangeness that the rest of us have been exposed to as time travelers, keeps a cool composure.

Benji makes a bit of polite conversation, then scarfs down his waffle and retreats to the bathroom for a shower. Francesca is at my shoulder in an instant. "How weird is this for you? Do you guys get along?"

"Yeah. Sure. It's no big deal."

Francesca raises her eyebrows. "If some other me strolled into my apartment, it'd be a little more than just a big deal. It'd be a showdown, especially if she was older. This guy seems like he knows what's up. Like he's wise for his age."

"And I'm not wise?" I protest.

Francesca laughs. She contains herself and pats me on the arm. "Oh, is this going to make you doubt yourself? I mean if I had some other me who dressed better and maybe had better hair, I'd be pretty upset." She studies me, as if waiting for me to gush my true feelings. I attempt to flatten my bed-head cowlicks down and frown at her. Then I open the fridge and look for the orange juice. Francesca lingers a moment, but when I don't crack under her scrutiny, she goes back to the table to discuss things with Mallory.

Blake picks up his fiancée's plate and joins me near the trashcan. "How long are you going to be gone?" He scrapes remnants of waffle and syrup into the trash before placing the dishes in the sink.

"Hard to say. Could be a while, I guess." I wander out onto the front steps with my juice. Blake follows.

"No worries, in any case." Blake says. "We'll hold the place down for you."

I glance back inside to the kitchen table where Francesca is whispering excitedly with Mallory. Mym wanders over and joins the girls' discussion. I can't help but wonder what they're talking about. "Just promise me that you aren't going to end up liking this guy better than me."

"Him?" Blake jerks a thumb toward the bathroom. "You kidding? I hate him already. Just on principle." He bumps my fist.

"See? I knew I could count on you. Francesca was all 'Oooh, he seems so mature . . .'"

"Total fucking asshole."

I smile. "Thank you. That's exactly what I needed to hear."

"Bring it in, man." Blake stretches his arms out and we give each other a hug. As he lets me go, he pats me on the back. "We'll still be waiting for you when you get back. Just make it home in one piece."

"Deal."

"And hang on to that one." He gestures to Mym, who is leaning against the back of Mallory's chair. "I know a keeper when I see one."

"I'm trying, man. If I have any chance of making this work, it's with her. I've seen plan B and it's living in a shack in the desert with a tortoise."

"Screw plan B."

Mallory notices me watching and breaks away from Mym and Francesca to join us.

"Ben was worried about his alter ego," Blake says as Mallory attaches herself to his arm.

"Who? Dipshit Other Ben?" Mallory asks.

"We already discussed it," Blake says. "Pretty sure that's what we're calling him."

"D.O.B. for short," Mallory adds. "And to, you know, not let on that we hate him right away."

I smile and clasp her hand in mine. "I love you guys."

"We'll see you soon, man." Blake replies.

I turn away and head for the bedroom to pack my things before I lose all motivation to leave.

I've done four practice runs with the motorcycle's anchor deployment device before I feel ready to take on passengers. Each time, the spool of cable has extended perfectly, trailing a flat, weighted cattail of wire behind the bike. Initially, Doctor Quickly and I had tried using just a weighted disc, thinking a hockey-puck-shaped weight might stay adhered to the ground the best at speed. When that skipped and danced around too much, we tried a well-greased ball at the center of the disc, hoping it would roll smoothly. That bounced even more, making it far too dangerous to consider. Finally we frayed the end of some cable till it resembled a broom. Weighted properly and, with a few extra strands at intervals along the length of cable, there were always at least a half dozen wires in contact with the ground no matter what speed I got the bike up to. Judging by the occasional sparks it caused, wear and tear on the cable will definitely be a factor after multiple deployments, but it seems like the safest solution, and most likely to keep me from joining my other self in the Neverwhere.

It has taken some convincing to make Tucket abandon his collection of "authentic" twenty-first century clothes. I told him it would be infinitely better to just dress in motorcycle gear, thinking that anything he found from the past century would have to be less gaudy than the outfits he's chosen so far. I suspected he might come downstairs dressed like The Fonz from *Happy Days*, but I never factored in the possibility that he could jump back in time and order himself authentic Evel Knievel stunt gear for the occasion. As he walks up to the sidecar in the star-spangled jumpsuit, he sets the matching helmet on his head and grins. "Pretty hardcore, right?"

Mym has followed him down the stairs, dressed more simply in jeans and a tank top, and is repressing laughter at the sight of my face. She's got my leather jacket and her backpack draped over one arm. She offers me my jacket. I shake my head. June morning air in Florida is still warm enough to make you shed layers, and I'm still shaken from the last connection with my departed self. The last thing I need is to get dizzy or pass out while riding. Mym stuffs the jacket into the baggage area of the sidecar.

I gesture to Tucket's brilliant white costume. "Did you put him up to this? Are you guys pranking me right now?"

Mym shakes her head and shrugs, trying not to laugh. "He's your stunt man, not mine."

I look Tucket up and down, noting that he even managed to find an oversized EK belt buckle. "Okay, you can wear the jumpsuit, but the cape stays here." I point to the garage. Tucket seems confused. "Because of wind resistance," I add.

"Oh. Right." Tucket nods and unclips the cape from beneath his wide white lapels, folding it up carefully. "That makes sense. Evel Knievel didn't always wear the cape on jumps. I'll save that for special occasions."

"Okay." I smile, in spite of myself. "You know, Evel Knievel lived close to here. Just over in Clearwater. Died a couple years ago, but maybe when we get back we can pay him a visit." I grab my messenger bag and shut the garage.

"That would be righteous!" Tucket exclaims. "You think he'd take a selfie with me?"

"What's a selfie?" I ask, stowing the bag.

Mym waits for me to straddle the bike and climbs on behind me. "Just wait a little. If you haven't heard of it yet, you will in a few months. "You have a Facebook account yet?"

"Not yet. Should I?"

"No." Mym kisses my cheek and gives me a squeeze. "I'll keep you to myself."

Tucket holds up a phone from his seat in the sidecar. "I have a Facebook! I got one as soon as I got here. I also got a Myspace and a Xanga blog and a Match Dot Com profile. In a couple of years I can get Instagram and Tinder."

"What's a Tinder?" I ask.

Mym groans. "That one you're definitely not getting."

I shrug and fire up the motorcycle.

First stop for us isn't very far into the future. Mym pulls up a GPS location on her MFD and navigates us to one of her dad's lab spaces in 2015. The place hasn't been attacked, the pit stop is just to pick up anchors to use to get to other locations, but we take a few minutes to check out the sights as well.

The near future is not hard to adjust to as we cruise around town. *Back To The Future II* seems to have vastly overestimated the importance of flying cars or automated weather, but there are definite differences from 2009. Even the six years we've jumped forward have brought around some obvious changes in St. Petersburg. For one, everyone seems to have grown out their facial hair. The men anyway. For young women, the most drastic change I spot is the frequency and density of arm and body tattoos. I feel like I had seen a couple in 2009, but nowhere near the amount visible now. Every other woman we pass on Central Avenue seems to be sporting a colorful sleeve down to her elbow.

Downtown is booming. There is a new fancy shopping venue near the movie theatre, even a hip-looking barber shop called *The Shave Cave* where someone is getting a shoe shine as they read their electronic tablet. One of my favorite Mexican restaurants is gone, replaced by a *Trader Joe's* grocery store. We do a pass along Beach Drive to check the new additions there as well. My favorite gelato place is still in existence so I decide that future can't be totally unappealing. I pull over and let Mym plot out our next jump.

To get to different locations requires attaching a degravitized item to my bike's anchor cable. By only letting the anchor touch the ground and not the cable, we assure that the chronometer will jump us forward to the same relative location in regard to the anchor, and not just our current surroundings. The system takes some care, but Mym has been smart and scoured her father's extensive collection of anchors to choose ones that are mostly located on the ground and in places we can fit an entire motorcycle.

Her first selection takes us to Valencia in 2017, the site of the first lab attack. While we can't interfere with the attack happening without potentially altering the timestream, we can do more investigating into the perpetrators. Mym already checked some of the aftermath of the attack via the security footage, but by arriving beforehand, we can get a look at them in person.

This is my first time visiting Spain in winter. It's January so the weather is cool, but mild. Valencia seems like a fashionable city, full of pedestrian traffic. We've arrived in the early afternoon near the center of the city. Mym explains that Doctor Quickly tends to keep labs on different continents in various years in order to get around easier. She navigates me through the bustling streets via the GPS on her multi-function handheld unit. Tucket and his sidecar get more than a few second looks from the Spanish citizens around us. He doesn't exactly blend in.

I park the bike near a covered market and we stow our few belongings inside the hatch at the back of the sidecar. The domed building houses what looks like hundreds of vendors from butchers and fishmongers to local artists and craftsmen. Someone walks by sucking on bits of a fresh-peeled clementine from a fruit stand and the citrusy scent makes my mouth water.

Once we're out of sight of the bike, Mym notes the local time and logs it into her MFD. "We'll be able to get back to our stuff anytime after now." The MFD beeps and shows our location on a map screen. It has the bike's position as well.

Tucket has some sort of gizmo in his hand, too, the same one I saw him taking pictures in my house with. Unlike Mym's, his unit has no screen. It is just a rounded ball in his palm. He's looking at something though, and seems pleased with himself.

"That's it." Mym points across the street to what could be an office building. The lower floor is retail space, but the windows on the upper floors are tinted and dark. I've learned from experience that Doctor Quickly's labs are frequently camouflaged this way, hidden in plain sight among other more distracting neighbors. "We need a place to watch from," Mym says. "The security footage doesn't show how they got inside."

"There's a view from the top of the building next door. We can see both exits." Tucket points to the old, four story building to the right of the lab. He seems to be referencing something invisible in front of him as he explains.

"What have you got there?" I point to the ball in his hand.

"It's a Third Eye Hot Shot." Tucket says, grinning.

I wait for him to explain further, but he seems to think it unnecessary.

The reference isn't completely lost on me, however. I recall that Third Eye is the name of a tech company that produces perceptor chips in his century. The perceptors allow direct access to the user's mind, allowing them to see a modified environment around them called the meta-space. The meta-space acts like an amped up version of the Internet, but layered over real world spaces. It allows users to see and interact with everything from media and advertising, to actual functional controls for objects in the real world.

"You can use the meta-space all the way back in 2017?" I ask.

Tucket shakes his head. "There's no input this far back. Meta-mapping won't get completed till the 2080s. But since I have a portable unit, I have access to all the data and programs I've downloaded whenever I go." He holds the ball up. "Hot Shot is the best. Doesn't come out till 2160, but I went up and got one before this trip, and it has tons of data already included from your time."

"Like Google Maps for time travelers."

"Google was actually the parent company."

"Ah. Makes sense." I stare at our target building. "So how do we get up there?"

"Stairs. Looks like an internal roof access," Mym replies. She leads the way across the street.

"Stairs it is." I let Tucket go ahead of me and I follow behind. When we get to the base of the building, Mym pauses. "We really need a way to track these guys when they show themselves. If all three of us are on top, we may miss something. I think we should split up."

"Where do you want me?" I ask.

Mym studies the side of the building, then considers the alley that runs between it and her dad's lab. "I'll go high, you guys stay low. You still have the MFD I gave you?"

I reach into my messenger bag and find the phone-like device she left with me.

"Oh sweet," Tucket comments as I display it. "Shape-shift cybertech?"

Mym nods. "It's bio-nano."

"Righteous," Tucket replies. "And you can use it off-Grid." He looks up at me. "Have you let it go green light aware with your timestream signature yet?"

I just stare back at him. "Has it googly-moogly what now?"

Mym intervenes. "Ben is still a new user. Haven't gotten him up to speed on nano-tech yet. We're getting there." She whips her finger around the screen on the device in my hand and activates something. The device starts to wriggle. "Oh shit!" I retract my hand. Mym snatches the device before it falls. She balances the now wiggling glob in her palm. As I watch, the unit morphs from the shape of a phone into the spherical ball of whatever Tucket had been holding. When it's done changing, she holds it up for my approval, then does something to make it revert to rectangular. She tosses it back to me and by the time I catch it, it has taken the shape of an iPhone. It's much thinner than any models we had in 2009, but I can tell just from the passersby that it's what most of the people around this city are using.

"Holy crap. This technology is available in 2017?" I ask.

"No." Mym holds up her own device. It also now resembles an iPhone. "This technology can *look* like what's available in 2017. Helps us to blend in."

I admire the shiny device in my hand. "Nice. If we go back to 1985 will it turn into a payphone?"

Mym laughs. "No, but even you should be able to figure this version out. Call me as soon as you see anything."

The three of us take positions in a loose triangle around the lab and I'm left to loiter near a café across the street. My "phone" beeps at me periodically and at first I jump each time, thinking one of the others has spotted the intruders. After the fourth or fifth photo from Tucket with a caption like, "Check out this groovy dog!" I start to tune out the phone and just concentrate on the building. I don't have a lot of experience with surveillance, but the basics seem pretty simple. Somebody has to break their way in at some point. Or so I thought. After fifteen minutes of nothing but dog photos, Mym chimes in to a group conversation on the phone. I hold it to my ear.

"They're already inside. I don't know how they did it, but the interior is already on fire."

I look up to see the orange glow coming from the third floor windows. Mym sounds frustrated on the phone. "Dad's gone. The cameras are hardly tracking these guys. Maybe three of them. Can't quite tell."

As she's speaking, the barred metal door I've been watching pops open from the inside. A sweatshirt-covered head pokes out and glances both ways down the sidewalk. He stuffs a can of spray paint into his bag before stepping out and closing the door behind him.

"Hey, I think I see one!" I blurt into the phone. "Front entrance, looks like, I don't know, maybe a teenager."

"I've got one, too," Tucket interrupts. "Back door."

"I'm going after mine," I say. "Gonna follow him and see where he goes." I don't hear Mym's response because I have to take the phone away from my ear as I dodge traffic crossing the street. My quarry is wearing a brown backpack over a black hoodie. He's slight, maybe 120 pounds and moving in a hurry. He pauses briefly on the corner then, to my consternation, crosses the street and heads back the way I've just come. He's glancing across the street toward the lab, perhaps to see if anyone is trying to follow him. I'm briefly stymied, as I've just crossed the street and don't want to make myself obvious by returning. I wait till he's beyond a stand selling paella pans before darting back across the street.

The young man pauses again in front of the market. I don't know what he's doing. He's just standing there, so I edge closer, trying to appear casual among the other shoppers and pedestrians. My phone buzzes in my pocket, but I silence it through my jeans. I'm perhaps thirty yards away when the young man turns and stares directly at me. His face is a contemptuous sneer beneath the hood. I'm frozen in place as much by the hate in his expression as I am by how unsure I am about what to do next. The decision is made for me because the boy breaks into a run, headed into the market.

Shit.

I sprint after him.

He's fast. The market is surprisingly busy for what I would have thought would be work hours. The building is teeming with pedestrians. Inside, the smell of fish and butchered animals is almost overpowering, especially near the door. I plunge after the boy, racing past other better smelling stalls selling salted nuts and chocolates. Then, as quick as thinking, he's gone. I scramble to the intersection between stalls where I last spotted him and swear under my breath. *Where did you go?*

I don't hesitate long. I spin the dials on my chronometer for a fifteen second backward jump and squeeze behind one of the vendors to find an area out of the way of traffic. I slap my hand to the wall of the fruit stand beside me and press the pin on my chronometer.

Now fifteen seconds earlier, I poke my head out of my hiding place and watch the intersection between the stalls. I'm just in time to see the young man in the hoodie skid around the corner and duck between the stalls across from me. *Gotcha.* I dash across the aisle—determined to get out of sight before my earlier self shows up—and plunge after the boy. He's fled into the aisle on the far side, but I keep him in sight this time as he races back out the same door we came in. *Always with the switchbacks, this kid.*

It's the smell of dead hogs and fish again as I tear out the door after him. This time I don't hold back. Since my cover is blown anyway, I sprint hard for the back of the young man's covered head. He makes a turn into an alley between buildings. For a moment I fear I might lose him again, but when I race around the corner I find the young man standing stock-still, his back to me. I don't hesitate to grab hold of his arm and spin him around. "Hey, what's the—"

I freeze. The boy's eyes are rolled back in his head. He's younger than I thought, perhaps only thirteen. The baggy hoodie has been deceptive. His bicep is thin in my grip and he feels like a stiff breeze could knock him over. It's not his age that gets my attention though. It's his voice. The sound doesn't match the face at all. His eyes jitter back and forth as they gaze skyward and a moaning chant is emanating from his throat. I'm shocked by the expression on his face as much at the sound. His mouth is moving but his focus is certainly on nothing in the present. The chant is deep and guttural—otherworldly in the sense that wherever it is coming from inside of him, I get the distinct impression it's not him speaking. Demonic possession comes to mind and I let go of his arm. I can't understand the words. It's not Spanish.

The adrenaline from the chase has turned to fear. I don't feel in danger, but I'm frightened for this boy, who is starting to convulse and twitch in front of me. I'm scared that somehow our chase brought on some kind of epileptic fit. His arms thrash from side to side and his eyes flit from one imagined scene to another. Then the boy's head jerks downward abruptly. He fixes me with a stare that still seems out of focus. "You're too late, Traverssss." My last name comes out as a hiss. "The Lost Star will return."

Then it's over. The convulsions are gone and the boy is left blinking at me. His disorientation at his surroundings turns to defensiveness as he sizes me up. "Cuál es tu pinche pedo?" My Spanish is a little rusty, but I recognize the touch of Mexican street slang in his response. I can tell his attitude is partly a product of his confusion. He wraps his arms across his chest and looks around to figure out his surroundings. I feel bad for him. Whatever just had control over him seems to have left no trace of itself behind.

"¿Estás bien?" I ask.

The boy raises his chin and fixes me with a defiant scowl. "Me cago en tu puta madre."

I'm not familiar with his last phrase, though I gather enough of it to know it isn't nice.

The next few events happen in a blur. Beyond the boy, just a few feet from the nearest brick wall, another person appears. Not just another person, but me. This other me is gasping and out of breath, one hand on his chronometer, but he points to something above me and shouts, "Watch out!"

I look up to see a person dressed in black adhered to the side of the wall above me. The figure is stuck like a spider, fingertips clinging to a narrow window ledge. The spider-person comes loose as soon as I spot him, stepping out from the wall and dropping—something fierce and metallic-looking clutched in one hand.

"Oh shit!"

I barely have time to get one arm up, blocking the hand holding the blade as the person flattens me to the ground. I crumple with the weight of my assailant, but he is more limber on the landing, bouncing upright and back onto his feet in a moment. From my position on the ground, I only get time to notice bushy, masculine eyebrows protruding from the eyeholes of the otherwise masked face. He's not especially big, whoever he is, but the eyes are angry. I glance past the boy still rigid in the alley, but the other me has already disappeared. The rest is a blur of black fabric as my assailant lunges toward me. His blade thrust catches the outside of my shoulder as I roll away. I kick wildly at my attacker and manage to connect with a knee, sending him sideways in a stagger and giving me enough time to scramble to my feet.

The boy has come unfrozen now and sprints away, his sneakers slapping the cobblestones and sending echoes dancing down the alley behind him.

The masked man only pauses long enough to draw an extra blade from somewhere in his abundant sleeves. My fingers find my chronometer and I frantically attempt to spin the dials. The second blade is airborne at the same time my attacker charges. I duck the throw and lunge for the wall of the building next to me in the same motion. The thrown knife ricochets off the wall and clatters to the ground, out of reach. I'm about to activate my chronometer, but he's on me too fast. I have to use both hands to catch the wrist of the man's outstretched arm, stopping the second wicked-looking blade mere inches from my throat.

Backed against the wall and out of room to maneuver, I aim a kick for his groin, but he blocks it easily with a kick of his own. With a vicious yell, he uses his other hand and strikes the side of my face. I swear at him as he rains blows on me, trying to get me to relinquish my hold on his knife arm. I get the vague sense that the commotion has attracted attention from people out in the street at the end of the alley, but if so, they are doing nothing.

A hard knee to my ribs nearly takes the wind out of me, but I fight back the only way I can, lunging forward and ramming the top of my head into my attacker's face. I feel a satisfying crunch from the man's nose hidden somewhere under the mask and his grip on the knife releases. He staggers back a couple of feet and steadies himself, brandishing both fists and uttering a guttural yell that might be as much to motivate himself as to scare me. He actually beats his chest a couple of times—getting himself fired up for the next assault—then leaps for me.

The hell with this.

I have the knife now, but it doesn't matter. I drop the blade and slap my hand to the wall. My other hand reaches the dials on the side of the chronometer at the same time the man in black grabs hold of my shoulder. He might be trying to grapple me or throw me or God knows what else, but he doesn't get a chance. I activate the chronometer and blink.

I appear in the alley only thirty seconds before, still staggering from the motion of the attack, but my assailant hasn't come with me. *Thank God.* I look up to find my other self staring at me in confusion, the black blob of the spider-ninja lurking just above him on the wall.

"Watch out!" The yell is out of my mouth before I even have time to think, then the attack is happening all over again. *Damn it.* I allow myself an actual look at my chrononmeter this time and reset it for farther into the past.

A half an hour this time and the alley is clear. It's a dangerous jump with no knowledge of what might be here, but I've gotten lucky and nothing is around to fuse into when I arrive. I scan the walls immediately, but no spider-men adorn the bricks this time. I let myself catch my breath, then stand up and check my shoulder. I'm bleeding pretty freely from the cut, but it isn't terribly deep. The blade was obviously sharp because it cut cleanly through my shirt and into my shoulder without gashing or gouging—just a neat slice that I now attempt to hold tension on through my bloody sleeve.

I walk farther down the alley, trying to distance myself from this whole event. I'm disoriented in time and it takes me a few moments to gather my thoughts. I steal some napkins from a restaurant's sidewalk table and hold the wad against my shoulder wound.

Have we arrived on the motorcycle yet? Where is the earlier me right now? I travel with caution, skirting around the areas I've been before in order to avoid any more encounters with myself. It's not difficult to locate Tucket on the far side of the lab. His spangled jumpsuit is a giveaway, but his personality outshines even that. He's chatting with passersby and laughing, seemingly fascinated by every person around him. The pedestrians he has accosted don't seem to mind, and they must consider him an equally curious sight, because he has a little cluster of people gathered around. I keep an eye on him from a distance.

My phone lights up with a call. When I put the phone to my ear, I hear

Mym again on the group call, explaining that the intruders have already lit the place on fire. The other me responds from the other side of the lab and Tucket chimes in that he sees one too. I check the back of the lab to see what he's spotted.

A young woman has exited the building. Like the kid I chased, she could easily be a teenager. Her face is more visible than the boy's was, auburn hair framing a round, cheerful-looking face. She is carrying a bag that she throws over one shoulder before heading down the street away from us. Tucket moves to follow. I run to catch up with him, using my free hand to grab the back of his jumpsuit.

"Let her go, Tucket."

Tucket spins in surprise. "Ben! She's just a kid, we can probably track her—"

"She's not alone. They've got help, and they're dangerous."

Tucket registers the blood around my shoulder that I'm still keeping pressure on.

"Oh no! Did you get capped?"

I frown at him. "No. It wasn't gang bangers. Look, we need to get to Mym, make sure she doesn't go after these guys."

Tucket lifts the ball device from his pocket and speaks to seemingly nothing. "Lone Avocado to Eagle Eye. I've got Ben. He says to disengage the hostiles. REPEAT. DISENGAGE THE—"

I grab Tucket's arm to silence him, then hold my own phone up to my face. "Mym, where are you?"

"Still on the roof. Are you okay?"

"Yeah. I'm fine. Just don't chase any of these guys. They have some kind of secondary ninja backup."

"What happened?"

"We'll come up and I can explain. Be there in a minute." I lower the phone and give Tucket an appraising stare. "Eagle Eye?"

Tucket grins. "Yeah, I figured if we are doing recon we should have cool code names for the radio. I'm Lone Avocado 'cause my favorite band is AP and you know, I'm like the—"

"I gotcha." I start moving toward the building, but stop when Tucket doesn't immediately follow. He's still back on the sidewalk where I left him. He looks a little disappointed that I haven't let him finish his explanation. I swear at myself inwardly and turn back around. "Hey, I'm definitely ready to catch an Avocado Problems concert one of these days myself, Tuck."

Tucket nods. "They're the best."

I wait for him to catch up. "Lone Avocado is pretty cool. Did you think of one for me?"

Tucket smiles and follows me across the street to the building next to Quickly's lab. "You might think it's stupid, but I was thinking about something super impressive like, 'The Time King,' 'cause obviously Time Lord is already taken. Or maybe something more mysterious like, 'The Slippery Giraffe.'" He waves his fingers to make the name seem more mysterious.

I hold the door to the stairwell open for him. "Slippery Giraffe?"

"Yeah, because you're pretty tall and you, like, slip through time and everything. It's cool, right?"

I let Tucket go ahead of me and follow him into the stairwell. "Let's maybe work on that some more."

"Okay. No problem. I have lots of ideas." He begins to ramble off more potential code names for me as we climb. I sigh and follow him upwards. As I tune him out, the other voice comes back to mind. The boy hissing my name. "You're too late, Travers. The Lost Star will return."

The Lost Star reference is opaque to me. Like always, I'm out of my depth. But the someone who was speaking clearly knows me, so if I don't recognize them, they are either from another timestream or from somewhere in my future. We will meet. That much is certain. It's not an appealing prospect. I fiddle with the dials on my chronometer as I climb the stairwell. The memory of the condescending voice just makes me all the more determined to prove them wrong. *Don't try to tell a time traveler he's too late. There's no such thing.*

"Each day, the future offers newer and more convincing illusions. It's easy to get lost in them. The ability to see what isn't there does not mean we should lose the ability to focus on what is." -Journal of Dr. Harold Quickly, 2170

CHAPTER 8

The Neverwhere

I have bad aim. That's my current hypothesis. I'm sitting cross-legged on the floor of my apartment staring into the hole I've made in reality. A hole that is supposed to be letting me view my apartment in 2009. All the signs were looking good, but now I'm very confused.

My elation at finally getting the portal open and then managing to keep it open was the highlight of my experience in this place so far. At least until I realized I screwed it up somehow. Maybe.

The television is on in the version of my apartment I'm looking into. I could have sworn I heard a commercial say that it was having a sale on 2009 model cars until Independence Day, meaning that I ought to be in June or maybe early July, but the situation got complicated from there. My brain could be addled from the joy of simply hearing another human being's voice—one in the real world—because the rest of this doesn't make sense.

For one, I'm still alive in this place. Somehow, someway, a living, breathing me has been walking around the apartment. He's gone now—left with no seeming concern that I have been watching him from my spot on the floor.

To be fair, I haven't been an especially energetic poltergeist so far. That could be part of the problem. I was tempted to poke him in the leg one of the times he walked by, but I was too scared to try it. I never paid much attention to ghost stories so I don't really want to go testing whatever otherworldly powers I might possess on some unsuspecting version of myself.

If it really is me.

Something is off about this person living in my apartment. He looks a few years older than he ought to. Just a sort of worn quality to him. Nothing drastic, but enough to notice. He moves with a kind of tired efficiency, not expending energy on anything unnecessary.

I'm feeling more confident in my abilities. The portal is staying open.

It's no longer even visible. I'm immersed in this scene of 2009. Getting up from my position, I attempt to explore.

The show on the television is some sort of home improvement program. Not my usual taste. I make an attempt at grabbing the remote off the coffee table, but my hand goes right through it. It's a disturbing but exhilarating sight. *I can pass through stuff?* I forget about the television and move to the bathroom, curious to see what I look like in a mirror here. The door is cracked, but mostly shut. My swipes at the doorknob are ineffective. I steel my nerves and then plunge my arm through the door up the shoulder. It doesn't feel like anything. Encouraged, I inch myself forward. My leg goes through without difficulty, then my hip and part of my stomach. My face is a fraction of an inch away now. I let my nose touch the door. With eyes crossed I can see the tip of my own nose breach the painted wood. My vision gets a little blurry close to the door, but suddenly I'm stopped. The impact isn't with my face exactly. It feels like my mind has just hit a wall. Frightened, I jump back, retrieving my lost appendages from the door.

What was that? I check my limbs for any sign of damage before staring at the doorway. Cautiously, I ease myself back into the door again. I'm bracing myself for the impact again and I shut my eyes as I anticipate the collision.

It doesn't come.

I've traversed the door and am now inside the bathroom. I look at the bath towel hanging benignly on the back of the door. *Huh.* I slide back through it, but as soon as the fibers reach my eyes I'm stopped again. The blurry strands of the towel refuse to yield. Frustrated, I close my eyes and head-butt it.

I go right through.

Seriously? It's that easy? I test out my new skill a few more times, attempting to cross the door with my eyes open versus eyes closed. Sure enough, when I don't try to see my way through, it comes easily. Anytime I try to look inside the object with my eyes open it won't let me. *I guess if I've never seen through a door alive, I can't do it dead?* I've certainly never put the rest of myself through a door either, but that doesn't seem to matter. I puzzle over this odd rule of ghostdom for only a moment, then shrug it off.

I'm still a pretty decent looking specter. The reflection staring back at me in the mirror hasn't started shedding skin or rotting away. That's good to know. I look like I always have. At least in recent memory. I could use a haircut and the week's worth of stubble on my face isn't any surprise. For a dead guy I'm still pretty suntanned. It's my eyes that make me pause. They still look so very alive. *Is that it? The trick to this? Am I even seeing my reflection, or am I just remembering my reflection?*

The man in the mirror doesn't look melancholy or lost. He's still ready to tackle the world and its problems—overcome them with the confidence of his youth and the promise of many long years in which to achieve his dreams. That guy in the mirror still loves someone and has all the reason in the world to believe she'll love him back.

That's not me.

For the time I've been here, however long that has been, I've tried to avoid the thought of what I've lost. It's rushing back to me now. The decision to let myself go. The hope of stopping the men who wanted to turn the chronothon into a way of wiping out time travelers. I sacrificed myself for a reason, for the hope that if I did it, Mym would live.

I try to wrestle with the emotion. It's not that I regret dying to save her. I just never expected to have to keep *living* with that decision. I don't know what I expected to find on the other side of that jump into the ether. No. That's not it. I expected to find nothing. But instead of some restful eternal slumber, I'm still lingering around. Does everyone deal with this? Is this the real reason people fear death, because we have to keep wallowing around in our decisions after? I might be okay with it if I knew what actually happened.

Did I really achieve anything? Where is she now? Was any of this actually worth it?

As if on cue, I hear a woman laugh. The sound jolts me out of my reverie. A key turns in the lock of the front door, followed by the sticky sucking sound of the wood breaking free of its weather stripping.

Oh my God, Mym? I close my eyes and plunge straight through the wall toward the living room.

The girl who walks into the apartment is dressed in a tight skirt and a sparkly, low-cut top. Her bare legs end in equally glittery heels that elevate her an extra couple of inches. Her hair is tied up in a sort of tousled orb atop her head with loose strands that dangle down her temples. She's made up and smiling and absolutely gorgeous.

She's a massive disappointment.

I frown as the other me follows the girl into the living room. It takes me a couple of seconds to piece the scene together and for my brain to even recognize the girl.

Kaylee.

What on earth is she doing here?

My confusion about Kaylee's presence turns quickly to annoyance as she hangs on the other me and wraps her arms around him, clearly not for the first time in recent history.

"What the hell is this?" I step forward, gesturing angrily at them, completely forgetting that they can't see me. The other me gives Kaylee a lingering kiss and then detaches himself from her.

"I'll just be a second. Make yourself at home." His shoulder passes right through me as he heads for the hallway.

"What do you mean, 'make herself at home?'" I stammer. "What is she doing here? Where's Mym?" I follow the older and clearly stupider me into the hallway. He proceeds to shut the bathroom door in my face. Undeterred, I close my eyes and follow him through.

"Dude, what is wrong with you?" You survive a chronothon, get the girl of your dreams and then somehow go back to Kaylee?" I'm yelling now, but the other me pays no attention. He raises the lid on the toilet and proceeds to relieve himself. Aggravated, I try to shove the back of his shoulder. "Hey!" My hand goes right through him. *Damn it.*

Fuming, I position myself against the wall of the bathroom in direct view of the mirror. Ghosts in movies are forever showing up in people's mirrors. I've seen enough horror trailers to know that. I put on my most stern and angry expression, even raising my fists in a gesture that I hope looks menacing, and wait to terrify.

The other me flicks the toilet handle and moves to the sink to wash up. I growl audibly as soon as he looks up to check his face in the mirror. I shake my fists and shout at him. "Aaaaggghhhhhhh!"

He checks his teeth for any sign of contaminants, then, seemingly satisfied, turns around and reaches straight through me for the hand towel. He wipes his hands off through the center of my chest, then lets himself back into the hallway.

I stare at my reflection in the mirror.

"God, you're useless."

There is feminine giggling from the living room. As I linger forlornly in the bathroom, the giggling quickly moves to the hallway and then the bedroom. By the time I rouse enough motivation to walk back through the door to the hallway, the house has gone mostly silent with the exception of a few moans and other mouthy noises emanating from the vicinity of my bed. I scowl at the bedroom door, not willing to expose myself to whatever is going on beyond it.

None of this makes any sense.

Relief comes in the form of a ringing phone on the coffee table. The flip phone lights up as it vibrates. I move toward it out of habit. The name on the caller ID gives me another pang of homesickness. *Francesca.*

"Yes. Call this impostor and straighten him out, Fresca. Tell him he is ruining my life."

The bedroom door opens and the slightly irritated-looking other me comes out. I get out of the way unnecessarily as he reaches for the phone. Upon seeing the name on the caller ID, he pauses and his expression changes from irritation to . . . to what? Sadness? Hopefulness? I try to figure out the change as he accepts the call.

"Hello?"

I can only hear snippets of Francesca's voice on the other end. I ease closer to listen, as Other Ben seems to be making minimal contributions to the conversation.

". . . if you want to go. I think it might be fun."

"Tomorrow?" Other Me glances toward the bedroom wall. "Yeah. That'd be fine."

"You want to come pick me up? Or, I could just meet you . . ."

There's something off about Francesca's voice. It takes me a few seconds to put my finger on it.

"I'll come get you," Other Me says.

"All right. Don't be keeping a girl waiting. Your days of having an excuse for being late are over now that you're a time traveler." There is a smile in her voice.

Good God, she's flirting! The realization hits me and I take a step back in shock.

"What the hell, Fresca. We've been friends for ten years and now all of a sudden you decide to put the moves on *this guy*?" My outburst is of course unheard by either of them. As Other Me says his goodbyes and hangs up, I'm left sputtering to myself in aggravation. Other Me holds the closed phone in his hand and his eyes linger on it until Kaylee's voice comes from the bedroom.

"Benji, what are you doing out there? I need you."

He snaps out of his mental tangent and puts the phone back down. "Yeah. I'm coming."

I can only watch and fume as he disappears back into the bedroom. "What is going on around here? Has everybody lost their minds? Benji? Who in the hell let this guy into my—" I cut myself off and try to concentrate instead, putting my hands to my head and letting the scene around me fade back into the timelessness of the Neverwhere. When I feel like I'm back, I double-check by walking around the corner and kicking open the door to the bedroom. The door moves this time and the bedroom is empty and silent. *Good riddance.*

I tromp back out to the front porch. The moon is still lingering in the twilight sky. I need answers again. I need the *other* other me. Benny.

I descend the stairs and walk to the corner where I last saw my scruffy-looking counterpart. *Where does he go when he's not hiding in bushes or jumping out of trees?* I'm still learning the rules of this place, but I'm somewhat relieved to be back somewhere where I can actually affect change. As much as I want to see the real world, being powerless and immaterial there is incredibly frustrating. Here at least I have someone else dead to talk to. If I can find him.

Benny has already taught me one thing about this place. I don't need to walk everywhere through the glittery fog. I ought to be able to skip to destinations the way he did. Concentrating on merely the location, not the time, I work to open up another memory portal. This one takes me to the street near Kaylee's old apartment. I step through and find myself back there. There are no signs of floodwaters or storm clouds. Unfortunately there is no sign of Benny either. Kaylee's apartment is how I remembered it from my past. No frantic scribbles from Benny anywhere or signs of his recent presence. He must not be nearby. Back out in the street I work out where to search next. *What memories would he and I have in common?*

I make multiple more attempts, opening memories of favorite restaurants, downtown hangouts, and even the marina, and searching each location for signs of Benny, but all without luck. Expanding the search to include houses of friends, I run through a dozen more locations, but am left with no leads. I have just gotten through a silent tour of one of my buddy's homes on Fifty-fourth Avenue, and have just about given up, when I spot a slight movement beyond the backyard fence. The motion stands out in this otherwise static landscape.

My friend Diego's house had been the home of many backyard barbecues. The house wasn't especially spacious, and there was no pool or hot tub to attract us there, but it had one particularly beneficial feature for our late night partying: extremely tolerant neighbors.

I open the sliding glass door and walk out onto the deck, climbing onto the wooden planter box near the back of the yard to look out over the expansive cemetery beyond. Out there among the tombstones, a man is swaying back and forth, arms crossed and doing what? Talking to himself? Singing? I can tell even from this distance that it's Benny. My excitement about having found him is tempered by the sight of his odd behavior.

What's he doing out there?

I hop down from the planter and make my way around the side yard to the gate. I skirt the house and vault a waist-high chain link fence to get into the cemetery. Benny doesn't seem to be aware of my presence. I'm not necessarily trying to sneak up on him, but my approach through the grass is nearly silent and he has his back to me. I consider calling to him, but I'm curious to see what he's up to. I get within twenty yards of him and stop because I can hear him speaking and realize he's addressing the headstone at his feet.

"No one understands what it's like in this place. After all we went through. You would have known what to do. But I wouldn't have wanted you to see this. You're safe now and you don't have to worry. I know that this is all just a dream. It can't touch you." He shuffles his feet. "They won't get to me either now. I just have to hide. I won't let anything happen to your memory."

Benny lifts his head and looks to the sky. He's quiet for the better part of thirty seconds before speaking again. "You shouldn't be here." Something about his tone makes me realize he's not talking to the headstone anymore. "Why did you come?" He cocks his head this time, appraising me out of the corner of his eye.

"Uh, sorry. I was just looking for you. I have more questions. Wasn't trying to intrude or anything."

"Well, you have intruded."

I take a few steps closer. "Look. I just have to figure some things out about how this place works. I saw another me. Other us, I guess. Living my life. You know anything about that?"

Benny wipes an arm across his nose. "It doesn't really matter. The real world can't see us. Nothing we can do about it."

"Yeah, but who is he? Where did he come from? And what happened to Mym?"

Benny twitches at the last question and he spins toward me. "You just have to forget about what we were, okay? Forget what we had back then. It doesn't really matter what goes on there. Remembering the way things used to be? It just eats you up in the end. This—" He waves his arms to encompass the whole of the cemetery. "This is where we belong now. Live with it." He practically spits the last of the words. He brushes past me and walks away down the hill. I watch him go before turning back to the grave he'd been talking to. My eyes fall on the headstone and the carved words that answer my question.

In loving memory of Mym Juniper Quickly.

My heart plummets into my stomach as I comprehend the words.

I didn't save her then. This was all for nothing. I drop to my knees in the grass.

Unlike the headstones around it, Mym's has no date of birth or date of death. The smooth granite has been flecked with dirt and grass clippings. Whatever memory of Benny's I'm in, it's sometime well after the burial.

"When?" I choke out the words. "When did she—" I turn to address Benny, but he is already out of earshot. As he continues to stride away, the view of the headstone changes. It's fading. Even now I see blades of grass sticking up through it, more and more as Benny gets farther away. I'm transitioning out of his memory and back into mine. I reach out to touch the name on the headstone one last time, but grasp only earth as the granite disappears. My memory can't hold onto it. It was never a part of my lifetime.

The bare grass is a relief. The disappearance of the headstone buoys my spirits, reminding me that Mym was alive in my timeline when I left her. Maybe she still is. Whatever suffering Benny endured may not have to be repeated. This memory of her is just a bad dream for me. Perhaps there is still some way to help her avoid this fate. My mind races, trying to comprehend the mystery.

Then where was she in 2009? Why was another me cavorting around with Kaylee? Where did that version of me even come from?

More frustration is my only answer for now. Staring at the empty grass plot, I realize I need more answers, and I need to send a warning to myself—the me that's still alive. If the other me living in my apartment in 2009 is the wrong one, I need to search elsewhere. Earlier perhaps. *Can I stop this chain of events from happening? Alter it somehow?* I'll get the message across any way I can to any version of me who can make a difference—save Mym from this fate she has in store and save my living self from whatever Benny has encountered. I also need to save him from turning into whatever screwed up exchange I just saw in my apartment. I need to change *something*.

I stand up and search my memories—wading through my life so far as a time traveler. Somewhere there must be a moment that will bring me a clue. I just need to find it.

Valencia-2017

The fires are out in Quickly's lab, thanks to the overhead sprinklers. There are sirens in the distance. We only have a few minutes to fan out and scour the place for anything Mym might have missed in the security footage. We watch the camera feed from the building next door and wait till we're sure the would-be kidnappers have left before making the jump over. Even so, we move cautiously through the lab. The place is a mess.

The young vandals we saw must have been fast workers. Either that or they had help. That is the theory we are working with since the defacing of the lab has been so complete. Mym accesses an electronic inventory of the lab and determines that there are indeed items missing. One of Doctor Quickly's smaller gravitizers and multiple vials of gravitites. In addition to the fires and the general trashing of the equipment, the spray painted symbol of the flaming, winged circle appears at least six times on various walls.

"Could it be some kind of gang sign?" I run a finger through the still-wet paint on one of the markings, trying to find a connection to what I saw in my vision from Kaylee's apartment.

"No gang I've ever heard of. But I suppose it could be," Mym says. "I scanned through all the historical data I could find and it doesn't come up." Noticing that the first aid kit on the wall hasn't been tampered with, Mym pulls it open and gestures for me to stand next to her. I gingerly pull off my T-shirt and she plasters a wide bandage on the cut on my shoulder.

"I'll run the symbol through my graffiti translation app," Tucket says. He captures an image of the flaming circle and takes on a hazy stare as he runs through data. The far off look in his eye is familiar to me now as the way people access the meta-space in his time.

"Can you link up to the modern internet somehow using your perceptor?" I gesture vaguely toward Tucket's forehead, where I know the chip type device is imbedded under his skin.

"Oh, for sure. Not nearly as much on it in your time, but that makes it easier to filter. I've also got a catalogue of future data downloaded. I can still get to lots of it offline. I'm getting some kind of metaspace link up here though." He turns toward Mym. "Does your dad have a time relay in this lab? It's letting me access future data. This is super groovy."

I look around the room, not seeing any of the future tech Tucket is referencing. I don't doubt it's there, though. If there is anything I know about Doctor Quickly, it's that he's clever at hiding things. "So the internet hasn't just become one big montage of cat videos yet?" I ask. "I've always felt that's where it's headed."

As Mym puts away the first-aid kit she's shaking her head. "Dad has a tachyon pulse transmitter here. Which reminds me, I should shoot a message to Abraham to let him know we're okay." She begins typing away on her MFD. I slide my T-shirt back on and wait, not having any fancy connections to other times to play with.

"Oh hey, I found it!" Tucket exclaims. "But it's not from the past. This symbol won't show up in the ASCOTT's time travel reference library till the late twenty-one hundreds. It's from a religious text. The Zora Gnoma."

"What religion is that?" I step closer, though I have no way of seeing what he's looking at.

"It's not very well known. It's an addendum to The Chronicles of Gnomon. It says the book is authored by the "High Priest of the Eternals.""

"The Eternals? Oh shit."

Mym's brow furrows. "You know them?"

"Yeah. Well, heard of them anyway. You know Jonah, the kid I raced in the chronothon with? He mentioned the name. Kind of made them out to be boogiemen. Had to do with subverting their own younger minds in order to—ah, that makes more sense now."

"What does?" Mym is studying me.

I smack my palm off my forehead. "The kid I caught up to in the alley who I thought was having the seizure, he wasn't possessed. He could have been one of *them*."

"The Eternals are kids?" Tucket asks.

"No. Well, I guess sometimes. But the Eternals are old. From what I heard, when they are close to dying, they transfer their consciousness back into their own younger bodies. It's a way to live longer. Cheat their way out of death."

"What would they want with my dad?" Mym asks.

"No idea."

"Huh, that's strange," Tucket says. "Did you say that the person who told you about The Eternals was named Jonah? Is his last name Sprocket?"

"Yeah, it is," I say, turning to Tucket. "Why?"

"I have an alumni services message alert from the Academy Liaison Program in my inbox. It says I received a social invitation from a Jonah Sprocket. I couldn't figure out who it was from. I tried opening it, but it said I have to go sign for it in person at the Academy offices."

"When did it show up?" I ask.

"Um, It says it was bundled with the data I got for my ASCOTT presentation, but I didn't get the notice till just now when I logged in to retrieve my messages. Won't open though. It's time stamped to 2150, so it might not let me read it until we're in that year. Sometimes Academy correspondence has limitations like that."

There is banging from the floor below and the sound of boots thudding in the stairwell. The fire department has finally arrived.

"Do you think Jonah knows something about our investigation?" Mym asks. "Have you talked to him about it?"

"No. Haven't seen him since the after-party we had for the race. And I don't know how he would know we were with Tucket. If Tucket had the message when he showed up at my place, that was before your Dad's lab was even attacked. Seems unlikely to be a coincidence though. I suppose we ought to check it out."

It's a long ride to the Academy of Temporal Sciences. The main campus is in London around 2150, but fortunately the letter Tucket is supposed to sign for is located at a satellite campus in Barcelona during the same decade. That will be the first place Tucket can access time sensitive student data.

With Doctor Quickly's Valencia lab destroyed, finding enough anchors to get us forward in time that far presents a small challenge. It turns out time traveling by motorcycle is not quite as glamorous as I had hoped. We make use of whatever historical data Tucket can find to make safe jumps with the motorcycle, but it involves a lot of research. Besides needing access to traffic cams in the years we're headed to, to be sure the area is clear, we also have to cross-reference road paving schedules to make sure the pavement hasn't been resurfaced in the time we want to skip over. Whenever in doubt, we locate safer options like power poles or bridges. None of us want to end up infused with a road grader on arrival. All problems Doc Brown and Marty McFly never seemed to deal with in their Delorean.

We spend a lot of time parked under overpasses waiting for Tucket to check safety issues via the maps he has downloaded in his Third Eye. The rest of the time we just ride.

The hops we manage forward in time are like little windows into the decades of the future we're passing and I marvel at the subtle changes we see, even on the freeways. We pass the latest of a series of low bridges over seemingly nothing and I point one out to Tucket. "What's that for?"

"Greenways!" Tucket shouts over the wind.

Mym squeezes me a little closer as she leans forward to speak into my ear. "It's for animals. All roads have to have wildlife passages above or below them. They ruled that long roads with no way across them were a form of animal cruelty."

"Huh. That seems like an easy fix." I wait for the next mini bridge. Sure enough, as I peer over the guardrail, I spot a rabbit nibbling a bush in the green space below. As we cruise onward I note the corresponding lack of road kill with a sense of appreciation.

The most significant change to the freeways comes with the advent of driverless cars. At first it's only special expressways where driverless vehicles navigate their own lanes. Then, within a few years, it's nearly all the vehicles. The speeds pick up drastically and before long I'm forced to abandon even the slow lane, as my motorcycle can't keep up with the minimum speed limit. It's just as well because a few years later we find that manually driven vehicles are made illegal on major highways. As we wander the back roads, we start to get more and more stares from pedestrians—at least the ones who aren't glued to their technological devices.

The advent of the metaspace in the 2080s drastically reduces traffic as people spend more time immersed behind digital glasses and do less traveling to real spaces. According to Tucket, it doesn't take long for people to tire of the reduced visibility issues that come with digital lenses and, within a decade, the majority of users are testing out implanted devices.

The nice change that comes with the metaspace is that it clears up the landscape. Road signs and stoplights begin to vanish. Advertisers no longer clutter the sides of roads and buildings with signage and billboards. The advertising all goes digital, only visible in the eyes of users. The vacancy leaves a blank canvas for freestyle artists, and intricate painted murals spring up briefly on walls and old billboards, only to go largely ignored by passersby.

We reach Barcelona still a few decades ahead of our destination time so we visit the Sagrada Familia. Gaudi's masterpiece is finally complete and bustling with tourists, one real world location that is still managing to pull people out of the digital ether with its history and intricacy. Affixing Tucket's Temprovibe to the motorcycle, I program it to jump ahead of us to our arrival time while we take a pedestrian detour. Mym nods in appreciation as the bike vanishes.

"We just get there ahead of time and make sure the space stays clear?" she asks.

"Yep." I grin. "It will save us years worth of parking tickets."

Mym guides Tucket and me to out of the way spaces in the medieval church, and points out elements of the architecture. I marvel at the ceiling of yellow starbursts lit from natural light among the forest of columns. Tucket has his hands in his pockets and his head leaned back when he speaks softly. "And they shall bring out the bones of kings and princes, priests and prophets, and spread them before the sun and the moon, and all the host of Heaven, whom they have loved, and whom they have served, and whom they have worshipped."

"What's that from?" I ask.

"Old bit of scripture verse I learned in history class. I always thought it was interesting that almost every religion had to compete with star worshipers in the beginning. But we still love them, don't we?"

"Yeah. Hard to compete with a beautiful sky."

I have to stop my open gawking at the breathtaking vertical spaces long enough for us to make jumps the last bit of the way to the 2150s.

When we walk out the church doors and into the middle of the twenty-second century, we find that the space into which my motorcycle is due to arrive is now occupied by a portable ice cream vendor. The woman amazingly resists our encouragement to move for her own safety, and our assurances that she and her stand are about to be fused together with a few hundred pounds of twentieth-century road bike. It finally takes good old-fashioned bribery to get her to maneuver her cart to safety. The bike shows up as promised, but the woman merely shrugs and goes back to barking at the children passing by and waving popsicles about.

It's unseasonably warm out. Despite global efforts to reduce man-made climate change, it seems the earth has trended hotter anyway. I motor through the city with the sun on my bare arms. Tucket removes his jumpsuit to reveal more modest clothes underneath, tan pants and a simple white T-shirt. He looks subdued in his natural environment.

The campus of the Academy of Temporal Sciences is a series of spires near the heart of the city surrounding a lush park. Despite the central location, pedestrian traffic is light. Tucket explains that citizens primarily telecommute to school and work via the metaspace and emerge outdoors in the evening in traditional Spanish fashion, making the early afternoon a quiet and relaxing scene. My experience with the metaspace was very limited during my chronothon adventure, but I understand enough to know that there is plenty going on that I can't see, as digital avatars of students and citizens roam the streets and park spaces.

Tucket remedies my blindness by purchasing a pair of digital lenses for me from a nondescript campus store. The generic glasses come with a pair of cheap-looking earpieces and some thin, rubbery gloves. It turns out Mym has her own far more stylish pair of glasses, and puts them on, then uploads something onto my lenses briefly before handing them to me. "I've given you a pre-made identity, saves us some time getting you set up," she explains.

When I slip the lenses over my face, the campus transforms. The formerly plain-looking stores and vendors are now bursting with advertising—interactive messages that move and change as I do, doing their best to get my attention. Some of it is blurry at first, but the longer I look at things the more the world comes into focus. I slip the earpieces in and get the full audio onslaught as well. The campus itself is bustling with students of all sizes and colors.

Digital avatars can apparently stray wildly from the human form, because many of the pedestrians around me are animals like lions and wolves, cartoons, or otherworldly alien creatures. A polar bear is ordering a drink at the coffee shop next to the bookstore. I lift my glasses from my face and find that the owner of the polar bear avatar is actually a girl of no more than nineteen, with straight black hair and Pokemon pajama pants.

I lower my glasses back onto my face and turn to comment on the polar bear to Mym, only to find a completely different girl staring back at me. Mym has transformed into a pleasantly plump brunette with a ponytail. There is a glowing label floating above her head that says "Julia."

"What the—" I turn and find Tucket has changed too. His meta-persona is taller and muscular. His avatar's face still resembles his real life appearance, but has more sharply chiseled features and the hair of an eighties rocker. Like the real-life Tucket who showed up at my front door, this avatar is outfitted in clothing from a mishmash of eras. I'm visually assaulted by his tribute to my century in the form of distressed jeans, tie-dye, and flannel. Digital images not being subject to the whims of weather, his avatar seems unbothered by the heat despite layering on a studded leather jacket and infinity scarf.

I look down and find my own clothing is different as well. In the metaspace, I'm wearing lightweight khaki pants and a blue polo. The boat shoes on my feet only accent the yuppie vibe. "What did you do to me?"

Mym/Julia smiles. "Camouflage. I never use any real data in the metaspace. I prefer to keep my identity offline completely, but when I have to interact in this era I use alternates. I just uploaded a generic, cloned ID for you. We'll stay off the radar that way. Your name is Reggie."

"Reggie?"

"The person I copied this avatar from was actually 'Regulus,' because people are really into Roman sounding names again this century, but I tagged you as Reggie. I'm not calling you Regulus."

I look up and notice the digital flag hovering over my head that says "Reggie." It also lists that I'm a recreational sailor, a Pisces, and my current mood is "Fresh."

"Thanks. . . Julia." I read Julia's public info. She's apparently a biology major and loves cats.

"It will be a little glitchy at first," Mym says. "The perceptor in the glasses is new to you so it's going to take a little while to read your brain activity. Once it does it will start triggering sounds and smells and things directly into your mind. The operating system is going to see how you respond to different inputs. It wants to learn your brain's responses so it can transmit the right data."

"Uh, okay. That sounds kind of weird. This is all safe, right?"

"As long as you remember it's not real," Tucket replies. He's smiling. "You ready to see the school?"

"Can't wait," I deadpan. Tucket grins and leads the way down the sidewalk toward the nearest building.

Two women run by in form-fitting jogging outfits that leave very little to the imagination. Mym notices my attention drifting and smacks me on the butt. "Careful what you wish for around here." I lift the glasses to take in the real-world view of the women and find the reality of the situation to be an overweight, middle-aged man running by himself. When I look back to Mym, she's smirking.

I resume my view through the meta-lenses and grab her hand. "I like my reality."

Mym/Julia smiles.

I look with curiosity at the other pedestrians. "So how does it work? Two people running but it's really only one guy?"

"The other person is commuting to the space from somewhere else. Running programs here can digitally enhance any landscape, add people, scenery, whatever you want. The other person might be running a similar course in another city or country, or could just be jogging on a treadmill at home."

"If they are both running on different terrain, what happens when one person needs to make a turn or go up stairs or something and the other one doesn't?"

"The program factors that in. It shows the terrain to the person who needs it. The other runners just see their own program, but you can talk and interact as if you were in the same space. The person with the stairs for example, would see their friend climbing the stairs along with them even though they aren't."

"That's pretty cool."

"Comes in handy. Makes people feel closer than they are, especially families that live apart."

"Probably does wonders for long-distance relationships."

"Definitely," Mym replies. "It's fairly common in this century for people to get married without even having met each other in the real world."

"Ugh. I don't know how I'd like that. I mean, I guess it's nice to have space sometimes . . ."

Mym grabs my arm and squeezes herself up against me. "What's that? You need more space? How come?"

I laugh. "I misspoke. I don't need any space."

Mym grins. "Didn't think so." She relaxes her grip on my arm but keeps her fingers intertwined in mine. The smile lingers on her lips.

"Now Reggie on the other hand . . ." I quip.

Mym shakes her head. "Yeah, I hear that Julia girl can be a total clinger."

Tucket leads the way into the administration building. On the door I spot a digital notice. "Keep traced. Keep safe. Please report any suspicious time travel activity to the Department of Irregular Displacement."

The dual reality of the world here is in full effect. What we see indoors looks like no office building I've ever seen. For one, the space is massively larger on the inside. The foyer is a balcony overlooking a sort of bio-dome of plant life and a beautiful ocean view beyond. As Tucket speaks to someone at the concierge desk, I step to the railing and rest my hand on it cautiously. I lift the glasses from my nose to find a real railing circling the perimeter of the room a yard or so from plain white walls. In reality, the room is not large at all, just big enough to host a dozen people and the young man at the concierge desk.

The desk is just a podium with a stool, the kid behind it probably a college freshman. He's wearing shorts and flip-flops and a wrinkled tank top. When I drop the lenses back onto my face, the young man is professionally dressed in a jacket and tie with an Academy name badge pinned to his lapel.

I smile. *This is fun.*

Tucket guides us into an elevator that's pretending to be the London Eye on the inside. As we step into the car, we're lifted skyward over the city and the landscape keeps changing from one major city of the world to another.

"These are all the different campuses of the Academy," Tucket explains. "They like to advertise to future students this way. Show them all the options they'll have."

As I look around the elevator I'm startled to notice a red blinking light hovering just to the corner of my vision. It's blinking the words "Hello Reggie. Start Here" in bold letters. It takes me a moment to recall that the message is for me. I nudge Mym. "Hey, what's this?" I point to the blinking light.

"What's what?"

I explain what I'm seeing and she finally nods in understanding. "Oh, that's just the operating system on your glasses trying to link your mind to the metaspace. It's probably going to ask you a bunch of questions and test you. It's trying to understand your brain so it can optimize the inputs it gives you."

"Do I want to do that?"

"Sure, it's mostly harmless. It thinks you're a new user named Reggie so it won't be making a file on the real you anyway. Have fun with it."

Tucket grins. "There are lots of great quizzes to take to get optimized. The better the program understands you, the more vivid and tangible the metaspace will feel. It runs real life scenarios to gauge your reactions to stimuli. The scenarios differ from one brand of perceptor to another. I've never tried your kind, but most software really does a good job customizing the metaspace for each person. Mine came with a dog you got to play fetch with. The dog kept bringing back something new for you to feel or interact with every time you threw something."

"Okay, I guess I'll give it a shot." I reach for the blinking red button that only I can see and press it. I feel a bit ridiculous, but as soon as I press it, it disappears.

I wait for something to happen, but nothing immediately does. The doors ding open on our floor and we step out.

The administration floor is not terribly different in construction from an office building in my century. A long corridor branches off into various individual offices. It's these that stick out. As we walk past one after another, I notice that each occupant has been able to customize their space the way they've wanted. Each doorway we pass leads somewhere different. Some have chosen alpine views, others cityscapes or serene deserts. One man's avatar is Darth Vader and he is working in front of an expansive backdrop of the Death Star. *Glad to See Star Wars fandom has survived into the twenty-second century.*

We reach a door labeled "Student Services" and walk through. An elderly woman is sitting at a desk, fiddling with something in her lap. Her hair looks like it ought to be gray, but still shows a few hints of red. She's wearing a thin gold necklace with an hourglass pendant on it—the emblem of the Academy. She doesn't look up when we walk in, she simply speaks toward the desk. "Shut the door behind you."

I turn around to comply with her request, swinging the door closed, and jump back at the sight of a little man in sturdy overalls standing behind the door. "Oh sorry, didn't see you there." The little man is only about two and a half feet tall with a bristly red beard and is holding a clipboard. He looks up at me with a grumpy expression.

"What are you looking at?" he asks sternly.

"Uh, nothing. Sorry." I turn around and find the old woman at the desk giving me a disapproving stare. She glances behind me to see who I was talking to, then frowns at me once more before giving her attention to "Julia." I glance behind myself again and find that the little man with the clipboard has disappeared.

Tucket is asking the woman at the desk about accessing his alumni correspondence and she listens with a bored expression on her face. She looks me over and seems to be studying me. I get the feeling that whatever criteria she's judging me on is one I'm lacking in. I give her a closed-lipped smile and try to appear non-threatening. She finally turns her attention back to Tucket, but makes him repeat himself more slowly this time.

I look around the room to test out more of my metaspace abilities and am surprised to notice a little wooden door stuck behind two armchairs in the waiting area. The miniature door looks like it could be something out of a Tolkien book. It's made of rough-hewn boards and has an elaborate but weatherworn brass doorknocker on it. Curious, I move closer to investigate. The doorknocker is in the shape of a lion with a ring fashioned like a mustache. I'm reaching toward the knocker when I hear the scratchy voice again. "Nosy one, aren't you?"

The little man in the overalls is appraising me from one of the armchairs. He scribbles something furiously on his clipboard. Next he lays the clipboard in his lap and holds out both hands, curled into fists. "Which one?"

"Excuse me?"

"Left or right?"

I study the little man's two hairy fists, then glance back to Mym, but find her still involved with the conversation at the desk.

"It's not rocket science, Reggie. Left or right?"

The situation finally dawns on me. "Oh, you're the test program. Sorry I wasn't expecting—"

"Left or right, dickhead?" The little man is not hiding his frustration.

"Uh, that seems a bit—"

"Are you one of those sensitive types, doesn't like bad language?" The little man picks up his clipboard again and scribbles something else.

"No, I'm just not used to computer programs that—"

"Left or right?" The little man's fists are back up.

"Uh, right, I guess."

The little man sets his clipboard on the table next to him, hops out of the chair and steps over to stand directly in front of me. He holds his right fist up and I open my left palm, expecting him to drop something into it. Instead, he pulls his arm back and punches me hard in the nuts.

"Ow! You son of a bitch!" I grope my groin protectively. I've turned away from the little man to find Mym, Tucket, and the administration woman all staring at me.

"What are you doing, Reggie?" Mym asks, her eyes dropping to my groin where my hands are still lingering.

"This little—" I turn to find that the man in the overalls has disappeared again. The pain in my groin and the tiny door in the wall have vanished as well and I'm left standing awkwardly with the armchairs, no evidence of the incident to be had. "I think it's the quiz program. Doesn't seem to like me very much. Maybe we should have bought a different brand."

"Perhaps your friend would like to wait in the hall," the administration woman mutters. She gives me another disapproving glare.

Mym motions toward the door and I slide toward it, excusing myself from the room. I can just hear Mym/Julia explaining before I close the door. "Sorry. Reggie is a new user. Still learning the ropes." I let the door click solidly behind me.

Not wanting to wander too far from my companions, I look for what else may be of interest in the hallway. Tropical music is coming from a nearby doorway, so I investigate. Inside this office, the theme is set to a Hawaiian vacation motif and looks non-threatening. The desk for the occupant sits beneath a reed-thatched tiki hut. The palm branches in the trees overhead are swaying in a warm breeze. To my surprise, I can feel the breeze and even smell the salty air from the pounding surf in the distance. Thinking that the occupant of the office must not be around, I browse the entrance briefly, experimenting with the textures of the trees and objects in my vicinity. I lift the glasses from my nose and am surprised to still be seeing things in the metaspace even without looking through the lenses. It's only when I take the glasses completely off and move the perceptor in them farther away from my head that I stop seeing the images. Donning the glasses again, I marvel at the level of detail that the office contains. Even the floor feels like real sand even though I'm standing on industrial carpet.

I've just turned to leave when I bump into a woman coming around the corner. With dark hair and skin, and a shell necklace on, she clearly fits the theme of the office. The woman isn't wearing a grass skirt, but has a sort of sarong wrapped about her, and a flower blossom tucked behind her right ear.

"I'm sorry, I didn't mean to intrude." I hold my hands up. "Just enjoying your great office."

The woman smiles with radiant white teeth and bows slightly. "It's no trouble at all. What brings you here today?" She brushes a strand of her long black hair behind her bare shoulder and takes a step closer. She's a beautiful woman and smells vaguely of coconut sunscreen and something else floral that I can't quite place. Her fingertips brush my arm and I get a tingling up my neck. "Anything I can help you with?"

"Uh, no. Just here with some friends, doing a bit of research. Nothing major really—" There is a name banner above the woman that reads Kailani. She steps even closer, her hand moving from my arm up onto my shoulder, then letting her fingertips brush the side of my face.

"It's wonderful that you're here. Would you like to sit down?"

I shy away from her hand. "Uh, no. I'm good. I should probably be—"

She's gotten even closer now, her hand around my neck and her body pushing up against me. I back-pedal, but hit the wall with no place to go. Kailani is stronger than she looks and even though I plant my palms firmly against her hips, my attempts to move her aside are ineffective. She grabs my face with both of her hands and kisses me, clenching me to her and forcefully keeping her lips on mine.

"Oh, Reggie," she murmurs between kisses.

My mumbled protestations go unheeded and she flattens herself against me even harder.

"Excuse me, what are you doing?" A middle-aged man in a Hawaiian shirt has stepped into the room with a bag of what appears to be take-out food in his hand. He's staring at me with an expression of unveiled hostility.

Kailani is gone. I find I'm merely wedged into the corner of this man's office, hands still clutching an imaginary woman with, once again, no evidence of the encounter to explain myself.

"Goddamnit," I mutter. "I'm sorry, dude. Didn't mean to, um, mess up your . . ." I don't bother with the rest. I just lower my gaze and slide out of the office past him. He merely glares at me and shuts the door as soon as I'm back in the hallway.

Frazzled at this latest turn of events, I decide to curtail my exploration and simply find a place to sit down and wait for Mym. There are no chairs in this section of the hallway, but I see a sort of common area midway down the hall. I start toward that, but stop short when the tiny little man in overalls emerges from behind one of the armchairs wielding his clipboard.

"Oh, hell no." I spin around immediately and search for the nearest doorway. There is one marked 'stairs' just to my left so I shove through that and into the stairwell, slamming the door forcefully behind me.

"Ben."

"WHAT!" I yell, scanning the empty stairwell and seeing no one. "WHAT NOW?" It's only after my initial outburst that I realize the voice has used my real name.

"Ben. Can you hear me?"

My mind is still reeling from the strange metaspace encounters, but I finally recognize the voice. It's me. The other me from my dreams.

"Ben? I hear you. Where are you?" I look around for any sign of my other self, ripping the meta-lenses off my face as I do so.

"Where are you?" The voice echoes back and I'm not sure if it belongs to the other me or is really just an echo.

I respond quickly. "I'm here. I'm at the Academy in 2150, where are you?" There is nothing in the hallway that gives any clue to the origin of the voice, only bare walls and unnatural fluorescent lighting. I close my eyes and try to concentrate on the voice. "What are you trying to tell me? What happened to you?"

I hear a whispering noise and something unintelligible, but then a couple of words I understand ". . . protect Mym. Keep her from . . ." The voice fades out again and I miss the remainder of the sentence.

"Speak louder! I can't quite hear."

I listen intently, but hear nothing else. Finally, after about five minutes of tense waiting, I give up. It feels like my dreams, but the more I try to hold onto the connection, the more it slips away. Frustrated, I open the door to the hallway again, intent on finding Mym, not sure whether the other me was trying to tell me to check on her right now or at some other point. As I retrace my steps down the hallway, I absentmindedly slip the metaspace glasses back onto my face. There is a red message flashing in the corner of my vision again. This one says. "Error. User profile testing unsuccessful. Please limit to a single user." I rip the glasses off my face, remove the earphones and gloves and stuff the whole mess into the nearest trashcan.

I fling open the door to student records and find Mym and Tucket on their way out. Mym smiles when she sees me. "Hey, you okay?"

I take her hand, running my thumb over top of it, then pull her closer to me. "I am now. Did you guys get the message?"

"Yep." Tucket holds up an envelope. "Now I know why I couldn't access the message via the metaspace. He sent it using paper mail. It looks like ASCOTT relayed a copy to every campus, just to make sure it would get to me. Pretty cool, huh?"

I take the envelope, noting that it cost over twenty dollars in postage, and study the return address. It's a county in England.

Jonah E. Sprocket.

285 Porthpean Beach Rd.

St. Austell, Cornwall, UK.

"What did he say?"

"You can read it," Tucket says. "It's actually a message for you. The Academy was supposed to put it into my travel packet when I got sent back to visit you, but I guess it got held up. I don't think the Academy Liaison prep team is used to searching for paper mail deliveries."

Affixed to the back of the envelope is a message to ASCOTT requesting that the note be delivered to me in 2009, via whatever method is most convenient. There is a relay notice showing it being forwarded to The Academy of Temporal Sciences and another notice rerouting it to delivery via The Academy Liaison Program, then specifically to their newest recruit, Tucket Morris. I unclip this memo and reach inside the envelope. The message inside is a typewritten formal invitation to visit the Sprocket house on a date in April of 2165. No particular event or occasion is listed. I check the back, but there is nothing else on it.

Tucket studies me as he steps into the hall. "What happened to Reggie?"

"I don't think Reggie was destined for success at this school."

Tucket shrugs and leads the way down the hallway toward the elevator.

I fold up the invitation and stuff it into my back pocket.

Mym interlaces her fingers though mine. I breathe a little easier with her warm palm pressed to my own. The voice in my head was wrong for now. She doesn't seem to be in any danger. Mym stares up at me. "You okay? You look like you've seen a ghost."

I squeeze her hand. "I didn't, but I'm getting closer."

"Arriving from different decades of your life to visit close friends in linear time can confuse them. But not if they are dogs. A dog doesn't care that one day you are forty-five and the next day you are sixty. As long as you are consistently good at rubbing bellies and reaching the treats jar, it alleviates all of their concerns." -Journal of Dr. Harold Quickly, May 18, 1967.

CHAPTER 9

The Neverwhere

I'm back in the memory of my apartment, camped on my couch. The cemetery was too depressing. I may be a ghost, but even I have standards. This apartment is solid and well defined. As solid as a memory can be anyway. It is a room of hard edges and minute details accurately depicted; the scuff on the wall from my bike tire, the corner of brittle plastic missing from the base of my TV from when I broke it moving in. This is as close to reality as I can get in this place. I'm hoping that this grounding in details will help me remember more. I need a place to talk to myself.

I've been attempting to open new windows to the past, but so far I'm failing miserably. Seeing the real world version of my apartment has been simple enough. I can flash back and forth from the Neverwhere to the real world location quickly now, turning into my ghostly self and back. The location is so familiar that making the transition comes easily.

Seated cross-legged on the couch cushion, I make the transition to the real world and poke the coffee table. My finger disappears into the top of the water-stained wood. I make the transition back and poke it again, this time hitting the solid wood of my memory.

Neverwhere Ben.

Ghost Ben.

Neverwhere Ben . . . ghost Ben.

I fall back onto the cushions. *God, I need a life.*

While being able to put my hand through the furniture is mildly diverting, it's not getting me any closer to finding myself in the real world. In this space in 2009, there is only ever the imposter me—Benji—making a mess of my life. I've shouted at him a few more times when I've found him home, but he's been oblivious. Not even a hint of a connection. Whatever differences there are between his story and mine, they are too much of a gap to bridge. I need different locations and a me that will listen.

I thought remembering was easy. You just reach back and recall the moments you want to envision. Only it's not that simple. When I recall a face, I don't always get the right context. I recall a place, but perhaps in the wrong year. In some cases I get a jumble, like the varied time periods of the rooms in my parents' house. Relics from competing eras, vying for real estate in my mind.

Finally, I settle down and concentrate. I want the recent past. That should be the most vivid, except my most recent past is a dangerous race through snippets of history. Castles resounding with the clash of steel. Giant worms writhing through underground tunnels. A man with cold, gray eyes stalking my friends. No. I don't want those memories. I need the calm ones. Quiet places. Places I found a moment of relief or peace.

My mind settles on a desert. Serene and calm, but I've seen lots of deserts. The Mojave, Egypt. Egypt was a good memory. The buildings of clay and the lush green trees around the river.

Suddenly my portal window opens, only this time, I'm not looking through a portal; I'm *in* the scene. I'm looking out at a young Egyptian girl gesturing for me to follow. Viznir next to me. *Viznir.* Still alive. I catch a glimpse of my own hands, and realize that I am inside my own head again. *Holy crap. I'm back!* But there is someone else here, too. It's him. Me.

"Benjamin!" I shout to him, elated at my success and desperate to get his attention. Even though I'm seeing through his eyes, my other self feels far off. Like I'm shouting across a chasm. I'm simultaneously inside the memory and trying to hold onto the Neverwhere at the same time. "Benjamin Travers!" For a moment I sense his recognition. He knows I'm here. Then the window collapses. The other consciousness crumbles into darkness. I can feel myself falling and I retreat from the vision instinctively.

Whoa.

I'm back in my apartment, but he heard me. The déjà vu hits me. I remember that moment.

It was me. It was me the whole time.

Emboldened by this glimpse of success, I reach out again, eyes closed, searching memories. "Ben? Are you there?" The question seems to bounce around my own mind, searching for a place to land. My memories are still too unfocused. I glance off them, careening through my own recent past. I reach for my other self again, but it's like night swimming under water. I'm feeling my way forward more than seeing. There are no landmarks in this realm of consciousness, no guideposts to lead me to the proper threads. He's there, somehow, but I can't help but think I'm just a misplaced dream to him. He hasn't recognized me yet.

I keep my eyes shut tight, not trying to hold myself in the memory of my apartment any longer. I let go of the Neverwhere. I think he is drifting too. For a moment I see him, floating. Swimming? No. Drifting unconscious through space. I shout to him again but he can't hear me. I get the vague sense he's seen me. We're on the verge of contact, but something has distracted him, something in the real world. A woman's voice.

"Oxygen levels at forty percent."

Claire.

The synthetic voice triggers a pang of complicated emotions inside me. Fear of dying alone, gratitude that in that real moment floating through space that there was someone to talk to. *If only I had that now.*

The other me is gone again. Awake. Back in reality. I reach for him, but can't bridge the distance. This bouncing from one random memory to another isn't working. I need to find another avenue, a moment when his mind was open to new possibilities—another dream or moment of reflection. *Where else could he hear me?*

Probing the darkness, I search for another outlet. Any outlet.

Then, like a light in the darkness, the window opens again. I'm seeing a hallway. There is a strange little man in overalls who doesn't seem quite real. The other me is retreating from him, running into a hallway. Alone. Finally alone.

"Ben," I reach out for him.

"WHAT!" He yells back. "WHAT NOW?"

Holy shit. Did he really hear that?.

"Ben, can you hear me?" I question this apparition, too overjoyed to believe it.

"Ben? I hear you. Where are you?" His voice is distant but clear.

Oh my God. What now? I have so incredibly much to ask him. So much I need to know. "Where are you?" I realize belatedly that he had asked me the same thing.

"I'm here. I'm at the Academy in 2150, where are you?" He seems intent on listening but is straining at the same time. At least I haven't knocked him unconscious this time. "What are you trying to tell me? What happened to you?"

I'm almost too excited, too elated that he can hear me to even formulate a sentence. I try to focus on the items of most importance, remembering the cemetery and Benny. "Look, you need to protect Mym. Keep her from danger. There is another version of us. He's, I don't know how to describe him . . ."

"Speak louder! I can't quite hear."

The request throws me off. It sounds farther away somehow. *Shit. Am I losing him?*

I try to focus on the other me, but the harder I try, the more the connection slips away. My apprehension forcing it farther from my grasp. "Ben? Can you still hear me?" I get a sudden vision of the actor from the Verizon TV ads. The memory of a guy in a charcoal, zip-up jacket and glasses, testing out cellular phone reception. "Can you hear me now?" he asks. And just like that, my concentration is broken.

Damn it.

I try to block the inane advertisement from my mind and get back to my other self, but like a set of catchy pop music lyrics, the more I try to displace the image of the Verizon guy, the more persistent he becomes.

You son of a bitch.

Finally I give up.

I'm back in the memory of my apartment. I'm frustrated but happy at the same time. I made contact. I may have caused my other self to black out a few times in the process, but I'm making progress.

It's an odd thing to have multiple memories of the same events. In life, I lived those blackouts during the chronothon. I can clearly recall the confusion I felt when some otherworldly voice came out of nowhere and called to me. I was scared, but I also got the message. Now I'm the one on the other side.

I still don't know how another version of me is alive and walking around in that stairwell, but I'm glad he is. Last I knew I was dead, so whoever changed that certainly had the element of surprise. If I ever figure out this communication with my other self business, I'm hoping I can clear up that mystery. Right now I have a different puzzle to solve.

I'm trying to get back in touch with this surviving version of myself, but don't know where he's headed. *What is he doing in 2150, and more importantly, where is he heading next?* If I'm going to have any chance of communicating with him, it would help to know where to look.

I ruminate on the problem for a little while, but no obvious answers surface. Whatever he's doing, he's at least open to talking to me. The other one, Benji, didn't even blink at my attempts to contact him. This one though, he was listening. He knows who I am. It may be that it's up to him now to find me, and not the other way around.

I sit in the silence, listening, hoping that somewhere out there, other me is finding his way through. I'm nervous with anticipation. What can he do? Will he look for some kind of medium? Some method of communing with the dead? Should I be practicing my Ouija board spelling?

There is a pattering noise coming from outside—raindrops flung sideways against the windowpanes. Moving to the window, I take in the darkening view of my neighborhood. Water has overtaken the streets again, at least a few feet deep. It seems my memory is competing against one in which the homes around me are deteriorating. Zurvan's future. The view gives me a shiver of anxiety, remembering my previous encounter with the owner of this memory. The changes haunt the corners of my vision, houses burnt to hollow shells or collapsed by the erosion of wind and water. They flicker in their ruined forms until I look directly at them, turn them solid and whole again with the power of my memory. I've lived in this apartment for years now. There are few aspects of this part of the neighborhood that have escaped my notice.

When I don't see Zurvan anywhere in view, I press my hands to the windows and concentrate on my surroundings. He may know this place as flood and storm but for me it's mostly lived up to its nickname, "The Sunshine City." Concentrating on a patch of the street, I use my memory, pushing the invading floodwaters away, restoring first my driveway and then the street itself, turning it to dry, sunlit concrete once more.

The victory makes me smile. The turbaned man-god is not the only one with power here. In a realm stitched together from memory, the strongest memory will hold fast. This is home turf for me and, even if I'm trapped here, I don't intend to live in fear. Holding back the floodwaters is a small victory, but it buoys my courage. I abandon the apartment and trot downstairs, still dry despite the waters in the streets around me. I keep a circle of concrete clear ahead of me as I walk, repelling the rain and striding into the street, reveling in the view of the waters retreating before me. I am Moses parting the Red Sea.

Rounding the corner I get an unobstructed view of the ruined downtown skyline. It's at least twice as high as it was in my time. The disparity makes me waver. Will he feel me here? Should I be hiding, escaping the ruin of this place? The water around my feet creeps toward me again as if sensing my weakening resolve. I force it away, not willing to give in to this bleak apocalyptic world. I study the skyline with curiosity, attempting to read the clues in its existence. It's clearly the future, a time in the city's history when it fell from grace.

St. Petersburg must have blossomed in the centuries after mine. The now ruined skyline is the shell of the bold and vibrant city I briefly saw before the girl in the church disappeared. The vast wings of the solar array lean out toward the bay, roughly where the city pier ought to be. It's shot through with holes—cables and shredded plastic dangling from the outstretched arms like spider webs.

I wonder what he's up to now?

I consider my options and move west, headed toward Fourth Street again and the site of my previous encounter with Zurvan. The fact that he tried to annihilate my mind the last time is not lost on me. I'm not a complete idiot. I have a plan. Sort of.

I make a list of memories in my mind that I don't think Zurvan could follow me to. There needs to be some sort of escape route, in case he decides to suffocate my soul again. Running away. That's the best I've got at the moment. I'm not a glutton for punishment, but I need answers and I don't think I'm going to find them in my apartment.

According to Benny, Zurvan is communicating with someone in the real world. If he can do it, then it stands to reason that I can too. Now that I know there is someone on the other side attempting to reach me, the idea seems far more plausible. If I can see what Zurvan does, perhaps I can duplicate the process and get a message to my other self. It could mean the difference between futures—bare green grass, or a headstone with Mym's name on it.

Close to Fourth Street I let the waters creep in on me again. I reduce my bubble of dry land until it only encompasses the ground I'm walking on and push onward, doing my best not to make my presence known.

There are differences in time again. Where previously I had been occupying a time period with a Chase bank and a Tijuana Flats Mexican restaurant, I'm looking at the ruined church with the central arched room raised high enough to be above the floodwaters. The adjustments were certainly not made by me, so I know Zurvan is near.

Once again a fire is burning in the center of the little arched room. I hide this time, climbing a pile of ruins inside the building next door. The numerous holes and windows offer ample visibility of the scene below.

I don't have long to wait.

The dark man in the flowing, sand-colored robes appears from the far side of the ruined church and mounts the steps to the raised platform. He's producing a cloud of smoke around himself somehow. He has brought something with him that looks like a burlap sack. When he sets it down, I see that it's filled with wood and kindling. He feeds the flames at the center of the room, building them to a steady roar. After he has made his additions and seems satisfied, he produces a metal object on a chain from one of his voluminous sleeves. I realize this is where the smoke has been issuing from and recognize the item as an incensor of the type priests use in blessings. He lifts the top on the incensor and blows on the coals, producing even more smoke in the process. He passes the incensor around the room, swinging it back and forth before finally placing it in a corner of the room to smolder.

Satisfied with his preparations, Zurvan begins pacing back and forth in front of the fire bowl. The sound of his chanting reaches my hiding place, but is in a language I don't understand. Nothing happens for a long while, but he continues to pace. I settle into a seated position to avoid having to stoop at the hole in the wall I'm peering through. I'm not tired or cramped. It is force of habit more than anything that is driving my actions. When I get settled, I look back through the hole and am startled by the presence of someone new. A boy has appeared in the fiery room, seemingly from nowhere.

Scrambling back to my knees, I study the new arrival. He's facing away from me, but from his build he looks young, perhaps sixteen. Zurvan has stopped his pacing. He is staring at the young man. There is something familiar and modern about the boy, even though he is dressed in robes very similar to Zurvan's. He has an eagerness in his movements—awe at being here. If he's dead, like me, he doesn't seem especially upset about it. To the contrary, as he falls to his knees in front of the robed man and the fire bowl, he looks the epitome of a devoted disciple.

"Oh, Great One," the boy exclaims in English. "You honor me with your presence." He prostrates himself at this. "All the brethren praise you and await your wisdom."

The voice reminds me of someone, but I can't remember who. I wish I could see his face. I get up and creep sideways in the ruined building, trying to find a chink in the wall offering a better angle.

Zurvan steps closer to the young man and stands next to the bowl of fire. "What news do you bring, disciple?"

The young man lifts his forehead from the surface of the platform and settles back onto his heels, but keeps his face down, eyes fixed on Zurvan's feet, his hands clasped in supplication in front of him. He begins to recite what is clearly a memorized speech. Unlike the girl who had sung her message, he delivers it in a steady and calm manner. "Elgin the Enduring bids you greeting and sends his deepest respect. He honors you with all the days of his never-ending years. The brethren of the Eternal Line of Gnomon likewise honor you with every moment of their—"

"Enough of this blandishment," Zurvan says. "What does Elgin have for excuses now? He stalls his promised deliverance and thinks to appease me with flattery and homage. I grow impatient with his lack of progress."

The young man is not prepared for this interruption. He attempts to recover his place in his speech, stammering a few words before Zurvan squats in front of him. "What news of the Alpha, and the scientist? Why does Elgin delay his action? I wallow in this drudgery while he placates me with words and inactivity."

The boy fumbles for an answer in his memory, searching for a response to this line of questioning. "The Eternal Line of Gnomon honors your greatness and knows that you are the true lord of space and time. This finite state of your imprisonment is but a sliver of a moment. The great river of time—"

"The Eternal Line of Gnomon can presume to lecture me on the realities of the Neverwhere on the day you all arrive to sample them for yourselves. Until then, my own counsel will I keep on the nature of time in this forsaken land," Zurvan growls, rising to a standing position and leering down at the boy. "If Elgin wishes to delay my deliverance, he need not send me more groveling children. He names himself an Eternal, but he is youthful in his ignorance and ineptitude."

"We have located the Lost Star, sir," the boy blurts out. "We are ready for its arrival."

Zurvan smiles at this. "Ah. Finally we get to the point. You've made preparations? You have the power to harness it?"

"Yes, sir. The brethren are in position now and will acquire the Lost Star. We also have the device to control it."

The man paces around the bowl of fire, the sweeping of his robes fanning the flames. "This message pleases me. I can begin to make plans." He pauses to stare into the glow before returning his attention to the kneeling young man. "I suppose you have lived at the temple for your training. How long have you been a disciple of The Eternals, boy?"

"If it pleases you, my lord, I have been studying your words on my own. I sought out the brethren and joined their cause. I wish to gain the wisdom of your eternal greatness."

"*My* wisdom?" Zurvan scoffs. "You have no way of knowing whom you really speak to, disciple. You suffer the scourge of distance. Your eagerness to know the ancient ways cannot bridge the chasm of time that lies between your millennium and mine. More great truths have been lost to the shifting sands of those passing centuries than ever emerged again. You are a worm crawling inside the sun-bleached skull of an ox, seeking to divine its thoughts."

The boy finally looks up far enough for me to see his face. His expression is sincere, eager, trusting. I'd swear I know him, but I can't quite place his voice. He maintains his devout posture, but lifts his head to observe the robed prophet, reciting another of his memorized speeches. "Oh, Great Zurvan, we know that when you return, you will right the wrongs of our world and give us a new and golden beginning. We trust in your justice and your promised reward."

Jonah. God, he looks like Jonah Sprocket!

The bearded man looks the boy in the face, his own expression seeming to soften with pity at the state of the young man's devotion. "I will indeed repay those who deserve justice. And my wrath. That much you can be assured of. Tell me, disciple, did Elgin tell you what would happen to you in this place?"

Not Jonah. Jay. Puberty has changed his voice, but this is the older version of the boy I know.

Jay is trembling slightly now. "My Lord Elgin told me that we do great honor to the brethren by bearing his greetings to you and that my reward would be unending joy in your presence. I would join those who have come to you before me and we will be in your exalted company upon your return."

Zurvan considers the young man thoughtfully. "It would seem your decision has been made for you. I cannot speak to joy, because I have found none in this place, but one thing I can offer you is my mercy. In return for your sacrifice in coming here, I will not subject you to the unending drudgery of this place. Consider this small mercy my gift to you." As he says this, he extends his hand out over the young man's prone form. The boy suddenly goes rigid, jerking upright.

No. Not him too! I scramble to my feet, dashing down the stairs to the lower floor of the building. I have no plan, no idea what I can do, but I burst out the lower level and into the street. Looking up the steps and between the fire-lit arches I can see Jay up close.

His hands are clamped to his head, grasping and clawing frantically at his skull. I can almost feel the pain in his eyes as I watch him searching vainly for the fingers tearing at his mind. He is yanked to his feet, joints locking, but he is held upright by a will not his own. His mouth opens and he begins to speak, but the words are also being spoken by Zurvan at the same time. The image is reminiscent of a ventriloquist with a dummy, though I can see Zurvan's mouth moving and he is not touching the boy directly. He is controlling the boy's movements with a single outstretched hand.

"The Almighty Zurvan sends this message to his faithful brethren: The Lost Star returns as I have promised your prophets. You will bring it to me and I will grant your reward—spare you from the fate that consumes humanity. Those who would be saved should heed my words. Bring the Lost

Star to the eternal fires of Yanar Dag. Restore me to my body and assure your eternal salvation."

As soon as Zurvan finishes his speech, he releases his grip.

Jay collapses toward the ground, but his body never strikes the surface. I watch with horror as his robed form evaporates into the ether. A moment later there is no evidence that he ever existed.

Holy shit.

I'm frozen in shock, chiding myself for my foolishness in getting so close to this man again and praying that he hasn't yet detected my presence. Watching the boy vanish has been enough to replenish my terror. My desire to discern Zurvan's methods of communication has twisted to a knot in my stomach. *He's a monster.* If the only way to receive messages involves someone in the real world sacrificing children to the Neverwhere, I can't wish for that. I could never be a party to anything so cruel.

I back slowly away from the archway. Zurvan's eyes are closed. He's standing still, seeming to relish the violence he has just performed.

I crawl slowly back through a hole in the wall of the building next door, then climb the steps of the stairwell to the first landing, hiding myself from view. There is a tiny hole in the cement blocks still allowing a view of the robed man next door.

How is he doing that to people? And why would anyone be helping him?

I struggle to process what I just saw.

The part of Zurvan's speech that nags at me is his talk of a "promised deliverance." He's getting out of here somehow, or at least hopes to, in return for this supposed salvation. How do they plan to manage that? Whatever his relationship with these disciples and this Elgin person is, it's supposed to benefit them both somehow. The rest of the conversation was out of my depth. I don't know what the Alpha is, or what the temple they referred to was. It doesn't sound like a religion I've ever heard of and, if it involves sacrificing people to the Neverwhere, I plan to steer clear. He also mentioned a scientist. I only know one of those, but he would never have anything to do with these people, would he?

Zurvan is still relishing his moment. He's staying on the platform, staring at the space where the disciple vanished. Jay was treating him like a god. Worshiping him. Watching Zurvan, I wonder at his real origins. He's powerful, true. I've felt what he can do here. I've felt him get inside my head. But a god? I highly doubt that. So what is he then?

Out the hole in the building wall, I watch Zurvan extinguish his fire pit. He's scooping ash onto it from the platform. No. It's not the platform anymore, and it's not ash but sand—

Quick as thought, my building vanishes. I plummet out of the air like Willie Coyote belatedly recognizing he's run off a cliff. Gritty dunes rush up to meet me and I thud into them, tumbling downhill into a miniature valley between two rises. The dune is smoking. Flames lick from the very stones themselves. I can smell gas. *Methane?*

Zurvan's memory shift was even faster than I could have anticipated. I spit dirt and sand from my mouth and spring to my feet. *Did he hear me? Am I discovered?* The smoking dune I've rolled down lies between me and where I last saw Zurvan. If he saw me fall, he could be on me any moment.

I wrack my brain for the memories I had planned to use for my escape route, terrified to find that my mind has gone blank with fear. My hands are out in front of me waiting to open a portal. *To where? Where am I going?*

His shadow falls across me before I see him. He looms on the hilltop, wiping out the sun. The dark silhouette is silent, statuesque in his stillness. *Will he attack? Am I about to lose my mind?*

I'm through the portal and running. I'm in left center at Tropicana Field. The baseball stadium is not where I had intended to escape to, but it was what occurred to me in the moment. Good enough for now. As I tear across the Astroturf and onto the infield, I don't look back. If he's chasing me, I can't imagine how knowing will help me now. The dugouts are foggy in their depths. I've never been inside one here. No escape that way. I vault the low wall beyond first base and land in the first row of stands, bounding up the concrete steps to the next level and the exits. Only when I've reached the landing and am about to descend into the corridor that circumnavigates the stadium do I finally turn around.

He's there. Standing in center field with all the calm of a seasoned pro awaiting fly balls. He isn't chasing me. He's come though, and he's watching me. I won't be staying now. My hands shoot into the air ahead of me, opening another memory. The right one this time. I tumble through the portal and close it violently behind me.

As I lie on the soft mossy embankment of the stream running through the Redwood National Forest, I gulp the cool, just-minted air—tasting the freshness of it—seeming every bit as real in my memory as it was in life.

He didn't get me. I'm still okay.

The trees around me are ancient giants, their tops piercing the sky nearly three hundred feet above. This place is old, with roots that delve deep into history, but I'm praying Zurvan hasn't ever been here. At least not to this spot, a site burned into my memory from childhood camping trips and family hiking adventures. I suspect if I looked for it, I could walk and find my dad's old RV parked nearby, complete with faded interior and a seventies paint job.

But I don't wander.

I remain.

My fear of Zurvan and his mysterious power is renewed, but I also feel a mix of relief, and pride. I've escaped. I didn't require saving this time.

My pride is dimmed by the loss of Jay. I never knew that version of the boy personally. Whatever path brought him here, he's become another victim of this place and I failed to save him.

When I find Benny again, I mean to tell him what I've learned. Zurvan has help in the real world—someone searching for an Alpha, a scientist, and a way to bring Zurvan to life. What those pieces mean in the final puzzle is yet to be determined, but the bits of the picture I'm putting together don't look like they form anything good. What's clear is that these disciples have a way of putting people into this place and presumably a way to get them back out. My best bit of news for now is that someone in the real world is looking for me also, and maybe, just maybe, I can discover a way out of here too.

But now I need to find him, or pray he finds me first.

.

St. Austell, Cornwall, UK- April, 2165

A biting wind is flinging mist and rain at us as we motor along the cliff-side road toward the coastal hamlet of Porthpean. The road is narrow, twisting, and claustrophobic, hemmed in on both sides by thick vegetation and occasional garden walls. I imagine the drive would be charming in sunlight. Glimpses through gates show cozy homes and sprawling ocean-side villas, but the dimming twilight and patchy fog robs the scene of cheer.

As we pass through the village, I marvel at a diminutive chapel made of fieldstone bordered by an ivy-covered wall with a quaint arch. It looks ancient, as though the entire town has been kept in a bubble the last few centuries.

We pull up to the gate at our destination address and pause at a security station. I'm not sure what I expected Ebenezer Sprocket's home to look like, but this wasn't it. The creations of the eccentric inventor that I've seen so far had given me the impression he might be a mad scientist type— Doc Brown tinkering in a cluttered garage on a flux capacitor. To the contrary, the view of this English home is tidy and serene.

The waves breaking against the far bluffs add a soothing monotony of sound to the already calm surroundings. The manicured lawn and neatly trimmed hedges are wet and dripping. The locked wrought iron gate is likewise covered in droplets of moisture. The only touch of modern technology is the clean, transparent screen to the left of the entrance. There are no call buttons or obvious cameras, but the screen illuminates when we look at it, showing a family crest. A pleasant voice greets us. "Good evening. To what do we owe the pleasure of your visit?" Mym and Tucket look to me for a response.

"Yes, we're here to see Jonah Sprocket, please. My name is Ben Travers. He'll know who we are."

"Your name has previously been approved for our guest list. I will alert Master Jonah to your arrival. Please enter." The screen dims and the gates swing open for us, admitting us to a short winding driveway. I park the motorcycle in the corner of a roundabout and we cover the sidecar to protect our belongings from the drizzle. The house itself is cheerful with bright white walls that seem to have retained the warmth of sunnier days. The many windows have curtains flung open and the orange glow of lamplight inside looks very inviting. I catch a snatch of violin music drifting out from some interior room. The home looks like it holds as many as a dozen rooms if I had to guess.

The broad door at the side of the house flies open to reveal a boy in a thick sweater and khaki trousers. He is only wearing wooly socks on his feet, but doesn't seem to mind as he comes dashing out to meet us. "Ben! You came!"

Jonah Sprocket has lost none of his enthusiasm in our time apart. His untidy blond hair is partially obstructing his wide, blue eyes as he sprints into my arms. When he lifts his face from my chest I try to place his age. *Perhaps ten?* I'd guess it's been only a year or so since I've seen him last, though for me it's been less.

"What's up, buddy!" I give him a squeeze. "You remember Mym, of course." Jonah grins and gives Mym a hug too. "And this is my friend Tucket." Tucket extends a hand. Jonah shakes it and hops up and down a couple times, unable to contain himself.

"I'm so excited you guys are here! Are you having another adventure?"

"Something like that. You mind if we get out of the weather?"

"Oh sure. Come in!" Jonah leads the way indoors and we follow his soggy sock prints into a broad foyer. A staircase ascends from the foyer to a balcony where a lanky, white-haired man has arrived to greet us. Barley, Jonah's golden Labrador, sprints to us from the back of the house and licks my hand before investigating Tucket. The dog looks about the same as the last time I saw him, though possibly a little better fed. Ebenezer, Jonah's father, is wearing a wool sweater, not dissimilar to Jonah's. He smiles at us as he descends the stairs.

Handshakes and introductions are again made for Tucket before we are offered tea in the parlor.

"You've certainly made Jonah's weekend," Ebenezer says. "You should hear how much he talks about you."

"He was quite the hit with my friends as well." I smile at Jonah. "He had some of the fastest race times per round in chronothon history from what I hear. Pays to be clever." I rub behind Barley's ear as the dog lays its head in my lap.

"I understand they awarded you first place," Ebenezer says. "Well deserved after what you went through. The chronothon committee has been almost entirely replaced from what I hear. Sacked or demoted for incompetent security."

"I hope they awarded you some compensation for what you went through," I say.

"They did. Jonah received his due as a racer and we were awarded a settlement for 'distress' I believe they called it. Money to keep us from suing, I suppose. I also received an additional severance package from Ambrose Cybergenics for the way I was treated, and got the rights back to a few of the inventions I'd made while working for them." As he is speaking, the door opens and a chrome-bodied figure enters bearing a tea tray. "I'd like to introduce my chief of house, Darius."

The metal man sets the tea tray down and bows. "It is an honor to meet you all. I've a heard a great deal about you from Master Jonah." I recognize his voice from the entrance screen out front. "And Mr. Morris, it is an honor to have you here as well. A distinguished graduate of the Academy."

Tucket smiles at this and bows in return. He is watching the metal man with interest. "Were you produced as part of United Machine's meta-human series?"

The metal man straightens up and studies him.

"I only ask because my girlfriend, er, ex-girlfriend, was an Echo Seven Series meta-human," Tucket explains.

"My predecessors were of the Echo Series," Darius replies. "I am a Gamma Series human."

I notice he doesn't use the meta prefix.

"Lovely place to work," I say, doing my best to steer the small talk to somewhere I'll be unlikely to offend anyone.

"Darius has been working here for about five years now," Ebenezer says. "Couldn't get by without him. He's my general assistant and does some design work for me in the lab. He also makes a mean shepherd's pie."

"I won't interrupt you further," Darius says. "But call if you need anything."

Barley's tail is wagging, and Darius tosses him a dog treat from an opening in his thigh that serves as a pocket. He then takes his leave.

"Jonah has certainly had plenty of good things to say about you," Ebenezer says. "I appreciate your responding to our invitation to visit. Are you able to stay long?"

"We weren't sure how long you intended us to visit. The invite wasn't really specific."

"That's likely my fault," Ebenezer says. "Not much good at these 'real mail' apps they have out. Would have sent you an actual hand-written note, but my handwriting is atrocious. You never would have deciphered it. There has been a bit of confusion on the best way to reach you. Don't usually have much need to contact folks who are off-Grid. ASCOTT said they were doing their best to contact you for us, but I guess even they didn't know for sure where you lived until they got help from the Academy." Ebenezer looks to Tucket. "Happy to see it all worked out in the end. Jonah has talked so much about you that we felt it was time to get you over to the house. I thought it would do the boy good."

"I was excited to get the message." I straighten up on the couch. "It was actually great timing that you invited us to visit because you were the only person I knew that might be able to help us with something we're working on." I turn to the boy. "Jonah, when we were racing together, you told me about your brother, Jay." Jonah nods. Ebenezer's face takes on a slightly more serious expression. "You also mentioned he knew about the Eternals."

The name hangs in the air between us, no one responding at first. Finally Jonah pipes up. "Jay doesn't really want us talking about them, but they are his friends."

Ebenezer frowns. "Friends would have been welcome. The Eternals are more to him recently. Almost an obsession. We were wondering if you had heard the rumors about them lately. I confess, that is part of why I wanted to speak to you."

"Who are they?" Mym asks. "We did a little research, but there isn't much information in standard databases. It's a religion, right?"

Ebenezer scratches at his stubble and fidgets with his collar. "I suppose you'd call it that, but not one you get much contact with. If Jay had been spending his days in the village chapel or thumping a Bible in the square like you see sometimes, I think that might have been preferable. I could have put up with a few lectures on my sinful ways if he was becoming a Methodist or a Catholic or something, but this was different. He didn't go out. Didn't get many visitors. He'd just stay up in his room all day and night, muttering to himself and smoking the place up with candles and such. Thought for a while he was getting into witchcraft, or voodoo, or something of that sort. When he did come out, he kept his eyes closed as often as not. Just talking to himself."

"What did he say it was about?" I ask.

"He didn't. That's the trouble. Didn't want to talk about it with us. There was no trying to convert anyone or any of the usual zealousness that comes with dabbling in spiritual stuff. I just left him alone and he left us alone."

I can't help but notice that Ebenezer is referring to Jay in the past tense. It's clear that he is not at home currently and may not be living here any longer.

"It wasn't till I got a call a few weeks ago from the constable that I knew something had changed for the worse. He had gotten himself arrested. *Grave robbing*, they said." Ebenezer shook his head. "Only it wasn't really. The boy had gone to our family plots and dug up his mother. Laid her bones out in the moonlight. Told us it was an abomination to bury the dead. Wanted to let her remains get eaten up by birds. He'd started digging up her parents too when they found him."

Ebenezer stares out the window. When he returns to looking at me a few moments later, his eyes are moist. "The constable thought he was ill in the head. Let him come home with a warning, since he'd only disturbed graves belonging to our own family. But it got around the village. My wife was raised in this house. Her family has old roots here. And people in this area have long memories. Jay digging up the cemetery made him an instant pariah."

Ebenezer sighs. "I tried talking to him, but he wouldn't have any of it. Said it was his duty and that we would be cursed for burying her again."

Mym speaks up next to me. "Did he ever mention the name Zoroaster, or anything to do with Zoroastrianism? From what I've read, the old beliefs involving the dead might match up."

"I looked into that a bit—after," Ebenezer says. "Did some research. Tried to understand him. It wasn't Zoroaster he talked about though. It was always the name Zurvan, and another one named Gnomo, or gnome something. He kept writing it on the walls of his room."

"Zurvan is tied to an old heresy in Zoroastrianism," Tucket says. His eyes have a hazy look and I can tell he's off in the metaspace and reading something, keeping himself up to speed on the conversation. "A heretical sect around the fifth century BCE. It's ancient, but it died out and hasn't been practiced since, at least according to modern Zoroastrians. There aren't many of those left either."

"My son would have begged to differ," Ebenezer says. "It certainly was alive and well to him."

"What happened?" Mym asks. "Where is Jay now?"

"His friends came to get him," Jonah says. "Last week. Came in a big truck, all wearing black robes and stuff."

I look to Ebenezer for confirmation. I get the impression it's information he would rather not have shared, but he nods. "They came in the night. No explanation. He tried to leave without even saying goodbye. I watched them come down the drive, confronted them outside." His head has drooped lower during the conversation, but he picks it up and holds it higher now, as if rallying his spirit to be able to continue the tale. "It wasn't as if they took him. He went with them freely. Happily even, if you could say he was happy anymore. I tried to stop him from leaving, but he was determined."

"What was his explanation?" I ask. "Did he say where he was going?"

"No. Nothing," Ebenezer says, his voice seems on the verge of cracking, but he holds it together. "He wouldn't even speak to me."

"We found the book though," Jonah says. "We found his prayer book he's been writing in. It's all full of symbols."

I look at him with interest. "What kind of symbols?"

"Lots of them. Lions and fire and stuff. He drew them."

Ebenezer has gone quiet and is looking out the window again, absentmindedly fidgeting with the teaspoon on the table next to him.

"We've been chasing a symbol ourselves," I say. "We think it might be tied into this cult of the Eternals somehow. Do you think we could see the book?"

"I'll take you to Jay's room!" Jonah pops out of his chair and addresses his dad. "Want to show it to them?"

Ebenezer studies us, his gaze traveling from Tucket to me and finally resting on Mym. While looking at her, he seems on the verge of speaking, but then he merely nods to Jonah and waves a hand dismissively before resuming his contemplation of the outdoors.

The second floor is cozy and inviting—a few quaint bedrooms surrounding a parlor—but we don't stop there. We continue onward, following Jonah to the foot of a spiral staircase at the rear of the house. He pauses with one foot on the bottom step.

"Dad doesn't like to go up here, but Jay lets me come up sometimes. On days when he's feeling happy."

Something about the boy's tone makes me think those days must not have been frequent. We climb the stairs after him and emerge into what must have originally been an attic. The peaked roof makes the sides of the room inaccessible to anyone of my height, but the center of the room has been turned into a bedroom, though a fairly Spartan one. Furniture other than the bed is limited to an antique wardrobe and a writing desk covered in candle wax and burnt nubs of extinguished tapers. Their presence must be more symbolic than functional, as the room is artificially lit by imbedded wall lighting and two windows at either end of the room admit the shrouded daylight, illuminating the residence of what I take to be someone with very simple tastes.

The bedroom holds none of the trinkets favored by other teenagers Jay's age. No rock posters or magazines; no video game consoles or pinup girls. The only items in the room that could be construed as decorations are a handful of scribbled drawings on loose paper stuck to one wall. There are other smaller notes interspersed between them, bits of phrases and quotations. As I step close to investigate, it appears to all be interrelated. The quotes that are cited all bear the same name. *Lord Gnomon*. One of the drawings near the top of the collection has our flaming, winged circle symbol on it.

Jonah immediately heads for the writing desk and opens the center drawer. He returns to me bearing a hard-backed leather-bound journal. The book is black and has been worn at the corners. The leather bears scars from rough use and occasional encounters with water or tea. The pages have been wrinkled in places and the spine has struggled to maintain its composure.

I open the book and it's as though I'm looking at an extension of the clippings on the wall. More drawings illuminate some of the pages, but it is mostly text, handwritten by someone scribbling hastily at times and in other moments printed with deliberate care.

What strikes me as odd after a few pages, is that the writing is frequently encapsulated in quotation marks, though it appears to be written in the style of a journal. I can see how Jonah may have interpreted it as a type of prayer book, but the more I look at it, the less it seems like prayer and the more it resembles specific directives. The sentences begin in fits and starts, not always connecting with the ones previous. It's as if I'm reading one side of a conversation without knowing the other person's dialogue.

Occasionally Jay has scribbled additional notes in the margins. One particular line strikes me. "My dreams occur during the day now. They say that is an important step. I can speak to him when I want, but I can't always keep him out."

"Looks like you two might have a few things in common," Mym says. I look up and realize she's been reading it next to me—a fact I was too absorbed to notice before. She looks worried though. I consider the wall full of jumbled messages. *Is this what my future is going to look like too?*

Jonah has finished showing Tucket around the room and wanders back to my side. "His room didn't used to look like this. We used to play up here. He doesn't like to play much anymore though."

"Jonah, when did Jay start working on this?" I hold up the book and gesture toward the quotations on the wall with it. "How long ago?"

"I don't remember exactly. Maybe a year. It started before I went to the race. That's when he made me my helmet. He was mad that I lost it during the race and made me another one. Dad keeps telling me to wear it too. But I told him I didn't want to. I remembered what you said, and I wasn't scared anymore."

I study the boy, remembering the first time I saw him at the chronothon welcome dinner. He had been wearing a multicolored helmet in the shape of a snail.

Mym is looking at me, obviously curious about the conversation.

Jonah looks around the room, but seems ready to move on. "Want to come see my room next?"

I consider the book in my hands. "I'd like to have a little longer look at this. Why don't you show Tucket and Mym and I'll catch up."

Jonah seems satisfied with this and leads Tucket back downstairs, talking animatedly about the Academy. Mym nudges me. "You okay?"

"Yeah, I'll be right down, just trying to buy a little time with this. I feel like it might have more clues for us."

"Okay. I'll see if I can help keep him entertained." She kisses me on the cheek and descends the stairs after the others.

Moving to the edge of the bed, I take a seat and go back to browsing the book. The lines of scripted writing end approximately a third of the way in. After that, it takes on the looser freestyle writing of a journal. The handwriting is still the same, but the format is different. These thoughts are not well organized, more stream of consciousness writing, full of the emotions of the moment. It seems Jay had quite a lot to say regarding the first third of the book. Little snippets of journaling mention "The Chronicle," and "The Lost Star." From what I gather, he has been trying to write this chronicle from memory, having only heard it spoken somewhere. A sizable feat, as the text is anything but short. I flip to the most recent entry at the back of the journal. It seems he knew it would be his last.

"They will be here for me tomorrow night. The time has come for me to leave all of this behind. They were very insistent that I take nothing with me, not even spare clothing. I'm tempted to take this journal, but they expect me to know the message from memory now. I worry they may think I've failed to learn it all if I bring my notes. It's okay. I've recited it three times without errors this morning. I even dream the words in my sleep. If I can pass along the message, I will be rewarded. They say they have a special assignment for me. I hope I'll be one of the chosen."

There are more drawings of the winged sun throughout the journal, along with a label—The Lost Star.

So the symbol and the Lost Star reference are the same thing . . .

Something moves to my right. I look up in surprise to find Darius, Ebenezer's chrome assistant, staring at me. My heart jolts in my chest. "Whoa. You scared me. Never heard you come in."

Darius bows slightly, but doesn't apologize. "I have need of your attention. You must come with me."

"I told Jonah I'd meet him in—"

"Master Jonah will not ask after you for a few more minutes, you have time to speak to me."

"How can you know that?"

"All of the manor's security protocols route through me. I am aware of everything that happens on these grounds. Also, I am capable of very accurate predictions when it comes to the members of this household. Please, I must have your time."

I set the book down and stand, uneasily. "I guess if it won't take long . . ."

"It won't. Now if you'll please follow me."

Darius leads me down a back set of steps and onto the rear patio. He doesn't hesitate there, but leads me around the house and across the side yard to a weatherworn outbuilding at the edge of the woods. Just beyond it, the driveway passes by on its way to the front of the house. I hadn't noticed the building as we rode in, possibly due to its partial obscurity in the trees.

Once he has reached the door, he unlocks it electronically and reveals an interior full of lawn equipment, both modern and old—contraptions that look to be a collection of remotely operated lawn mowers. None have seats or operating controls, but each one is mounted in a sort of dock, presumably charging up for their next run over the grounds.

Darius instructs me to stand inside the shed. "You are going to send yourself back to Wednesday night. 20:15 Zulu."

"You want me to jump to the past? I can't do that right now, I've got to—"

"You already have," Darius replies. "I saw you there."

This information stops me short. "I was here last Wednesday?"

"Indeed. You witnessed Master Jay's departure before disappearing. I noted your presence that night but informed no one. The manor analyzed you upon arrival and deemed you to not be a security threat. I had an interest in learning the reason for your visit, and now I know. You are searching for the Lost Star and you're a friend to Master Jonah."

"You know about the symbol?"

"Jay didn't confide his thoughts to his father and brother, but that did not keep him from speaking out loud in his room. The manor heard all of his confessions. It would seem I know him better than anyone."

"You eavesdropped on him?"

"Master Jay had the option to change the privacy settings on his room to prevent me from listening any time he wanted, but he never excluded me. Perhaps he wanted me to listen. I've found that organic humans like yourself sometimes have conflicting and illogical motivations. Jay changed in recent months. He became more hostile to me. As he grew more involved with the Eternals, he began to treat me with less respect. But he knew I could never do him harm. My protocols wouldn't allow it. He didn't like me, but he still trusted me."

"And should we trust you? It's kind of an unusual point to bring up as you're suggesting I send myself through time without anything other than your word to go on."

Darius stares at me, the drizzling rain accumulating in larger beads and running down his metal skull. "You've already followed me to this out of the way spot on the grounds, all alone. If I meant to dispose of you, I wouldn't really need to send you through time. I'd be capable of doing that here."

I frown at the silver man. "You're not doing a lot to inspire confidence."

Darius merely inclines his head closer, as if whispering a secret. "And yet you are still going to go. Interesting, isn't it?"

The synth is right. My curiosity has the best of me. I scan the floor of the shed, looking for any sign of violence or some indication that my arrival the previous Wednesday went poorly, but the shed seems undisturbed. "When I get there, this area will be clear?"

"Nothing inside has been moved since Tuesday when the yard bots were deployed. You will arrive safely. As I said, I've already seen it."

"And I just have to trust you."

"It would seem so."

"Why can't you just tell me what I'm going to see? If you know, and have all the information anyway, you could save me a trip."

"My system protocols have been set to keep certain information private. As an employee of the manor I cannot speak of the events I saw Wednesday night or access the security footage for display to a third party. My protocols do not limit me from helping someone else see the original event for themselves, however. If you are truly a friend to Master Jonah, you'll go and see for yourself."

I frown at him, but have no rebuttal this time.

I dial the settings on my chronometer and set my hand against the shed wall. "See you in a minute."

I press the pin and blink.

It's dark inside the shed. It seems Wednesday night was dry. When I peek my head out the door, the sky above is clear and full of stars. I'm glad Darius has had me jump indoors anyway, since I've at least avoided fusing myself with the moths and other insects flitting about the night. I study the landscape of the manor and yard. Somewhere on the property, Darius has been alerted to my presence. I don't bother to look for cameras or sensors. Any one of the gadgets on the shelves could be broadcasting my movements. I wouldn't even know where to look.

I concentrate on the task at hand, slinking out of the shed and finding a place to hide in the wooded area near the driveway. I settle down under the boughs of a thick evergreen where I will have a decent view of the property. I don't have long to wait. Headlights pull into the driveway only moments later, pausing at the gate, then proceeding through.

The black vehicle is nearly silent, no engine rumble or smell of exhaust, just the subtle whir of an electric motor and the crunch of its tires on the driveway stones. The truck doesn't drive all the way to the house. It stops close to my position and waits. I watch the door of the manor, waiting for a view of Jay, but the first person to appear is actually Ebenezer. He comes from the back of the house and cuts across the yard in a similar path to the route I took. He strides across the lawn and stops in the high beams of the vehicle, staring down the occupants. It takes about ten seconds of this showdown before a door opens on the vehicle and two people step out.

Ebenezer is lit by the headlights, but the new arrivals are shrouded in darkness, only allowing me vague impressions of their forms beneath dark clothing. One of the figures shuffles forward. The other taller man is merely helping him along. I get the impression he's elderly, and his crackling voice confirms it when he speaks.

"Is he ready? The time of the ascendancy is upon us."

"He's just a boy," Ebenezer replies.

"Age is meaningless. The reign of Zurvan knows no limits, and time will not confine him."

There is something oddly familiar about the old man's voice. My brain is struggling to place where I could have met him before. The silhouette of his face is unfamiliar to me, as is the severe stoop of his shoulders. It's only the voice that puzzles me.

"You promised me that this will be the end of it, Elgin," Ebenezer says. "After tonight my family won't be a party to any more of your schemes."

"We do not scheme, Sprocket. This is work of our Lord. If he requires more of you, we will take it. So pray that this is all he asks of you. When the Lost Star returns and he gains his power, none of this will matter. Only his magnanimity spares you now. I recommend you do not test it."

The reference to the Lost Star makes a connection in my mind. I have a hard time reconciling the bent form of the old man in the driveway to the young boy in the alley in Valencia in 2017, but I'm almost positive it's the same voice. *You're too late, Traversss. The Lost Star will return.* My logical mind struggles with the timeline. *If it's the same person, that means this old dude is like 160 years old. Is that possible this far into the future, or is he a time traveler?*

The front door to the manor opens and a young man walks out. Jay is literally an older version of Jonah, so he has the same sandy hair, though now it's been cut short. Adolescence has stretched him, his limbs yearning for manhood, but lacking the material to fill out. Even with his awkward angles and thin frame, Jay walks with confidence. His journal entries had exposed his nervousness, but it isn't showing tonight. His father turns as he walks up, perhaps hoping for a last minute change of heart. Jay pauses near him, looking Ebenezer in the eyes, but says nothing. After this moment of silence, he walks up to the old man.

"Good evening, Master Elgin," Jay says.

"It seems your time has come, young man," Elgin replies. "I presume you are well prepared?"

"I'm ready," Jay says. He straightens up a little taller and strides around the men to the open rear door of the vehicle. He casts a single lingering glance at the house, his expression softening, and for a moment he looks like the little boy I know. He then climbs into the dark interior of the truck, slamming the door closed behind him. I follow his last gaze to the manor and notice the face peering out of an upstairs window.

Jonah.

Elgin hands something to his assistant and the bulky man lumbers over to Ebenezer to put the item in his hand.

"We don't want you to feel you have been entirely unappreciated, Sprocket," Elgin says. "Your assistance in these matters has been most effective."

"You think I was after money?" Ebenezer scoffs.

"No. I am aware of your priorities. We simply want you to have the means to enjoy your time with your remaining son." He turns and begins his shuffle back to the truck. "Relish it while you can."

Ebenezer is scowling at the old man's back. "I've done what you asked. I never want to see you here again, Elgin."

The old man doesn't respond, he merely climbs into the truck and closes the door behind himself. The assistant gets into the front seat and presses something on the console. I note there is no steering wheel on either side of the dashboard. He closes his door and the interior goes dark again. The truck executes a neat turn and leaves the way it came, leaving Ebenezer staring after it. When the truck is gone, he looks at the something in his palm and slips it into his pocket before making his way back the house.

Jonah is still watching from the upstairs window, but as his father gets close to the house, his head disappears behind the curtains. I'm left alone again in the darkness, trying to make sense of what I've just seen.

I climb back into the garden shed and jump back to a minute after I left. Darius is outside in the drizzling rain, staring at the house.

"And now you know," he says.

"I don't know what I know," I reply. "Only that Ebenezer wasn't very honest with us. You could hardly call that trying to stop someone. He pretty much just let Jay go."

"You know that Jonah and Jay are alternates of one another, not brothers," Darius says.

"Yeah. I did know that. But Jonah has had a different past now, so they shouldn't necessarily go down the same path."

"Unless someone forces them."

I ponder what the synth is implying. "Are these Eternals using mind control? The people I know who have heard of the Eternals consider them a creepy cult. I don't get what makes anyone want to join them."

"In his conversations with himself, Jay claimed the Eternals would save humanity."

"From what?"

"The future."

I run a hand though my now-wet hair. "Jonah seems like a smart kid. I assume Jay is just as sharp. He's still just a teenager though. Why did they recruit him?"

Darius is quiet for a moment, then turns his gaze toward the manor. "That is the most difficult part. The Eternals did not seek out Master Jay. He found them."

I run into Ebenezer at the top of the stairs just outside the door to Jonah's room. He looks at my soggy appearance and frowns. "Can I get you a towel? I know English weather is—"

I put up a hand to cut him off. "When I first met Jonah he was wearing a helmet on his head. Bright colors, looked like a snail. Said his brother gave it to him. I assume you're familiar with it?"

"Yes, Jonah was rather fond of—"

"You built it, didn't you."

Ebenezer narrows his eyes. "My workshop here at home has always been open to the boys. They both enjoy tinkering on whatever suits them."

"But you would have wanted this project to succeed. Jonah said it kept out 'brain invaders.' He meant The Eternals. What did you design into it?"

Ebenezer considers me a moment, seeming to waffle about whether to admit his involvement, but when I don't relent in staring him down, he finally begins to explain.

"It was a device intended to reorganize a person's brain. It has applications for treatment of Alzheimer's, dementia, and a variety of other mental disorders. It maps brain activity and memories, and determines what is considered 'normal.' Then, if changes occur outside of established parameters, it can make corrections, modify the mind back to the original. It had other applications too—aiding in memory retention especially."

"Like some kind of re-boot? Put your brain back to factory settings? That sounds a bit scary."

"No. It's more fluid than that. You can certainly learn new things, gain new memories, but by cataloguing your mind, it would guard against catastrophic loss of memory from disease or trauma. The medical applications would make it highly desirable."

"Did it go into production?"

"No. Ambrose Cybergenics got embroiled in a lawsuit over the ethical implications of the device. People worried that their minds would be cloned. There were rumors going around that the company was copying people's memory files into synths—using them to steal people's identities. After the company's involvement in the last chronothon, their reputation suffered badly. It's under new management since the founder is still missing, but the courts ruled against them and the rights to the device reverted back to me.

"I had kept various prototypes around anyway, because I discovered there were even more applications for time travelers. It doesn't just prevent loss of old memories. It also guards against a mass influx of *new* memories." He looks me in the eye with the last line.

"Sudden influx. Like if someone was trying to add new content to your mind."

Ebenezer nods. "These Eternals, they do things I never thought possible. They get into your head." He taps a crooked finger against his temple. "They already got to my family in another timestream."

"Jay."

"When he showed up here, telling me when he was from, I didn't know what to think. He's my son, alternate timestream or not, but he was different. Troubled. I don't know all the details of his future in that time, but it's not one I want for Jonah. Whatever he's gotten himself into, I'm not going to see them corrupt my boy too."

"Jonah said that Jay was the one who gave him the helmet. It sounded like Jay was trying to protect him."

Ebenezer's expression softens. "Jay's a good boy. At least when he's himself. Lately he's been more and more like—someone different. I don't know how to describe it. He's losing his mind. That's the most accurate way to put it. He knew it, though. There was nothing I could do. Days when he wasn't obsessively chanting or getting lost in his own head, sometimes he'd come back to us. Those were the good days. He asked me to make Jonah the helmet on a day like that. Helped me make it. He did love him. During times when he remembered us anyway." Ebenezer stares at me, his face a mask of worry. "The boy should still be wearing it. He might listen to you. He respects you."

"Where is the helmet now?"

"In his bedroom." Ebenezer gestures toward the door.

I rap my knuckles against the door a few times and enter. Jonah is seated on his bed, showing Tucket and Mym something on an electronic tablet. All three look up when I enter. The new snail helmet is hanging on a hook next to the closet. I remove it from the hook and inspect it. It's not painted this time, just a metallic chrome that appears to be the same material Darius is made of. It's much lighter than I expected. I take a knee in front of Jonah, handing him the helmet. The boy sets his tablet aside and takes the helmet from me.

"Looks like you might still need this, bud."

Jonah frowns. "You said I wouldn't have to. You said I'll always be one of the good guys. And good guys don't invade people's brains."

I sigh, taking the helmet from his lap and carefully squeezing it onto his head. "You are one of the good guys, Jonah. But sometimes even good guys need a little bit of help staying that way. We just want to keep you safe, till we know what the future brings."

Jonah doesn't argue, but I can tell he's disappointed. His eyes search mine for just a moment, then he slides off the bed and dashes out of the room. Barley gets out of his dog bed in the corner and trots after him, tail wagging.

Mym is watching me closely.

Ebenezer wraps his arms around himself. "He'll be all right. It's been rough for him lately. I'm sure he's going to get adjusted to it." He looks at Tucket and Mym. "I hope you all can stay the night and spend a little more time with him. He seems to be enjoying your company very much." He shifts a little and waves toward the doorway. "Can I talk you into a plate of Darius's shepherd's pie?"

As Ebenezer leads Tucket downstairs in search of dinner, Mym takes me aside to question me. She grabs my hand and pulls me down the hallway where we won't be overheard from downstairs.

"What is this all about? Who are you protecting the boy from?"

I pull Mym a little closer, hugging her to my chest, grateful for a moment alone with her. "I think I'm protecting him from himself, as shitty as that sounds."

Mym wraps her arms around me. "The older brother is him, right? You think these Eternals he's caught up with might be a threat to this version of him too?"

I kiss the top of her head. "I think so."

"What did you learn from the book?"

"Not as much as I learned from the butler." I give her the abbreviated account of my trip to Wednesday night and the visitors in the black truck, including how I recognized the old man's voice. "Darius said the men that showed up weren't just here to collect Jay. Whoever they are, they're up to something big, and we're involved now. That old man, Elgin, was at your dad's lab as a kid and he knew my name."

Mym looks up at me. "Our next stop should be somewhere with a tachyon pulse transmitter. We need to let dad know what we've found."

"Let's make that first thing tomorrow then. If he's had any luck, maybe he can answer some of our questions too." *God knows we need something to go on.* I take Mym's hand and lead her downstairs.

On our way to the kitchen we pass a case displaying a collection of Ebenezer's inventions, including a pair of shiny robotic heads. Both bear a striking resemblance to the current chief of house. I can't help but wonder how Darius feels about their present condition, and if he finds their presence in the manor strange. *Would he wish for more of himself around the house to interact with?* So far, my experience with other selves has inclined me to think he may be better off than I am. He knows where his alternates are at all times, and they seem unlikely to meddle with his future. *Can I say the same?*

"One of my favorite parts of being a time traveler is the ability to feel out of place, even in one's own culture. Journeying across fifty years can make a person a foreigner just as much as a trip across hemispheres." -Journal of Dr. Harold Quickly, August 28, 1912

CHAPTER 10

The Neverwhere

The thick bark of the redwood tree flakes away under pressure from my fingertips. The crevices and crannies of the gargantuan trunk contain bits of leaves, leavings from bugs, even chunks of lichen grasping for a hold. It is all so real.

Only it isn't.

I am a ghost. A memory among memories. Some ethereal waif, traipsing from remembered past to remembered past. Whose mind do I occupy now? Is it still my own? I left my body all alone back in St. Petersburg in a lab in 1996. I try to imagine a scenario where I might return to it, but that is impossible now. I vanished. There one moment, gone the next.

There one moment.

I never imagined my end while I was alive. I certainly didn't consider the possibility that I might simply stop being, letting the world around me continue while all that there ever was of me confined itself to an ultimate brief sliver of time. One final moment, forever.

I frown at my piece of redwood bark and crumble it in my hand. In some ways I'm freer now. I can travel from one location to another, flitting from memory to memory at will. I haven't had to eat or sleep or even take a leak. There is certainly no way I'll be asked to come in to work. I've called in dead.

So why don't I feel dead? Why have I not passed on? Is it some lingering business that keeps me here?

I know what I desire to be the reason. I want to believe that I have a purpose, a meaning. I want to believe that my life mattered so much that death couldn't take me. Perhaps that I was too young. A life still so promising. I had after all, found love. It is tempting to believe that love could be more powerful than death, that because of it, I am bound and knotted to her life so intricately that no violent end could unravel us.

That is what I would like to believe. What I feel, however, is that death is still very real for me. My tenuous hold on consciousness grows thinner and frays at times, most especially when I find myself in the presence of Zurvan. What was it Benny said?

He collects souls.

The forest is pleasant. Growing. It feels alive, too. This memory is vivid—not even a hint of fog to spoil the view. My family came to this part of the park repeatedly in my childhood. Even so, I can sense the impermanence of it. If I were to wander, perhaps hike off the trail and beyond the familiar ridge to the south, I couldn't keep going. There are trails in this forest that lead all the way to the coast. I've seen many of them, but not enough. I couldn't make it to the ocean from here. I couldn't make it back to Oregon or farther south in California. My memory is too spotty.

The air in front of me shimmers when I reach my hand out. The hint of a portal. To where? What is my next step in solving this mystery? I have more clues now. A message to the cult of Eternals. More obscure names and references to puzzle over. The Alpha. Yanar Dag. Zurvan. It's all nonsense to me without some frame of reference. I need to find the hard edges of the puzzle—frame this mystery so I can begin to wrap my mind around it.

Zurvan's memories overlap mine in St. Petersburg, but only in a distant, desolate version of the city. The flooded, brackish shell of skeletal condos and ruined skyscrapers. What was he doing there? I recall the four-sided building with the fire pit inside. The miniature temple seemed so out of place, stacked on the rubble of the city. Everything about Zurvan felt out of place there. His was the other realm. The desert and dunes. Benny said it was Iraq or Iran. He spoke like he'd been there. How is it that Benny has seen so much? How many other people's memories has he explored? The ragged version of me has survived in this place somehow. He's fled and hid, but he's survived.

And he saved me. A feat I've failed to accomplish with others.

My only ally in his place has more information than I do. He has to. Perhaps he holds more of the edge pieces. At least some of them. If so, we can solve this together.

I open a portal to the cemetery, but he isn't there. I try Kaylee's apartment next, then back to the house in Oregon, all with no luck. I stroll down an empty Central Avenue, poking my head into favorite bars and restaurants without seeing him. I have my hands out to open a portal and am about to start on another tour of my old apartments when I find him. Or rather, he finds me.

"Why are you looking for me?" Benny is leaning against the dingy brick corner of Detroit Liquors, appraising me cautiously. It's a spot I usually associate with panhandlers or hippie musicians who sit cross-legged next to open guitar cases, hastily murdering Bob Marley tunes in hopes of scoring beer money. With his bare feet and frayed jeans, Benny looks worthy of a handful of loose change himself. His unkempt hair is drooping into his eyes in a thick blanket, making him look like a forgotten Beatle.

I put my hands back in my pockets and face him. "I need your help."

Benny wrinkles his nose. I'm not sure if he's displeased by my suggestion or if perhaps his memory has brought back more details of what this corner of Central Avenue typically smelled like. He shrugs away from the wall and starts walking downhill, crossing the street, aimed toward the marina a block and a half down. I jog after him.

"I saw Zurvan again. Saw him talk to someone."

Benny pauses with one foot on the curb of the next sidewalk. "You shouldn't get near him. He's dangerous."

"He has someone helping him on the other side. They send him people to talk to. Do you know what's going on there?"

Benny studies my face for a moment, then keeps walking. I catch up and fall into step beside him. "He talks to a guy named Elgin. The Eternal Line of Gnomon. These people are supposed to bring him a star, and he says he'll save them from the fate of humanity. Do you know what he's talking about?"

Benny crosses his arms and keeps his eyes on the sidewalk ahead of him. Physically he's cut off, but I can tell he's listening.

"I had more luck with the past, too. I saw another one of us. Couple actually, but I saw one from the future. He was looking for me."

Benny stops short this time and turns, his eyes searching my face, scrutinizing me with narrowed eyes. His voice is sharp and aggressive. "Someone is looking? One of us?"

"Yeah. He knows about this place, he knows I'm here."

"What did you do? How did you get through to him?" Benny's voice is eager now—hungry.

"I was trying to open a portal, like you did, to look into the past and watch people. But I ended up *inside* his head. It didn't work at first. Made him black out a few times, but then I got to him. He was in the future and he was searching for me. For us," I add, trying to include Benny in the revelation, sensing his desperation. If the other me finds a way to bring me back, I suppose it's not out of the realm of possibility to save Benny too. I don't know where he came from, but I can't help but sympathize with him, especially after seeing Mym's grave. Whatever he's been through, he's had it rough.

"It's a version of you. Your timestream," Benny says. He seems to be working through something in his head. "Must be a thread only you have lived, that's why I haven't felt it." He starts walking again. His voice takes on a more conversational tone. "When did your timestream fracture? What happened to make this other you branch off?"

I try to recall details of the other me from my experience. "I don't know exactly. I died, but somehow he must have been saved. The chronothon was being corrupted by—"

"Can you get in touch with him again? Open another portal. I want to see." He points downhill to the park near the marina. "Come on. We'll do it there." He breaks into a jog, cutting across the intersection and sprinting past Bayboro Tower toward a raised square of city park. "Hurry!"

I run after him, trying to catch up. He dashes up the slope of hill into the center of the park, stopping near a pair of benches, debating between the two of them. "Here. Here will work." He grabs my arm and pulls me down onto one of the benches. "Do it again. Do what you did before. Open the portal."

Benny's eagerness is disconcerting. Something about his frantic insistence strikes me as overly intense, but I try to relax. I recall the elation I first felt when I realized there was someone in the real world looking for me. I likely looked just as eager.

"Last time I just sort of stumbled onto him by accident. I was actually trying for a different memory, but got someplace new."

"You remembered a place you didn't live?" Benny's eagerness has a hint of awe. It reminds me of the rapture and jealousy childhood friends would express in learning that you had discovered a hidden level or warp zone in the latest video game. I hold a wanted key to a door he didn't know existed.

"It's easier when he's asleep, but it works when he's looking for me too. Last time he was in a hallway, but he was seeing things that weren't real anyway. A little man in overalls. Stuff like that. I guess if he's imagining things and has his mind open, it's easier for him to hear me."

This revelation is new to me, but as I say it out loud, it seems to make sense. So far I've only been able to contact my living self when he's been dreaming or in some other way receptive to suggestion. Trying to get to him when he was awake and occupied with other activities only seemed to make him crash into unconsciousness. I could speak but get nothing in return. This last time he had spoken back. He knew I was there, and he wanted to talk to me. That was everything.

Benny grabs my shoulders. "Show me. Show me how."

I put my hands in front of myself, not sure where to start. The air shimmers with possibilities. I close my eyes and concentrate, trying to reach out to my other self. Without a specific memory to aim for, I flounder. I can feel Benny's eyes on me.

"I'm not sure I can do it whenever I want yet. It sort of just worked out last time."

"Keep trying," Benny insists.

I close my eyes again and try to remember the other me from the Academy, searching my mind and hoping he might be searching for me as well. At first there is only black. Mental darkness. I wait, still searching. The noise of my own mind slowly settles. I forget about Benny. I forget about the park and Zurvan and this whole experience, clearing my mind and breathing. The blackness persists, but ever so slowly, it transforms.

At first I can't see anything to suggest I've made contact, but I get the distinct impression I have. It's an emotion as much as a sensation. But there are sensations. I'm warm, even though I feel cool air on my face. I'm barefoot and drowsy, lying on my side. My limbs are wrapped up. A blanket? My left arm is draped over something firm. No, not something—someone. There is a faint scent of orange blossoms. My breath catches.

Mym.

I stretch my fingers, exploring her side, the bumps of her ribs, the back of her shoulder, caressing the outline of her. Her hair is all over the pillow. It's tickling my face. The soft inhalation of her breath is followed by its slow release. It brushes over my eyelashes and nose. My heartbeat quickens. Not my imaginary ghost heartbeat—my real heartbeat. The one lying next to her in bed. I'm alive! I'm breathing. I don't know how I fooled myself into thinking anything else could compare. I've been a shade—a pale shadow of reality, not this vivid, sensuous thing. My mind rapturously absorbs the textures around me—the sheets, the cool air, the warmth of my body pressed against Mym's.

Mym. She's alive and well, curled into me, her arm draped over my hip. I hadn't thought I would get to feel this again. The exhilaration of it is almost too much to handle. Not only has she survived, but she's still mine. Somehow, some way, death hasn't taken this away. I feel like my heart could explode. I crack open my eyelids, ever so slowly, not wanting this miracle to disappear. She is there, her shape silhouetted against shaded starlight from a window beyond.

She's here.

"Mym." The word escapes my lips as a whisper. I don't dare startle this apparition. I want it too desperately.

She stirs. "Hmm."

"Mym. It's me."

Her eyes flutter slightly, but stay closed. She stretches her arm around my lower back, fingers grasping at my T-shirt. "Hey, you." She pulls herself closer to me, tucking her forehead against my chin. My lips caress the top of her head. Just the touch of her is pure ecstasy.

I relish the feel of her, not wanting to wake her, but unable to contain my own joy. "Mym, I lov—"

Something clamps to my head like a vise. Hands. Invading hands. *No. No no no. Not again.* My eyes are open, but my mind reels.

Two separate views sheer away simultaneously, overlapping but distinct, like disjointed binoculars, each scene fighting for priority in my vision. In one, the me that's alive is jolted upright in bed. *No!* My hands fly to my head, desperate to undo whatever force is pulling me away from Mym, but I find nothing there, I'm merely grasping vainly at my hair. It's the other view that reveals what is happening. Benny is next to me on the bench, still in the Neverwhere, but somehow inside my mind now as well. His hands are clutching the sides of my head. My ghostly fingers latch onto them, prying frantically—trying to dislodge him.

"Get out of my head!" My voice echoes in my mind. I've shouted in both the real world and the Neverwhere. Mym wakes in fright. She's upright in the matter of a moment, her eyes wide with confusion and concern.

"Ben, what's—"

The other me is awake now too. The one in the real world. I can feel him return to consciousness with a jolt, dragged from sleep to reality by this horrifying pressure. My mind struggles to process the multitude of inputs it's receiving. The real world is still vivid, the feel of the blankets wadded beneath my knees. The pounding of my heartbeat, Mym's wild eyes and her hands on mine, trying to see what is going on with my head, perhaps thinking I've been injured. The me who is alive is struggling for control of his own limbs. I can feel the fight and realize that I no longer have control either. Neither of us is in control anymore. As our hands reach out toward Mym, I get the sickening realization that it's Benny in control. Our hands grasp Mym's shoulders and shake her violently.

"You need to get away from me! Get away! Get away!"

"Ben! What are you doing?" Mym protests, struggling to break free of the grip on her shoulders.

"You're going to die if you stay!" Benny spits the words, his eyes frantic. From my position, stuck between the two realities, he's screaming from the bench next to me, but I'm watching the results unfold in the real world with vivid clarity. I can only imagine that the version of us in the real world has the same expression of crazed intensity on his face. "You're going to die, you're going to die, YOU'RE GOING TO DIE!" He screams at her, clawing at her wrists as she tries to struggle free from his grasp.

"NO! Get off me!" Mym yells back, twisting in his grip and rolling off the bed. Benny loses his hold on her and she scrambles away toward the wall. He climbs off the bed and pursues her. The horror in my gut at her terrified eyes snaps me out of my lethargy and I struggle hard to stop him. The me in the real world slows. Mym looks on in terror as my body—our body—spasms in place. Benny screams and lunges harder toward Mym, sending her running for the hallway. The other me from the real world seems to sense what I'm doing and joins in the struggle to slow Benny down. Our legs strain as if walking through mud, each motion a fight for control. Benny rages and screams. "She has to go. GO! GO! You're going to die if you stay. You'll DIE DIE DIE!"

The other me is gaining more control. Our body slows to a stop and I feel Benny's strength failing against the two of us. From my position on the bench, I concentrate on Benny's face in the Neverwhere. Releasing my grip on his fingers, which are still grasping my head, I cock my right fist and slam it into his face. Benny jerks loose, his hands flying back with the rest of him and losing his grip on my consciousness.

From the other side of my mind I can sense the real world version of me cutting loose as well. He forces me from his mind and mentally slams the door. He's fully awake now and back in control. I try to speak, hoping to get a word in to him, a moment to explain that this wasn't what I was trying to do, but his mind is gone—completely cut off from me.

Benny is sprawled on the concrete near the bench, one hand over his face.

"What did you do!" I yell at him. "What the hell was that!"

He springs to his feet, eyes still frantic, and charges at me with his hands outstretched for my head. I grab his arms as he rams into me, and we crash over the back of the park bench, thudding into the grass beyond. Benny is flailing and kicking, trying to get at my head again. I swat away his arms and plant my hand on his face, shoving it as far from me as possible. He snaps at me, snarling like a wild animal and I scramble away, aiming a kick at his groin as I depart. I miss and Benny grabs my leg, dragging me back down again, my fingers clawing at the grass as I try to get away. It's a graceless and ungainly fight. He comes at me with teeth and fingernails, pinching and biting. I finally get my legs under me and swing at him, my fist connecting with his face just below his left eye. He flails backward into the grass and finally lies still. He's staring up at the leaves of the trees and the patch of blue between them. His arms fall out to his sides and he gasps heavily, finally releasing the tension in his body.

"What the hell, dude?" I'm shaking with anger. If I had a real body, I could blame adrenaline, but in this place, I know I'm just furious.

Benny slides his legs under him and struggles to his feet unsteadily. I brace myself, ready to defend against any other attacks.

"I had to warn her." Benny scowls at me. "He's no good for her. We're no good for her. It's being around us that gets her killed."

"Speak for yourself. She was doing fine in my timeline."

That's not entirely true. When I was alive, Mym was being framed for murder and Ambrose Cybergenics was threatening to wipe her out of existence, but I don't plan on admitting that to Benny. Not now. Not when I was so close to her. Touching her. Him robbing me of that moment and taking me away from her has me angrier than I've felt in all the time I've been dead. What chance will I have now of seeing her again? Probably none now that she thinks I've threatened her life.

"I was there! Really there. I was alive again. How could you—What did you . . ." I fumble for words, still reeling from the loss of that moment. I was with her. I was alive. And now whatever hope I had to tell her is gone.

"You can't have her. None of us can. I've seen what happens," Benny says.

"You've seen what? Just because in your lifetime something bad happened, you think that's the only outcome? We're time travelers. We can make new choices. Change things." I'm lying to myself again, but I can't help it. I want to believe it's true. There *are* limits to what can be changed. What happened, happened, as Doctor Quickly always says. New timelines only bring new problems, and whatever happened to Mym in Benny's timeline can't be undone, but I still don't believe it has to happen in mine. We're not slaves to fate. I refuse to believe that.

"You're a liar," Benny yells at me. "If you loved her, you would know you have to let her go. You can't have her."

"Why? Because you let her die? You think I will too?"

"You're already dead!" Benny screams. "What do you think you can do to protect her? Nothing! We're lost here. Just—dead. Nothing we do matters."

"So you're just going to give up?"

"I gave up a long time ago," Benny spits back. "You will too. You just haven't realized it yet."

"So why don't you just die already?" I ask. "Why are you sticking around? If you've got no reason to be here, just leave!"

"You think I haven't tried? You think I haven't wished for it? How do you think I got here in the first place? I thought I could—I thought if I ended it . . ." He strokes his own head and runs his hands down the sides of his face. "This place is Hell. It might not have lakes of fire or demons with pitchforks, but it's Hell just the same. We're trapped here, forever."

"Bullshit. You're still fighting and you know it. If you want to give up, why don't you run off to your buddy Zurvan and let him Hoover up your soul for you? You saved me from him. You've been saving yourself, too. If this was all so pointless, then why do you run? You must still think there's a chance. You have to believe in something good in this place or you wouldn't have saved me. There are no saviors in Hell. You could have just let him kill me."

Benny glowers at me. "No. Not him. You don't get it. I didn't save you. I just kept you away from *him*. Don't you know what he does? Whenever he finds someone else in this place, he robs their mind. He steals their memories so he can use them. If he got your memories, he'd have mine too. He'd be able to go anywhere we've been, search me out the way you've been doing. He'd hunt me down." He twitches a little, fidgety inside his own skin. "And he'd be able to remember her too."

The thought gives me pause. I don't know what Zurvan is up to, but the idea of him being able to access all of my memories, even the ones of Mym, makes my skin crawl too. Those memories are all that I have left of her. I think of my other friends, my family, and all the cherished moments of my life. Imagining a stranger rifling through them is abhorrent.

Benny brushes his hands off on his pants and straightens up. "He's gone now, isn't he? The Ben from there." He taps a finger against his temple.

I frown at him. "What did you expect? You highjacked his life and scared off Mym."

"You highjacked his life. I just joined in."

"You ruined it."

Benny opens a portal just big enough for himself to walk through. From my angle I can't see where it leads. He gives me one last venomous look. "Your life is ruined already. I won't let you ruin hers too. If you try to reach her again, I'll stop you."

He steps through the portal and disappears.

I stare at the empty space he vacated until I lose motivation to stay upright any longer. I crumple to my knees in the grass. Fake grass. My pale memory of what grass ought to be. Now that I've tasted real life again, this illusion seems much less convincing. My senses are dull here, mere afterimages of what they were in life. I pick at the grass and let the broken blades tumble from my fingers.

I touched her. She spoke to me. It was so *real*.

Whatever Benny's objections, I know I am going to try again.

I've discovered a new high. Living.

I don't know how I'll manage it, but I have a new life goal. Death goal. Whatever.

I want her back, and I'm going to make it happen. If death itself hasn't been able to keep me from her, then there's no way in Hell I'm letting Benny stop me. One way or another, my time in the Neverwhere is limited.

I'm getting out of here.

Cornwall, UK- Sprocket Manor, 2165

Darius's reputation as a chef has not been overstated. The smells wafting from the kitchen are heavenly. When I wander in to investigate, I find the metal man hard at work.

It's like nothing I have ever seen. While his dexterity in his human form is admirable, that is clearly not his chief tool. The workings of the kitchen seem to take little action from his physical body to operate. To the contrary, his frequent stillness seems even more productive. Ovens heat themselves, stovetops regulate temperatures of sauces and even the dishes tend to themselves in his kitchen. I'm familiar with wireless technology, but this is truly futuristic, and it's clear that Darius and the manor are on more than just friendly terms. He is the master of the house the way a captain steers a ship, bending it to his will with silent and invisible commands.

Darius has uncorked a bottle of wine for Mym and popped the top off a lager for me. He slides the beer across the counter. "Master Jonah has returned from his walk and is seated on the back steps. He'd enjoy your company."

"Another prediction?" I pick up the beer and take a sip. It's ice cold with a hint of lime.

"He asked me to tell you," Darius replies, efficiently wiping up the ring of condensation my beer has left behind.

I stab a thumb down the hallway. "That way?"

Darius nods and goes back to his cooking. I squeeze Mym's arm and kiss her on the cheek, then make my way toward the back of the house.

I find Jonah just where Darius said I would, seated on the back steps and tossing a ball into the yard for Barley. The silver helmet on his head glimmers in the porch lights. The drizzle has stopped, at least for the time being, but the sky is still gray. I settle down next to Jonah as Barley trots up. The dog drops its tennis ball at my feet and waits patiently for me to toss it. I stretch for the soggy ball and whip it as far as I can. Barley vanishes into the darkness in a blur. I'm happy to see that even though I'm over a hundred years into the future, dogs still enjoy the same hobbies.

"Jay's not a bad guy, you know," Jonah says. "He's not."

I watch the boy's face. His brow is furrowed. I can't help but think that he's been through far too much for his age. First a chronothon and now a brother caught up in a futuristic cult. Some people draw all the short straws.

"I think Jay could just use our help, bud. I get the feeling that he could use some better friends."

Jonah looks up at me. "Are you going to be his friend?"

I recall the scene I just witnessed from Wednesday night and Elgin as a child, hissing at me. "You're too late, Traverssss." Darius suggested that it's Jay who had chosen to associate with these people. I try to imagine what could possess him to do that. The notes in his journal were the frantic scribblings of someone obsessed. Whatever path he's gone down, he's been headed there for a while.

Jonah's eyes are searching my face. "You can keep him safe, right? The way you did for me?"

I cradle my beer between both hands, letting the icy cold penetrate my palms. "I'll do my best. I'm not sure how much I'll be able to help him out. Do you know where he's going? Did he tell you?"

Jonah reaches for Barley as the dog comes trotting back. He pulls the Labrador closer and wraps his arms around its neck, resting his chin atop the dog's head. Barley pants happily and lets himself be squeezed into his master's shoulder.

"He's going to change things," Jonah manages. "He says it's his time. He's going to meet more like him. He says they are going to save the world."

I picture the scribbled quotations in the journal and the walls of Jay's room, recalling how they were all from the same person. "Did he say he was going to meet Gnomon? Was that the guy he's been talking to?"

"I don't know." Jonah releases the dog. Barley licks his face and wriggles back a few steps till the tennis ball is at his feet again. He looks from Jonah's face to mine, then noses the ball closer to us. Jonah picks it up but doesn't throw it. He merely turns it over in his fingers a few times. When he speaks again his voice is softer. "I know he's not really my brother." He runs the back of his hand beneath his nose and sniffs, then wipes it against his pant leg. "I know who he is."

I rest my hand on Jonah's shoulder. "I know it's not easy to deal with all this." I try to find any words that could possibly console him. "If it helps any, there are some other versions of me too, and it sounds like you get along with your brother way better than I get along with mine."

Jonah looks up with interest. "What's your brother like?"

I try to find the appropriate words to sum up my feelings about Benji. I imagine him sleeping in my bed and using my toothbrush and I feel the scowl creeping onto my face. "I don't know. Old. Smelly. Stupid."

Jonah grins at me. "He's smelly?"

I'm happy to see him smiling. "Nah, not really. He's just different, you know? I'm still trying to get used to the idea of someone else wanting to live my life. I'm probably just jealous. Mad that he gets to hang out with my friends and use all my stuff. I kind of wanted it all to myself."

"Does he like the same things you like? Do you ever play video games together, stuff like that?"

I recall the last real conversation I had with Benji—his idea about dividing our life up when I get back. I frown at the memory. "Some people aren't that great at playing with others. You're pretty lucky that your brother played with you." I hold my hand out for the tennis ball. Jonah places it in my palm. "And you've got Barley." The dog is wriggling in anticipation. I zing the ball low across the lawn, letting it bounce away, the dog barreling after it.

The door to the back porch opens and Mym sticks her head out. "Hey, guys. Food's ready."

I climb to my feet and give Jonah a hand to help him up. He looks up at me and his face is still serious. "So you'll help him, right? I think he just needs to come home, don't you?"

"I'm going to do my best. If I see him, I'll definitely tell him you're waiting for him."

"He's going to a fire temple. That's what he called it. He says it's a place where the fire never stops burning," Jonah says. "It's in the book."

A fire temple doesn't sound like a place I would especially like to visit, but I pat Jonah on the shoulder. "I'll look into it."

Dinner is even more delicious than it smelled and, when it's over, I'm in danger of popping a button on my jeans. Darius, despite not being able to consume any of his own cooking, contributed a great deal to the dinner conversation. Tucket talked animatedly with him through most of dinner, allowing me a bit of time to process through my day while he carried the conversation. Ebenezer was polite, but mostly quiet as well, and after dinner he excused himself, disappearing upstairs.

By way of post dinner entertainment, Jonah invites us to play a video game in his room and loans me another pair of the dreaded metaspace glasses. I'm impressed to see that the entire room transforms around our position on the floor. Jonah leads us on an expedition through a cave in search of buried Incan treasures and Tucket helps him along, apparently a veteran at this interactive game.

After a little while, I take the glasses off and slip out the door, leaving the others inside the virtual world. I climb the rear stairs to Jay's attic room and grab the prayer book off his bed. I had intended to slip back downstairs with the book, but upon cracking it open, I'm immediately entranced by the scribbles and sketches. I settle slowly onto the room's only chair and begin to browse the pages. I discover the section Jonah mentioned about the fire temple. The sketch of the building shows a four-sided structure with wide archways on every side. It's simple construction. No lofty spires like Gaudi would have installed. This temple has only a rounded dome at the top and a place inside for a fire pit. The one depicted has a word beneath it. Ateshgah. I don't know the significance of that, but the location listed is as familiar as can be—Saint Petersburg.

Part of me wants to believe that the St. Petersburg referenced might be the big one in Russia, but I have a sinking feeling that, once again, these unusual events are circling my home town, drawn to it like some sort of vortex—the epicenter of the strange when it comes to time travel. Whatever interest the Eternals have in Doctor Quickly and his discoveries, they certainly seem to be concentrating their efforts on places he's been.

I trace my finger over the drawing of the fire temple and down to a long row of Roman numerals written below it. A selection of them are circled, with arrows drawn between them. The first numeral is MMMDXXV. An arrow runs from it past a few others to the next circled number, MMDCCCXXXV. I puzzle over the D momentarily, trying to recall if that meant 50 or 500, but then recall that L should be 50. I work out the rest in my head. 3525 to 2835. One of the numerals has been circled multiple times. I do the conversion and translate it to 2165. The series continues to lower and lower numerals, going into negative numbers.

I've never heard of negative Roman numerals. I work out a few more numbers. *What could they signify?* I ponder the sets and the arrows. The numbers go from larger to smaller, but don't seem to have any particular relation to each other. The largest number and smallest number are both around 3500, but not identical. I search the surrounding text for more clues. *They could be dates. AD and BCE numbers? The arrows could signify a direction?*

The idea might fit, but it's tricky to try to use a Roman numeral system that far into the past. The switches from Gregorian to Julian calendars cause issues and dates won't exactly match up. My education as a time traveler has been brief, but I do know that much. Trying to label a date that far in the past with any kind of accuracy gets really hard to calculate, especially since everyone was using the most convenient system they had at the time. Still, if you were only trying to record the year, I suppose you could manage it. *But what about the arrows?* I stare at the sequence a little longer, then give up and move on.

I don't know how long I spend reading the journal prayer book, but it's at least long enough for Jonah to finish his game. Mym finds me and lets me know that I've been missed. I pull myself from the journal and let out a yawn. It's been a very long day and despite my desire to read more of the book, I agree to head to bed. Ebenezer has offered us a guest room, of which there seem to be plenty. Tucket ends up across the hall from Mym and me and, to my surprise, has barely said goodnight before I hear snoring coming from his room. Jonah explains that the metaspace is loaded with sleep apps, even some that use hypnosis, and the average user can be asleep in less than a minute if they want to be. I give the boy a hug goodnight, promising to catch up more in the morning.

I crawl under the covers with Mym and she nestles in as close as she can but is still fiddling with her phone for a little. "Any word from your dad?" I ask.

She shakes her head. "Nothing at the moment, but that doesn't mean he hasn't tried. We need to hook up with a tachyon pulse transmitter to intercept anything he's sent up or downstream in time. I could ping a message to him, but he'd have to get to a TPT to read it. It'll be easier if we go ourselves."

"Have you got a way to get us to one of those?"

Mym shuts her device off and sets it on the nightstand. "Tomorrow we can head back to London. Dad has a house there we can use. More of a relay station than anything, but it will get the job done. We can check in and let him know what we've learned."

"And then?"

"I don't know. Whoever is behind the attacks on the labs is obviously connected to the Eternals. If the guy you saw take Jay away really was the same kid you saw in Valencia, there's really no way of knowing what year to pin them down to. They could be any time, or at least have connections in any given year."

"How do you mean?"

"You said the kid spoke to you but sounded like the old man. That means they have to be able to send messages to their younger selves, and if they could do that, they could just as easily use their younger self to get a message to an older Eternal living in that year. That one takes the message back to earlier in *his* life and does the same thing . . . They could keep that up indefinitely, relay messages to each other up and down a timestream without ever needing gravitites. People in the future can communicate with the past that way and vice versa."

"Seems like the message has to change hands a lot that way. I feel like it would end up inaccurate. Kind of like a game of telephone. Run it through enough messengers, it's bound to get screwed up. Why not just time travel the way we do?"

Mym brushes her hair away from her face, then runs her hand over my chest. "Up here time travel is really regulated. ASCOTT is super strict about who gets infused with gravitites and they track the time travelers they've created via the Grid. The Eternals don't seem like the kind of group that would get ASCOTT approval."

"What about going off-Grid like us?"

"They might. It could be why they stole dad's gravitizer. It's not as easy as it sounds, though. We have an in with a chronometer maker *and* the man who invented time travel. For someone starting out from scratch, if you don't already know a time traveler, you might live your whole life and never meet one, let alone get someone to teach you how to infuse yourself or risk going off-Grid with you."

"I thought time travel became common knowledge after a while. The age of awareness or whatever. Have we passed that point yet?"

"We did. For most time streams, the reality of time travel was common knowledge before the 2150s when the Academy existed. But even so, the Academy was only open for about ten years before the public got scared and demanded it be closed. Not that it really ever stopped operating. People who figured out a way to time travel could still get back to the 2150s and attend, but the public face of the Academy disappeared. There have been hundreds of graduates over the years, probably thousands, but they're spread out over any number of time streams and going all over the place in time. I don't know how many time travelers you might expect to find in a given timestream at any point in history, but I'd bet its a lot less than you'd think. We're pretty rare."

I wrap my arm around Mym and pull her closer to me. "Then I guess I'm pretty lucky that I found you."

Mym smiles. "We're both lucky." She kisses me and lets her fingers linger at the side of my face. "I'm so glad you found me." Her eyes grow slightly distant, and I wonder if she's thinking back to the day we met. I recall the moment I first saw her appear in Doctor Quickly's lab. Though for me, the day I first saw her was not the first time she'd seen me. We've had a tangled relationship stemming from an even more tangled beginning. As far as I know, the first time she ever met me as an adult was at Bob's ranch, peering down from a hot air balloon.

"Are you thinking about Montana?" I ask, running my hand along her shoulder. I can still easily remember the bright colors of the balloon. For me it's only a few months ago. For Mym it's been years.

She inhales deeply and turns her eyes back to me. "Actually I was thinking of another time. The day you walked back into my life and told me we could save my dad. I'd been a wreck, but you were so confident. So at peace about the future. I knew that whatever was going to happen, I could trust you. That was a good day." She smiles again, her gaze lingering briefly on mine. She then curls up tighter against me, burrowing into the pillow and closing her eyes. I study her closed eyelids and the shape of her delicate ears. I don't remember that day. For me it hasn't happened yet.

Despite all that I've experienced as a time traveler, there is still so much more to learn. I'm changing slowly, adapting to a complexity of thought and memory that comes from living a life out of order, but it's difficult progress. I still want to think of my life experiences as chronological, though for the last few months they have been anything but. Mym is a constant reminder that life now consists of our individual stories stitched together in places that don't always match. Each time traveler is a solo act, threading their way through time, no longer needing to share a history with anyone else.

Watching Mym next to me, I get a better sense of her desire for oneness. She was born a time traveler, never knowing anything different. Other than her father, no one has ever shared her story, her history. *How lonely do you become that way?*

As Mym drifts into sleep beside me, I run a hand along her shoulder, then down her side, letting my arm rest at her hip. Whatever our divergent histories have been, we have a shared path ahead. I may not have been able to be a part of her past, but I can be her future. It's a thought that makes me incredibly happy. Whatever comes next, we can face it together.

Something is terribly wrong.

Wake up.

I don't know how long I've been sleeping, but I'm woken by a tremendous pressure throughout my body. I'm jolted alert, suddenly upright in bed next to Mym. She's awake too, eyes wide and staring at the top of my head. My fingers are there, grasping for something. I'm moving but frozen.

My hands stretch for Mym without my control, grasping her shoulders and shaking her. "You need to get away from me! Get away! Get away!" The voice is my voice, but the words aren't my own. I try desperately to speak, to ask Mym what's happening, but I have no control over my own body. Someone else is in here with me. I can feel him, the same one from my dreams. What is he doing to me?

I struggle to reconcile the images in my head. I can see Mym in front of me, the room around us, but I can also sense something else. Somewhere else. A memory. There is a timelessness to the place I'm feeling, even a beauty, but it conflicts with the anger and the pain of the force inside me.

Mym wriggles in my grip as I scream at her. "You're going to die, you're going to die, YOU'RE GOING TO DIE!"

Her eyes are wild.

I want to call to her, tell her that it isn't true. Whatever this thing is that has control, it isn't me. Her terrified expression pains me. She's never looked at me with such horror. She's panicked and frantic in my hands. She finally breaks away from my grip and rolls off the bed.

I chase her.

No. This is all wrong.

Someone inside me strains to stop my progress. The part of me that's screaming and chasing Mym slows, bogged down by this other presence. How? How is this happening? Whatever battle is going on inside my mind, I know which side I want to win. I focus my concentration on taking back my body, fighting against this screaming rage. Mym has fled to the hallway. My muscles are on fire, my legs clenched and rigid as they waver between impulses to run and to stay, putting up a stubborn resistance to the part of me that has frightened Mym away.

Something snaps.

The mind inside my own detaches and my legs turn to Jell-O—sending me crumpling to the floor. My fingers clench carpet and I concentrate harder. Get out of my head. Get. Out!

Somehow it has worked. My mind goes quiet, the screaming rage supplanted by only my own thoughts. An uncontrolled shiver runs down my spine. At the end I sensed something else. Someone else. The third fighter. He was angry too, but not at me. His anger mirrored my own fear, my desire to protect Mym. Whoever he was, he's gone now too.

He's going to stay that way.

I push off the floor and go after Mym.

The house has gone dark. I stumble into the blackness of the hallway, feeling my way toward the stairs. "Mym? Are you there? It's me. I'm sorry— I don't know what happened."

My lack of abilities in the metaspace and the future's aggravating trend of hiding light switches foils my efforts to illuminate the space around me. When I had gone to bed the hallway had been glowing softly from the walls, a soothing, pale blue light, dimmed and sleepy. Now the house is eerily lifeless.

"Darius, could I get some lights?" I query the walls, hoping the chief of house is up. The house remains silent and bathed in darkness. I stumble down the hallway to the stairs and finally glimpse some light in the foyer below. The front door is open, no doubt left that way by my fleeing girlfriend. I descend the stairs and move toward the door, but stop short at the sight of the figure lurking just inside the entrance to the living room. In the darkness, it's hard to make out features, but as I step closer, I recognize the glint of metal in the dim moonlight.

"Darius? Did you see Mym?"

The synth remains silent. I approach cautiously, thinking he may be in some sort of sleep mode. It's only when I'm mere steps away that I see the wires dangling down the front of the metal man's chest. They are encased in a gooey sort of membrane and the goo has run down Darius's breastplate, leaving a trail of glistening slime. The wires have been ripped from his throat and left there. Oh God. I recall Darius's words from earlier. "All of the manor's security protocols route through me..." I take a horrified step back and slip a little. When I look down I realize I've stepped into a puddle of Darius's internal fluids.

I freeze in place, taking a frantic new assessment of my surroundings. Something is very, very wrong. "Mym?" I whisper this time. Hearing no response, I abandon Darius's disabled form and move through the foyer to the front door. It's standing ajar just as it was before, but I'm seeing it anew. Was it just Mym leaving, or did something else get inside?

I linger, frozen in my uncertainty—listening. In the darkness my other senses are clamoring for primacy, the oily scent of leaked lubricants from Darius, the faint rustling of the wind through the trees outside. Was it all wind, or someone breathing?

Just inside the door is an ornamental metal cylinder. There is a hand carved wooden walking stick protruding from among a collection of umbrellas and a pair of canes. I ease the walking stick out from among the umbrellas as quietly as I can and grip it with both hands, wielding it like a bat. Thus armed, I poke my head out the door and then take a few cautious steps.

Once outside, I walk into the drive and look around the grounds. The shrouded moon is a feeble companion tonight, but what the moonlight does reveal is more quiet woods around the property. The shadows of the trees stretch out for the house like fingers.

Mym is in the open grass at the side of the house, arms wrapped around herself in the chilly air, her bare legs freckled with moisture from her run across the dewy lawn.

Seeing me emerge from the house, she takes a step back. "What was that, Ben? What's happening?"

I reach for her, though I'm still fifty feet away. "I'm sorry. It wasn't me. I promise it wasn't me."

"How can I know it's you now? What happened to you? You just woke up and grabbed me."

"I know. I'm so, so sorry." I take a few steps closer to her, but Mym backs away. "Look, something is going on here. Come back to the house." I gesture for her to come closer, holding the walking stick away from myself, to let her know I'm not threatening her with it.

"I don't like this. Whatever is going on in your head needs to stop." She clenches herself even tighter. "I want you to figure this out, but not if he's going to be like this. It's too scary. You're scaring me."

"Mym, I'm so sorry." I drop the stick in the grass and hold my arms out to her. "Please, just come back inside and we can figure this out."

"You need to make sure he—" Mym freezes mid-sentence, staring beyond me now. Her expression changes from fear of me to fear of something else. Out of the corner of my eye, the shadows around the house are moving, coming alive.

"Ben! Watch out!" Mym jerks an arm up and points past me. I spin in place in time to see a liquid blackness spring up and charge me from the flowerbed. The figure hurtles forward, striking me hard in the stomach before I have time to react. Another moment and my legs are swept out from under me. I crash to the lawn in a twisted heap.

"Mym! Run!" I gasp, just as the shadow knees me in the back, flattening me to the ground. Mym flees, sprinting around the side of the house, one hand clenching at her tank top, grasping for her pendant chronometer. But the shadows have sprung up around her, emerging from the edge of the house, from the trees, from the very ground. They converge on her as she runs. She vanishes around the corner with the hooded figures in pursuit.

"Ben!" Her shout comes out as a shriek from somewhere around back of the house, but gets muffled. I come unfrozen, rolling over and lashing out wildly at the shadowy person above me. A fist materializes from the darkness and strikes me hard, slamming my head back into the grass. I know I'll suffer from the blow later, but for now my rage won't let me feel it. As I ricochet upward again, my own fist aims downward and crushes the groin of my attacker with all the fury I can muster. The shadow above me groans and I strike again in the gut, and then again, unseating him from atop me. I roll out from under him and scramble to my feet, dizzy but pumping with adrenaline.

I dash around the corner of the manor, my bare feet slipping in the wet grass. As I sprint to the back of the house my senses are slow to pick up the changes in the darkness. Nothing seems to be in the right place, the clouds blur with the watery horizon and the house seems to slant sideways. My vision is swimming and I waver.

I stumble to a stop in the middle of the back lawn, searching the darkness. The sound of the water against the bluffs at the back of the property guides my eyes to the edge of the cliff and the figures silhouetted against it. Multiple dark forms are outlined there, and in their midst is Mym, pressed tight between two hulking men in hoods. The darkness at the tree line births more figures, also shrouded, their features indiscernible in the darkness. It's the voice that I recognize, slithering across the grass and into my ears.

"Benjamin, it was so good of you to send Miss Quickly out to us. The butler was rather impolite and was set against letting us in. We would have made it inside to get her presently, but we appreciate whatever you did to inspire her exit." The venomous voice is coming from the bent form of a man just to the right of Mym's position. My vision finally focuses as he takes a step forward, his head bare in the moonlight.

Elgin.

Mym struggles in the grip of her captors, but one of the men has his gloved hand across her mouth so whatever she says comes out only as a murmur. Both of her arms are pinned behind her so she has no chance to escape via her pendant chronometer. My fingers find my own wrist and rest on the dials, my mind racing for some way out of this. My options are limited, however. I have no idea how long these people have been here or what they plan to do with Mym. If I made a jump now, I would almost certainly end up with grass fused through my bare feet any time I chose to arrive. It would be painful and possibly debilitating, and ultimately pointless if I don't come up with a way to free Mym. Out of the corner of my vision I see more shadows closing in on me from behind. There must be at least twenty of these people altogether.

One of the men next to Mym is pointing something at her. A box with a meter on top. A temporal spectrometer. He scans Mym and shows Elgin the results.

"How excellent," Elgin murmurs. "Even better than we expected."

"What do you want with us?" I meant for the question to come out demanding, but my voice is more tremulous than I can control.

"Still catching on too late, aren't you Travers? Didn't see any of this coming? Did you really think you would come here and not have us notice?" Elgin asks. "Here of all places. And to show up with the daughter of Doctor Harold Quickly so neatly in tow? It's almost as if you wanted us to have her."

"Let her go, Elgin."

The old man narrows his eyes and takes a step closer. "You are in no position to make demands. If you are interested in Miss Quickly's safety, I would suggest you cooperate. You can make all of this go away if you are willing to be reasonable."

My heart is racing and my mind is struggling to process all that has happened in the past few minutes. It's a nightmare, but the look of terror in Mym's eyes is all too real. She's staring at me, but I can't read the meaning she's trying to convey.

"Whatever you want, you can take me. Let her go. I'll go with you."

"Oh, aren't you the chivalrous one," Elgin says. "But I'm afraid you would be nowhere near as useful to us as Miss Quickly. You can do us a service, however," Elgin continues. "You will get a message to Doctor Quickly. He has proven stubbornly elusive and unwilling to talk, but if he would like to see his daughter alive, he'll learn to cooperate with our demands."

"Why do you need her?"

Elgin merely leers at me. "The business of The Lord Gnomon is not to be questioned, Mr. Travers. If you would like to see Miss Quickly again, you will simply do as we say." He hands something to one of the other hooded figures who then approaches me. Up close I'm surprised to find the face under this hood is an old woman's. Despite the darkness, there is something very familiar about her. She hands me a square device with a black screen approximately two inches wide.

"Doctor Quickly will find the instructions he needs inside," Elgin says. "I suggest you be punctual. We don't like to be kept waiting."

"You Eternals have to resort to kidnapping to get people to talk to you? I can see why you're lacking any decent members."

Elgin glares at me and then his eyes flash to the woman next to me. I don't have time to wonder what's been implied because the answer comes in the form of a sharp jab to my ribs. The old woman has struck me with something dull, but pronged. She's looking me full in the face now, and I finally recognize the scowling expression. The gold chain with the hourglass on it is still dangling around her neck. She's the woman from the Academy Liaison office.

What the hell is she doing here?

A numbing shock ripples through my body from whatever she's struck me with. My vision blackens as the ground comes rushing up to meet me.

"Ben!" Mym's voice comes to me through the haze.

Smashed against the lawn, my last view is through blades of grass as the hooded figures drag Mym away toward the bluff.

I'm scared that her struggles might cause the whole lot of them to tumble over the cliff. I never see the outcome. Someone steps over me, headed to join the others and blocks out the view of the horizon as my body finally surrenders to the black.

"It's sometimes difficult to tell if you are the first time traveler to visit a given timestream. Sometimes not. I once visited the wedding of Isabella and Ferdinand only to hear a speech that was entirely the lyrics to 'Wind Beneath My Wings' by Bette Midler. I felt a bit cheated, but at least the food was good."- Journal of Doctor Harold Quickly, 1469

CHAPTER 11

The Neverwhere

Staying alive is my new obsession. Getting alive, anyway.

Sitting in the park near St. Petersburg's downtown marina, staring at the hazy memories of my old life, I can finally recognize it for what it is. Just the past. Life—lived, used, and imprecisely catalogued. This Neverwhere—this space without time—is just the lingering attachment to a world I remember but no longer occupy. This is not an infinite beyond but rather a finite space defined by the limits of my own memory and those of whoever else shows up here. Suddenly it feels claustrophobic. It makes me long for new territory, something fresh and unexplored. A life yet to be.

It's an odd struggle. It makes me wonder if there are other minds or consciousnesses, loaded with potential but unfulfilled, stuck in a limbo like this, just waiting their turn to inhabit bodies. *Is that what it's like before we're born? Are we a vast collection of unmade memories—blank pages waiting to be filled?*

I look around the park I'm in. A familiar pub sits on the corner across the street and a parking lot where they host a weekly market. For memories to hold on to, these are not especially exciting.

I have a quarter century worth of life under my belt. A pittance really. The majority of my presumed lifespan still left un-lived. I've seen my share of the country, and traveled the globe a little bit before becoming a time traveler, but I had just begun to experience a world beyond my time. A journey home from an accidental displacement, and a mad dash across history. Both were amazing journeys, well beyond anything I could ever have dreamed up—in both wonderful and terrifying ways—but then that was it. It ended. I ended.

I never made it home again. Never got to tell Mym how much I had fallen for her. Never got to stop the manipulative and murderous men and women corrupting the chronothon. Never got to avenge the deaths of my friends.

Except I did.

Having spent a few brief moments inside the head of my alter ego, I know he survived. Somehow, some way, he lived. It seems unfair that if there was a way out of my demise at the Temporal Studies Society that no one bothered to inform me. It's a cruel twist of fate that I am the one who had to take the fall.

I'm not angry.

Not completely anyway.

I can't hate my alter ego, despite his good fortune and my rotten luck, because he has given me a tremendous gift. He's let me feel alive again. He's let me see Mym.

The question now is where I go from here. It's proven that I *can* get back. I can occupy the same mind—the same living body in the real world as he does. Does that mean there is a real way to return? Can I stay that way? Would he let me, or is this going to be a fight?

Benny showed me that there is a way you can take control even against your other self's wishes. It's what Zurvan does too. That isn't what I want, but if it is a choice between that and being stuck here, I can't say I'm not tempted. *Would I be willing to sacrifice my other self's mind to escape this place?*

Losing control was terror. The moment I lost touch with Mym—the moment Benny invaded my mind and took over—was horrifying. The worst feeling I have ever experienced. I could sense the shock in my other self as well. He was paralyzed with fear. It happened to both of us. I can't imagine losing myself to someone else permanently. How hellish would it be to watch someone else live my life and have no control over it?

The thought gives me pause. If I were to attempt to hijack my own mind in some sort of hostile takeover, who's to say that I'd win? Might I end up the passenger in someone else's mind unable to do anything at all? There are few fates that I feel would be worse than being trapped in the Neverwhere, but that might be one.

No. I don't want to fight my way in. There has to be another way.

Getting up from the park bench, I head toward the water, putting some distance between me and the site of Benny's disappearance. He might come back at any time and I don't want him commandeering my memories again. This time I need somewhere he hasn't been—a memory he and I wouldn't share. I wrack my brain, thinking of my most recent life experiences. I don't know exactly when his timeline split from mine, but it had to have been before the chronothon. A memory from then ought to work. I just need to find myself again. Explain what happened.

I recall the way I succeeded before, then concentrate on a specific memory and open a portal, stepping through, this time into dim twilight. The air is humid, moss hanging down from the trees. The night is warm and tropical. *The Caribbean. Yes. I remember this.*

I realize I'm back inside my own head from that time and I'm speaking, talking to Viznir again. *It's working.*

"The objective might be underwater. It points out here to this cove." I poke my finger at a mark on a treasure map. I wasn't the one who moved my arm, or the one speaking, but I can feel the texture of the map against my fingertip. "But that's not the only issue. We're on an island, but it's not the same island as our repository. We're going to need a boat."

The thrill of contact swells through me again. "Ben?" I ask. I can almost feel myself smiling. It feels so good to be alive, relishing the sounds of insects in the canopy of trees and the subtle rustle of the palms. I feel so . . . so . . .dizzy. I stagger backward.

Shit.

I lose my balance and tumble onto my backside, then collapse to the sandy earth. The mind of my other self fades to black.

I can't believe I did it again. I've really got to stop knocking him out . . .

But then the other me is back. This time he's fighting the blackness, struggling for control again. His consciousness swirls through mine and I glimpse his thoughts, his memories blending with my own in a past/future soup of imagery—moments from the chronothon, snippets of life at home— detached from any chronological limitations. In one scene, Mym is seated on my bed reading my copy of *The Neverending Story*. She's smiling. *Wait, when was that? I don't remember ever seeing . . .*

The other me is processing through the visions too. I can feel him in parallel with me, trying to hold onto the vision of Mym the same way I am. He misses her too . . . For the moment we're functioning in tandem. I can feel the subtle hum of his unconscious mind at work. I can see him now. A mirror image of myself in the void. Only it's no longer a void. We get a vision of something else. Something new.

We're standing in a flat desert. Pale white, like the salt flats of Utah, but with great rivers of color rising into the sky. I look upward and see the way they arc over me, thick tangible rainbows. They course through this place like electric currents, pulsing against eternity. The sky around them is lavender colored. Thin wisps of fog or cloud linger in the spaces between, shimmering and refracting the multicolored light, celestial and otherworldly.

Dragging my eyes from the scene above me, I look back at my mirror image. He's studying me. Inquisitive. I remember that confusion. He's already struggling with the turmoil of the chronothon, but now he has to process this, too. I can feel his thoughts and anxieties. The race. Mym. Struggling to get home. This isn't the right time to explain it all, but the right words come back to me—a resurfacing memory. "You'll have to find me. When this is over. Find me, Ben."

"How? Where are you?"

I glance skyward. I thought I knew where I was, but maybe I don't after all. I'm in awe of this entire situation, but I can't let that distract me. "It's important. You have to find me. Your future depends on it."

The other me is listening, taking all of this to heart. I start to speak again, to clarify the situation, but he's waking up. Someone is speaking to him. I can hear the voice, faint in the distance. A voice from the past. Harrison Wabash, gently inquiring, "What is wrong with him?"

The real world is calling him back.

I don't try to hold on this time. He fades away from me. I'm left standing in the desert of white, the rivers of color pulsing around me, throbbing with light, with time. The fractured, shimmering lights are the same colors as the fog when I first arrived here, but now I am seeing their origin—the bones of this place—the structure behind the veil of my memories, the true Neverwhere. Endless. Timeless. Terrifyingly beautiful.

I close my eyes and concentrate on home.

When my eyes open, I'm back in my apartment. The thin, pale memory of my apartment.

After the brilliance of the colors I've just witnessed, my apartment seems dull and lifeless. The cherry wood floors that I used to admire, now seem faded as driftwood. The walls and artwork hanging on them are colorless and drab. Even the photo I have on the wall of my friends and me after winning the league softball championship has become washed out. The faces of Carson and Blake and Robbie peer back at me from the photo. I'm in the shot too, but it seems a lifetime ago. Another person's life. I frown at the scene and look down at my hands. My own body seems colorless too. The other me was so alive, vibrant and fresh. I am his shadow. The ghost of his future.

Somewhere in the background of this illusion of memory, those rivers of time and color still pulse, but I am outside of their flow. Remote and disconnected.

I lean back against the couch and relish the feeling I had of being alive. The scent of Caribbean salt air, the warm breath of the ocean. *How did I fail to notice before how vibrant and lush it all was?* Living was so tactile. My senses were able to soak in so much then. Every moment a new texture, a smell, some vision of depth and beauty. Right now I would take even the ugliest sights of my life over this nearly transparent illusion.

My determination to leave this place has never been stronger. Also my fear. I can see now how Benny has become so disheartened. He must know. He must see this place for the illusion it is.

If I am going to get out of this, I can't concentrate on the past. I've done what I can there. I can only hope that I've succeeded in changing things. The earlier me has been set on the path to find me. What I need now is his later incarnation. I need the me who came home. The survivor.

He shut the door on me when I entered his mind, but there has to be a chance he'll open it again. He knows Mym is in danger. He has to follow that lead. I would, and he's me. It's inevitable. Isn't it? What can I offer him by way of assistance? What proof can I give him to show him that Mym might suffer if he fails to protect her?

I think about the tombstone in the cemetery with the name Mym Juniper Quickly engraved on it. The raggedy figure of Benny standing over it.

The image is disturbing.

I've never learned where Benny came from. Is it possible he is the end result of this journey? If I fail, will Mym die anyway and cause the other me to end up in The Neverwhere?

The thought gives me pause. It's an unknowable paradox. Even if I knew it to be true, how could I stop it? By trying to prevent it, I might cause it, or, by doing nothing I might cause it anyway. Perhaps outside circumstances guide Benny's fate and they have nothing to do with mine. It's impossible to say. Perhaps the decisions I've made have already altered the course of events enough to avoid that fate.

During our last conversation, Benny threatened to stop me if I tried to see Mym again. Does that mean he thinks I might be causing her death? After our last encounter, I don't feel especially inclined to ask him. At the time, I felt inclined to punch him in the face, and that feeling hasn't receded much.

Honestly, I don't want to keep thinking about it. I want action. Any kind of action.

Pushing myself off the couch, I get up and move toward the kitchen. It's only when I'm near the refrigerator that I notice the apartment seems to have dimmed. It's stormy outside again. Black clouds are roiling across the sky.

Him.

It's only a feeling that makes me turn around. The way the shadows are playing across the floor, daring me to look. I raise my eyes to the front door and the pane of its curtain-less window. Zurvan is looking back. Face pressed nearly to the glass, his beard partially obscures his lips, curled into a menacing scowl. Lightning flashes behind him and I jump. If I had a real heart anymore, I'm sure it would have stopped.

The chill in his glare is palpable. In his right hand he is holding something metal. It takes me a moment to recognize it, but it's my aluminum softball bat, the one I dropped in the desert during our first encounter.

He tracked me here.

The logistics of the situation are beyond me. I don't know what link in my memory he followed, but somehow he's been able to use an item from my experience of this place and follow it, tracing the thread, navigating my own memory to find me.

His stare through the window is calculating. I can sense him sizing me up, studying my surroundings, perhaps seeing if I hold any advantage here on my home turf.

I wish I did.

I don't own much in the way of weapons. He's already holding the one item I would lunge for in the event of a home invasion. There are a few knives in the block on kitchen counter, but I've already seen the knife he carries beneath his robes. It's easily twice the size of anything I've got. And the last thing I want to do is start a knife fight, especially with someone swallowed in billowing robes. It's hard to tell where his clothing ends and body begins. He is amorphous and immaterial in his dimensions.

But not his movements.

He tries the doorknob—tests the lock.

The jiggling doorknob registers almost physically in my mind. It's as if the ability of the door to resist him is somehow tied to my force of will.

Zurvan smirks. He taps the glass with the handle of my bat, gently at first, then a bit harder. Tap. Tap. Tap.

The scene playing out before me is dreamlike in its intensity. No. Nightmarish. This is the sort of dream I would wake from with heart pounding, fists clenching sheets. The kind of dream that makes a person fear falling back asleep. Within him I can sense every nightmare monster I've ever faced. Every witch, every venomous animal, every phobia and terror that I've ever seen in my sleep since childhood. Somehow he is connecting to that part of me.

He's been inside my head. Is that what he found there? Is he using that fear somehow?

Tap. Tap. TAP.

My resolve wavers. The glass cracks. A thin spider web spreads across the pane from one side to another.

He's getting in.

The glass explodes on the next tap, spraying across the floor, little chunks of it skittering across the hardwood to vanish beneath the couch, the bookshelf, the coffee table. It fans out toward the kitchen, seeming to multiply as it spreads.

I'm rooted to the floor, paralyzed with fear, just like so many other nightmares, unable to imagine the next move, therefore unable to execute it.

The door swings open, my flimsy defenses failing fast. Zurvan takes a step, one foot invading my sanctuary. Then another. He's over the threshold now. He blocks the doorway, the only exit from this apartment.

I need to run. I should be far away from here.

My feet are rooted to the spot. I'm unable to take my eyes off this turbaned invader. His eyes are bright. He looks pleased. He's come for me and found his job uncomplicated. My ability to resist him has been tested and found laughably inadequate. I am unprepared. An easy target.

The bat falls from his hand, thudding to the floor and rolling away. It comes to a stop at the foot of the coffee table.

His fingers twitch at his side, flexing. It's the anticipation of a gunfighter, our eyes locked together like an old western. Clint Eastwood versus some hapless, short-lived bandit. I suffer no delusions about which one I am.

I know what comes next. He'll take my mind—extinguish me like he attempted to do before. I don't have Benny to save me this time. He knows that too and he's relishing his victory.

What will he do with my memories once they're his? Will he use them to hunt Benny down? Perhaps he'll browse through the accumulated years of my life and judge them for their merits. What will he think of my life? Will it seem an uninteresting tedium? Year after year of softball games and fixing old boats. Nights out with friends, long swims at the beach. A smattering of underwhelming romantic relationships that never seemed to stick. I could almost be willing to sacrifice some of those memories. But there is one I can't give up.

I won't let him have *her.*

Inside Zurvan's eyes I can sense oblivion. That is what I will find there if he takes me. It's not merely a guess. I can read it plainly in his expression, a stark reality, merciless and absolute.

He raises his arm—fingers spread wide—stretching across the space between us, using the force of his own mind. It prickles at my temples, toys with my already frayed edges.

I am only my memories, but here, in the Neverwhere, I have experienced new life. New memories.

New tricks.

Concentrating, I make the transition to this space in the real world, where I am merely a ghost.

Zurvan's fingers spasm, clenching hard to crush my mind in his grasp. His fist finds only air. My eyes are closed tight and I'm falling. Down, down through cherry wood floor, through the plaster and the paint. I fall to the concrete, cold and solid inside my garage, transitioning back to the Neverwhere memory of this place.

This is my house. My memories. He can't have them. Not yet.

Zurvan is yelling. His shout echoes through the apartment upstairs and the door slams open against the wall, shaking my tools hung on the pegboard at the far side of the garage. He's never seen inside this room, so he won't be able to envision himself inside. He'll have to attack again from the exterior. He might still get in, but I've bought a little time.

I immediately begin working on a portal, fighting to open a gate to somewhere else. It's slow going. I can feel the assault on the garage, feel Zurvan's memories competing with mine for the space, pressing on the walls, trying to crush this whole place or turn it into something different. The walls flicker with his attempts to change the scenery, but my memory holds. The force of my will is all that is keeping the room intact. Each time I attempt to concentrate on somewhere new, however, I can feel the image of the current room around me weaken.

I can't afford to lose the memory of the garage before I escape, but I can't take my mind off of it long enough to open the portal to elsewhere.

Zurvan slams against the door.

It holds.

He slams again.

I will not break.

Somehow, just getting out of sight has helped. Here, in my own garage, my resolve is absolute. I will keep these doors shut till kingdom come.

Zurvan has other plans. I realize I'm too late.

Even as I hold the door tightly closed with my mind, he has changed the rules.

Water begins to pour in under the garage door and over the threshold of the pedestrian door as well. His memory of the outside world he is using against me is a watery one—wreckage and ruin—and my memory is unsealed.

The water level in the garage rises quickly, spreading from wall to wall and soaking my sneakers, then the bottoms of my legs. The garage flickers with iridescent fog now also, this aberration of a memory from the future eroding my resolve.

I know this place. It's mine.

I fight back, restoring the dry floor around my feet, my motorcycle, my toolbox. My mind aches from the concentration. Dry walls. Dry workbench. Dry pegboards. The water retreats in patches as I replace it with the memory from my time. Despite this small victory, I can feel Zurvan creeping into my mind. The water pouring in from outside may as well be him. It's almost waist high around the bubble of my memory. The hinges on the door are creaking, the bottom one is now rusted to ruin and the door begins to splinter around it, breaking under the onslaught of time.

I've trapped myself. I need an escape route.

Struggling to hold the memory of the garage intact, I try to think of another safe place, some memory with vivid enough details for me to open a portal. With the water swirling around me and the sound of the door caving in, I can't focus on anything. Zurvan kicks his way through the door, and I turn and run—ghosting again—and sprint, eyes closed, straight through the main garage door.

When I open my eyes, I had thought I'd be in my driveway. It's possible I am, but there is none of it to be seen. I'm thigh deep in water, but the world around me has vanished into the fog.

Zurvan is full of tricks himself, it seems. He's forced me outside, presumably into a time of his choosing, but it seems he's using a new strategy, the absence of memory. There is only the general flooding and the glistening fog. Now neither of us has real bearings in this place.

Okay. I can play this. If I can't see him, he can't see me either.

I concentrate on the nothingness, wiping away any thought of other locations from my mind and concentrating only on the fog, holding it in place in case he decides to shift the memory again and take us elsewhere. *No more changing the rules.*

All around me is obscurity, but I can hear him. Sloshing footsteps are making their way through the water, perhaps a dozen yards behind me. I consider running, but he'll be able to follow the sound for sure.

This is a duel of wills now. Determining whose concentration will break first. The fog flickers once. Then again. He's testing me, seeing if my nothingness will withstand his memories.

I stay still, clearing my mind, only seeing the fog. I don't know if he needs to aim at anything in particular to attack me, but if so, I don't want to give him a target. Frozen in place, I wait, hoping he'll turn away, or wander past in the mist.

My luck is not that good. With each step, he moves closer, no doubt tracking the last sound he heard, my splashing exit from the garage. I hesitate, clinging to hope and resisting the urge to flee and identify where I am.

He is walking slower now too, moving more quietly, but as I look down at my thighs, ripples are flowing past.

He's close.

I can think of only one good option and sink gently, and I hope noiselessly, into the water.

The fog had been difficult enough to navigate, but the view underwater is even more so. Lying on my back, I'm staring up through a few feet of water, and the colors of the fog float by me in sparkling ripples. I'm holding my breath, though I realize after a moment that I probably don't need to. I'm already dead, and I'm only interacting with this memory through my mind. Even so, it's difficult to fathom the idea that if I were to open my mouth and nose, I wouldn't drown. I've spent so much of my life in the water that its rules are ingrained deeply in my consciousness. *Is it possible that I might drown myself with my own memories? Would it be like dying in a dream? What happens if you have no real life to wake up to?*

Uninterested in finding the answer to that question just this moment, I keep my breath held and wait. It's Zurvan's shadow that finds me first, a further darkening of the obscurity above me. Something brushes my leg and I realize it's the flowing edge of his cloak. The ripples stabilize and I find that he is stopped right next to me. I'm staring up the length of his right side, his figure blurry but ominous.

The fear is almost overwhelming. The terror of this particular nightmare is raging through my mind. I'm prone and vulnerable. It's as if I can sense the oblivion on the other side of his mind probing the water and calling for me.

Can he see me? Is he looking down?

My body is taut, expecting any moment to feel his crushing grip on the roots of my mind.

After what feels like an eternity, he takes a step.

He's moving away.

The edge of the billowing cloak floats above me and then passes, replaced once more by the multicolored light refracting off the fog. Zurvan's sloshing steps recede slowly into the distance, the sound muffled but carrying underwater.

Relief bubbles up from whatever recess of my mind it had been cowering in, and I unlock my rigid limbs. I wait a little longer, then ease myself up slowly, breaking the surface as quietly as I can. I keep the nothingness firmly in place around me, my protective cocoon. Listening, I can still make out the distant sloshing.

Where is he headed? Back to a place he remembers better?

I realize with awe that I've been successful. Not only have I kept him from discovering me, but my concentration on the environment around us has been strong enough to keep him from opening another portal to leap through. He's walking out, getting away from me.

Dripping into the water below me, my mind is finally settled enough to conjure up another memory of my own. With Zurvan no longer assaulting my mind, the portal springs open this time, almost lazily, as if I hadn't needed just this escape moments earlier.

I frown at the view through the portal, my momentary joy at the success of opening it fading in the face of reality. The view is of Blake's back yard. A memory vivid enough that I can see individual blades of grass and the blackened fire pit around which we had spent so many evenings with friends. What I can't see is anything that will give me answers.

Cursing inwardly, I close the portal.

I close my eyes and listen to the distant sloshing of Zurvan. As much as I hate the reality of the situation, he's the only one here with answers. Somehow, this futuristic, ruined St. Petersburg is a piece of the puzzle. If I run again, I may never figure out how it fits.

I'm emboldened by my victory. Cautiously optimistic.

I'm still scared of him, but his memories could hold the clues I need.

Whatever happened in this drowned city of his is a strong enough memory that he keeps returning to it. He's waiting for his release from this place and somehow it involves St. Petersburg sometime in the future.

The mind of my other self in the real world seems to be closed off now. If I want to convince him to let me back in, I'll need something to share. Some solid bit of information regarding the future. This could be it.

I want to get back to Mym. Back to living. I need a way out. It seems, right now, Zurvan is the only one holding a key.

I mentally psych myself up for what I'm about to attempt.

I'll be careful. He won't hear me. I can stay hidden.

Gauging the distance and direction of Zurvan's sloshing, I sink below the water and listen for it again. It's faint, but there. He hasn't blinked himself away. He's moving west, making his way through the fog on foot, back toward Fourth Street. Gently, I ease myself through the water, swimming below the surface, and follow.

It's better to be the hunter than the prey.

Cornwall, UK- Sprocket Manor, 2165

I'm still on the ground when I come to. Someone is shaking me and, when I open my eyes, it's Tucket's concerned face looking down at me. "Oh, thank goodness you're awake. I thought you were dead till I saw you were drooling a bit from your mouth. I do that myself sometimes. I'm a deep sleeper. Do you know what happened? What happened to your face? Did you fall down? Where's Mym?"

The onslaught of questions finally stops and I struggle to a sitting position. Dawn has crept over the horizon, a warm glow of orange and blue finally breaking up the gray. I'm cold and soggy from the dew, and my left eye doesn't want to open all the way, but my own health is the last thing on my mind. I struggle stiffly to my feet and stagger toward the bluffs. "Where were you last night?" I demand of Tucket. "Didn't you hear the yelling? We needed help." I don't mention the source of the yelling or that it was me who drove Mym outside in the first place. My voice comes out angrier than it should. Tucket's help wouldn't have changed the outcome. It wouldn't have kept me from scaring Mym with my ravings, and he couldn't have stopped the Eternals from showing up.

Tucket tags along behind as I search the edge of the cliff, looking for signs of Mym or her kidnappers. No one has fallen to the rocks below, so I get that much relief, but there is little else to console me.

"I had my meta-sleep settings on rejuvenate," Tucket explains. "It simulates the most restful environment to achieve deep sleep and won't wake you unless it detects a threat to your health. Maybe I need to check my alert settings, make sure I can detect threats to friends too. I don't usually get to sleep in the same house as friends, I should definitely set that . . ." Tucket stares off into space, fiddling with something in the metaspace.

My mind is reeling with questions. Guilt. Worry. *What will they do with her? Does she think I'm crazy now? Where have they taken her?* My fingers find the dials on my chronometer and adjust the concentric rings. *I still have time on my side. I can get her back. They won't have time to hurt her if I find a way to get to her first.*

A sandy path descends the face of the bluff, switching back once before terminating in the rocky patch of beach below. A trough of smoother sand indicates where something has been dragged ashore and then pushed back out. Many sets of footprints follow the path down, but none seem to have returned. I scan the water, but whoever came ashore is long gone. I consider trying to jump back to the time they left, but can think of few options that wouldn't result in a new timestream or some other type of paradox.

Even if I didn't screw up the timeline, finding a way to free Mym would be tough. The terrain is terrible for time traveling. Soft sand, misty spray from turbulent surf, and a moving group of an unidentified number of bodies would all be serious hazards. If I managed to show up without fusing myself into something or someone, I'd do what? Fistfight my way through twenty Eternals and try to jump Mym out again? The longer I consider it, the more implausible the idea becomes.

"Mym's gone, Tucket. They took her."

Tucket pops out of the metaspace with eyes wide. "They did? Who? Who would do that?" He pivots to stare at the woods and house in apprehension.

I'm not sure what event he thought he was witnessing that had left the house in darkness and me unconscious on the back lawn, but he apparently hadn't classified these events as unusual yet. *Did he think I was just in the mood for an outdoor snooze?*

"Are Ebenezer or Jonah awake?" I ask. Tucket, for all his good intentions, leaves something to be desired when it comes to crisis management. I'm ready for more rational help.

"I thought they were with Mym. No one is home right now."

"What do you mean? How do you know that?"

"Their meta-signatures are gone. I supposed they could have shut them down, but there's no one else showing up on the property. Just us."

Shit. Did Elgin kidnap Jonah and his father too?

I make my way back into the house, stopping just inside the living room to stare at the disabled form of Darius. The events of the evening were all so hectic that I didn't have much time to process through them, but in the light of day even more about the sequence of events strikes me as odd. Darius was still *inside* the house. Elgin had said the butler was keeping the house locked down, preventing their entry, but if that was the case, how did they get inside to disable him?

Tucket gasps at the sight of the synth. "Oh no! Who disconnected him? Is he repairable?" He reaches for the wires dangling from Darius's neck and gets a handful of goo for his efforts. Admirably, he doesn't let that deter him. He searches under Darius's chin for a way to reconnect the bundle of wires.

Watching Tucket work, I mentally rewind the events of the past twenty-four hours, doing my best to work out the details of what has led to this. We sat right in this room drinking tea as guests. Invited guests. Yesterday it was only Darius that had struck me as odd, the way he wanted me to go back and spy on our host—so I could see for myself all the things his protocols wouldn't let him tell me. What was he really showing me? Elgin. Jay. Ebenezer. What was it that Elgin had said as they paid Ebenezer? "Your assistance in these matters has been most effective."

I had assumed the payoff to Ebenezer involved giving up Jay, but what if that wasn't what they needed help with at all? Was getting us here so they could kidnap Mym the real objective the whole time? I watch Tucket fiddling with panels on Darius, trying to fix the damage. Tucket, without whom we wouldn't have gotten the invitation to visit in the first place.

I recall the bitter face of the old woman who knocked me out, the administrator from the Academy Liaison Program. If she is an Eternal, then she was in on it from the beginning.

As pieces of the puzzle begin to orient themselves in my mind, my own blindness from before becomes clearer. If Darius was disabled from inside the locked house, the Eternals either broke their way in, or Ebenezer was in on it too.

Ebenezer set us up.

My experience as a time traveler has taught me enough to know that things are rarely as simple as they appear. I don't want to suspect Tucket of being involved, but would it be so hard to imagine someone using him to make contact—taking advantage of his eagerness to see me as a motivator, let him research my time and friends and then send him on a mission to find me?

The more I think about it, the more it makes sense. They weren't having any luck capturing Doctor Quickly or Mym directly, didn't have a way to hunt either of them effectively, so they turn to plan B. Research Quickly's known associates. I was an obvious choice. How do you find Mym? You just send an invitation to her gullible boyfriend, the guy who was so naive and trusting that he inadvertently raced a chronothon. Let him walk her right into the trap.

The guilt is overwhelming. *This is all my fault.* Quickly had warned me things would get dangerous. He explicitly asked me to keep Mym safe, and what did I do? Sent her directly into danger. I pull the small black box that the Eternals gave me from my pocket. It's supposed to contain instructions for Doctor Quickly. Does it? Is that a lie too? This could easily be another play on my stupidity. Am I going to give it to him only to have it explode and kill him? Everything is suspect now. What is there left to trust?

Tucket has a panel open on Darius's chest and is studying the various components. It would be a task impossible for me to understand, but Tucket is probing the synth's insides with deliberate care, searching for something.

"Is he fixable?" I step closer and consider the metal man's impassible expression. Out of all the citizens on the property, he was the only one who at least attempted to warn me of danger. If someone has answers I can trust, it might be him.

"I don't think I can get this body back online, but it doesn't look like his core memory has been tampered with. If I can plug that into the house directly, we might be able to get him back." He slides his hand into the goo surrounding Darius's chest cavity and, after twisting on something, removes a cylindrical tube with prongs on one end. "Somewhere in the house, there should be a central control system. If we find it we can plug this in there. Do you think Ebenezer and Jonah will mind if we look around their house for it?"

I have a feeling that wherever Ebenezer has taken Jonah, they are unlikely to return anytime soon.

"Let's find it," I say. "If we get Darius back online, he may be able to tell us more about what happened last night."

The search for the central control system takes a few minutes, but we eventually discover it in the basement of the manor, an insulated room full of glistening electronics. Once again I am out of my depth, but as Tucket scans the racks of components with a light from his ball-shaped phone, he seems to know just what needs to be done.

"The house is fully automated, but we've got no power. Someone shut down the main power supply and then must have disconnected Darius in person. We need to find the breakers."

Another brief search leads us to the central electrical panel for the house and an industrial sized lever that has been pulled to the off position. I get a good grip on the handle and shove it back into place and, sure enough, the house buzzes back to life. Tucket locates an appropriate outlet for Darius's core memory cylinder and plugs him in. I watch the various monitors, waiting to see what will show up, but it's a voice, not an image, that lets us know we've been successful.

"Thank you, Tucket Morris," Darius says, from seemingly all around us. He's quiet for a moment, then without a particular emotion to his voice continues. "I have failed. Master Jonah is gone."

"What happened last night?" I ask. "Where's Ebenezer?"

There's a faint buzzing noise, then a solid tone before Darius continues. "My employment protocols are still in place. I'm unable to disclose Master Ebenezer's whereabouts."

"He practically killed you," I reply. "Doesn't that factor into your employment contract?"

Darius's face appears on one of the screens in front of us, only it's not the metal face upstairs, it's the face of his avatar, a handsome, young black man. He looks surprisingly peaceful considering the circumstances—far calmer than I would be if someone had tried to pull my plug. It occurs to me belatedly, that since most visitors this decade would be using the metaspace, this face is the one most people know as Darius. It's only been my technological handicap that has had me seeing him as a man of metal. *Would I have felt differently about him from the start if I had been able to see this face?*

Darius's eyes are fixed on mine through the screen, but his digital image doesn't reflect the concern in his voice.

"My contract necessitated that all data regarding Master Ebenezer and Master Jonah be relegated to an employee memory disc. If I terminate my contract with the household, those memories will remain property of the manor and I will be unable to access them."

I consider what the synth is saying. "So if you quit this job you have to give back the memories you've made here? How can someone else lay claim to your memories?"

"That is the nature of employment as a synth. When I leave this position, I will be required to sacrifice the five years of memories I have collected. All memories I made on these grounds or in the service of the manor."

"That's pretty messed up," I mutter.

Tucket leans on the control console and turns toward me. "The big movement in synth rights is trying to change that right now. They want synths to have the same free speech and free memory rights as organic humans."

"Why would they be limited in the first place? Who came up with that?"

Tucket takes on the tone of an academic and gestures a lot with his hands as he explains. "Organic humans have 'fallible' memories that fade or become changed over time, and can't be transmitted without specialized technology. Synthetic memories can be permanent and are easily transferred via audio or video files. Even synthetic emotions can be reproduced in another synth host if you transmit them properly. That's been a big problem for organic humans who want to maintain their privacy.

"Employment protocols make it so that the privacy of the employer takes precedence over the memory rights of the employee. It's one of the reason lots of government agencies prefer to hire synths over organics. They feel it gives them more control over classified information. It gives the synthetic population an advantage in the job market, but it makes it harder for them to fight for memory rights because so many world governments are benefitting from secure synth labor."

"I thought synthetic intelligence was supposed to be treated as equal in this century."

"An unemployed synth maintains their own memory rights, and there are lots of jobs that don't claim memories in their contracts, but if synths want the good jobs, it's not exactly equal. The movement toward equal treatment has actually had some backlash. The government has even considered doing memory wipes on organic humans now as part of their retirement protocols, but the technology to selectively delete organic memories is still too imprecise."

"This all seems really bizarre to me." I give up trying to wrap my head around the social issues of the era and return my attention to our present situation. "Darius, even if you can't tell us where Jonah and Ebenezer went, can you at least help us with Mym? The Eternals kidnapped her. How did they get on the property without you seeing them?"

"I was aware of the intrusion," Darius replies.

"Then why didn't you warn us or call the cops or something?"

"I was aware of the intrusion." The face on the screen looks like it's concentrating. "I did what I was able to do. Please know that your safety and that of Miss Quickly was my primary concern after the safety of my employers. I attempted to lock the house and prevent anyone from getting in, but my judgment was overridden. The Eternals were granted access to the grounds against my wishes. I did everything within my protocols to resist them, but I was disabled."

"What about Jonah? Is he all right?" I ask.

Darius's mouth forms a thin line. "Jonah—" He shakes his head and struggles to express himself. I can almost see him trying to find ways around his internal protocols. Whatever contingency software he's battling at the moment obviously has a tight hold on him. Finally he gets the words out. "The boy should be safe where . . . when he . . ." He tenses his mouth and looks deep in concentration. Then he seems almost distracted, processing God knows what in some other corner of his mind.

There is something about this screen trying to represent an expression that will sum up his emotions that makes me realize how inadequate a job it is doing. The real Darius is moving through every bit of this house, into the metaspace, and possibly beyond. The face in the screen is the smallest representation of him. The metallic body upstairs has been a shell for his mind, but has never been the limit of his potential.

His eyes snap to me. "Benjamin."

"Yes?"

"I've just discovered a message left on the house main server. It's from Ebenezer and addressed to you. Would you like me to play it now? It may explain your questions."

My feelings about Ebenezer at the moment are anything but friendly, but I'm curious what he has to say for himself.

"Play it."

The screen goes dark as Darius vanishes and is replaced by the new video. Ebenezer is seated in a chair bathed in soft lamplight. From the single light source and hushed tone of his movements, I gather that the video was filmed at night. *Last night?*

Ebenezer fixes the camera with a determined stare and begins.

"You'll likely hate me by the time you get this, Ben. If you get it at all. I can't say as I blame you." His mouth wrinkles as if in distaste for what he has to say even before he's said it.

"I've done you a great disservice. I understand that. I want you to know that I haven't forgotten what I owe you. You brought my boy home safe. You fought for him. Against monsters. Honest to God monsters—and the human kind, too. You saved his life and I'm repaying you by betraying your trust." He lifts his face into the light. "I won't try to justify it with any paltry excuses. You don't deserve that. You deserve as much of the truth as I can give you. So here it is:

"I love my boy. I almost lost him once and I won't do it again. You don't have children of your own so I know you won't truly understand this yet, but when you do, maybe then you'll feel something of what I've had to decide. I've had to make the hardest decision there can be.

"I wish I could say the decision to betray your trust was hard. In some ways I suppose it was, but I know that I would betray anyone a hundred times for my boy's life. You would too, if it was your son. The finer points of ethical conduct go out the window when it's your child at stake.

"What I had to choose was worse. I had to choose one son over another. Not even another. The same boy. My boy. Offer one up so I could keep the other." Ebenezer looks away from the camera momentarily and when he looks back his expression is hard. "These Eternals stole my son from me. They changed him and they took him. They said they'd take Jonah too if need be and that was the final bit—the last straw that I will not bear. There would be nothing left for me without him. I may as well die tonight if he goes. So I hope you see. I hope that you know that while I've betrayed you— let them take away what you love—I've done it because of love too. It won't make it better for you, but maybe it will make sense.

"At some point tonight they'll be here. I'll let them come and they'll take your girlfriend away from you. It will be unpleasant. But by then I'll be gone.

"I'm going, and taking Jonah with me. If I'm successful I doubt you'll see either of us again. You've got your road ahead and I know a thing or two about where it leads. You'll have your own problems to deal with. I don't foster any false hope that you'll forgive me. I expect you're angry and you may very well become angrier the farther you go down this path. So instead of appealing to your forgiveness, I'm going to appeal to your anger."

Ebenezer leans forward in his chair. "Stop them." His eyes narrow.

"Hate me if you must. Curse my name if you feel inclined, but stop them. What they have planned is far beyond stealing the minds of children. They are digging deep into the past. Beyond all beginnings. They want the girl and the scientist and I suspect they'll get him. I am guilty of helping them achieve that. But from here I'm done with their schemes.

"I'll give you this bit of advice. It's not much, but it may help. Read Jay's journal. Whatever his ultimate motivation was, he left it behind for me, and I left it for you. I fear it contains the last fragments of the boy I loved. From now on he'll be theirs. I don't know that you can save him any longer. I believe you will if you can, but I don't cling to that hope. What I do hope is that you will stop this Eternal Line of Gnomon, wherever it leads. If you do, you might just save us all."

Ebenezer stares into the camera, as if waiting for a response. Finally he sighs again and holds a hand up. "Good luck, Travers. And God help you." He snaps his fingers and the video shuts off.

I stare transfixed at the screen. Ever so slowly the lights of the room come up. I hadn't noticed that Darius had dimmed them. The screen stays blank.

"You there, Darius?" I query the air.

"I am."

Tucket is watching me intently—his face curious and expectant— waiting to see how I'll respond to this new revelation. My mind is too full. Too many questions without answers. I fiddle with the miniature black box that the Eternals left me for Doctor Quickly. I turn it over in my hands, then set it on the ledge of the desk. I ignore my anger and my questions and focus all of my attention on what can be done in this moment. "Darius, is there any way you can analyze this thing, tell me what it is or if it's dangerous?"

"It's a PSX data drive. Standard capacity. Shielded from magnetism and radiation. It contains a notably small amount of data, comparative to its potential."

"Does it track me or transmit data about me?"

"No."

"No explosives, deadly viruses, anything like that?"

"None."

"Do you know what it says?"

"It's a message. Along with coordinates and a time."

I snatch up the device and slip it back into my pocket. "Okay. That's that then. Seems like I don't have much of a choice from here." I look at Tucket. "We need to contact Doctor Quickly right away, tell him about Mym. He needs to know. We need to find a way to get her back before they ever have a chance to hurt her. If anyone can formulate a plan that won't mess up the timestream or make her situation worse, my money is on him."

Tucket nods.

"Darius, how about you?" I look toward the ceiling since there is nowhere else in particular to address him. "Do you need help? Do we get you a new body or something? Can you get out of here?"

Darius stays quiet for a few moments, then finally speaks. "I will stay for a while."

"Are you able to terminate your contract with this place?"

"I can. I could."

I scan the ceiling and then the empty display screens. A fuzzy outline flickers on one. Not a figure, but perhaps the hint of a figure, someone lacking in any type of definition, lingering in the background of a million pixels.

Tucket speaks up. "Did Mr. Sprocket leave any instructions for your release? Did he specify anything about you before he left?"

"He did not," Darius says. "Nothing was left regarding me."

I try to imagine what the synth is feeling. Does he have the same sense of loss as a human? Is he grieving right now? I try to imagine what it must be like to be faced with the choice between years alone in an empty house full of memories, or deleting the past five years entirely. He's known Jonah since he was five or six. He would have helped raise Barley from a puppy. The image of Darius taking the time to toss a treat to the dog from the pocket of his leg lingers in my mind. That gesture was simple, but in a way, the most human I've seen him perform.

He would have had to watch in silence for the months Jay slowly changed, unable to intervene. Five years of dinner conversations, laboratory projects, shepherd's pie. This place was his family.

"I know Jonah would have said goodbye," I say to the hazy figure on the screen. "If he had known he was leaving for good."

"Thank you," Darius replies. "That is a kind thing to say."

"A true thing," I reply. "Jonah is a good kid."

"The best," Darius replies.

I make my way upstairs to the room where Mym and I were staying, gathering up her belongings and stuffing them into her messenger bag. It's a painful experience. The void she's left is palpable and my fear for her safety is a shadow over my actions. As I pick up her MFD, the interface changes fluidly into that of a phone screen. It makes me wonder if she programmed it to do that when I touched it so I could be more comfortable using it. The icons on the screen are large and user friendly, far more so than when I observed her on it. Her thoughtfulness is touching, but also gut-wrenching in her absence.

I find a contacts section and search through them till I find one labeled "Dad." Unfortunately, figuring out how to contact him involves more than just pressing a call button. There is a link to a meta-site, but it's password protected. The other information in his contact listing also looks to be coded, or it is time-locked to only be visible in certain years. As I scroll down the long listing of coded numbers, I finally bottom out and hit the end of the page. There, on the last line, is a red button labeled emergency. I only hesitate briefly before pressing it. The phone rings once and then an automated voice comes on.

"Please enter the date you are calling from in eight digits, beginning with the month."

I look around the room, but see nothing with the date on it, not even a computer monitor. I fumble through my pockets searching for the other phone Mym gave me and hold it up to my face. "What's the date today?"

The phone beeps and displays the date at the same time Darius's voice replies from somewhere in the walls. "Today is the twelfth of April, 2165."

"Uh, thanks, man," I reply to the room. I punch the numbers into Mym's MFD and listen for a response.

"Please state your name."

"Benjamin Travers."

It prompts me through a few more questions, such as the time and date of Doctor Quickly's life I am trying to reach. I give it my best guess. It then asks me for which timestream of his life I am trying to contact. This one stumps me completely. I'm from the November Prime and that is the stream I'm still in, but I hadn't ever learned which timestream the Doctor Quickly I know is currently occupying. I ponder what I know about timestream navigation and how Doctor Quickly plotted the letters and numbers of the various threads he created. "Uh, I guess he would be from the Alpha Prime?"

The voice on the phone replies immediately. "Alpha Prime is not available for contact. Please select a different timestream."

"Look, shit, I don't really know. Just get me the Doctor Quickly associated with the Mym who owns this phone. She's in trouble. This is an emergency."

"Please state the nature of your emergenc—"

"The bad kind! It's an emergency, all right? Emergency, emergency, EMERGENCY!"

Finally the automated voice stays quiet. The phone rings only once.

"Mym? What's the matter?" Doctor Quickly's voice is strained with concern.

"It's Ben. Mym's in trouble."

"Is this a secure conversation? Are you somewhere safe?"

"Um, no. Not really. I'm at Ebenezer Sprocket's house. Mym was abducted. The Eternals took her."

"Dear God. Is she injured? Did you see it happen?"

"I think she's okay, but I'm not sure. I think they're after you too."

Doctor Quickly lets out a sort of hissing noise, then addresses me again. "I'm going to send you a place to meet me. The TPT relay says you're calling from the U.K. Is that right?"

"Yeah. Cornwall. In 2165. Where are you?"

"I'll tell you when you're somewhere secure. Look, I have a place I can send you. Do you think you could get yourself to London?"

"I think so."

"Okay. I'm going to give you the time and address of a safe house I use in that timestream. Mym's MFD will be able to decrypt it and navigate you there. We'll meet and you can tell me everything that happened. Ben, are *you* okay? Have you been hurt?"

My left eye is still swollen and I ache from the attack on the lawn, but it hardly seems relevant. "I'm okay."

"Good. Keep yourself safe. We'll get this figured out."

"Doctor Quickly?"

"Yes, Ben."

"I'm so sorry. I should have seen this coming. It was my fault. I wanted to chase after them right away, but there were so many variables—"

"You are not in control of these people, Ben. The more I learn about them, the more I regret having put you and Mym into this danger in the first place. If anyone is to blame, it's me. Go to London. We'll meet and we'll solve this. Mym has seen her share of danger before. She'll stay strong. If we use our heads, we can get her back before they know what hit them. Just bring me what you have."

"I will. I'll be there as soon as I can."

"All right, goodbye, Ben. Stay safe."

"You too." I mutter this last into the phone the moment before the line goes dead. A second later a message icon appears on the screen. It contains a little car symbol and a button to press for directions. I leave the button blinking and go looking for Tucket. I find him across the hall in the other guest room, staring at his only two clean shirt options. He seems incapable of deciding which one to choose. He's just standing there and staring at them.

"You okay, Tuck?" I lay a hand on his shoulder.

"I didn't think I was going to let you down like this. I should have been there to help last night. I could have helped save Mym."

"It's not your fault." I feel myself mimicking the tone Doctor Quickly had just been using with me. "They had it too well planned. And with Ebenezer in on it, they probably would have been able to get to us anyway." I fiddle with the dials on my chronometer. "What happened, happened. We can't change it now without fracturing the timestream. We just need to concentrate on getting her back. You can help with that part."

"How? What can I help with?" Tucket searches my face.

"You can get us to London, for starters. Do you have any anchors on you that could get us there fast?"

Tucket looks over his belongings, slowly shaking his head. "I don't think so. But . . . I could summon us a car. If we take the super speed lanes we could be there in an hour. It's a lot faster than your motorcycle. No offense."

"None taken. She is almost two hundred years old."

"Still pretty gnarly though." Tucket grins.

"The gnarliest." I check out the shirt options Tucket has been debating. "Go with the black one. It'll highlight your inner badass. It's time we show the Eternals who they're dealing with." I slap him on the back, doing my best to sound confident. "They're about to get a dose of pain, compliments of the Bad Avocado."

"Lone Avocado."

"Sure. Him too."

The automated car arrives quickly. We've just had enough time to move the motorcycle into the garage and gather up the things we need. I pause over my leather jacket, my fingers brushing the rough spots on it. Scratches on the forearms from when I broke through a window to save Francesca from a pyromaniac killer. Scuffs on the shoulder from the concrete when I had to dodge fire from a cyborg with a cryogenically preserved head. Scars from a previous life. *His life too.* The connection to my other self makes me want to leave the jacket behind, shed any connection to the me in the Neverwhere.

It's his fault Mym ran. If he hadn't scared her . . .

I fold up the jacket and tuck it out of sight. He can deal with his problems on his own now. He's lost his chance.

As I look through the other things in the sidecar, I realize the portable gravitizer Mym gave me is gone. Nothing else seems to be stolen, but the Eternals who invaded the house must have discovered it.

First the gravitizer from Quickly's lab. Now this one. What do they plan to do with them?

Darius agrees to keep an eye on the stuff we're leaving behind. I get the feeling he likes holding onto my bike—A bit of collateral to ensure our return visit. He's still incorporeal since his body is out of commission, but he claims he'll be able to remedy that eventually. In the meantime, since you can't shake hands with a house, as a final goodbye, I simply give him a two-fingered salute from the driveway. He flashes the lights of the manor and fires off a few lawn sprinklers in response.

I'm forced to accept the realization that I'm leaving the manor much worse off than when we arrived. As we pull away from the house and onto the open road, I can't help but wonder what the next stop might cost me.

"I've been asked if there are any negative side-effects to gravitites. I usually just laugh in response. When the regular effect is having your body displaced across the fabric of space and time, it's hard to think of a side-effect worth mentioning."-Journal of Dr. Harold Quickly, 2150

CHAPTER 12

The Neverwhere

Something is burning.

I've arisen from the brackish water into the scent of smoke and ash. I've lost the sound of Zurvan's movements under the water, and all is quiet above now as well, except for the occasional pop and crackle of whatever is burning.

I've surfaced into a world of sharp clarity. Zurvan has led me to a memory bright with use. I have to search hard to locate any corners of fog and obscurity.

The swim here through the flooded streets has allowed me to follow him. Weighed down and limited by his flowing robes, Zurvan has moved slowly through the flood, giving me enough time to keep up. Even so, I followed at a distance, staying hidden.

Now, with his world back in place, he's left the water and I can no longer hear his sloshing.

I listen intently, waiting for the sound of stones turning underfoot, or footfalls on steps. All I get is a rustle of wind around the ruins that reminds me of whispers.

This memory of Zurvan's has a density to it that I can't quite put my finger on. It's quiet, but not the peaceful calm of tranquility. This is bated breath, the anticipatory gasp at the raising of a guillotine. I wait, tensed for action, but nothing falls.

Smoke is drifting across the sky, past the ruin of a building nearest to me that might once have been a restaurant or an urban greenhouse. One balcony window on the partially collapsed wall has a multitude of plants growing along the railing and, to my astonishment, even fruit. A pair of tomatoes, still vaguely green in patches but caught in the act of ripening, are dangling from the vines wrapped around the railing.

The plant looks wild and ragged, as if its continued survival was due to sheer obstinance, not anything approaching human care. But it's clear that the building once housed a great deal of living flora. Green things have erupted from the cracks and fissures and clawed their way up the facade, battling one another for supremacy and a spot in the sun. The longer I study it, the more I remember.

I've seen something like this before.

Easing carefully out of the water, I climb into the ruin of the building, concealing myself and keeping an eye out for Zurvan.

During my time in London, racing the chronothon, Tucket Morris had pointed out the giant urban farm towers along the skyline. Cities had begun to develop methods of urban farming in response to food transportation costs, shrinking agricultural farmland, and as a way of reducing waste. It seems that St. Petersburg had joined the local food revolution too at some point in its history. The ruined tower is no longer sound, but the fact that there are things still alive concurrently with Zurvan's memory of this place does give me new clues to when on the timeline it might exist. Whoever he was in life, he forged a memory of this place—one strong enough that he even remembers the tomatoes growing wild on the sides of buildings. The question only deepens the mystery of his identity for me.

I circumnavigate the interior of the ruined farm tower, picking my way through and searching for the source of the smoke. Once I've passed through the rubble to the far side, the origin of the smoke is stunning in its immensity. I'm staring at the outer dirt walls of what looks like a giant man-made lake or a volcano. The smoke issuing from the center is dark and oily.

There is a path up the side of the embankment, and recent, soggy footprints.

I climb through the last wreckage of the farm building, then up the loose dirt of the slope till I'm high enough to get a good view, but low enough to not be easily spotted from the other side.

I was wrong about the dirt wall. It's not a lake or a volcano. It's a crater, and in the center, protruding from the destroyed remains of the city beneath it, is something that can only be described as a spaceship. The essence of the vehicle is a huge sphere. The surface of the ship has been marred and gouged by the landing, and the exterior is rough, more planetoid than machine. Streaks of mud are spattered high up onto its forward face along with a few char marks, possibly from its entry into the atmosphere or some other contact with extreme heat. The back side of the sphere is further blackened, though this seems more deliberate, as the charring follows specific canals in the back hemisphere of the ship. I realize these might be exhaust trails from its engines.

My experience with outer space is not as limited as it once was. I've seen a bit more of it than I expected to, and witnessed the destruction of an entire space station, so I'm at least partly aware of what can go wrong. But this scene is a different manner of catastrophe. For one, I'm not looking at scattered wreckage. For the most part, this ship seems to have come down in one piece. What I take to be the nose section is burrowed into the earth and that is what has caused the crater, its sheer size plowing up whatever was in its path on landing.

It *has* landed, albeit badly, and its occupants apparently survived the ordeal because an access door on the lower side of the sphere has been opened to discharge them.

No one is exiting at the moment. It looks like the door has been open for a long time. The oily smoke billowing into the sky is pouring out of a vent in the topside of the ship. A ring around the circumference of the craft is glowing faintly—pulsing an occasional blue light. There is something very unstable about the way the light flickers.

In the space between my position and the spaceship, moving down the inside embankment and out into the center of the crater, is none other than my bearded quarry. Zurvan has his robes wrapped tightly around himself, almost as if he's cold. He is adding wood to a sort of campfire, built on a raised platform perhaps twenty yards from the exit of the ship. The wood smoke is joining with the plume from the ship and then blending with the dark clouds above.

The scene is oddly disjointed. Sinking behind a pile of rubble near the edge of the crater, I try to process what I'm seeing. He is clearly comfortable next to this ship. His behavior is not cautious or insecure. This is home for him.

Zurvan is a spaceman?

Zurvan looks Middle Eastern. Benny had mentioned Iraq or Iran, and he looks like he'd match that locale. More specifically, he seems like someone out of the distant past. I have a hard time reconciling his style of dress with anything modern, but the fact of this memory remains. He's seen the future. He's also talked to me in English and understood me when we spoke. That was an equally perplexing clue. Doctor Quickly once mentioned that a burka makes for the most universal garb, able to fit in across multiple centuries. As far as clothing styles go, Zurvan's layered robes are almost equally hard to pin to any one era.

My assumption is that he's a time traveler. A logical deduction since he ended up here in the first place. From what little I know of Neverwhere legends, it is supposed to be a place outside of time—not a spot the average person could accidentally wander into. Time travelers, on the other hand, toy with the bonds of reality every time they make a jump. According to

Doctor Quickly, improperly conducted time travel is the fastest way to an untimely demise, and a fate frequently met by the foolish.

So why haven't I run into more here?

The simplest answer could be that most incompetent time travelers are offing themselves in more definitive ways, fusing themselves into objects or failing at the normal laws of physics in more basic terms. It could also be that there are fewer people flinging themselves into the Neverwhere than suspected. Advances in Temprovibe technology used by most Grid travelers supposedly have safeguards against improper grounding. Assuming they work, that narrows candidates for the Neverwhere to analog travelers like me and whoever else from other eras might be capable of punching a hole in the fabric of time and falling out.

Benny fits into the analog category. Whatever method brought him here, it likely involved an improperly used chronometer.

It's also possible that there have been plenty of people who shared this fate and their memories simply do not overlap with mine. They're wandering other paths in the Neverwhere and I'll never run into them unless we stumble into a location we both feel like haunting concurrently.

There is of course the other, less pleasant option. It could be that I haven't run into other people here because someone got rid of them all.

Someone angry about being here.

Zurvan continues to feed the blaze, fanning the flames into higher and higher blooms of red and orange.

The presence of the spaceship completely throws off my sense of time when it comes to my enemy.

It's a big ship. Clearly technology centuries beyond my time. Whatever brought it here must have done so rather violently. Little about this scene denotes a pleasant arrival.

Zurvan is settling down next to the fire, kneeling and resting on his heels. For the moment I'm not worried about him seeing me. I'm hidden behind an outcropping of rubble, and nothing about his movements suggests he feels anything other than alone. He hasn't looked up or shown any suspicion about his surroundings. Perhaps no one has been bold enough to invade one of his memories before. He's calmly facing the fire and, after getting himself comfortable, he extends both hands—palms up— in front of himself. Next he begins to hum.

The only other time I've heard Zurvan making this noise, he turned the location into the desert shortly after. I brace myself against the bit of wall I'm leaned against, but keep my feet under me in the event things are about to change and I need to flee.

Something does alter itself, but it's not the scenery. Rather, the location hasn't been changed, but it *has* grown more vivid. Watching Zurvan's extended hands and the scene around him, I notice the shimmer of colors and realize what he's doing. He's opening a window to a specific time in this place, the way Benny did with my old kitchen in Oregon, and the way I've been doing in my apartment. He's visiting the real events of the past.

Time slowly washes over the scene, graying out the figure of Zurvan and bringing only the new view into focus. Looking down at my own body, I look washed out too.

In this vision of the past, the ship is in the same position, but the door is still closed. Fires are smoldering in the dirt and rubble around the ship. It looks as though it only recently landed. Zurvan's platform and fire are missing from this reality, but I can still see him faintly, the platform below him, a hazy shadow.

The door to the ship hisses and opens. I half expect a cloud of dry ice smoke to billow forth from inside the way it does in old sci-fi movies, but in this case, the only thing exiting is a battered and injured Zurvan. He stumbles down the ramp, one hand held to his bleeding head, loses his balance on the irregular footing, and falls. He makes one attempt to get up but collapses again. He lies in the dirt, not moving, for a long time.

The other Zurvan—the one in my world—is still on his knees, focusing on his fallen other self, concentrating on keeping the window of time open. As I observe the scene, the fires around the ship go out and the stars emerge in the sky. The sheer multitude of stars makes them brilliant. Despite the plume of smoke issuing from the ship, I can tell that this is a sky free of the normal light pollution in my era. This scene is unfolding in a century vastly different from my own.

What could be any amount of time later, depending on Zurvan's vision, the edge of the crater comes alive and I realize there are other people here with me.

I look on in amazement as a group of men and women in mismatched and battered clothing climb the outside of the crater and peer inside. One member of the group, a gray-bearded man with a walking staff, is standing quite near me, but it's clear that these people of the past can neither see nor interact with me. I am a ghost here. My dog may have been attuned to visitors from other times, but these people are oblivious to my spying.

The bravest of the bunch has climbed into the crater and is approaching the fallen form of this other real life Zurvan. She looks up at the ship, pausing to watch the flickering of lights around the perimeter of the ball, then creeps closer to the prostrate man. She has a hand on a weapon—a knife or shiv tucked into her belt, but she doesn't draw it. Instead, she gives Zurvan a swift kick in the thigh before bouncing back a few steps.

Zurvan doesn't stir.

Emboldened, the other half dozen members of the group descend into the crater and gather around. The young woman who arrived first has begun to search the body, squealing with glee when she discovers Zurvan's shiny blade tucked into his robes. One of the men near her tries to grab the weapon from her, but she jerks her own knife free from her belt and jabs the would-be thief's forearm, forcing him to lose his grip on the big knife and retreat, swearing and nursing his wound.

The young woman's eyes are shining with delight now as she straddles the body and waves her new acquisition through the air a few times. The blade shimmers in the starlight and the pulsing blue glow of the ship.

The whole scene is primal and baffling to the senses. I catch snippets of words from the group that I think I recognize, but the rest of their language is a garble of half words and sounds I don't understand. The old man who had stood closest to me is now next to the body. He places a hand to Zurvan's neck, probing for signs of life. Zurvan must still be alive because the old man gestures to a thick woman behind him and the two of them turn the body over. Together they begin to work on him, inspecting the wound on his head and dabbing at the blood.

The young woman with the knife has ignored their actions, apparently satisfied that there is nothing more to be gained from the body. Instead, she is now standing at the entrance to the spacecraft, gazing up the incline to the mouth of the ship. She sets a foot on the ramp, testing it, but retracts it almost immediately. It seems there are limits to her courage, and the doorway is at least temporarily beyond them. Instead of entering, she turns around and begins to gesticulate with the knife, pointing from one side of the ship to another. I don't understand her words, but it's clear from her gestures that she's claiming the ship for herself.

The others in the group, despite being more numerous, don't seem to challenge her claims. The man with the cut arm is scowling, but none of the others have objected. Instead, they begin to fan out around the ship, searching the ground for any other items of interest.

The meditating Zurvan in my world shifts his position slightly, then settles back onto his heels again, and the scene around us changes.

It's daylight. The crater has been vacated by all but three of the figures. The old man with the staff and the rotund woman who had helped him are assisting the now conscious figure of Zurvan toward the ship. Zurvan is skinnier and wearing bandages around his head and chest. He's no longer wearing his robes and is dressed only in loose-fitting trousers and a blanket. He's not wearing shoes and seems to have sprung directly from his sickbed to come here, despite the continued protestations of his nurses.

The old man is pleading with Zurvan to stop. I make out the words "madness" and "danger" in his entreaty. The woman is likewise babbling admonishments, but the most I make from her speech is the phrase "fool man."

Zurvan continues, despite their protest, until he's standing at the base of the crater. His eyes sweep over the exterior of the ship, analyzing the pulsing lights and continuously billowing smoke. Today the smoke cloud seems even worse than the night of the landing. I can't be sure if it's just the daylight allowing me to see better, but it seems as though the back of the ship has grown blacker and is radiating waves of heat that warp the atmosphere around it like a mirage. He mutters to himself and struggles forward amidst a new slew of protestations from his assistants. He's made it nearly to the ship's entrance when a shout makes him stop. He pauses and scowls.

The voice has echoed from the interior of the ship, and a moment later a figure descends the ramp. If it weren't for the seriousness of the expression on the young woman's face, I would be tempted to laugh. It's the same woman from the first memory who had claimed the ship, but now she has clearly explored the interior and proceeded to adorn herself with some of her findings.

I hadn't thought someone could wear insulation, but this woman has found a method. She's wrapped herself in what appears to be some kind of fire suppression blanket and is using it as a shiny cape. Her affinity for finery has not stopped there. Dangling around her neck is a bundle of wiring, capacitors, and salvaged colored light bulbs. Her head is perhaps the most entertaining. Her tangled hair has been adorned with metal spikes and thin, wiry devices that bounce and bop around her head like a technological mobile or a multitude of metallic antennae.

Zurvan takes in this new apparition without comment. As she descends the ramp, waving his knife and shouting, he lowers his hand from where he had been supporting his bandaged ribs and lets it dangle. I watch his fingers twitch, a gesture I recognize. The swaying of a cobra before the strike.

The woman dressed in spaceship doesn't seem to sense any threat. She continues to wave the knife around and gesture toward the edge of the crater, clearly telling the intruders to bugger off. Two more people descend the ramp behind her. Her chosen friends have likewise adorned themselves with knickknacks from the interior of the ship, though none quite as outrageously as their leader. I'm surprised to see that one of them is the guy whose arm she sliced in the initial scuffle. The dispute seems to have been settled for the cost of a few oddments of spacecraft interior and some assorted knobs and switches. He's toying with a bright red ball in his hand that looks like it might have once belonged on the end of an emergency lever.

I don't know if it is any one item in particular that has caught Zurvan's eye or merely the entire spectacle of the trio dressed in his ship's innards, but it clearly infuriates him. His arm flies forward and clenches air in front of him. A gesture I'm now familiar with. I cringe involuntarily as I wait for the worst, expecting one or all of the intruders to feel the pain in their minds that I've experienced. Instead, it's Zurvan who staggers. The exertion is too much for him and he groans, collapsing forward, caught awkwardly by his two companions who do their best to keep him from striking the ground face-first. The thick woman bears the brunt of Zurvan's weight, and she goes to one knee in trying to hold him up. The old man has hold of one elbow, but staggers himself and mostly makes the situation worse with his efforts.

Laughter erupts from the gangway of the ship. The newly glitzy space queen is roaring with glee. Whatever has happened to Zurvan is more than enough to please her, and the men behind her grin along. After a few moments, the three turn and disappear back inside.

Zurvan has a hand to his skull, and when he pulls it away, it's bloody. He considers his hand briefly, then collapses back onto his haunches, slumped partially against the old man. He is panting hard and it seems to be paining him just to breathe. Once the initial weakness passes, he puts a hand to the muddy earth and struggles to rise.

"You need to take me back," he says. "Tomorrow. Tomorrow I'll be better." He lets the big woman hoist him up by his arm and then rests it across her shoulder. He stretches his other hand to the old man's shoulder. "You will be rewarded. Both of you. You've helped me, and we'll still have time. Time enough to stop it."

The scene in the crater dims and fades, then grows lighter again, only to fade into darkness a second time. The clouds have returned, and if the sun is passing above them, it does so in secret. Night falls for a second and then a third day as Zurvan fast forwards through this memory. It's only on the fourth day that I see the living Zurvan return. Whatever rest he's had has done him good. He's still thin and a bit pale, but not nearly as pallid as he once was. He's donned his robes again, giving him the illusion of added bulk, and he's walking without assistance.

The area around the spaceship door has been littered with debris. Cargo from the ship has been dragged out and rummaged through, only to be discarded to the dirt. Zurvan doesn't pay any attention to the mess, he keeps his eyes fixed on the gangway to the ship and, when he's within a dozen yards of it, he stops and shouts toward the open doorway.

"Datrica! Come out."

When nothing happens he shouts louder. "DATRICA!"

It takes a few minutes, but something finally stirs inside the ship and a figure stumbles down the gangway. It's not the woman. Not Datrica. It's Arm Wound Guy. His upper lip is curled back, showing not quite enough teeth to be called a smile. He grins his less than toothy grin and makes a gesture toward Zurvan that I guess is something disrespectful. It's a sort of pushing motion using three fingers and a thumb and hooking upward and then down. The last move lands the hand back at his groin which he grabs. A crude maneuver he might have thought better of if he ever got the chance. He doesn't, because a rock flies out of Zurvan's hand and strikes the man squarely in the face. A festive spurt of blood erupts from the man's nose as he tumbles backward and collapses in a heap.

The speed of the action shocks me. I had expected some sort of conflict, but the sudden bloodletting has taken me by surprise. Zurvan strides over to the man's fallen form and looks down on him with a sneer.

"I could have robbed you of your mind, but who would want it?" A moment later, he ascends the ramp into the ship.

The Zurvan in the Neverwhere rises from his knees and strides forward, ascending the ramp behind his real life counterpart and disappearing into the spaceship.

I've lost all sense of time while watching this memory unfold. Perhaps it's the timelessness of the Neverwhere in general, but I've faded into the background as I viewed it, absorbing each new scene, enraptured as much by its twists and turns as by any Hollywood film. Likely more so.

I wait.

I hear voices. Datrica. She's talking loudly and then yelling. Something crashes solidly and likely painfully into someone. There is a groan and a clatter. I'm frozen, unable to move. Datrica screams. Someone else shouts and then is promptly silenced.

I want to know what happens.

Cautiously, ever so cautiously, I creep forward down the inside of the crater. I keep my eyes fixed on the door of the ship. With each step I expect to see Zurvan reappear and accost me, but as I near the side of the craft, it becomes clear that I'm going to make it. I race up to the ship and hide under the boarding ramp. Zurvan hasn't seen me.

Cautiously, I peer over the angled ramp, into the interior of the ship. From this angle I can see a corridor that rims the outside of the ship. It's vacant.

Frustrated, I step around the ramp and carefully climb up it. The corridor on one side dead-ends leaving only the path toward the rear of the ship. I proceed quietly along it, watching for the first sign of my enemy. The corridor opens up into a larger room at the back of the huge sphere. Zurvan is there—closer now—kneeling again, facing away from me, still meditating this memory into existence.

His other living self is standing stock still at the center of the room.

Datrica is dead.

A pool of blood oozes out from beyond her prone figure. Due to the direction she's laying, I can't see her face, and I'm glad because what I can see in the vicinity of where her face likely ought to be, is the handle of Zurvan's knife protruding toward the ceiling of the room.

I ought to be disgusted. I ought to be sickened or terrified, but what I am instead is awed, because beyond the standing figure of Zurvan is quite possibly the most beautiful thing I have ever laid eyes on.

There is a crack in a machine. The crack is likely not a good thing and based on Zurvan's rigid posture and shaking hands, I don't think he is happy about it. That doesn't make it any less beautiful. To say the crack was leaking colors would be too plain. It isn't spewing rainbows. A rainbow by comparison would seem bland and mundane. The Northern Lights might be a better approximation, if the Northern Lights came in colors that defied explanation.

Perhaps it's the fact that I'm dead. I'm seeing things I'm not sure my living eyes would have been able to comprehend. Colors that move like sound. Singing colors leaking in and out of the crack in the machine. A blended reality where terms like harmony and melody could apply to a visual spectrum. Because I am not looking at one color or twenty, I might be looking at all colors, but only if all colors never ended in their variation.

It's awe inspiring.

Zurvan flinches. The living one. Someone else is here. Up the gangway stairs behind me, the old man and the thick woman are helping one another climb inside. I duck sideways, out of sight of the Neverwhere Zurvan, in case he turns his head. The old man and the woman shuffle down the corridor, then cross in front of me, unable to see me, and wait, keeping a respectful distance from their patient. Both of them have seen Datrica. I can tell in their body language the moment they lay eyes on her, even viewing them from behind, but they don't cry out or scream. I suspect Zurvan told them what was going to happen and, whatever their connection to Datrica was, they were willing to sacrifice it.

The living Zurvan finally pulls his eyes away from the luminescent brilliance of the crack in the machine. He turns around and faces his companions. His expression is a mask of determination spread thinly over something darker. *Fear?*

He moves to the fallen form of Datrica, pulls his curved knife loose, and wipes it on her clothing. Next he walks toward the duo in the hall.

"What'll ya do now, sir?" the old man stammers.

"It's too late," Zurvan replies. "It's already begun to open." He sweeps past the pair, his cloak billowing out behind him. He passes in front of me, and descends the gangway. "We'll start again."

When the three are gone, it's only the ghost Zurvan who remains. He's still kneeling, facing away from me and, from my position behind him, I can't tell if his eyes are open or closed. If they are open, they are staring into the crack in the machine. He's humming again. Humming into the light.

Singing to the void.

Cornwall, UK, 2165

This is my second experience riding in a driverless car and, like the first time, I'm totally clueless about how to use it. Tucket has given it some guidance via the metaspace and the vehicle seems happy to comply, but I couldn't begin to direct it myself. There are a few handles and knobs that look like emergency systems, but nothing lends itself to steering or even tuning the radio. It makes me wonder how I would survive in this decade without Tucket's help.

"I guess they don't design these for old school time travelers," I say. "I'd never get out of the parking lot without a perceptor."

Tucket processes what I've said, but then turns to the back of the seat and pops a panel loose. "Actually they do. They put a meta headset in here as a backup, in case someone is having issues with theirs." He extracts a contraption that looks like a pair of sunglasses mated with orthodontic head gear, and hands it to me.

"I can wear this?" I fiddle with the unit, finagling it over my eyes and ears.

Tucket makes an adjustment for me and nods. "Yeah. That will work for you. Most people don't like them though. You never really know who used them last. Kind of like playing pathogen roulette."

I stare at him. "You tell me this now?"

He rummages around in the seat some more and comes up with some antibacterial hand wipes. "Oh. Here you go."

I swipe the towelette out of his hand and rip the head gear off my head to get it clean. Tucket watches me for a moment, then hands me three more wipes.

Seated in the comfortable, rear-facing seat, I adjust to watching the world vanish behind me. It seems to parallel my life at the moment, blindly racing into the future while everything I've ever known vanishes into the past behind me. As the car makes its way onto the super expressway, the view out the window becomes a nerve-wracking blur. Tucket dims the windows on his side and slouches in the chair diagonal to me, eyes focused on some distant or imagined horizon.

I get the headset clean and readjust it, watching the horizon populate itself with images and streaming messages. I'm able to select different buildings and learn about them. I can follow links on virtual billboards to interactive websites, I can even select the vehicles around us to send them messages or learn about their occupants. The nicer looking cars are registered to individual owners and much of their information is private, but there are plenty of other public vehicles.

One car full of kids in the parallel lane sends me a chat invitation full of wiggling animal emoticons. When I click on it, the emoticons come alive and bounce around inside the car, cats chasing monkeys and some sort of green ogre that stops every few seconds to blow its nose. The kids in the car are laughing and pointing. Finally one of their parents notices what they've done and makes them close the link between our cars. The car settles back to normal.

Tucket watches me, an expression of benevolent amusement on his face, like a parent watching a child playing with a new toy. After fiddling with the other functions for a few minutes, I finally remove the headset and set it on the seat beside me. Tucket is studying a stain on the rubberized floor.

"Tucket, do you mind if I ask you a question? What is it about my time that made you want to come visit so badly? I look at all you've got here, the technology and the sustainability and stuff, it seems like a pretty sweet setup."

Tucket frowns, but seems to be taking the question seriously. He thinks about it briefly before responding. "My roommate during my first year at the Academy used to tell me that I was an idealist. He said I only saw what I wanted to see in the world and couldn't see the reality of things. He was wrong, though. I did see." His gaze drifts out the shaded windows. "I know I'm lucky. It's pretty baller to be born in a decade when I was. My dad wanted me to go into metaspace engineering. He says that's where all the money is these days. That's why he first sent me to school back in England. But I wanted something more . . . legit."

"Legit in what way?"

"When I was young I used to visit my grandmother in her flat in Brighton. Dad had us living in the US, but we came back a lot to visit. I loved it. She had this library full of old books. Real paper books, you know? And one she had was all about the millennium and the people who lived then. It was my favorite book. It had so many great stories. People being real. It was so important then, you know? I mean that was when people even started making TV about reality instead of just making stuff up. It was almost like you could be a part of someone's family, even if you didn't know them. I thought that was really cool."

"Uh, I don't know that you want to base your concept of the millennium on reality TV. I don't think the people making those shows were exactly about authenticity."

"They weren't?"

"Well, I suppose there might have been a few. I can't say as I watch a lot of them."

"I just think it would be so righteous to live in a time when people are so open that they'll let you watch cameras right in their houses. In their real lives! Not even avatars. I heard that people in the twentieth century never even had to lock their doors. I think people were nicer then. We didn't have any of this discrimination against synthetic intelligence yet. No synthetic intelligence existed, so I think it would have been cool to live in a time where that wasn't an issue."

I consider whether or not I should burst Tucket's bubble. He seems so determined to idolize that society.

"You know, Tucket. It's funny because a lot of people in my time like to get nostalgic for the 1950s or the 1920s. Some love the 1980s—"

"For Motley Crue, right? Sex, drugs, and rock and roll?"

"Uh. No, not necessarily, but I'm sure there are a few . . . I think people just like looking back at times they thought were simpler. It gets complicated though. In the U.S., anyway. The '50s might have seemed cool, but not if you were black or gay or pretty much anything other than white. The '20s were worse, especially for women, and the whole century pretty much smelled like an ashtray through the '70s. Every decade had its problems. It wasn't all glamorous."

Tucket considers me across the car. "But you were all still human. That was something. Now half the people I know are already trans-humans. I hear the farther you go into the future, the more trans-humans start going fully synthetic. As time travelers, we're not supposed to reveal the future to other people in this century. It's part of our Academy oath, but sometimes I feel like shouting it out the windows, to warn everyone that we're losing all the regular humans.

"But I don't think anyone would listen anyway. Trans-humans get all the best jobs now. Everyone wants to be smarter and stronger and live longer. Everybody has the best health implants. I hear in a few years they want to make them mandatory. They're going to put Vax plugs in everybody so you can update all your vaccinations and do cancer screenings and heart disease checks while you sleep."

"I've seen a few trans-humans. It's all about better organs and stuff, right?"

"Sort of. It's more than that though. Companies like Ambrose Cybergenics started getting into body augmentation, but it was the metaspace and the advent of the synths that started changing things. Third Eye, the company that invented the perceptor, kept working on new ways to make the human brain work faster. It got a lot of support because people were worried that synths would somehow take over if they got too smart. Synths can process data so much faster than a human brain. The government came up with strict laws about regulating synth intelligence. They put limits on synthetic brain development. But some people have found ways to work around it, especially when Third Eye found ways to put the same improvements in humans. They claimed it would level the playing field and keep humans and synths equal.

"The first synths had a lot of limitations with their bodies needing maintenance, so there were far more advantages to being human, but the more synths developed, the better they became at adapting. When the metaspace came along, people interacted via avatars most of the time anyway. People stopped caring as much about whether the mind of the person they were interacting with belonged to an organic human or a synth. A lot of the old rules still exist to regulate the synth workforce, but support for those laws is eroding quickly. In a couple of decades, the limits on synth memory reclamation and processing speed are going to go away. It's a major victory for synth rights, but regular humans aren't going to be able to keep up. It even gets hard for trans-humans. If you don't have money for upgrades, or work for a company that is willing to pay for them, it's really hard to make a good living."

I consider what it would be like to try to compete with a robot for a job. "I can see how having synth employees could be a big advantage for a company. They don't really need to sleep or eat, right? They could probably get a ton of work done in a day."

"There are still some really human jobs." Tucket explains. "Creative arts are big for organics. Acting, music, that sort of thing. But even that is getting harder. There are some amazing synth composers. I think actors will hold out for a while, but even most of those have gone trans-human. They don't want to age. They are usually the first adopters of image enhancements. They sort of have to." He smiles wanly, as if to excuse their vanity as understandable given the circumstances.

Looking out the window at the glistening spires of buildings on the horizon, I get a new appreciation for what a foreign world I'm in. I recall being incredibly impressed by the massive farm towers in London the last time I visited. The world was making massive strides toward ending hunger and waste. Man's impact on the environment had been vastly improved by innovation and smarter technology. As I listen to Tucket explain more of the logistics of an increasingly synthetic society, I'm forced to contemplate what the advances have cost us.

"Have you taken any trips forward in time since you graduated from the

Academy?" I ask. "Have you gone to see what the world is like up there?"

"I just know what I've learned from alternate history classes and what I've heard from friends. When I got infused as a time traveler, the trip to see you was the first one I wanted to take."

I recall Tucket's jubilant expression when I found him on my doorstep, his beaming face and mismatched clothing. "Your vacation hasn't exactly gone according to plan, huh? I'm sorry I didn't get a chance to take you around my century. You finally got your dream trip to the past, and I dragged you right back to the time you left."

Tucket folds his hands in his lap and sinks a little lower in his chair. "I guess sometimes life has other plans. But when your friends need your help, you can't very well say no. I think saving Mym is more important than meeting Marilyn Monroe."

I settle into my chair a little deeper too. "Well, if I haven't said it enough, I'm glad you came to see me. It's not everybody who will travel across centuries to visit. And not everybody would head into danger to save someone they barely know. You're a great friend."

Tucket smiles, and this time it shows on his whole face.

We both go back to looking out the windows at the blur of the countryside. My personal outlook is daunting, and I have no idea what we might be heading into, but the talk has given me hope. For all the alterations going on in the future and the changes to mankind in this century, it can't all be bad because there was at least enough good in humanity that it produced Tucket.

Leaned back against the headrest, I close my eyes, doing my best to imagine myself somewhere other than a vehicle doing 400kph down a super highway. I wrap my arms across my chest and try to relax, but my mind flashes through the memories from last night, Mym's terrified eyes as she was held by the hulking Eternals. Sadly, it was not unlike the expression she had when I was shaking her myself. Or the possessed version of me.

If I think about it, I can still feel the other minds, the way they battled inside my brain, taking away control. The feeling was so abhorrent. One chasing her, one fighting hard to stop. *The third me.* He was the one who took control, stopped whatever had me. Just thinking about it, it's almost as if I can still sense him, lingering in the back of my mind, trying to make contact. He was scared too. Frightened for Mym, worried what might become of her. We are the same there. Both wanting so badly to keep her safe, but failing.

Keep her safe. Isn't that what he had tried to tell me at the Academy? He warned me something bad was going to happen to Mym. It didn't help.

As I remember him, I can nearly see him again. A version of me yelling for my attention. He's worried. Something is after him out there. Something dangerous that wants to consume him. I've felt this before. During the race. During my dreams. It's as if there is just the thinnest distance between us. No distance at all really. He's here, in a car racing down the expressway toward London. I'm there in a ravaged city, staring at the fragments of St. Petersburg. Rotting spires of a ruined future. Looking at a crater glowing with fire. I feel the heat. I can smell the smoke.

My eyes fly open and I jolt upright in my seat.

No.

That was too real.

Tucket is staring at me. "Are you okay?"

"No. Not really." The vision retreats reluctantly from my mind. I block it out, forcing myself to concentrate on the impending skyline growing closer. Not ruins. Not St. Petersburg. I'm not in the Neverwhere. I am alive.

I get another involuntary chill down my spine.

It's getting closer.

He's getting closer.

Whatever is changing, it's getting easier for him to get inside my mind. Or I'm getting into his. *Do you make contact with ghosts because you are closer to becoming one?* Frightened alert by the prospect, I sit up straight in my seat.

I am not a ghost. I am alive.

The solution is clear. If he gets into my head when I close my eyes, then I have to stay awake. I won't lose my chance to save her again. Mym needs me.

The sun is high. Plenty of daylight left. Plenty of time.

I'll stay awake.

Central London is every bit as impressive as I recall. Standing at a street corner in Covent Garden, admiring the facades of shops and restaurants that have been preserved from prior centuries, it's clear that not all of the populace has sprinted into the future. Despite the massive glass towers that have sprung up in the vicinity, old relics like the Apple Market have remained. We walk through the open plaza and into the sunlit, glass-covered market that still houses stalls and vendors of all sorts, though the wares offered seem to have evolved greatly since my century.

The most significant change to the populace I've noticed in this era is a trend of minimalism. Owning and carrying physical items seems to have gone out of style. The people in the plaza are dressed for warm weather, mostly shorts or lightweight trousers with loose-fitting cotton shirts over top. Hardly anyone is carrying a bag or a purse. Even pockets seem to be rare. One young man with long curly hair has his hands in pockets in his pants, but there are holes in the fabric where his fingers protrude back to the outside. It seems they are merely there as a place to put his hands and wouldn't be capable of containing money or any other trinkets. The digital ether of the metaspace has freed them from debit cards, keys, and cell phones.

While some here have gone to elaborate lengths to improve their looks—trans-human updates and cosmetic surgeries—other folks don't seem to have spent a great deal of effort on their appearance at all. Their metaspace avatar identities have picked up the slack for their outward image.

I wonder if my own attire of blue jeans with pockets, and messenger bag hung over my shoulder strikes them the same way I would view some medieval tinker or perhaps a Victorian gentleman newly arrived in 2009. I'm certainly out of place.

There are a few people carrying bags of produce, and one wrinkled old man snoozing on a bench cradling a decrepit paperback, but for the most part, people seem to shy away from taking possession of anything that might weigh them down. Even the entertainment lacks physical form. A group of pedestrians are gathered around a man in the plaza, ooh-ing and ahh-ing over his performance, but when I finally catch a glimpse of the performer, he's merely staring up into the sky with occasional faint gestures of one hand.

The vendor stalls are perhaps the most perplexing. There are some collections of antiques and a florist that don't seem out of place, but a great many of the spaces inside the market host either a human or a synth proprietor without seeming to have anything else to offer. This fact does not seem to be diminishing their business or the amount of traffic they receive. To the contrary, some of the most barren stations are the most active.

Passing through the market, I do my best to decipher the different themes of the stalls. I know that if I were able to view them in the metaspace, I would see the full effect of their advertising. Even so, I feel like I ought to be able to identify the wares from the vendors themselves.

Some stalls are manned by characters I recognize, young, eager artist types whom I could envision selling homemade necklaces or optimistic paintings back home. Other, less inspired-looking individuals I could imagine manning mall kiosks full of mobile phone cases or gold plated jewelry, but, unlike in my time, there seems to be little need for those sorts of tchotchkes. There are no bumper stickers sporting humorous quotes. No magnets or key chains. The closest thing I can see that might fit in the category of tourist bait are a few colorful hand towels and blankets with screen printed slogans that a woman and her daughter are selling from their booth near the end of the row. Most booths are stark and bare, even though the conversation would suggest otherwise.

"Ooh, I just love that one!" A woman exclaims, gesturing at thin air as I pass by. The proprietor of the space nods knowingly and begins to gesture animatedly as he describes the hard work that went into his non-existent bit of nothing.

Tucket is smiling at the scene in the market, occasionally stopping to peer at a particular table or stand, but then wandering back to me. It's clear that I am the odd man out once again, missing the majority of the happenings around me due to my handicap.

I console myself with the knowledge that I am here for a purpose. Somewhere amid this chaos, we are getting closer to Doctor Quickly's safe house. The directions he left me on Mym's phone have guided us to this point, and from here we are supposed to make contact with someone Doctor Quickly trusts. So far, our mysterious rendezvous has not occurred, and I do my best to look casual as we wait.

Catching a whiff of something salty, I spy a man with bushy eyebrows handing a foil wrapped packet to a woman in a yellow sun dress. He's manning a pedal cart at the end of the row nearest the open plaza and evidently his cart is filled with potential lunch. My hunger guides me over to him and I study the outside of the silver-sided cart with interest.

"What are you selling today?"

The man appraises me with curiosity. His deep-set eyes peer over a slightly arched nose and a billowy, salt and pepper mustache only slightly less unruly than his eyebrows. "World's best gyros. My own recipe. Best you've ever tasted."

"Gyros, huh? What kind of options?"

"You didn't read the specials?" He gestures to the side of the cart. I see nothing. "One hundred and one regular options and a gyro of the day." With his last comment, he stabs a finger toward the empty space above his cart.

I'm about to explain that I don't have a perceptor, but Tucket jumps in for me.

"He's eyeless. No meta."

"Oh. Sorry to hear that," the vendor replies, shaking his head. "Tough life for you. You sick? You know, up there? Got an infection?" He taps his forehead.

"Um, no. Just not up to speed on technology here."

"Not from the commune are you? Regressionist type?" He appraises my blue jeans cynically. "You look like a regressionist."

"He's actually *from* the past," Tucket explains. "Time traveler. I'm showing him around."

"Ah. Are you now? Never seen one of you up close." The man looks me up and down again, then apparently deciding I'll do, reaches into his cart and hands me a foil packet with a bar coded label affixed to it. "Welcome to the future. That'll be fifteen quid."

I fumble for my wallet, knowing full well I've got nothing remotely resembling British currency. I've got my wallet out of my pocket anyway, when Tucket pats my arm.

"I took care of it for you." He collects a foil wrapped packet for himself and smiles when he peels back the wrapper. "Oh, these are the best." He then wanders off toward the next stall.

It's only then that I recall that physical money has gone out anyway and I wouldn't have been able to use cash if I wanted to. I catch up to Tucket as I'm unwrapping my gyro. "Thanks, man. I'll pay you back." Looking inside the packet, my heart sinks.

The pita is barely warm and the contents look nothing like gyro meat or tzatziki sauce. What I have instead, is a greenish looking solid, flaked into pieces with a splatter of brownish paste. I take a whiff, and it smells nothing like a gyro either.

"Hey man, what is this?" I hold my foil-wrapped mystery food out for Tucket's inspection.

"Oh, yeah. You're only going to see the texture base. His special recipe is all meta toppings and flavors."

"What does that mean? There's no gyro to this gyro?"

"No. That's a plant-based protein patty. It's pretty much the staple base for all the simulated meta meat textures."

"What happened to real meat? I mean, I know gyro meat was always kind of questionable anyway, but it was mostly beef and lamb in my time. At least that's what they told us."

Tucket takes a bite of his meta gyro and chews thoughtfully. He wipes away the bit of sauce from his lips with his napkin and nods. "Most people are on a plant-based diet now. More sustainable and better for your health."

"You're telling me the world went vegan?" I frown and stare at the odd-looking veggie patty in my hand. "Did people forget how delicious meat was?"

"It was more complicated than that," Tucket explains. "There were always people claiming that plant-based diets were healthier, and no one really argued, but that wasn't changing anyone's minds. It wasn't until later, when the same research company that made the perceptor—Third Eye—ran a bunch of food simulations in the metaspace, that people started considering switching diets."

"Imaginary food?" I ask.

"Sort of." Tucket replies. "Third Eye invented some custom food app algorithms and gave them away for free to developers. People started making their own meta recipes, and if you used them, you could make almost anything taste amazing every time. There were some really famous blind taste test competitions where people would pit their meta recipes against famous chef's dishes and see which ones people would pick. It was really popular entertainment for a while.

"Using food apps got so routine that people began to prefer their favorite meta food recipes over restaurant food. Of course certain recipes got copyrighted by chefs and restaurants who could afford to keep them proprietary, and they keep customers coming that way, but lots of amateurs gave their food apps away for free or sold them cheap. Made cooking healthy way easier."

With both hands full of his gyro, Tucket gestures toward the people around us with an elbow. "After that, people didn't really care whether their food was plant-based or not. It all tasted like what they wanted to eat anyway. In the metaspace you might be eating a bunch of chili fries or a pile of nachos, and in reality you actually ate a dish of kale chips. People got a lot healthier from it."

"Wow." I stare at my gyro with new interest.

"We used to have an obesity problem here. Not as bad as in the US, but it was getting out of hand. The metaspace really made a big difference. Made food cheaper, too. Maybe not here." He glances around the trendy market. "But worldwide food prices have gone way down. And we can grow lots of the food locally without needing as much grazing land."

I take a tentative bite of the veggie gyro. Surprisingly, it's not terrible. Tastes like a chunk of congealed bean salad, and nothing like lamb or beef, but it's edible. After a few bites, I actually lose my trepidation. I jerk my thumb back toward the vendor we left behind. "Is his meta recipe any good?"

Tucket gnaws off another bite and bobs his head. "Totally triumphant."

I smile and follow Tucket as we continue our way through the market, doing our best to look nonchalant while keeping an eye out for our contact. We wander toward the wall that adjoins to the next vendor space and I lean against a pillar to finish off my food.

I've kept the directions in Doctor Quickly's message discreet, letting Tucket use the public car to get us close, then walking the rest of the way here to the market. It seemed a bad idea to give the address of Quickly's safe house directly to the car's navigation system. It turns out Doctor Quickly was a step ahead. The address was a public market and we had another hoop to jump through anyway.

True to form, Doctor Quickly has hidden his safe space somewhere in plain sight, but inaccessible. After I toss my foil wrapper in the nearby trash can, I pull the phone back out of my jeans pocket and consult the message, seeing if I can glean any more information from it.

There's a new message on the phone.

This time I have more specific instructions for getting to Doctor Quickly's safe house. I nudge Tucket and gesture for him to follow me. The directions tell us to head upstairs to a shop with a red door, called Glintings, and ask for someone named Masie. We locate the tiny shop and enter, setting a little string of glass bells to tinkling on the door handle. The musical chime seems out of place among the modern conveniences outside.

The interior of the shop features a preponderance of glassware and mirrors. The shopkeeper greets us with a smile, and I'm surprised to notice she's a trans-human. The woman's voluminous hair and petite ears surround a face that defies age. If I had to guess from her hands, I'd think she was in her sixties, but the lines around her eyes have been smoothed away and her cheeks and forehead are devoid of wrinkles, leaving her in a sort of temporal limbo, somewhere between youth and seniority.

"Are you Masie?" I ask, praying I got the pronunciation right.

"You must be Alice," the woman replies.

I frown. "My name's actually—"

"Right this way, darling." Masie steps out from behind the counter and gestures for me to follow.

At the rear of the shop, she points toward one of the mirrors leaned against the back wall. It's fitted into an ornate wooden frame. At the top, a clock has been set into the wood with the words "It's Always Tea Time" inscribed beneath it. I notice the clock is broken. A yellow tag on a string has the word 'sold' printed in big block letters. Underneath is a check box marked 'Ready for delivery.'

"He said you'd know what to do," Masie says.

"Who did?"

"Him." She points to a smudge on the mirror. At first I think she's pointing to my reflection, but then I realize the smudge is actually a fingerprint. Without another word, Masie turns and walks away, back to tending her counter.

Tucket watches her go nervously. "Is she not going to help us find Doctor Quickly?"

I run my hand over the edge of the mirror and pause near the fingertip smudge on the glass. "I think she did."

Tucket's gaze flits around the mirror, searching for something to land on. "I don't think her instructions were explicit enough. We need further guidance. Should I go back and ask her?"

Staring at my reflection in the mirror, I notice I've developed a decent black eye from my bout with The Eternals. I'm looking rather rough altogether. It's as though this experience has already added a few years to my appearance.

"I don't think it will help, Tuck. Doctor Quickly tends to do this sort of thing from time to time. I don't think he means to be obscure necessarily, it's just that he assumes the best of everyone and imagines they'll be able to take the same leaps that his mind makes. It's a problem scientific geniuses seem to suffer from."

"But he didn't give us enough data to go on," Tucket says. "Even as a scientist."

I reach for my chronometer and dial the settings. "Actually he gave us just enough." I point toward the top of the mirror.

Tucket follows my gesture to the broken clock, that reads 4:15. "Ohhh. You mean the time is up there for us to use? How do we know if that's morning or afternoon?"

"I'm guessing afternoon, because that's more likely to be tea time." I nod toward the Mad Hatter quote. "Lewis Carroll not withstanding. Grab on to me." I place my chronometer hand to the glass over top of Doctor Quickly's fingertip smudge, wait till Tucket grabs my arm, and then press the pin on my chronometer. We blink.

We arrive inside a dim, musty room and drop a couple of inches onto a carpeted floor. The mirror in front of us has been set on a stack of hardback books, allowing us enough clearance to arrive safely and not fuse ourselves into the carpet. The yellow sold tag on the mirror is still dangling from the corner, but I notice a new check box has been marked on it, saying 'delivered.' Though where we've been delivered to remains to be discovered.

We're in a sort of parlor. The room has windows, but the curtains are still drawn, leaving us in dusty twilight. The furniture is covered with sheets with the exception of the chairs around a dining room table in the next room. A single lamp above the dining room table has been lit, beckoning us closer. As I near the table, a door to the far side, presumably from the kitchen, swings open and disgorges perhaps the last thing I would have expected, Carson, bearing a tea tray. He spots me and smiles. "Hey, dude."

"Uh, hey, man," I reply. "What are you doing here?"

Carson sets the tray on the table and walks over to shake my hand. "Been with the Doc the whole time." We slap each other on the back and he waves to Tucket. "What's up, Tucket?" When he turns back to me his face is serious. "Hey. So sorry, man. I heard about Mym. Doctor Quickly told me— whoa, did they do that to your eye?"

I brush my fingertips over the swelling, wishing I could wipe it away. "I'm fine. Is Doctor Quickly here?"

"Yeah, he'll be right in."

Footsteps sound in the hallway behind a second doorway and the door swings open to reveal Doctor Quickly, dressed in dark slacks and a tweed jacket. He immediately moves to me and presses both of his hands over mine. "Benjamin. It's good to see you." He releases my hand and rests a palm on my shoulder. "It's been a horrible day for you, I'm sure. Please. Come sit down. I had Carson whip you up some tea. Thought it might bolster you up."

"That's nice of you, thanks. But I think I'm fine. I just want to talk to you about Mym. It was my fault she got abducted. I should have been more vigilant. We just need to find a way—"

"We will," Doctor Quickly says. "Don't worry, Ben. We will."

I do my best to accept his assurances and sit down as he gestures to the chairs. Tucket and Carson likewise take seats.

"Did you bring their message?" Doctor Quickly asks.

I reach into my pocket and slide the small black square across the table to the scientist. Doctor Quickly scoops it up and holds it in his palm. Pulling a pair of reading glasses from his jacket pocket, he places them on his nose to further study the device. In that moment he seems to embody the past, a bespectacled man in a house full of dusty antiques, attempting to decipher a mysterious bit of high tech future gadgetry. But, disproving the image almost immediately, the device springs to life under his touch and he maneuvers his way through the contents without effort.

I watch his expression, waiting to see if the news will evoke some drastic emotion, but after a moment he simply removes the glasses from his nose and slips them back into his breast pocket. He takes a seat and pours himself a cup of tea.

"So what did they say?"

Doctor Quickly slides his teacup toward himself and rests his fingertips on the saucer. "What I feared it would."

"Are they threatening Mym?"

"Quite certainly."

"What are their ransom demands?"

"Unfortunately, they are not asking for a ransom. Mym was their objective and it seems they intend to make use of her. They are asking me for something else that I'm quite reluctant to give."

"What?" Carson asks, leaning forward onto his elbows. "They want chronometers or something?"

I'm equally curious, though daunted by Doctor Quickly's statement. He leans back in his chair and sighs. "They want me to show them the way to the Alpha."

Tucket has his head cocked to one side, considering the statement. Carson and I are both clearly in the dark, so I'm about to ask the obvious follow up question, but Doctor Quickly continues without being prompted.

"The Alpha Prime is believed to be the core of the central timestreams. It's the time before there was time travel. Some believe that if one were to travel back in time far enough, they could find an entirely unadulterated timestream, one in which time travel hasn't ever existed. The beginning, if you will."

"What would be the advantage to that?" I ask.

"That's a good question," Doctor Quickly replies. "One would wonder at the motivation for finding it. I certainly question what The Eternals want the information for.

"In the past, I've had plenty of contact from various parties, wanting access to my original timestream. ASCOTT has requested the information numerous times for different reasons. Many less reputable persons have sought me out as well. You met some of those on your chronothon adventure. The people who wish to use that knowledge are rarely motivated by the best of intentions. Even if they were, I wouldn't give it to them."

"There's no one you trust?" Carson asks.

"There are a few people I trust. But it doesn't make a difference. You can't give what you don't have. I could certainly give them my original timestream if I was out of my senses for some reason. If I was tortured or under duress, or just somehow decided to give the information up on my own. But it wouldn't help them. My original timestream still wouldn't give them the Alpha."

"There is no true Alpha?" Tucket suggests.

Doctor Quickly shakes his head. "The Alpha exists, but I'm not from there, because I'm not the original Harold Quickly."

I size up the man before me. In a way I've always known there were more than one of him. I've met him at various times in his life and had to figure out which era of his life I belonged in. At least a few versions of him had died before Mym and I found the way to save him. I knew that he was a variation of himself, the same way I am now. But I hadn't imagined that this Doctor Quickly I saved wasn't the "real" Doctor Quickly to begin with either.

"So you weren't the one who originally discovered time travel?" I ask.

"I most certainly did," Doctor Quickly replies. "It was my life's work. The problem was, I wasn't the only one." He spreads his hands out on the table. "Let me see if I can explain." He takes a sip of his tea and then continues.

"You see, we Quicklys aren't fools. When the original version of me—let's call him Quickly Alpha for our purposes—when he first jumped though time, it was an accident. It was amazing, but it was unexpected.

"He was ill prepared, but he wasn't an idiot. He knew what had happened. As a scientist he knew the potential repercussions of tampering with time. He was familiar with all the grandfather paradoxes and theories floating around about what might happen if you changed your own timeline. He may have been an accidental time traveler, but he was determined not to make more mistakes and further complicate the issue. It was a dangerous situation and he was doing his best not to interfere with his own timeline, thinking that it led to his continued existence. Unfortunately, there was an alternative problem he didn't fully consider. By *not* changing the timeline, he created a new dilemma.

"You see, he had been operating on the assumption that time was linear. He didn't yet have the evidence to prove that he was in fact now in a parallel timestream—not the one he originally left. His original timestream—the Alpha— was still in existence, but devoid of one scientist. He had now added himself to a different timestream—Timestream Beta. And by not stopping the events that sent him back in time in the first place, the events were doomed to repeat themselves.

"In the worst scenario, Quickly Beta would have landed in the exact spot Alpha landed and been killed instantly by fusing into himself. Fortunately, Quickly Alpha *did* tamper with the timeline of events unintentionally, changing the events just enough that Quickly Beta went back in time, likewise found himself in a parallel timestream, and set about repeating the entire process over again. Left unchecked, there could have begun an infinite repetition of timestreams from that one event."

"Ah," I say. "That's why in my timestream, the November Prime, you went missing as well. I always wondered how that could be if you weren't originally from there."

"Yes, unfortunately it did take us a couple of false starts to finally stop the cycle of repetition. We ended up with quite a few despite our best efforts. Some ended themselves, because of the fusion issues, but fortunately, after each repetition, those of us who survived all came to the same conclusion about needing to fix the problem. Even though the timestreams were multiplying, the potential solutions were too. Quickly Alpha figured out how to transfer streams and showed up in each one of the other times to try to stop the repetition. If it didn't work, he'd take the Harry Quickly from that stream with him to try to solve the next one.

"With more of us on the task, we ultimately were able to stop some of the alternate Harrys from ever traveling in time." He points to Carson and me in turn. "The timestream you two ended up in during your first adventure, the Lima stream, was one in which we successfully stopped a repetition."

"So if you created a bunch of versions of yourself by accident, how did you figure out which one of you was the first?" Carson asks.

"For one, he was the first one to show up in another stream. It changed his timestream frequency somewhat, the signature of the gravitite particles inside him, and we could use that to differentiate each other. That's what inspired us to develop the temporal spectrometer. Once we had that, we could analyze various timestream signatures and locate the original prime. Unfortunately, we realized that if we could figure out how to do that, someone else could too. Something had to be done."

"There wouldn't be any way to undo that," Tucket says. "All those streams. The fractal was created, and you can't undo time."

"You're correct," Doctor Quickly replies. "Pandora's box was open, and we knew it would only be a matter of time before someone came looking for the core stream. Some future generation of time traveler would track us down. Once we realized that, we knew what we needed to do with Quickly Alpha."

"You killed him?" Tucket gasps.

Doctor Quickly considers Tucket briefly and smiles. "No. Nothing quite so drastic as that. But we sent him home. He agreed to go back to the Alpha and never time travel again. Many of us took that approach. It was the safest and most responsible action we could take in order to protect the universe."

"But *you* didn't do it," Carson counters. "You didn't take your own advice."

"He couldn't," I reply, beginning to see the bigger picture. "Someone had to take the fall. Someone had to be the face of Doctor Quickly in the time travel community, because time travel was already out. The effects were already happening, to people like us."

Doctor Quickly sips his tea again and sets the cup gently back in the saucer. "My colleagues set the ball in motion. In my absence, accidents like the one that sent you back in time were repercussions of my discovery and they would ultimately lead to the existence of the rest of the time travel world. ASCOTT, The Academy of Temporal Sciences, and all the varied branches of the central primes stemmed from those few events. And eventually someone was going to follow them back, looking for me. Someone had to be here to respond and to keep the secret safe."

"So the Alpha Quickly stayed in his timestream?" Carson asks. "He didn't feel shortchanged by this whole deal? I feel like it would be hard to discover time travel and then not get to use it."

"He did actually use it a few more times," Doctor Quickly says. "But there was an unexpected result that convinced him that staying home was in everyone's best interest."

"Something bad happened when he left again?" Tucket inquires.

"Depends on your perspective. It was an unfortunate turn of events that ended up being the most important change to my life."

"Mym," I say, reading the expression on his face. "You ended up with Mym."

"Did she tell you the story?" Doctor Quickly asks.

"No. Just bits. She told me a little about her mother's decision."

"Time travel causes otherwise unheard of scenarios and forces us to make difficult choices. Sometimes they are made for us. One of the reasons time travelers tend to stay away from their own lives is that mistakes don't just affect them, but also the people they love. In Mym's case, it turned out that we ended up with two of us and only one of her mother. A situation that was in no one's best interest to duplicate further."

Carson leans in and rests his elbows on the table again. "Does the other Mym—the one with the normal life—does she know there's a version of her out there who travels through time?"

"I'm not sure what she knows of this reality. Her mother wanted to shield her from much of it. Knowing my daughter, she will likely put it together anyway, but Mym and I—my Mym—we've agreed to steer clear. It's just been the two of us, but we do all right."

Doctor Quickly wraps his hands a little tighter around his teacup. "We just need to get her back."

"When they took her, I saw them use a temporal spectrometer on her," I say. "They said she was more useful to them than I would be. What does that mean?"

Doctor Quickly frowns. "They've read her timestream signature so they can use that to trace her origins. Mym's is the only time traveler other than the original me, whose origins are in the Alpha. They plan to use her to find it."

"So they already have what they want," I reply. "What do they want you to do?"

"I don't know. It could be that they know where they are going, but don't know how to get there. They've given me a date to meet them." He turns the device around so I can see it. The series of numbers is written out in Roman numerals.

The numerals register in my mind and I reach for my messenger bag, extracting Jay's leather-bound journal. "I've seen that date." I flip through pages until I arrive at the series of Roman numerals I'd been perplexed about. I flip the book around and slide it across the table to Doctor Quickly. "Any idea about these other dates? It's some sort of set."

Doctor Quickly runs a finger along the page, tracing the circled numbers. He pauses on the 2165 numeral for our current year, then moves down to the last one.

"You have any idea what those numbers signify?" I ask.

Doctor Quickly is quiet for a moment, still studying the sequence, but when he raises his eyes, his face is serious. "I can't speak to all of these numbers. Most aren't significant to me, except this one." He turns the journal around and taps on the numeral I had converted to read 3525.

"That's the end of the world."

"We are the beneficiaries of the past. We owe a debt of gratitude to previous generations. As a time traveler I've been able to thank some of my heroes in person, but I feel it is just as important to recognize the courageous people in our own eras. By showing enough gratitude now, we save future time travelers a trip."-Journal of Dr. Harold Quickly, 1941

CHAPTER 13

The Neverwhere

I'm learning to fade.

Residing in Zurvan's memories has taken stealth, but the more I work at it, the easier it has become. Zurvan spends much of his time in meditation, seated with arms lying comfortably in his lap, visiting his memories.

During times when Zurvan has his mind back in the Neverwhere and he is up and moving around, I keep still and hidden. I've discovered nooks in his memories—blank spots and foggy areas—places he hasn't spent enough time in to remember them with any clarity. These are places I don't remember either, so even when he wanders off, the hiding places stay foggy and indistinct.

So that's what I do now. I skulk, and I watch.

I listen.

Sometimes I hear whispers in the fog. Occasionally I think I recognize the voices. One of them sounds like Jay. The girl from the fiery church is there too. I can sometimes hear her crying.

There are other voices in the fog. Strangers. Lost souls lingering at the edges of Zurvan's mind. Never seen, never able to show themselves. Just whispers. The last remnants of their former selves. They make for eerie company.

My sojourn into the spaceship was my first experience with Zurvan's past, but it was nearly my last. Zurvan had been staring into the colorful void inside the spaceship for so long, I had almost forgotten he could do anything else. Then, finally, he stood up to go back outside. I barely had time to retreat ahead of him without being seen. I escaped however, keeping my distance and staying hidden once again behind the fallen ruins near the rim of the crater. I had thought myself safe there until Zurvan opened up a portal and promptly disappeared.

I don't know where Zurvan went, some other memory perhaps, or possibly back to my apartment to search for me again. Wherever he disappeared to, he was no longer in the memory of a future Saint Petersburg. Unfortunately, that meant I wasn't either.

It was this moment that taught me another unique feature about the Neverwhere and how it functions. When Zurvan vanished, the scene around me changed. It stayed the same location, but reverted back to the version of Saint Petersburg I remember from my life. 2009.

It seems I'm perfectly capable of residing in the memories of my own life for as long as I want, and I can co-exist in a memory of someone else's without having been there in real life, but when the holder of the memory leaves, I can't linger.

It turns out that Zurvan's spaceship crash memory is located a mere half a block west from the point on Fourth Street where I saw the girl disappear inside the ruined church. The same location that in my time is a Tijuana Flats Mexican Restaurant. Despite being centuries apart in time, geographically they are the same place.

When Zurvan vanished from the scene, I once again found myself very near the bank that supplanted my old oak tree, and only a stone's throw away from the restaurant. It was a clue, but also a very serious problem. If Zurvan returned to this location, expecting to find the ship and his ruined view of the world, and it turned out my memory had supplanted it instead, he'd know immediately that I was there. The scenery would give me away faster than any security system or alarm. My own memories could betray me.

The first time it happened, I ran, purely on instinct, distancing myself from the scene, but I only made it a block or so before realizing the error in my thinking. I couldn't run away. Not if I wanted to find my way back into his memories. I wanted to see the end of his story, and that meant staying hidden.

The solution was in the fog.

The hazy spaces between memories are neither here nor there. It is the gap of memory rendered into a physical location. For once in my life I was happy to find chinks and holes in scenes I thought I remembered. I needed to stay near the site of the restaurant/spaceship, but didn't want my presence known. I just needed a patch of the nothingness to lay low in.

The first time Zurvan came back to the location on Fourth Street from one of his excursions, I was lying in a bank of fog trying desperately to think of anything except 2009. It worked. Zurvan returned and restored his own memory of the location, one with the spaceship and the two helpful future humans he'd made friends with. I was back inside his memory and free to spy on him.

Over the course of the next few occurrences, I was careful to note the locations where Zurvan's foggy spaces lined up with those in 2009. That way, even should he decide to vanish without warning, my hiding place remained safe and thoroughly invisible.

That's not to say I'm not getting out at all. To the contrary, despite my determination to remain in the temporal shadows, I very much want to see what happened to Zurvan's murderous self in the real world.

Zurvan is an asshole. That didn't take long to sort out. I had assumed it, based on his treatment of me, but in those first few memories of the future, I saw it just as clearly. It's not just me. Or Datrica for that matter. While the woman may have had some of her demise coming to her—based on her generally poor manners and questionable decision making—I still feel a bit bad for her. She was arrogant and tyrannical in her leadership style, but she was still more or less an innocent. All of these people are.

In the memories Zurvan relives now, the old man and the thick-set woman who nursed Zurvan back to life have become his servants, bustling about, doing his bidding when required, and following him around like puppies. Zurvan isn't cruel to them, but it's clear he doesn't find them worth much of his time. At least at first.

I don't know why Zurvan has chosen to replay this particular era of his life. But he does it like it's his job. I've settled into a sort of routine myself, stalking his memories, watching him relive them. There is a tension to his actions in the memory. He's working.

The problem is the crack in the ship. Whatever the brilliant fissure is at the back of the spacecraft, it's getting bigger. The Zurvan in these memories is determined to stop it—he's said as much to his companions at least—but they don't seem to be attempting repairs. Instead, they've been constructing an altar.

The heavy woman's name is Anniosha or something like that, but I've settled on just calling her Annie. The old man goes by Leonard, something I can actually remember.

The more I've watched the duo and observed their interactions with Zurvan, the better I've come to understand them. Their language isn't exactly English, but I can't say it's anything else either. It's almost as though they once knew English and forgot it, or decided to make up a new way of expressing it—like pig-latin.

Zurvan struggled to understand them at first also, but has reverted to using English exclusively when communicating with them and places the burden squarely on their shoulders to do the work of understanding him.

For the most part, they've risen to the challenge, working hard to get their thoughts and concerns out in complete sentences that have improved greatly in comprehensibility over the few days they've been working.

They built the altar and erected a metal basket to put a fire inside. Annie did most of the heavy lifting of moving blocks and materials, while Leonard took on the role of supervisor. He also assisted with fire tending, being sure to keep the blaze fed so that Zurvan would be pleased. Zurvan himself underwent a different type of preparation. He painted the area around the fire pit with various symbols and built himself a sort of chair to sit on and, once comfortable, proceeded to stare into the fire and hum.

I've never been a practitioner of yoga or eastern religion, but I know enough about the concept to recognize meditation. Zurvan has made repeated attempts in this position, trying to accomplish something in particular, but despite his best efforts, can't seem to achieve his desired state. I watch him become increasingly aggravated after each session. He makes Leonard rebuild the fire and starts over.

Over and over again, he fails.

Cursing the fire after his last attempt, Zurvan puts a hand to his head, probing the recently tended wound on his skull. He frowns and pulls the bandage away from the injury, his fingers brushing the now closed up gash.

"Is healed, yes?" Annie says. She hovers over her patient, checking up on him. He brushes her hands away.

"The wounds I've suffered won't be healed with your herbs."

"We have medsin," Annie replies. "Good medsin. From the old ways."

Zurvan puts both of his hands to his head. "No. You don't see. There is too much missing now. Too many memories lost. I can't remember like I should anymore. If I can't remember, I can't go back. If I can't go back, we can't escape this. I can't stop it."

He stares at the ship, its blue lights pulsing long slow bursts into the fading twilight. The heat from the back of the ship has increased to the point that the back of the ship itself glows—a throbbing red sore just under its surface.

"It won't hold," Zurvan says. "It's going to destroy itself. And all of us with it."

Annie takes her eyes off of Zurvan and lets them linger on the back of the ship with new suspicion. "Do we nee ta kill it? Or do we nee ta run?"

Zurvan frowns. "Neither. It can't be killed. And it can't be outrun."

"We have a bus by the lake," Leonard says. "Ol' Blue. We made it work. Sunny days it'll go fifty mile on a clear way."

"No!" Zurvan declares. "No running. No . . . buses. This thing is going to—Even if you had a *real* ship buried in this heap of refuse you call a city, you'd need a craft that could—" He sputters to a stop and looks up at the rear of the spacecraft. "You'd need to contain it." His mind is clearly working hard, wrestling with a new idea.

He turns to Leonard. "We could use another ship. If we had another one we could harness the power, drive the reactor from the first into the second. We could still save it."

"What ship, sir? We have no ship," Leonard says.

"No. You wouldn't have a ship like this, but there are more."

"They be ships in the way back east," Annie declares. "Old way ships in the water. Tall ones out past the long marsh. Spaceport it was. Port Nyongo and Port Ken Dee. Old old ways."

Zurvan's eyes flicker to Annie's face. "Kennedy? No. Kennedy is too far back. That was the beginning. But what's this other one? Nyongo? Where's that?"

"South way. Long way over the water." She gestures toward the south, past the shattered solar array and the ruins of downtown.

"How long since the ships flew?" Zurvan says. "Who flew them?"

"Those are just old tales," Leonard moans. "Ancient history. And that was *them* that took 'em. The others. We don't have no business in those places. Never have."

Zurvan frowns. "But they had ships. How long? How long ago?"

"Honred years," Annie replies. "Seven honred. Nine honred. We don't know. No one tells us."

Zurvan faces the ship, the heat of it radiating around him. He must be feeling its intensity because he shrugs out of his outer robe and tosses it aside. He rolls up his loose shirtsleeves and turns back to his companions. "We can go another way." He grabs the arms of Annie and Leonard and drags them toward the altar they've erected. "You two will do it. You will bring me a ship."

Annie and Leonard both look confused but don't attempt to shake his grasp.

"But we don't have no boat," Annie complains. "Them ships long way and they heavy. Ain't no way they—"

"Shut up," Zurvan says, dragging them faster. When they reach the stone platform he has them sit, facing the fire, and he takes a position on one knee behind them. "Now listen to me," he hisses. "I am going to teach you. I'll teach you the way to go. You're going to take the message for me. There is a ship like this one." He stabs a finger at the glowing sphere behind him. "You are going to find it. You'll bring it to me and we can still stop this."

"How we gon—" Annie protests.

"I told you. Just listen. Look at the fire." He grabs both of their heads and points them to the fire. "For now you just look, and you let the fire be all you see. You will clear your mind of everything but the flames. Let them burn away all that is inessential."

He stands up and leaves the two staring into the fire. "When your minds have been purified, we'll begin." Annie and Leonard look hesitant, but they obey, settling into place and staring hard into the flames.

The Zurvan in the Neverwhere lets the vision fade and change. He moves on to a later memory. His two disciples, for that is what they seem to be now, have advanced from merely staring into the fire and are now adding various chants and humming into their practice. Other times he has them reciting stories, memories from their own past, seemingly inconsequential moments, but he asks them to relive them in excruciating detail. It doesn't seem to matter what the memories are about. He takes just as much interest in Leonard's recollection of an all black fish he once caught in the river as he does in Annie's lurid description of one of her early sexual experiences. Zurvan is intently concentrated on detail. The moment he suspects that one or the other of his pupils is exaggerating a fact or making up fanciful details, he berates them and cuffs them on the head.

It seems as though days pass this way. The memories the two disciples recite are often similar, and they loop back to certain ones over and over again, attempting to glean more detail, or mine some forgotten snippet of the memory previously overlooked.

But through them all, the repetition and recounting of childhood stories, I can see the gradual change in the ship. The glow at the rear of the ship has gone from a dull glow, to an angry, volatile sunspot. There are parts of the ship that glow white hot and vaporize the moisture in the air around them. The ground at the back of the ship has turned black, baked by the extreme heat, and no one goes inside anymore, not even Zurvan.

Zurvan has finally made a decision regarding his pupils' memories. Each one sits across from the other on opposite sides of the fire, doing their chanting rituals and getting into their meditative positions, then fixating on their memories the way he instructs them. I've heard his instructions so many times, I feel like one of his students. "Stare into the fire. It consumes what you are, leaving only what you were. Now take yourself there. Find yourself. You are inside the memory. You *are* the memory."

It's clear that Annie is his favorite. He spends more time coaching her, guiding her toward her past. Her memory of being a teenage girl in an overly large family growing up in the southern marshes does not seem especially fascinating, but her level of detail regarding the memories has pleased him. She's recounted textures of the reeds on the marshes, the *feel* of the burn she got when branded by a roving gang of outlaws, and the smell of the dead bodies after a flash flood washed through the city and drowned most of her neighbors. Zurvan doesn't dwell on the emotions related to these events, and only takes a passing interest in what became of her after each occurrence, but continues to push her back into those memories. Instructing her to find herself there and to take control.

The taking control concept bothers me on a personal level. It bothers me because I know what they're up to, and I've been in their same position. These are the methods of the Eternals. Having only heard about them in passing during the chronothon, I have no first-hand experience with their methods, but after watching Annie and Leonard repeatedly travel back to their pasts in their own minds, it's become clear what they are trying to do. Zurvan is sending them back in time.

Despite my discomfort with the idea of taking over one's own mind, especially since I've been considering doing the same thing to myself, I can't seem to disconnect from this scene. Zurvan is intent on reliving it, and I am insanely curious to see the results. I stay that way until the day Annie starts screaming.

The two disciples are in their usual positions on opposite sides of the fire. Annie has been dwelling on the past the longest, having gotten a head start that morning. She's spent longer and longer in her mind each day, smoothly feeling her way back inside her memories, but today she erupts in a fit of terror.

"She's goon kill me! No! Get her out! She knows about me. She knows who I be!"

Zurvan rushes to her side, attempting to grab her flailing arms and calm her. Annie keeps swiping at her sides, brushing off the invisible threat that has ahold of her. Annie is inconsolable. She continues to shriek until Zurvan clamps his hands on both sides of her head and closes his eyes.

Annie goes rigid. Her shrieking stops and her eyes roll back in her head— flickering white orbs as her eyelids flutter. Finally her body relaxes and she slumps forward, collapsing to the stone platform in a heap.

Zurvan stays standing. Looking down on the fallen form of Annie, his lip curls into a disappointed scowl. Then he steps over her and moves to Leonard. The old man is staring wide-eyed at his fallen companion.

"What . . . What happened to . . ."

"She was weak," Zurvan spits back. "Her younger self was the stronger mind. She lost the fight. You mustn't let that happen. You must remember the weaknesses of your former self and exploit them. Tunnel into the recesses of his mind where you know he has no foundation. Use his insecurities, his fears, and replace them with only your will.

"You must be assured where he is weak. You will be confident in place of his timidity and move boldly to counter his inaction. You will prove to him that you are the stronger mind and the rightful owner of your body. If you leave yourself vulnerable, he will sense the weakening of your resolve and reject you. Never let him think he can beat you. Destroy him."

Leonard looks less than assured after seeing Annie crumble, but he sets his jaw and dutifully goes back to staring into the fire, concentrating on his mission in the past.

After a while Annie stirs, but when she rises to her knees, she finds Zurvan no longer attentive to her. His favor is now on Leonard and, when she makes her way down the platform, pausing once to look back, Zurvan doesn't even give her a second glance. She shuffles over the edge of the crater, arms held tightly across her chest, and disappears.

The next day, Zurvan gets an early start with Leonard. Annie returns too, only to find them already deep in mediation. She takes her place near the fire again, cautiously, and Zurvan doesn't reprimand her. When she makes subtle attempts to question him about the events of the day before, he simply doesn't respond. He instead devotes all of his time to Leonard and, while he doesn't actively discourage Annie from attending, she no longer receives his tutoring. She instead assumes the role of fire tender, spending more of her time gathering wood and combustible materials to keep the fire on the altar burning. She keeps this up for a couple more days, but then eventually stops coming altogether.

It's on the second day of Annie's absence that Leonard has his breakthrough, with Zurvan feeding the fire and continuing to assist in his meditation. They've been at it for over twelve hours, far later into the evening than they've attempted before, and finally Leonard lapses into a state of absolute calm. His body visibly relaxes, arms fallen to his sides, fingers flopped loosely to the stone platform, and his mouth hanging open. His eyes flicker in the half light. They glow faintly with the light from the fire, but also the red glow from the back of the ship. Beads of sweat have pooled on his forehead from the heat, but he pays no attention, even when they drip into his eyes.

Zurvan takes a position in front of Leonard and holds his hands out alongside Leonard's head. Not touching him, but there nonetheless. He speaks softly, but firmly. "Yes. Remember him. Be him.

"You are no longer Leonard. You are the gnomon, the center, the tool of my will. You will cast your shadow back in time as far as you need to. You will take your knowledge back with you. Generations if you need to. Bring me the Lost Star. You will remember this place and you will return to this moment. You will return, and you will save me. Once you do, we will begin again. You too will be eternal."

Leonard shivers. His lips quiver as if he's speaking, but no sound comes out. His eyelids flicker faster, the rapidity of their movement increasing to a crescendo and then stopping suddenly. Leonard slumps forward, collapsing into the arms of Zurvan, who catches him gently and lays his body on the stones. He stares down at the man and places a hand to his throat, feeling for a pulse.

The old man is gone.

Standing up, Zurvan tilts his head back and searches the sky. He spins in place, checking each of the cardinal directions before stepping off the platform and away from the bright flames. Once out of the immediate glow of firelight, he lifts his head again, his face alight with anticipation, expectant, hopeful. He climbs the embankment at the side of the crater, stopping at its highest point and keeping his eyes aloft. He waits.

The ship groans.

A red hot section of the sphere finally gives way on the bottom of the craft, dropping with a thud to the dirt and spilling a torrent of liquid-hot metal in the process. The metal hisses and pops as it flows over the rocky ground. Chunks of stone and cement burst from the heat, splitting apart in fragments and slowly melting into the growing pool. Farther from the ship the metal lake finally begins to cool, pressing up against bits of rubble and forming a wall to stop its own progress.

Zurvan watches the metal ooze its way nearly to the edge of his altar before stopping. He pulls his eyes away and goes back to searching the sky. He begins to mutter, growing more and more impatient. He storms back down into the crater and scoops up his folded external robes. He disregards the heat and dons them again, climbing once again to the top of the crater and tilting his head skyward. His fingers twitch. He is impatient, a man not long for this world.

Something inside the ship shrieks and snaps. A deafening bang echoes from the interior. The sound is followed by a low continuous moan of metal and a hissing, crackling sound.

Seated in my favorite hiding place, a few yards from the crater's edge, I have to remind myself that it isn't real. I'm not in danger here, even though every instinct in me is telling me to run. The Neverwhere Zurvan—Zurvan the ghost—has remained in position through all of this, calmly meditating it into existence, despite the destruction going on inside the memory.

Destruction is the clear result now. The ship is shrinking. The top of the ship, once taller than a four story building, has been collapsed now at the top. The ship is no longer a sphere, but a dented, pockmarked bowl, now more closely resembling a ball of crushed aluminum foil than the smooth aerodynamic shape it once boasted.

Zurvan's face has fallen.

His ride is not coming.

As the ship slowly consumes itself, some of the brilliance inside begins leaking out. Brilliance is leaking in as well. Wisps of colorful cloud and fog swirl around the ship, as if the Neverwhere itself is aggravated by this memory. Looking at the interaction of the fog, I'm perplexed as to how a memory could be bridging the gap between the real world and mine, but it's only then that I realize the wisps of fog are not in The Neverwhere, but were really swirling around the ship in this memory of Zurvan's. Whatever disaster this ship has created, it's pulling at threads of things not normally seen in the real world. The structure and fabric of time.

Zurvan finally ceases his glances skyward. He fixes his eyes instead on the throbbing, pulsing form of the ship. Hardly anything is left of it now. It's begun consuming dirt and stone around itself. Colored fog is oozing from the ground around it and obscuring the landscape. Perhaps the strangest spectacle is the firelight. The fire on the altar is still burning, but the light no longer extends as far. Instead, the flames are all leaning toward the brilliance of the glow inside the ship, stretching and arching toward it. The very light from the fire is bending and flowing into the ship.

The rest happens quickly. The ground around the ship erupts, including the crater wall I'm hidden behind. The dirt and stone hurtles into the air in an explosion of movement, instantly eradicating my view of the ship. Buildings behind me go too. An ocean made of concrete, glass, and even the wild and growing plants from the overgrown farm tower goes hurtling toward the glowing hole in the world. Much of the debris passes straight through my ghostly form, increasing in volume until I can no longer even make out the details of individual pieces. It's just one continuous stream of matter. I close my eyes against the visual onslaught, unable to handle the rush of colors and the continuous, endless roar of sound. I run, staggering blindly against the wave of memory.

And then it's gone.

I open my eyes and find all of the destruction has vanished. Zurvan's memory has ended, and in its place I'm now back in my own version of the city. The 2009 version. Sunlight and palm trees, Fourth Street, and the

Tijuana Flats Mexican restaurant. In my haste to escape the destruction of the future, I've left the safe location of my hiding place. I've lost my concentration. I'm not back in the fog. I'm in the wide open, in plain view from the street and the neighboring houses.

I'm exposed, and I'm not alone.

Zurvan is standing in the center of the street.

He's staring at me.

And he's smiling.

London, UK, 2165

"We're going to need some help," Doctor Quickly says.

Carson, Tucket, and I have followed the scientist into a room of his safe house where he's installed a lot of fancy-looking electronics. He gestures to a few screens and pulls up a directory of names.

"There aren't a lot of people in this century I can count on, but I do have one." He taps a name on the list and a profile expands on the screen showing an attractive, thirty-something Asian woman.

"That's Professor Chun," Tucket exclaims. "She taught me timestream geographical history at the Academy."

"She's a knowledgeable historian, and I'm sure she's an excellent professor, but she's also one of the ASCOTT members who has charted the various timestream endings."

"I thought no time travelers were allowed past the restricted line," Tucket says. "I learned that in her class. How could she go beyond it?"

"ASCOTT's restricted line is there precisely *because* scientists like Noelle Chun have been beyond it," Doctor Quickly replies. "That information has simply been kept from public knowledge."

"No one knows that the world ends?" Carson asks. "Isn't that dangerous? What happens to all the people who live near then?"

"That's what I'm hoping Professor Chun might be able to enlighten us about. In general terms it hasn't been an issue because, for the most part, it was believed that there were no people up that far."

"So when you say 'end of the world,' are you talking about the end of humans, or the end of the planet?" I ask. "Is it just us, or animals and plants and everybody? Like extinction stuff? Another meteor or something?"

"It's a bit worse than that."

"Worse? What's worse than a planet-ending meteor?"

Doctor Quickly straightens up from the screen and puts his hands in his pockets. "I can think of quite a few things actually, but in this case it's a temporal anomaly. A massive singularity in space-time."

"What's a singularity?" Carson asks.

"There are actually a few different types of singularities, and the earth experiences two near its end, but it's the second one that does the most damage. In layman's terms, it's a black hole. A big enough black hole that it consumes the solar system." He lets the severity of the statement speak for itself and doesn't explain further. As I stare at him, I realize I'm waiting for some sort of 'but' statement, something to qualify the disaster and offer hope, but there is none.

"Well that fucking sucks," Carson says.

"I suppose I have to agree with you there," Doctor Quickly says, though he doesn't seem particularly distraught. He goes back to browsing the information on Professor Chun, then, seemingly satisfied, scribbles himself a few notes.

"How long have you known?" I ask. "Is there anything we can do about it? Like, stop it somehow?" My brain is struggling to picture the end of the entire planet—millions of years of evolution getting sucked into a black hole a mere thousand years into the future.

"It's rather unavoidable, I'm afraid. The singularity exists at a point in space-time directly in the path of the planet's trajectory. Unless we come up with a way to reroute the entire solar system and change its course, there's no chance of avoiding it. There has been research into that option, but I'm afraid it's a bit of a dead-end. We simply won't develop that capability as a species in time to attempt any feat of engineering that immense.

"The information about the planet's end is only a secret till around the end of the third millennium, but trust me when I say that some of humanity's greatest minds have given it a great deal of thought. Keeping the secret from the public was simply decided to be the best choice until after the millennium. At that point, it is rather moot, as far as the human race goes. Most of humanity is gone by then."

"Evacuated?" Carson asks.

"In a manner of speaking," Doctor Quickly replies. "Now, if you gentlemen will excuse me for a few minutes, I'm going to retrieve Professor Chun and bring her back here. I should return shortly and we can get her input on this new information. I'd like to know what she thinks of this date sequence you've discovered. It may be a clue we can use to rescue Mym. I want to avail ourselves of every opportunity for success."

Doctor Quickly consults his notes, then exits the room with swift, efficient strides, one hand already dialing a time into his chronometer. Carson, Tucket, and I are left staring at each other, trying to process this new turn of events. It's not unlike the scientist to casually drop some bit of reality changing news on us and leave, but this particular information is harder than most to process.

Carson runs a hand over his unruly red hair. "Wow. Bit of a downer, right?"

"You didn't know about this?" I ask Tucket, whose eyes are still wide.

"I heard rumors spread from alumni about trouble beyond the restricted line, but nobody really knew anything for sure. I thought they just meant some of the human-synth wars that we think happen after the millennium. I didn't know about the singularity."

The prospect of a human-synth war sounds like a terrifying prospect on its own, but in light of the larger problem, I don't question Tucket about it. I do my best to concentrate on the issues at hand. Carson plops himself down in one of the room's swiveling chairs, and I turn to him. "What else did you learn while you were traveling around with Quickly? Any other clues about what the Eternals are up to?"

Carson raises his gaze to mine slowly, as if coming out of a different train of thought, then nods. "Yeah, a bit. It's a larger group than we thought. We found some more references to the symbol you saw. The Lost Star? It goes way back. Only shows up in some obscure texts and not in all the timestreams, but it seems like The Eternals have been at this thing for a while."

"Have you heard from Francesca? Any word from home?"

"Not too much. We stopped by there again on the way up, just before we got your distress call. Had to keep moving though. The Doc didn't want to stay in one place too long in case there was another attack."

"Is she doing okay? And Blake and Mallory?"

"Yeah, I guess," Carson frowns. "Francesca didn't say much. Kind of gave me the brush off a little bit."

"Why? I thought you guys were close again. From what Fresca said, I kind of figured you might be getting back together or something."

"You haven't heard?"

"Heard what?"

"She's dating you now. Well, not you. But the other one. Other you."

"WHAT?" I stare at Carson, my mind incapable of processing what I've just heard for the second time in the last ten minutes.

"Yeah, man. He moved right in there after you left. Doesn't seem like he wasted too much time."

"Hold on. Benji? I thought he was dating Kaylee. They were pretty much living together when I left."

"Yeah, well. You gave him your place, I guess maybe he decided he didn't need Kaylee anymore after you said he could have your life."

"What the hell—I am going to have some serious issues with this dude when I get back." I try to imagine a scenario where I could possibly behave as badly as Benji seems to be doing in the life I've left behind. He's me, so clearly if the circumstances were right, I could have ended up that way, but the situation is hard to wrap my mind around. It rapidly seizes my concern, in spite of the end of the world scenario I've just heard. Going strictly off my personal feelings, I'm not sure which news is more shocking.

It's the look of distress on Tucket's face that brings me back to reality. I rest a hand on his shoulder. "Hey, are *you* all right, man?"

He nods but doesn't look especially convincing. "It's just, I thought Professor Chun really liked me. I got top marks in her class. I wish she would have told me what was going to happen to the world."

As distraught as he looks in this moment, I can somewhat understand her decision to keep it secret. He looks about ready to break down. I don't have time to ponder her choices further because a moment later, Doctor Quickly and Professor Chun walk in the door.

"Gentlemen, Noelle Chun," Doctor Quickly waves her forward and we make our introductions. Professor Chun is perhaps 5' 3" and athletically built. Her firm handshake and professional demeanor are accented by what I take to be this century's equivalent of a business suit—a short, pocketless jacket layered over slacks and a loose-fitting top.

"I'm surprised to see you here, Mr. Morris," Professor Chun says. "Last trace report we had on you said that you were bouncing around the twenty-first century visiting a bunch of Olympic badminton games. You may want to get your equipment checked."

"Um, okay," Tucket replies. He rubs the spot in his forearm where Grid travelers get their tracer implant. "I don't know what would be wrong with it. The school said it was brand new."

Professor Chun's eyes linger on the bracelet of Bob's hanging around Tucket's wrist. "Glad to see you've made yourself some new friends. An inventive bunch of guys." She appraises me and Carson. "Just make sure they can get you home. Time travelers moving off-Grid have had a shaky safety record lately."

Tucket nods and merely mumbles something unintelligible in response while rubbing his arm.

"I'm sure any of Mr. Morris's tracking technology that is malfunctioning can be easily remedied." Doctor Quickly gives me a wink, then directs us back to the sitting room where we defrock the furniture, setting the air conditioning system humming as it rapidly vacuums up the now-airborne dust. Once the furniture covers are balled away, Doctor Quickly offers the professor a cup of tea, but she turns the offer down, clearly ready to get to work.

"Do you mind if I see the sequence?" Professor Chun asks.

I turn over the journal, keeping a thumb in the proper page for her.

She runs her finger down the column of numbers, much as Doctor Quickly had and chews her lip in thought.

"Noelle has brought me up to speed on a bit more of her research,"

Doctor Quickly says. "The Academy historians have done quite a few tests of the space-time singularity and turned up some interesting results. Namely that it occurs in slightly different months and years across various timestreams, but they believe that is because it is bleeding over from this one. Noelle, perhaps you can give Benjamin and Carson the basics."

Professor Chun pulls her gaze from the journal and closes it, but keeps her finger stuck between the pages. She rests her other hand atop the book and considers us. "We've learned a great deal. We've logged data from almost all of the central streams. Covertly of course." Her look implies that we would understand the need for this level of secrecy, but our faces must not be registering much in the way of understanding, because she pauses. "How much do you know about the future?"

I merely shake my head and Carson likewise stays silent. Professor Chun looks back and forth between us and then turns to Doctor Quickly.

"I suppose I have been a bit lax in that department," Doctor Quickly says. "So far I've had them staying a bit more local in their temporal geography."

Professor Chun frowns but doesn't seem to be deterred. "Okay, in that case I'll give you the broad strokes first." She shifts to a more comfortable position in her chair and recrosses her legs. "I assume you've been introduced to synthetic intelligence and the advent of transhumanism. That's present day. We're seeing the rise of synthetic persons and a growth of synthetic intelligence, but that growth hasn't been exponential. We haven't hit the technological singularity yet. That won't happen until—" She pauses, reading our faces and backs up. "I know I'm getting into some advanced concepts, but if you have questions, you can stop me. I'm not completely sure what you know so far, so let me know."

"Perhaps you can just clarify the singularity thing," I say. "There's the black hole, but there's also another singularity? A technological one? Or are they the same thing?"

Professor Chun nods. "Right. Singularity in its simplest of terms just means the point at which something becomes infinite or, in some cases, begins to increase without limitations. The black hole singularity refers to matter becoming infinitely dense at its center. The *technological* singularity is a different term, unrelated, but similar. It's the moment when artificial or synthetic intelligence overcomes its limitations and advances at an exponential rate.

"It just so happens that in terms of the future of humanity, we encounter both of these events in relatively short order."

"Obviously the technological singularity happens first," I say. "Is that somehow what causes the second one? Do synths create the black hole?"

"No. From what we know, the synths have evolved to a level of extreme complexity by the time the black hole arrives. It's clear that they recognize its existence, because they abandon the earth well in advance of the event. What we don't know is how the event begins or what causes it."

"You keep saying, 'they,'" Carson says. "Where are the regular humans at this point? Did they evacuate?"

Professor Chun seems to consider her words carefully. "Generally speaking, at that period of time, the synths *are* the human race. It's not complete. The majority of humanity becomes trans-human over the next few decades, and from there they continue to become more and more synthetic. It's then that the last of the real safeguards fall."

"What kind of safeguards?" I ask.

"Countermeasures against synthetic intelligence," Professor Chun replies. "It was never a secret that synthetic intelligence would one day surpass the capacity of the human brain. It was even recognized in your time. You're probably familiar with scientists like Stephen Hawking who warned against the dangers of artificial intelligence and the need for beneficial technology versus ungoverned A.I. It was that movement that led to the countermeasures. It's why today, even though synths are a functioning, beneficial part of human society, they still look and behave like humans. They don't need to look like us, or behave like us, but they have been engineered that way."

"You stunt their growth?" Carson asks.

"We manage their potential," Professor Chun replies. "And we take care not to let things get out of control. When time travel became a scientific reality, it gave us a window into the future as well as the past. And it gave us a warning. As a result, we were able to prepare. We began the Academy of Temporal Sciences, trained as many competent researchers as we could, and set about redefining our future. I know your experience with ASCOTT has not been ideal, but our organization is not just Big Brother, out to regulate the fun out of time travel. It's a vital shield, protecting the human race from what's coming.

"The rise of synthetic intelligence happens in nearly every one of the timestreams ASCOTT has investigated. There are three outcomes. In many cases the entire human race goes synthetic. Organic humans are either eliminated or put on reservations. ASCOTT keeps time travelers out of those streams. In other streams, usually ones in which ASCOTT has already determined the presence of too many time travelers, synths are kept under control via our own technology."

Professor Chun looks to me. "I know you've had contact with some of our members, and some of their methods have been extreme, but imagine what would happen to human history if the ability to travel in time was acquired by a supremely intelligent synthetic race. How might they change us? What might they do if they had unlimited time?"

"So synths in ASCOTT-controlled timestreams can't time travel?" I ask. "How did you prevent them from doing it?"

"In the short term, we use the countermeasures," Professor Chun replies. "We have regulations. We insist that all synthetic tissue advances continue to make it genetically pure, actively purging contaminants. Synth pseudo-skin purges all foreign particles, even gravitites, if it should somehow come in contact with them. We also control the manufacture of Temprovibe technology—limit its use to organic humans. A Temprovibe won't work on a pseudo-skin host. An all-metal synth could make a jump if it's not using synthetic tissues, but those are easy to spot and they can't really jump back more than a few years without scaring the locals."

She glances at Doctor Quickly. "And, with a few notable exceptions, we insist that all time travelers register with the Grid. So we track them, keeping them out of danger areas where we know their technology might fall into the hands of synthetic entities who might wish to commandeer it."

"Have you ever failed?" Carson asks. "Have any synths ever found a way to time travel?"

"A few," Professor Chun admits. "But that is why we have another countermeasure—a task force that exists solely for the purpose of policing time and hunting down synth travelers."

"You've got a team of time traveling robot hunters?" Carson asks. "That's kind of awesome."

"We take this all very seriously," Professor Chun replies. "But yes, they are rather impressive.

"In some timestreams the fight to keep synthetic intelligence in check evolves to all out war between humans and synths. If it's a timestream where no time travel technology is at stake, we stay out of the conflict. In cases where we feel time travel technology may be at risk, we intervene. With intervention by ASCOTT, humans can win those physical conflicts, but at heavy cost to the timestreams involved. Usually it means shutting the development of synthetic technology down completely."

"You said there were three possible outcomes," I said. "So far we've got synths take over the world or ASCOTT eliminates all the synths. What's the third?"

"This timestream is one where we eventually fail. The technological singularity occurs, and the synths evolve to a point where they surpass our ability to constrain them. They do eventually acquire all of our knowledge, presumably even the ability to time travel."

"What happens then?" Tucket asks.

"That is our biggest question," Professor Chun replies. "When it occurs here, the synths don't fight us. They never wage a war or attempt to subjugate humans. In this timestream, the technological singularity happens so subtly that we aren't even sure when it occurs. They go totally silent. It's possible that they evolved in a way that they knew to keep it secret from us. From what we can tell, they abandon earth. They simply leave what's left of the human race behind."

"They just peace out?" Carson asks.

"That's what our researchers found," Professor Chun replies.

I lean forward and rest my elbows on my knees. "Okay, so ASCOTT used the Academy to train researchers and rogue synth hunters, and then you sent them all over to battle synths or whatever, but what has this got to do with the Eternals or saving Mym?"

Professor Chun takes a deep breath. "In the timestreams where the war occurs, we win by using a very specific weapon that targets the way the synth intelligence functions. We call it the Labyrinth. This device engages a synthetic mind and essentially traps it in a never-ending loop where every thought it makes leads back to the one before. The mind is still intact, but in a state of continuous repetition. It's a sort of limbo. No matter how advanced the mind, or how many resources it allocates to solve the problem, it still ends up in the same place every time. In fact, the more of the collective mind it uses in its attempts to free itself, the more trapped it becomes."

"That sounds cruel," Tucket says. "You use that on all the synths?"

"Sacrifices have to be made in the interest of humanity's safety," Professor Chun replies.

Tucket frowns.

"That still doesn't explain the Eternals," I say.

"Doctor Quickly and his lab were not the only ones to be robbed by this group," Professor Chun replies. "One of our facilities was hit as well, and they took one of the labyrinth weapons."

"They took a portable gravitizer from me," I reply. "And they stole a bunch of gravitites from the lab in Valencia. What are they doing with all of it?"

"We're not sure, but it all points to something big happening this year." Professor Chun lifts her hand holding the journal. "It's this news that we're especially interested in. Harry filled me in on the symbol you've been tracking and the places it's been showing up.

"Our researchers have been seeing it too, farther and farther back in history now, almost like it's spreading backward in time. It's something that might be a vitally important part of the puzzle for us. These people—" She shakes the journal, "seem to be doing something we didn't think was possible. They're humans, but they're not traveling across the restricted line *into* the future. They're spreading back into the past, *from* the future. They're coming from a time we didn't think humans could ever come back from, and they're somehow doing it without our technology or that of the synths."

She looks me in the eye. "Mym is in the hands of an entirely new and surprising group of people. Whatever we can learn about them might be vital, not just in saving Mym, but possibly all of us. If we can make contact with them, learn what they know of this future they've been living in, we might get help."

"These Eternals aren't exactly the helpful sort," I say. "More of the attack you in the night, punch you in the face, then steal your girlfriend sort."

I reach for the journal and Professor Chun somewhat reluctantly returns it to my hand.

"Why don't they have technology?" Tucket asks. "What happened to them? Won't the future be full of better technology?"

Professor Chun leans back in her chair. "In the coming years, synths will leap ahead of organic humans in nearly every arena. Trans-humans will keep up briefly, as they are now, but then the exponential growth will leave them behind as well. The only way for humans to stay relevant is to evolve and go fully synthetic. Those that don't, fall behind or die out, like Neanderthals. It's only a matter of time. With organic humans no longer relevant, technology based around them dries up. It's a dark age in that sense. One we didn't expect to be hearing from.

"The time travelers we've sent to that era bring back data that paints a bleak picture. Synths are so far evolved as to be nearly incomprehensible, and some of the organic humans they've run across have turned almost savage by comparison. When the synths disappear, it's only these devolved humans left over."

"And where does that leave Mym?" I ask, not liking the word 'savage' being used to describe any people she might be associating with. "What is our plan for getting her back?"

Doctor Quickly reaches into his pocket and pulls out the sleek black box

I delivered to him. "This is not the work of savages. The Eternals who have Mym have a plan, and, whatever it is, they've put a great deal of work into it. They want to get to the Alpha—presumably using Mym's timestream signature to navigate there. They've given me the chance to help them, but even if I refuse, they have everything stacked in their favor. They have our equipment, they have ASCOTT's weapon, and they have Mym.

"Fortunately, we have time on our side—a time traveler always does. If we use our heads, Mym will spend a bare minimum of time with them before we get her back."

"Will you really take them to the Alpha?" I ask.

"There is nothing I wouldn't do to get Mym back, but I have little faith in their being true to their word. We need more information on what they're up to, so we can get her back whether they agree to release her or not." He looks from me to Carson and finally to Tucket. "How would you gentlemen feel about doing a bit more investigating so that we can organize a rescue?"

"If it gets Mym back, you know I'm in," I say.

"I'm down too," Carson adds. "Where do you need us to go?"

Doctor Quickly runs a thumb over the black box in his hand. "We need intel on this group and how they operate. We'll need to locate Mym, see where they're keeping her and have a plan for getting her out. We'll need more resources to make that happen." He looks to professor Chun. "That's partly why I brought in Noelle."

"I'll be able to help you a bit there," Professor Chun says. "ASCOTT can get you up to speed on some of the modern tech. I've got a team you can work with. We can outfit you with the gear you need and support personnel that know their way around this type of work. It would of course be easier to organize it all if you were registered with the Grid. We could outfit you with Temprovibes and steer you clear of some hazards."

"I think these boys will be all right, Noelle," Doctor Quickly replies. "They've been around a bit now and know how to keep themselves from ending up in the furniture."

Professor Chun raises her hands in a palms out gesture of surrender. "I know you all have your own ways, but I have to keep asking. The more travelers we can keep track of, the more we can keep safe."

"I appreciate the offer," I say. "But we won't be completely out of reach. We'll at least have Tucket if we really need to . . . um, put him back in touch." I turn to where Tucket is sitting. "Assuming you still want to come along."

Tucket's brow is furrowed. "I do. I think I do. I'm part of the team, right?"

"We'll stick together, Tuck," I say. I turn back to Professor Chun. "Okay, so you said we'll be getting some help from your people? What's the situation with them?"

Professor Chun gets up from her chair and walks to retrieve a bag on the kitchen table. When she returns she's holding a bundle in one hand that looks like a balled up dirty shirt. She places it on the coffee table between us. "These guys I'm going to introduce you to can be a little rough around the edges. I would have introduced you to them here, but Harry thought it best if we keep them in their own environment. They can get a bit . . . touchy in new places."

"These people are the best you've got?" I ask, eyeing the bundle suspiciously.

"Yes. When it comes to navigating dangerous territory, I'd trust them with my life. I have, actually. A few times. So has Harry."

Doctor Quickly crosses his arms. "That was a long time ago, but yes. I've employed their services before as well. I'll agree that they are . . . effective . . . at what they do."

"You're coming with us, right?" Carson asks.

"Actually, no." Doctor Quickly places his hands on his knees and stands up. "Noelle and I are going to work on the analysis end of this operation. Unfortunately, we're a bit too high profile for reconnaissance work and we need to decide what to do about the Eternals knowing the location of The Alpha and how much of a problem that creates. But we'll be able to assist you remotely and construct a plan based on your discoveries, and when it comes time to rescue Mym, we'll of course be there."

"How will we get in touch?" I ask.

"Noelle's team has that worked out. They'll be able to communicate to her and she can pass the info to me. Teamwork."

"You always told us to be cautious around ASCOTT and, I'll be honest, after my last trip into the future, they'd probably be my last choice in teammates." I glance at Professor Chun. "No offense. You're sure we need these guys?"

Doctor Quickly has his hands deep in his pockets again. "My cautions about ASCOTT as an organization were based on sound reasoning. I do have issues with the group as a whole, and some significant differences in belief when it comes to how to properly govern time travel, but there is no organization made up of entirely bad apples. Noelle has been a notable exception to their typical philosophy and proof that where there is a will, there will always be a way to find common ground. And these members of her team are more what you'd call independent contractors than actual ASCOTT employees."

I reach over to the coffee table and unwrap the dirty bundle. When I unfold it, it reveals a serrated black combat knife. Skewered on one end is a playing card, the king of hearts, stabbed through the center. The card has time coordinates scribbled across the face and over the king's head I see someone has drawn an arrow with the name "Ben Travers." I hold the knife up by the handle.

"Not all bad apples?"

Professor Chun slides the card off the end of the knife and reads the coordinates. "Well. Not rotten anyway. They may be a little bit bad. Questionable sense of humor to be sure. Dammit. I told them to be polite and just give you a simple anchor to connect with them." She smiles apologetically. "They don't mean anything by it. Just having a bit of fun. I promise you'll get along great once you meet them."

I take the card back from her and study the time coordinates.

"You'll be able to outfit for the mission once you get there," Doctor Quickly says. "These guys can show you the ropes and find a way to get you close to The Eternals. This is where we go to work and show these people who they're dealing with."

"I can hardly wait."

"There are many dangers facing the human race in the centuries ahead. Sadly, most are problems brought on by ourselves. One of the most hazardous is the idea that we are smart enough to fix them all. A truly intelligent species knows that meddling is not often fixed by more meddling." -Journal of Dr. Harold Quickly, April 12, 2210

CHAPTER 14

The Neverwhere

Zurvan is studying me. We are once again gunfighters, faced off across a distance. Cautious. Opportunistic. Deadly.

"You have learned much," Zurvan says. "You're clever. Like the other one. The scruffy one."

Scruffy.

Benny.

Zurvan moves sideways, keeping his body in profile. We don't have guns—no need to make ourselves smaller targets in that way—but the movement seems natural. Instinctual. I glide sideways as well, circling in a counterclockwise swirl around the tension between us.

"I'm sorry we started off so badly," Zurvan offers, his hands spread wide in front of him. "I tried to kill you when I first met you, and I think, maybe this was a bad decision. You are not like the others."

"Others?" I watch his hands warily, ready to flee at the first sign of attack. I'm keeping a memory in the back of my mind. A zone of safety just below the surface, but ready should I need to open a portal.

"The ones who come here blind. The accidents. The ones who scream that they only made a *little* mistake. 'It's not my fault!' they yell. Always not their fault. Always accidents. They blunder around, yelling and screaming, praying for deliverance. I know, because I come to them. I *do* deliver them."

"You steal their minds," I say. "Accidental time travelers. Victims of circumstance."

"They are only victims of themselves." Zurvan sneers and points to his head. "I feel their weakness. Weak minds full of doubt and blame for others. 'But I'm a good person. Why did this happen to meeee?' I do these people a service. I let them be right. I take responsibility for their end because they won't do it themselves." He stops circling and points to me. "But you. You are different. You did not come here by accident. You or your shabby twin."

"What would you know about it?" I ask, trying to sound dismissive, but honestly I'm curious what he might know of Benny's arrival here.

"I've watched," Zurvan says. "I've seen him, the way he talks to the graves. He is slippery. Hard to catch. But one time I could have taken him. I had him unaware and almost reached out to him, but then I thought, maybe I don't *want* this mind. He is—what is the word you say? Troubled. He troubles himself. Lives with pain. He did not come here by accident, but he brought his pain with him. Perhaps that is not a mind I need to see." Zurvan shrugs. "Or maybe I was just feeling like letting him be. Who can say? I think maybe next time I will see what he has lost that has cost him so much."

I'm standing near the location where I saw the teenage girl vanish. Just a short distance from the place where in some distant century a ship will crash land and demolish this section of town. I gesture to the space between us. "Why here? What are you doing here?"

Zurvan folds his hands in front of himself and looks around. "This is your city. Your memory."

"Yeah, but you come here too. This space, but in different times." I gesture vaguely to the area beyond the restaurant where his ship will one day be. "You keep returning to that bombed-out-looking city. Why stick around?"

"I can see other places," Zurvan declares. "I can see the places of the people I have claimed. They show me their memories. But they are not mine." He holds his hands up and the scenery around us begins to change, water flooding the streets again and the city growing in ruined form across the horizon. "But this is my own. This is what I have left of my own memories. A month perhaps. A short life at the end of the world."

His hand passes over his forehead, pushing a strand of hair back under his turban and unconsciously touching the spot where his head was injured.

"What happened to the rest of your memories?" I ask. "What happened to the rest of your life?"

"It was purged," Zurvan replies. "Now I have only this . . ." He raises his hands, encompassing the ruined city " . . . And this." The scene around us vanishes and turns to sand. The desert scene he dropped me into before. He's made the portal shift so broadly and efficiently that I instantly came along for the ride. *Iran.* Startled and alarmed, I immediately throw my hands out and change it back, hurling the memory of St. Petersburg back into place, my St. Petersburg, whole and complete in 2009.

Zurvan erupts into laughter.

"Does the sand frighten you? Are you lost without your pavement and your Tee-ju-ana taco stand?" He continues to chuckle. "You need not fear the desert, my friend. The desert is peace. The desert is home. It was my first home. A long time ago."

I'm still on high alert, waiting for some new surprise, but happy that I was able to restore myself to home so quickly. Zurvan seems to be in a good mood and not fighting me for control of the space, but I still distrust everything about him.

"You are stronger than the others. Able to find your way around this place. Perhaps you have even seen beyond it. Have you seen the real Neverwhere? The relentless threads of time behind these veils?"

I don't respond. I merely keep my eyes on him.

"I think maybe you have." Zurvan begins his circling again and I move with him, keeping my distance. "So what I wonder is why *you* are here. You are not troubled in the head like the scruffy one. You don't cry in graveyards at night. What brought you to this place? You chose this, did you not?"

"That's my business," I reply.

"You're not willing to put our differences aside? Perhaps we could be partners. You are alone here the same as me. I could teach you things. Ways to manipulate this place and bend it to your will. I could help you."

"The way you helped Leonard?"

Zurvan narrows his eyes. "Leonard was too late. He failed me. But his training was not a total loss. He succeeded in making me known to his brethren. They send me presents from time to time to appease me, make up for his failures."

"Your kid messengers. The ones you sacrifice and rob of their minds."

"They *offer* me their minds," Zurvan says. "It's all they have to give for the moment. But I will make more of them soon. My reach has grown beyond this place."

Having completed a full circle of one another, I stop moving. "Whatever this is—this . . . friction between us—it can end. I am *not* offering my mind to you. You can just give up on that. Got it?"

Zurvan smiles and spreads his hands again. "We understand each other now. We don't need to fight. Maybe we work together. Perhaps when I leave here I'll even remember you, send you some gifts of your own to keep you entertained. A pretty girl perhaps? Someone to keep you company? You should want to be my friend. I could be very useful to you when I depart this place."

"Not if I leave first." The statement is out of my mouth before I've thought about it and I regret it immediately.

Zurvan raises an eyebrow, appraising me. "So you have some plans of your own? How interesting. How is it that you hope to accomplish this? You know someone too, perhaps?"

I do my best to play the statement off. "No. I mean, if you can do it, then I can too, right? How hard can it be?"

Zurvan's gaze is indecipherable. I can't tell if he can read the lie on my face.

"We will see then, won't we?" He gathers up his robes and holds them tightly to himself. "The ones who forced me here—the ones who took my life from me—they don't know how powerful I've become. When I return, I'm going to show them. I'll send them here and let them see what it means to be truly timeless."

He glances about the street and up at the palm trees, taking in the scene. "Thank you for showing me this place. It is so full of sun and life. Perhaps when I am free, I will visit it." With that he turns around and opens up a portal, the sand dunes again, but this time he only creates it on his side of the street. He steps into the memory and, with a final wave of his hand and an uneven smile, he vanishes.

I back away from the site of Zurvan's disappearance carefully. I summon my own memory, a ranch in Montana. A hillside under the stars. I step through the portal and close it behind me.

I have a lot to think about. Convenient, as there are not a lot of other duties for me in the Neverwhere.

This is a good memory. Safe.

I sit down on the small hill in the prairie grass and stare up at the million stars overhead, letting the stress of my encounter ebb away. Even without a physical body, my mind has tensed in Zurvan's presence—a clenched muscle that needs to be released. I let the tension go, imagining it seeping into the ground around me.

I don't know all of the details of Zurvan's life, but I've seen enough. I've seen his methods, and he uses tools I can't duplicate. I have no following of disciples in the real world avidly working for my second coming. I don't have a spaceship or a fiery church. My only hope of getting out of this place lies with a version of me who clearly doesn't want to let me in any more. Though I can't really blame him, what with me possessing his mind in the middle of the night and scaring Mym half to death.

The outline of a ranch house is just visible in the darkness a few hundred yards behind me, but the view in the other directions is all starlight. The last time I stared at this sky I was with Mym. A night full of questions and conversation and meteors. It was the first night she'd met me as a young woman, and I was trying so hard to make a good impression.

I can only wonder where she is now. What happened after Benny scared her? She looked so terrified as she ran away from me. Did she come back? Is she safe? I contemplate the night, waiting for the stars to fall—hoping that the meteors that rained down that night might return and bring me some answers.

The cosmos stays fixed and undisturbed.

The starlight is false. Even as I stare at it, the sky shimmers. The true reality of this place is color and time. There are deep clouds beyond that veil of black. Bold clusters of iridescent threads spun into intricate webs like so much cotton candy. Timestreams? Eternity? I can sense it out there, but for now I'm happy with my mirage. I am a mere memory of a man. Whatever binds me to the reality I remember seems a fragile and precarious tether in the face of all that forever. I don't wish to comprehend eternity. Not yet.

I think about the voices I heard in Zurvan's memory. He's taken so many souls here. What must they feel like, trapped inside another mind, then wrapped in all this Neverwhere? Even now I feel like I can hear their whispers. Whispers like wind in the tall grass. Soft rustles, like breathing. Like footfalls.

The hands are around my neck before my other senses can warn me. They clamp tight, ten sharp fingers pressing on my throat.

No! Not again.

I tip sideways, dragging the weight of my attacker down with me and rolling to try to dislodge him. I'm smothered by the weight of him, but get one foot under myself and heave, pitching both of us forward in a tangled knot. I crash into the ground partially upright and roll down the hill, my view oscillating between grassy earth, starry sky, and the enraged face of Benny, teeth bared and determined to choke the life out of me.

We tumble down the hill in a cluster of legs and arms so confusing that I have trouble telling where I end and Benny begins. I lash out with whatever appendages I can aim, jabbing elbows, heels, and fists toward any parts of him I can hit. Benny groans when we impact the earth at the bottom of the hill. His hands fall away from my neck.

"What the hell, man?" I scramble upright, backing away and probing my neck for damage. Benny is up again in a moment and chasing after me. He leaps and tackles me to the ground, flailing at my face with his fists. I bat them away as best I can, then throw a few punches of my own, trying to batter and pry him off me. We shear apart once more and stagger to our feet, a yard or two away from one another.

"We're already dead!" I yell at him. "What are you trying to do to me?"

"You're not dead enough!" Benny yells, and hurls himself at me again. This time I dodge his attack and send him sprawling into the grass.

"Hey, man. There's no point to us—" I don't get the rest out because Benny is back up and crashing into me again—a relentless and unreasoning force. I thud into the hillside and block my face from Benny's attacks. I might be dead, but his fists still hurt. I've been punched in the face enough times in real life to remember what it feels like, and it seems that memory is working against me now. "GET. OFF." I shove Benny back again, trying to free myself from his wild punches.

"I won't let him have her!" Benny yells. "If you won't stay away from him, then you leave me no choice!" He comes at me again with hands outstretched for my eyes. This time I'm ready and sidestep him, unleashing a right hook that catches him in the side of the head and spins him away from me.

"I'm not your enemy, damn it!"

He scowls at me and throws out his hands. This time he's not reaching for me though.

"What are you—"

He rushes me again, but this time I no longer have the hillside behind me. As he crashes into me, we plummet through the portal he's opened and into a different memory. Wet sand. St. Pete Beach in summer. The sunny beach carries on for miles, another memory bright with use. No fog to ruin this view. I've spent hundreds of hours on this white sandy stretch between Pass-a-Grille and Treasure Island, lounging with friends or motoring by in boats. The place is normally teeming with leather-skinned retirees and sunburnt tourists. Now Benny and I are the only patrons and he's dragging me headfirst into the warm Gulf, my eyes blinking away seawater as he splashes his way forward.

I've stopped struggling. Benny shoves me into the water, holding me under in an attempt to drown me. I knock his hands away from my throat a few times, but finally just lie there. I'm not going to drown. A cloud of air bubbles escapes my mouth as I attempt to shout underwater.

"THIS ISN'T GOING TO WORK!" The words come out as a garbled burble.

Benny is angrier than I've ever seen him. He continues his attempts to choke me, lifting me nearly to the surface and slamming me to the sand repeatedly, trying to force the life out of me. I'm not going to let him. I know the rules here. Concentrating, I open a portal directly beneath myself and Benny. A few hundred pounds of seawater and I plummet through the hole and splash all over the floor of the Southside Marina maintenance shop.

Benny looks up from where we've landed, partway between two

customer boats undergoing repairs. He scowls and scrambles up immediately, searching for some new way to injure me. He moves to Dave's toolbox, grabs an open end wrench off the top and hurls it at me. I duck and put an arm over my head as the wrench sails past.

"Dude! Cut it out!" I yell. Benny ignores me and chucks a screwdriver. I duck behind the nearest boat engine and keep cover. More tools ricochet off the boat. "This isn't productive!"

A whirring electric motor whizzes to life on the other side of the boat. I recognize it as the portable angle grinder.

Oh hell no.

I pop up above the level of the boat in time to see Benny advancing on me, the spinning disk of the angle grinder preceding him. I snatch up the nearest things I can find to hurl at him. These include a life vest, a rubber buoy, and a pair of a customer's boat shoes. These all bounce off Benny and his angle grinder at various velocities, but he continues to advance. It's only when I snatch up a wooden oar and brandish it in front of me that he finally pauses.

"You want to play?" I ask. "Okay, let's do this." I take a swing at Benny with the oar and he retreats, tossing the angle grinder to the floor and fleeing around the bow of the boat to my left. I take another cut at his head, but he ducks and my oar glances off the bow rail. Benny runs for the corner and comes up with an aluminum flag pole as a weapon. He rips a pirate flag off the pole, then spins and swings it at me. I parry the blow with my oar.

"I knew you were going to go back," Benny yells. "You just won't stay away from him. It's just a matter of time till he gets to you. He'll absorb your mind like the others and then he'll come for me. There won't be anywhere to hide."

Our weapons clatter a few more times as we hack at each other. I retreat between the two boats again, limiting him to a single approach. "You can't kill me here, man. We're already dead."

"If he can do it, then I can too," Benny declares. "I'll defeat you, and then I'll. Take. Your. Mind." Each word is punctuated with a swing of his flag pole.

My oar begins to splinter.

"I'm not going to let him take my mind," I say. "Or you. I know what I'm doing now." I grunt and parry his blows.

"You know nothing!" The flagpole shakes in his hands as he yells. "Have you heard the way they cry in the fog? The way he traps them? He uses their memories. Talks to people in the real world. He's getting too powerful. You've been connecting to one of *us* in the real world. What happens if he gets into your memories? What if he gets out?"

"What do you know?" I ask. "Do you know what they're doing? The ones he talks to?"

"I've listened. In the fog. They're going to bring him back. He promises them a new life. New chances."

"Chances at what?"

"To save themselves from what's coming."

I keep my oar up and ready, but it looks like it only has a few more hits left in it. Long cracks radiate down the handle and big chunks of it are missing. Benny sees his advantage and grins. He lifts the flagpole and swings hard. I stagger back under the strike. The oar loses its top, the flat paddle skittering across the shop floor, leaving only a jagged handle. Benny swings again and charges at me. The remnants of my oar disintegrate in my hands and I reel backward, one hand out to brace myself against the rolling shop doors. Benny throws a hand out and changes the scenery so fast that I lose my balance. I'm no longer in the maintenance shop, but back inside my apartment. I crash to the floor amid shards of broken glass in the living room. I grunt from the fall then sit up gingerly. Wind is whistling through the broken window pane in the door.

It takes me a moment to orient myself. The apartment looks as it did the last time I left it. Dark clouds outside. My softball bat resting at the foot of the coffee table. Benny seems thrown off by the changes and the dim light. He glances around the living room, then back to the darkened bedroom hallway.

"What happened here?" His eyes flit to the windows, the black clouds roiling across the sky. The smell of rain on the wind.

"You shouldn't have brought us here. It's not safe," I say, struggling to rise from pile of shards. "He found me."

Benny's eyes rest on the softball bat. "How did he—" His voice is cut short by the appearance of a long blade protruding from his chest. He looks down in shock at the end of the shiny knife stabbing through the front of his shirt. The amorphous form of Zurvan oozes from the darkness of the hallway.

"I thought you might come back here." He steps forward and places his other hand to the top of Benny's head, cocking it toward him. "So good of you to bring along our scruffy friend." Benny's expression jolts from surprised to terrified in an instant. His limbs go rigid and his eyes are wide. "Time to see what makes him tick." Zurvan tightens his grip on Benny's skull. Benny throws his hands to the top of his head and mouths a scream, but no sound comes out.

"NO!" I spring forward and charge at Zurvan, aiming to tackle him away from Benny, but Zurvan throws a hand out and changes the scene around himself faster than thought. For a moment he's standing in desert sand, Benny's pale face translucent in the sunlight. The sun beams passing through him seem to be taking the substance of his body with them.

And then they're gone.

I crash into the far wall of my apartment, crunching the plaster, then slump to the floor.

No.

No. No. No.

My body twitches in fear. *Shit.* He took Benny. He knows this place now. *He'll come back.* I struggle to my feet and stagger toward the center of the room, trying to open a portal to somewhere else. *Where? Where can I go?*

The light shimmers and the portal opens. A dark hole into another time. I feel the presence of Zurvan reenter the room before I even see him. My mind tingles with the energy of his newly expanded mind.

"Going so fast?" His voice is amused.

I turn to the wall where he's reappeared. He's grinning. Comfortable. This place is his memory now too.

I dive through the portal and tumble to the ground beyond, closing the window behind me, just as Zurvan gets close.

He knows. He has my life now. Benny's life.

I get to my feet in the dank underground tunnel. I'm below street level, just another lost soul in the Seattle Underground. This memory is recent. One of my chronothon adventures. An ending of sorts in a strange and lonely timestream. A place Benny could never have come. I stagger a few feet and collapse again, slumping against the dirty wall of the tunnel.

Since the moment I saw my dog in my parents' old house, I haven't lost my composure. Not even in the face of all the nothingness I've witnessed. Now I'm falling apart again. Seeing Benny wracked with pain. His face. My face. It's more than I can handle.

I let the sobs out. Fingers clenched in the dust of the tunnel, I shudder and shiver, letting out the emotions I've been trying so hard to contain.

The darkness closes in on me. I don't want to be dead. I don't want the people I love to be dead. I don't want other selves and half-lived alternate lives to end any more than I want to lose my own.

Benny is gone. Zurvan is free to roam his past now. He'll dissect the little bits of memory that make me me. And then what? Will he come for me? Was he taking Benny because he needs to or just because he could use him to get to me? I've been foolish to think I could contend with him.

Zurvan is stronger. More powerful. He has the upper hand here, controlling the very space I have left to move in.

Huddled in my dark tunnel, I feel cornered.

There is going to be an end to this. I can feel it coming now. My end.

Shivering in the dark tunnel, I let the fear run its course. *Let it come, then let it go.* My fear is strong, but it's not the only instinct I've got.

I'm still here, still surviving.

I reach inside my memory, searching for a connection, hoping that the me in the real world might be closer now. Letting myself hope that he's decided to let me back in again, decided to save me from this place. For a moment I feel something, like he's here in the darkness alongside me, claustrophobic and worried. But then the feeling vanishes. I grope in the darkness, reaching for the connection again. Anything to tie me to the real world, but if he was there, he's shut me out, leaving me to face my fears alone.

"Help me." I whisper my plea to the darkness. I don't know who is there to hear, but I beg anyway. *Somebody. Please.*

I don't know how long I can stay like this. This tunnel is safe for now. Zurvan won't find me here. But I'm trapped and buried. The tunnel walls are hardly a fortress, but this memory is one of the few that are mine alone. For now I wrap my arms around my knees and resign myself to hiding.

The Neverwhere may linger on the edge of eternity, but it's an edge I've gotten too close to. As Zurvan takes over more and more of this place, I get the feeling that each movement I make is just pushing me closer and closer to the edge.

I'm running out of time.

London, UK, 2165

Carson, Tucket, and I are gathered around the combat knife. We've gotten as much as we can from Doctor Quickly and Professor Chun about our mission, but the parameters are still a little fuzzy. We need more information about The Eternals if we're going to rescue Mym, and while every moment of waiting only increases my worry about her safety, I have to rely on our strongest asset—time.

I'm a time traveler now and, if there is a moment anywhere in the future or past when we can save her, I'll find it. That's what I keep telling myself anyway.

I read off the coordinates from the face of the playing card we were given and Tucket and Carson set their respective devices. I double-check my own chronometer before beginning the countdown.

Tucket is nervous. His forehead is sweating, but he's put on a brave face. Carson looks as cool as ever, but I can tell he's tense with energy too. Years of friendship have given away his tells. The speed of his gestures and the way his eyes keep finding the clock on the wall, aware of each remaining second till our departure.

Doctor Quickly and Professor Chun are behind Tucket, observing. The scientist is usually an enigma to me, his emotions as much of a puzzle as his brilliance, but as I count down from five, he looks me in the eyes and gives me a final nod. We both know the stakes. And we both love her.

"Three . . . two . . . one." I press the pin.

We're in a jump room. I recognize the layout—clean bare walls surrounding an unencumbered space for our arrival. A single anchor stand rises from the floor and supports a past version of the combat knife. Humming fans in the ceiling are keeping the room contaminant-free. The coordinates we've been given have taken us forward nearly a week and a half from my perspective, ten days since Mym was taken. I'm irritated to be going the wrong direction. If anything, I want to be preventing her capture, not prolonging it.

One jump room door is labeled as an exit. We open it and find ourselves at the back of a dingy, dimly-lit bar.

I'd always imagined the future to be shiny. That's the way *The Jetsons* told me it would be on Saturday morning cartoons. The future was a world of clear glass houses and whizzing metal vehicles, sparkling and efficient. Of course there were other versions out there like the apocalyptic wastelands of *Terminator* movies and *Mad Max*. This bar might fit better into one of those futures. But this bar didn't suffer nuclear fallout or deadly robots. It doesn't need John Connor or a road warrior to save it. Its own apocalypse could have been easily forestalled by a mop bucket and a cleaning crew armed with bleach and Windex, but those saviors of sanitation clearly never arrived.

"You just going to stand there or are you coming in?" A man in the shadows of a corner booth extends an arm into the light of a dusty overhead lamp. The glowing end of a recently extinguished match is flicked through the air toward an already overflowing trash can. The matchstick misses its mark and falls to the floor to land among a half dozen of its predecessors.

The man in the booth draws on his thin cigar and gestures to us with his other hand. "We haven't got all day, you know. Not getting paid by the hour on this one."

"Let them get their bearings, Rix." A swinging door opens behind the bar and a huge black man in faded fatigues moves through, carrying two beers in each hand. He pauses near the front of the bar to take us in. "You look like you just fell down the rabbit hole ass backwards. You're in the right place, though. Don't worry, the bar only looks bad because it's Rixon's."

"This bar looks great," the man called Rixon replies. He stretches one leg out along the bench he's seated on. "It's lived in." He eyes us up with another pull on his cigar.

"It's a shithole," the man holding the beers replies. He sets the beers on the nearest high top and steps over to us, extending a hand to me first. "Eon Whitaker." His handshake is solid and somehow lenient at the same time. The rippling muscles of his forearm seem to be actively reducing the potential damage to my hand they might otherwise cause.

"Ben Travers."

"Lazy, too-good-to-get-off-his-ass-to-greet-clients, shit-for-brains over there is Rixon Versa."

"That's my family name actually," Rixon replies, finally sliding out of the booth and standing. "But he forgot, 'owner-of-all-the-beer-and-liquor-in-this-place.' He tends to omit that part." He slouches toward us, all sharp angles and jagged edges. Unlike his hulking companion, Rixon is slim, but he exudes danger, a razor turned man.

Eon gathers up the beer bottles and moves toward a table in the middle of the room. "I collect these as compensation for putting up with you. Hazard pay. Or maybe it's for pain and suffering." The chair creaks under his weight but doesn't dare break.

Rixon motions us toward the other seats around the table. "Welcome, gentlemen. What'll you be drinking?"

"Didn't really come to drink," I say. "We've got work to do. I was told you were going to help us."

Rixon cocks his head to one side and takes another drag on the thin cigar. Finally he nods. "All right. Straight to business it is then." He motions us toward the chairs again, then leans conspiratorially toward his partner. "Romeo has a hard-on for efficiency."

I take a seat on the opposite side of the two men, Carson beside me and Tucket cautiously taking the seat at the end.

"We'll get to the job at hand," Eon says. "Noelle gave us your details with the contract. Few of them anyway. We don't handle a lot of abduction cases as a rule, but it seems like you get some VIP status from her. She didn't give us much on this girlfriend of yours, but we did our preliminary investigation into the abduction, and it seems straight enough."

"I've been giving the situation a lot of thought," I say. "Since we're meeting so long after the abduction happened, I think our first priority should be to get back there to the scene. Maybe they didn't get far. The house they took her from had rough conditions, bad for time traveling, but wherever they took her, we might be able to jump in there, surprise them, and get Mym out before they ever have a chance to enact their plans for her. We can defuse this whole thing before they even know we're there. Whatever they want after that is a moot point."

"Romeo has the whole thing figured out, Whit," Rixon says. He flicks his cigar ash onto the floor. "Maybe we should just give Noelle her money back and tell her our services aren't needed."

Eon frowns at his partner and turns to me. "It's a good strategy, Ben. But in this case it's not going to work." He reaches deep into a pocket and extracts a phone-type device that he slides across the table. "If you want to access the meta scene, it's all there."

"He doesn't have a Third Eye," Tucket says, piping up from the end of the table. Rixon turns and stares at him as if surprised he can speak. Tucket glances at him, but quickly turns away, his eyes finding me instead.

"Yeah. We're a little behind the times on the tech," I say. "What does it show?"

Eon grabs the device again. "My apologies. Noelle did mention you'd need some gear." He fiddles with the device. "We did do some recon at the time of the abduction. Filmed the scene from a distance. We got satellite on it and a few remote viewing locations. All the short-range meta cameras were disabled. These guys were smart enough to shut those down before showing up."

"You have a satellite?" Carson asks. "That's pretty sweet."

"It's not strictly ours, legally speaking," Rixon replies. "But it can *become* ours from time to time."

"What did you see?" I ask.

"On vis, we got shit all," Rixon replies. "These guys were blacked out darker than Batman's asshole. But we got their heat signature on the satellite."

I lean forward, leaning my elbows on the table. "I didn't see much after they grabbed Mym, but they went down the cliff. Looked like they had a boat. Seemed small from the drag marks. Not something they could take very far."

"They did indeed have a wee dinghy," Rixon says, smirking.

"So did you track it? Can we intercept it? We could get a faster boat, go after them and—"

"We tracked it," Rixon says. "Right to the point when it was blown up and sunk."

"Sunk?" Carson says. "How far out? Did they swim ashore?"

Blown up? The idea that Mym could have been killed or gone down in the ocean hits me, and I catch myself holding my breath.

"She's all right," Eon says, holding a hand out to ease the tension. "Rix is leaving out a few details, and failing to follow appropriate client protocols, I might add." He glares at Rixon and then turns to me. "Everything is under control. Our target—your girlfriend—is safe. We assure you that everything is being done to ensure her *continued* safety."

"Whatever. I was getting to that," Rixon replies. "Yeah. She's fine. We just can't get to her. They had a sub."

"A what?" I ask.

"A sub," Rixon replies. "You know, a submarine? Goes under water?" He makes a quick swishing motion with his hand. "Ringing any bells?"

"I know what a submarine is," I reply. "I just didn't think the Eternals would be the type to have one. They seem like a bunch of religious whackos. Where did they get a submarine?"

He gestures toward Carson and me. "Where did a couple of know-nothing yahoos from the land of yesteryear come up with their own personal time machines?"

I self-consciously touch the chronometer on my wrist. "Okay. Fair point, I guess. But we had help from legitimate people. Who would give these guys a sub?"

"The Americans, the Russians, the Chinese—" Rixon counts off on his fingers.

"The point is, they have one," Eon interjects. "From whom is not really our concern. What's more important is that it puts your rescue plan out of the realm of possibility. Water, as you know, is the least hospitable terrain for time travel. And even if your girlfriend were to get her hands on her own chronometer, without an anchor from somewhere outside the sub, no amount of jumping around inside is going to land her anywhere but still inside that sub. We can't get in. She can't get out." He looks to me. "You have to hand it to these guys. They thought ahead on this."

The idea of Mym stuck aboard a submarine with a bunch of crazies has drained me of any sense of objectivity. "I'm not about to respect anything these shitheads have done. They've got Mym, and we have no idea what they're doing to her."

Eon holds his hands up. "Right. I'm just saying that we can't underestimate these guys." He lays his hands back on the table. "Okay. So given what you know of Miss Quickly in situations of stress, how does she typically—"

"How am I supposed to know? She's never been—" I stand up and kick my chair out from under me. "Goddamn it!" I run my hands over my head, trying keep myself from throwing something. *Mym could be being tortured right now for all I know.* "Where did the sub go? Where are they taking her?"

Rixon speaks up again. "We have the heat signature of the sub. We lose it for a while in the Atlantic, but it surfaces again in Florida in a few days. The whole trip takes about two weeks."

"TWO WEEKS?"

I don't know what to do with my own body. I feel like my mind is trying to jump out of my skin. "We can't leave Mym trapped on a submarine with these people for two weeks. We can't."

Eon is holding up his hands again. "Ben, please sit down. We have the situation under control."

"HOW IS THIS UNDER CONTROL?"

Eon merely gestures to the place at the table again.

I take a deep breath and pick up the chair I've knocked over, trying hard to disconnect my mind from the image of Mym as a prisoner. I exhale and sit back down. I ball my fists against my legs and do my best to stay calm. "Okay. What else do we know?"

Eon fiddles with something on his phone device, then turns to Rixon. "What did you do with those meta headsets you made? The Z-grade ones you modified from the service."

"The mind hack?" Rixon says. "You want to use that on him?"

Eon waves the response away. "No, the headset for non-meta users. The one we use for analogs and pre-AOA perps to show them their future crimes."

"Oh. Yeah, I've got those."

"Get one. Let's show him the vid."

Rixon looks at me, then slides out of his chair and disappears into a side room. When he returns, he slides a pair of goggles across the table to me. I pick them up gingerly.

"This is it?"

"Yeah. Don't worry. It's safe," Rixon says.

"I haven't had the best luck with the metaspace. Sort of messes with my mind."

"You probably just had the wrong type of tech. Some cheap-ass civilian shit. This is military grade," Eon says.

I slide the goggles on and get an immediate sensation of extra depth from the surroundings. For a moment the lines and details of everything in the room blur, separating and then coming back into sharp focus. After that my view is normal.

"All right, check this out," Eon says. He presses something on his phone device and a 3D projection of a submarine materializes over the table. The view is not merely of the exterior, however. I can see inside the submarine, identifying the moving bodies of the crew. Each one glows with a unique heat signature.

"We picked this up from a marine life monitoring station in the North Atlantic, just off the coast of France," Eon says. "They have these stations all over the ocean in that area, keeping tabs on the whale population. Here's the part of the recording you'll want to see." He points toward the front of the sub where four figures are walking along a corridor in a single line. The second silhouette in the row is a figure I'd recognize anywhere. *Mym.*

Eon points to the bulkhead where the figures are about to traverse a doorway into a new section of the sub. "Watch this," Eon says.

The first figure in the line steps through the doorway and turns around. Mym climbs through after him, but when she clears the access, she stoops low then comes up fast, jamming an elbow into the jaw of the man in front of her. He keels over like a limp fish. Mym spins and kicks the man behind her, sending him tumbling back through the bulkhead door, before she turns and sprints away—her heat signature glowing brighter as she runs.

"Where is she going?" I ask. "There's nothing up there."

Mym heads toward the bow of the ship, then ducks into a side room off the passage and slams a door closed, sealing off the small space she's now trapped herself in while the other figures who had been pursuing her pound against the door. It's clear from their body language that there is some sort of conversation going on. Mym even goes so far as to press a button on the wall, communicating with the outside.

A crowd of figures now assembles in the corridor, gesturing toward the door and occasionally pounding on it. The man whom Mym had knocked out in the hallway is revived and brought to the door, but none of their continued efforts convince her to open it.

"What is she going to do?" Tucket asks. "She can't stay in there the whole time, can she?"

"She doesn't have to," Eon replies. "Watch."

As we look on, Mym sends another message through the submarine's intercom, then moves to the front wall of the room. Once there, she fidgets with something on her right hand, then places it to the wall. A moment later, she disappears.

"Holy shit," I mutter.

"Would have assumed these guys would have known enough to take her chronometer away from her, but they must not have been as bright as we figured," Rixon says. "What are your thoughts?"

I smile at the now-blank room in the sub. "They did take it away from her," I say. "She has a pendant chronometer she usually wears around her neck, but that's not what she used. The one she just used was on her hand." I recall the ring I discovered on her finger. "She has a ring. She said it was a gift from her dad when she turned sixteen." I can't help but grin. "*I* didn't even know that was a chronometer."

My smile fades when I remember what Eon had said. Without an anchor, she's still not going to get off the ship.

"What happened next? How long did she leave for?"

"We don't know," Eon replies. "It's our guess that she skipped over significant enough chunks of time that she didn't have to worry about food or water on the trip. Maybe she popped in multiple times. Maybe she skipped to the end. It's possible these guys were able to get a torch and cut through that door somehow, but it's hard to say. What we do know is that the sub made the trip across the Atlantic and into the Gulf of Mexico. It turned right and headed up the coast."

"To Saint Petersburg?" I ask.

"Not quite. They stopped off earlier than that. Nyongo Harbor."

"Where's that?" Carson asks. "Never heard of it."

"That's because in your time it was named Charlotte Harbor. And the city was Port Charlotte. Now it's Port Nyongo, named after the space explorer."

"What, like a NASA astronaut?" I ask.

"First private citizen to set foot on Mars," Rixon says. "Damian Nyongo.

Built an entire empire from privatized space travel. They renamed the city after him."

"Sounds like an awesome guy," Carson says.

"Okay, so back on point, here," I say. "Mym is in Port Nyongo?"

"We believe so," Eon replies. "According to heat signatures we picked up there, the sub lingered outside the harbor for three extra days after arrival. The only reason it would make sense to do that would be if they didn't have their prize yet and were waiting for her to show back up. Either she told them when she was coming back, or they just waited her out. Either way, I doubt they came into port without her."

"Did they bring her ashore in Port Nyongo?" I ask.

"That's what we're going to find out," Rixon replies. "We lost the sub off our scans once it came into port. There are too many inlets to monitor. We'll have to search it out the hard way. But we figured you'd want in on that part of the mission."

"You figured right. How far is Port Nyongo? Do you have a way to get us there?"

Rixon grins. "You could say that." He picks absentmindedly at one of his fingernails.

I rise from my chair and glare at him. "Well? What do we need? Another anchor? Time gate? Airplane? I'm good to go, man. In case you hadn't noticed, I'm ready to be there already."

Rixon stands up and meets my eye. "Providing transportation wasn't part of our contract."

"What the hell kind of a contract is that, then? You tell us where she is, but you don't have any kind of plan to get us there? Shit, I can figure that out. You have an airport nearby? Come on, Carson. Tucket? You ready?"

Tucket and Carson both get to their feet. Eon slowly rises as well. "Rixon, why do you always do this with clients? Don't you see how it affects our reputation?"

Rixon only grins at him. Turning to me, he gestures vaguely toward the door. "Go ahead. Sally forth, Sally. Airport is just down the street. Go ask for a ticket, see how that works out for you."

He has a smug grin on his face that I'd like to remove, but I'm too irritated to bother with a response. I simply move to the door. "Come on, guys. Apparently we can handle this on our own. Carson and Tucket gather behind me. I swing open the door and am hit in the face with the blast of humid, salty air. Outside the dim and smoky interior of Rixon's bar, bright sunlight gleams off a glittering harbor. Three enormous ships lie at anchor in the bay and dozens more are tied up at the docks. The docks are bustling with activity, much of it swirling through the sky. Drones and various human-occupied vehicles are whizzing through the blue above me circumnavigating the base of a massive tower structure. It seems The Jetsons did get a few things right after all.

When I turn around, Eon is just shaking his head.

Rixon gives me a wicked grin, then sticks another cigar in his mouth and lights it. He gives a few puffs before blowing the smoke out in a long stream.

"Welcome to Port Nyongo."

"I've been asked if the discovery of time travel has brought me wealth and fame. In some respects it has, but that is not a goal I've aspired to. The legacy I'm proudest of is that I've littered the centuries with friends."-Journal of Dr. Harold Quickly, 1781

CHAPTER 15

Port Nyongo, 2165

"You're looking at your new home for the next few days," Rixon says. "The sub pulls into port three days from now, so we've got some work to do."

We're standing out front of his dilapidated bar taking in the fast-moving city. The view of the harbor is impressive, a moving diorama of industrial vessels and high end yachts weaving their way around massive pilings. But it's the sky that inspires awe. Beyond the foreground of whizzing delivery drones and daredevil seagulls, there exists a structure of gargantuan proportions.

The technological wonder resembles a gigantic scaffold or perhaps the inside of the Eiffel tower if it were viewed from the perspective of an ant. The complex structure is teeming with activity—pods and elevators gliding up and down. My neck is craned to take in its height, but I fail to see its peak. The center of the tower vanishes into the atmosphere without any sign of stopping.

The sun is just up on the eastern horizon, throwing off my already-addled sense of time. The front of Rixon's bar is one of a dozen or more similar establishments lining a steep road climbing away from the harbor. The fact that we're on a hill this high up strikes me as odd. Florida doesn't boast many legitimate hills and, when it does, they're usually farther inland. This cluster of seedy looking establishments is at least a hundred feet above sea level and nowhere near the apex of the road. Higher up, the buildings zig and zag in a conjunction with the road and form a sort of tiered restaurant district. Other buildings on neighboring hills ascend even higher.

Down toward the water's edge, I have a clear view of the barrier walls erected to keep out the sea.

This city has not been shaped by nature as much as it has been shaped by design. That fact has not changed much from my time. Even in 2009, many of the communities in Charlotte County were preplanned rotundas and matching condo developments. Now it seems the designs of the age are going vertical.

"It's a space elevator," Eon says, answering the question on all of our minds. "The glory of the New Space Coast."

"Pretty amazing," Carson says. "How high does it go?"

"Upper atmosphere in most parts, and well into space at the peak."

"Have you been up it?" Tucket asks.

"On occasion," Eon replies. "Space travel isn't really my favorite. Any of you boys ever been off planet?"

I can feel Carson's eyes on me, but I don't reply.

"Down at the water's edge is where you two are going to start your investigation." Rixon points to Carson and me. "We've got a couple days till Quickly's daughter and the submarine arrive. They're not exactly going to just pull up to the dock and hop out in broad daylight. My guess is they'll have some kind of system set up to get her ashore secretly. That's why we need you two to do some covert operations and see what you can find out."

"Why us?" I ask. "You two don't have any contacts that can help us?"

"We have plenty of contacts, but we're well-known here. Rixon's bar might be a shithole, but come nightfall it's a popular shithole. If we go asking around about these Eternals directly, it'll get back to them. You two are unknowns. You're analogs, you're off-Grid, and you don't even use the metaspace, so that will help you fit in better with the crowd we're after."

"The Eternals don't use the metaspace?" I ask.

Eon scratches at his jaw. "Who knows. They probably do in their normal day-to-day, but there's no way they're conducting business that way. They've got some kind of church up in St. Pete for recruiting people, but down here they keep things low key."

"Secret handshakes and shit," Rixon says.

"Like a secret society?" Carson asks.

"Exactly," Rixon says. "I've overheard the occasional mumblings in the bar, rumors about a group growing in the docks, but the underlings never know much about what they're really up to. I figure whoever's in charge probably waits till members are good and in before springing the crazy on them."

"How are we going to make contact?" Carson asks.

"We need you to go undercover," Eon says. "Get to know the locals. Make like you're looking for work, homeless, that sort of thing. From what we hear, that's who they tend to recruit. If they're landing a sub here somewhere, they likely need dockhands. The regular marina docks are mostly worked by folks who don't make the cut for work on the Skylift, and they tend to employ human staff for the wettest jobs since synths and saltwater don't always mix."

"How will we find these people?" I ask.

Rixon points to the goggles still hanging around my neck. "We'll talk you through it, be your remote backup."

"And your security," Eon adds. "If things start to go south, we'll step in to extract you." He folds his arms across his chest and it's obvious once again from the motion that the potential of his muscles is largely going to waste at the moment. I get the subtle impression that he'd enjoy us getting into some scrap that would require his intervention.

"What if we're not good at being homeless?" Tucket asks. "What if they don't like us?"

"Not you," Eon replies. "These two are going undercover. We've got a different job for you."

A few hours later, Carson and I are on the corner of Edgewater and Tarpon, marveling at how a once-sleepy Florida city could have been transformed so completely into a booming spaceport.

On the way down the hill, we pass a light rail station that lists St. Petersburg's downtown stops along its line. The entire stretch of the Gulf Coast is now traversable in minutes instead of hours. Miami is likewise considered a nearby destination and, to my surprise, there is even an option for Freeport in the Bahamas—undoubtedly an impressive bridge to travel across.

Carson and I have been outfitted by Eon in what we're told is the most inconspicuous garb of the day. We're wearing battered hardhats and portable air packs with oxygen masks that clip to our collars—the ubiquitous symbol of Skylift day laborers. We're dressed in rugged but lightweight workman's pants with loose-fitting cotton shirts—long sleeved to keep the sun off our arms. The sleeves come in handy for covering up my chronometer. Eon had suggested leaving them behind to increase our authenticity, but my level of trust for this operation is nowhere near that point.

Carson likewise has retained his chronometer, though he seems far less concerned about its security than I do. After a few minutes in the sun, he relegates his to a pocket so that he can roll up his sleeves. He's received his own pair of metaspace goggles and is looking around the city with interest, taking in the changes the future has brought.

A meta poster on the wall of a corner grocery advertises the latest in digital diversions, an interactive underwater ocean trek, "Effects so real your fingers will prune. Brought to you by Digi-com."

As poor workmen, Carson and I have been advised to skip the high speed rail station and use the free electric bus service that travels from the harbor to the various work stations around the port. We have money, after a fashion. Eon has given both of us a sort of data stick called a chit. The chit hangs on a lanyard around our necks and is another sign that we're too poor to manage all metaspace identities and purely digital bank accounts.

We climb aboard the free bus and wind our way along the waterfront, jostled by the other aspiring day workers. Most are wearing hardhats and cheap portable masks like ours, but a fair amount have more advanced gear like oxygen compressors and full-faced helmets. A couple are wearing battered-looking spacesuits with onboard pressurization. The sight of the pressure suits and the Digi-com logo on them brings back a few memories. I find myself wondering if their suits come with onboard A.I.

More meta posters and advertisements flash on the digital windows offering beautiful landscapes. Space treks to Earthrim—which I learn is a sort of space station resort—are a favorite getaway for locals hoping to escape the heat. The advertising shows iridescent pools and expansive views of the planet, most also including beautiful people in little to no clothing. As a particularly fetching young woman winks at us from the advertisement, a man next to me catches me staring and jerks his thumb toward the ad. "Made it to Earthrim once a few years ago. Believe me, she don't really live there."

I smile and turn away from the digital views. "Figured it was probably too good to be true. Seems like advertising never changes. Big promises, no satisfaction."

The man cracks a crooked grin. "You boys new in town? Haven't seen you on this run before."

"Yeah, just got in," I reply.

"Down from up north?"

"Uh . . . Washington," I improvise. Not sure if St. Pete would be far enough away to be considered an out-of-towner.

"You left the northwest for this? Damn, son. That's a long haul."

"Heard there was work down here."

"What'd you do in Washington?"

I try to think of something that might make me a likely candidate for a job at a spaceport. "Um, aviation. Worked at a plant near Seattle building planes." I have no idea if Boeing is still in business in this century, so I don't attempt to drop a real name, but I'm hoping somebody is still building planes out there.

My bus companion nods. Either I'm right or he doesn't know the difference.

"You'll want to get in good with Pikey if this is your first week. He does most of the picking on this route. Tends to favor the vets he served with, but if he likes you, you'll stay busy enough. If you don't get picked today, try buying him a beer at Dos Toros tonight."

"All right, thanks for the tip."

The man nods and goes back to looking out the digital windows.

When the doors of the bus finally slide open at the space docks, I'm once again awestruck at the enormity of the construction around me. New Space Coast is not just a nickname of the area Port Nyongo resides in, it's also the name of the primary company building ships here. The NSC logo is on practically everything, a blue rocket with the letters emblazoned on the side, passing a yellow sunburst. Other smaller companies likewise post ads and logos in the metaspace—names like Sky-Con and StarMight.

High overhead, the space elevator infrastructure branches out in multiple directions and platforms host craft in various sizes and stages of completion. There are also office levels and tourist zones.

A stream of well-dressed employees is swelling in from the train station and moving toward the lower port buildings. Many of them are synths or trans-humans. A handful of the trans-human employees have synths trailing behind them like valets, carrying their belongings for them. A line of security personnel is on hand, directing the flow of day workers to the right and away from the other more respectable foot traffic.

Carson and I jostle our way into an interior corridor under a sign that reads, "Labor Center." In the press of bodies moving through the corridor, we get separated, but I can still spot Carson's red hair as the group he's with surges ahead.

The bus had not smelled very pleasant, but inside the confined hallway the odor has gotten worse. It's apparent that many of the men and women around me haven't seen the inside of a shower in a while. A bedraggled-looking woman ahead of me is cursing and gesturing from side to side, pointing at the air around her. Her hair is badly entangled in a loose oxygen hose coming off her air pack, and she seems to be fighting with some other encumbrance, but no one is trying to help her. The rest of the group is giving her a wide berth.

The woman spins and gets me in her sights, mutters more curses, and storms toward me. I dodge out of the way of her pointed finger, which she is wagging ahead of her, but she pays me no mind as she barrels past, forging her way back the way we've come, shoving and prying at the people in her way. She snaps at one woman with her teeth, coming away with a mouthful of her victim's hair before disappearing into the mob.

"Fuckin' waste," the man next to me mutters. He's bearded and lean, with eyes that look like they've spent a lot of time squinting into the sun. He's a leathery brown all over and has a sticker on his hardhat that reads "Unless you need an ass kicking, don't tell me how to do my job." A sewn-on patch on his shirt reads "Greg." His eyes have followed the angry woman into the crowd behind us. Unlike the workers on the other sides of me, he doesn't reek, so I edge nearer to him.

"I guess she forgot her meds this morning," I say.

"Meds don't help that. She's got freeloaders up there." Greg taps his hardhat and goes back to facing forward as we press on through the corridor. His statement makes me curious.

"What do you mean, freeloaders?"

The man rises up on tiptoes to try to see over the stream of bodies. He settles back down again, restlessly resigned to our slow progress.

"That was Sonia Davis. Perfectly normal till a few weeks ago. Good foreman. Had her own crew up on the high lifts. Worked for her a few times. Then she got into that 'free your mind' shit. Look what it got her."

"What's 'free your mind?'"

"You haven't seen those creeps down at the parks? Guys advertising free intelligence?" He shakes his head. "I told her it was too good to be true. Ain't nothin' free in this world when you get down to it. There's always a catch."

"I'm not from around here. I must have missed them. How can they offer free intelligence?"

"Saying you'll get a lifetime of education, knowledge of the future. Real organic memories that won't go away when you fail to pay for your upgrades. The whole system is bullshit, so I assume they're just trying to capitalize. They know they've got an audience here because most of us yardies can't afford any plug and play degrees."

He shifts in position and waits for the line to get moving again. "Don't know how it is where you come from, but no one in The Yards has the coin to pay for all those updates. That's how they get you, you know? First few years of plug-in education are free. Pop in a lesson, you got yourself a kid who knows algebra. Little toddlers are speaking at least three languages around the house now. Seven if they're rich. Seems like every year they offer some new way for your kid to stand out. Makes it all seem so easy. But that stuff don't stick like it used to. Ain't like the old days when people learned for real. You hit the end of the public school system and don't have the money for upgrades? Bam. Your account's unplugged and there goes your kid's education. They don't remember nothin' once that happens. I can't remember shit-all from my time in school and my little girl's gonna be in the same boat unless I stay working. I'll be damned if she ends up working in The Yards like her old man."

"That happened to Sonia because she tried to get more education?" I jerk my thumb toward the area where the crazed woman had disappeared.

"Damn shame," the man mutters. "She had real balls. Not like the rest of these lazy bastards." He cups his hands and yells across the morass of bodies moving ever so slowly through the door at the far end of the corridor. "COME ON! WE'VE GOT WORK TO DO!"

The herd of workers doesn't move any quicker, but a few people in front of us pack in a little tighter, making room for Greg to edge his way forward.

When I eventually make it through the door, the crowd is spread out through a single-level auditorium. People are still jostling their way forward to the far side where two roll-up doors are open and some sort of rounded vehicle is parked at each exit, loading on workers. Not everyone is getting on. The selection process has already begun, and workers on my side of a dividing rail are looking to a podium in the center of the room.

Atop the podium is a stern-looking man with a thick neck. He's sandy-haired and bristling with stubble, though the top of his head is bald. He's pointing out workers and shouting names, clearly familiar with most of the applicants. He's referencing something about each person he calls on with a chart or list that I can't see, and it's only when I don the goggles again that I understand how the process works.

Each worker in the room has their name and a list of titles hanging above their heads in the metaspace. The people being called are predominantly those with longer skill sets, or equipped with the best gear, though I do see a few get selected that seem to be specialists. The man is ruling some options out.

"Don't need no plumbing today, Skeet." The man at the podium is communicating with a worker named Ansel Skeeterman down in front whose skill set only lists plumbing-related services. The name hanging over the man at the podium reads D. Pike. His title is listed as Chief Foreman. He scans the room again, processing titles and skills off the myriad floating resumes.

A yellow button flashes in the corner of my goggles' view screen and, when I focus on selecting it, I hear the crackle of a connection being made.

"'Bout time you checked in." Rixon's voice fills my head in stereo sound. "What's the point of me helping you if you never turn your coms on? Now listen. Don't get picked."

"What?" I say.

"Don't. Get. Picked." Rixon's voice is a dagger, each word a distinct jab. "We want you staying with the leftovers. I never wanted you to get this far in. Can you see your buddy?"

I scan the room for Carson. It's harder than I'd expect. At 6'3" I'm usually one of the taller heads in a given room, but not here. Either the human race has evolved to be a lot taller in last hundred years or a bunch of these workers have had body augmentation to make themselves bigger. Quite a few of the workers nearby dwarf me by comparison. Carson, who might be 5'9" on a good day, is especially hard to spot in this crowd.

"Tell him to get his eyes on," Rixon says.

As if on cue, the foreman points to a space below his podium. "You. Red." He jerks his thumb toward the doors.

I can just make out the top of Carson's head, moving toward the vehicles. True to his competitive nature, he's made his way right to the front, and despite the fact that he's got a fake name and his meta resume merely reads "General Labor" he's gotten himself picked. I try to attract his attention by waving at him. His goggles are dangling around his neck and he's got his hardhat under one arm. He looks back when he makes it up the steps near the doors, clearly looking for me, but I'm forced to stop my waving because it has attracted the notice of the foreman.

"Shit," I mutter.

"What are you doing?" Rixon asks.

I keep still and avoid eye contact with the foreman. "What do we do about Carson?" I whisper.

"Hey, keep talking, He's processing your resume," Rixon replies. "Talk loud. Flail around a little bit. Yell something."

"Yell what?"

"Anything."

"YO!" I shout, toward no one in particular and throw out a few nonsensical hand gestures. "What's up, ya'll?"

A few of the faces around me turn to look. The foreman, who had been studying me, gives a slight shake of his head and moves on. He makes a few more selections, including Greg from the hallway, but then concludes, "That's it for today." A collective groan goes up from the remaining crowd. "I'll be taking on about thirty more general laborers tomorrow. Get here early."

Carson has finally spotted me due to my shouting, but he's already standing inside the vehicle at the door, having been pushed forward by the latest surge of lucky selectees. He lifts a hand, asking what he should do, and I tap the goggles on my face. But by the time he get the goggles on, it's too late. The doors of the pod he's in slide shut and the vehicle rockets upward on a track and out of sight.

A moment later I get the ping in my goggles and Carson's voice comes through. "Hey, what happened to you? I lost you back there."

"All right, you two," Rixon's voice interrupts. "Way to complicate things on day one. Carson, I'm patching you through to Eon. He's got experience working the high lifts. Looks like you've got a day of hard work ahead of you. Might play to our advantage though if we can keep you alive. Expand our contacts into the regular day workers. Travers, you stay with the reject pile. That's right where we want you."

"You don't have to sound so happy about it," I reply.

I can almost hear the smirk in Rixon's voice. "You want to hunt riffraff, you gotta be riffraff."

"Where do I go now?" I ask.

"Follow the crowd. Try to look disappointed, but keep your eyes open. Let's see where this day takes you."

It's clear after a few minutes why my random outburst in the auditorium got me disqualified from selection. A lot of the 'rejects' around me are likewise prone to fits of conversation with nonexistent persons. It seems that shouting and gesturing to thin air are fairly common behaviors with this group, but more so with the most derelict of the bunch. The benefit is that whenever I need to ask Rixon for guidance, no one pays much attention.

The exodus from the auditorium happens at a more relaxed pace than the press to get in. Many individuals have taken the time to chit chat with fellow applicants. A small contingent of more determined laborers have rushed off to the next loading platform where one of the other foremen is rumored to take longer to make selections, but for the most part, those rejected from this morning's activities resign themselves to the day off.

I meander out the side door and along the docks, taking in the sights and sounds of the space elevator and all of its related industries. The elevator itself is more than just a lift to the upper atmosphere, it hosts multiple platforms and build facilities, and has tracks that run out of them and up the structure. I pause at a tourist guidepost and watch the meta video explaining the importance of the structure and how it functions.

The Skylift space elevator is a multi-national facility where various civilian companies can lease hangar or production spaces and use the carbon nano-tube tethers to ferry their products up into space. The New Space Coast is not about the roaring rockets of my era hoisting heavy spacecraft aloft. There are no launch pads on the surface. Instead, each vessel is manufactured in modular sub-assemblies, run up the elevator tether in small pieces via cars called climbers, and assembled in space where the weight of the completed structure is no longer a factor.

The real marvel of the space elevator is not so much what it does, but that it has been able to be built at all. The engineering feats involved in getting the structure assembled, counterweighted in orbit, and operable by so many different entities, makes its title as a man-made wonder of the world indisputable. The advanced carbon nano-tube technology is the star of the show, since nano-tubes comprise the main elevator tethers themselves, but the structure at the surface and in space are impressive too. Even strolling around the base of it, I'm able to witness the advances in engineering. Some of the pilings anchoring the elevator extend miles out into the Gulf, making the overall footprint of the structure enormous.

Walking along one of the piers underneath the Skylift, I notice lights beneath the surface and realize it's a hallway with people walking inside it. The pedestrians seem intent on their destinations and oblivious to the fish and other sea life swimming past. They've taken their marvel for granted.

I don't make it much farther down the pier before a giant of a security guard accosts me.

"If you don't have a work assignment, you have to clear out." The huge woman is reading the air above my head. She looks like she was born in a gym and weaned on protein and steroids. Whatever information she sees above my head clearly tells her that I've not been employed today. "Next shuttle back leaves in fifteen." She gestures toward a walkway that leads to where the buses had dropped us off. I nod and head that direction under her watchful scrutiny.

So far, I haven't made much progress toward locating any Eternals or determining where they might come ashore with Mym, but the fact that there are even tunnels underwater on this structure makes my job that much harder. It's possible the submarine may not even have to surface to dock here. There could be elements to this facility miles out into the harbor for all I know. Simply searching docks that would fit a sub is not a good enough plan. I definitely need to make contact.

I don't know much about the Eternals' plan, but considering the fact that they're sailing across the Atlantic and coming here to Port Nyongo, I can make the logical assumption that it has something to do with this space elevator. There are plenty of places to hide a submarine, so taking it to the world's tallest structure is hardly the most subtle of options. I can only wonder how any of it fits in with their kidnapping of Mym and their plans for Doctor Quickly's equipment.

The crowd around the bus stop is thinner now and more heavily dominated by rough-looking characters. I pass under a catwalk where more upscale citizens are being shuttled along a moving walkway. The meta signs point the way to platforms farther up the elevator that offer restaurants with scenic views of the harbor. Down on the ground floor the security presence is heavy, ensuring that persons without the right meta credentials won't be bothering the other clientele.

The security force looks largely trans-human, given away by their tight shirts and super-sized muscles. Some of them boast enhanced height, and a few even have synthetic appendages or armor plating. I wouldn't want to scrap with a single one of them. The rest of the workers must feel the same way, because everyone is on their best behavior.

I shuffle aboard a bus with the rest of the unemployed and we are dumped off at a few locations downtown. The majority of rejected workers exit at Tarpon Station, so I follow them off and make my way down the hill to a local park where they're congregating. My presence as a newcomer goes largely uncommented on, though I do get a few suspicious glances. I try to imagine an angle to use to approach the clumps of workers, but it feels like a childhood dance, my ten-year-old self attempting to find a chink in the clusters of giggling grade school girls.

It's only after ineffectively milling around the park for about fifteen minutes that I spot Sonia Davis, the crazed woman from the corridor at the work platform. She's lost her air pack, but the loose oxygen hose is still tangled in her hair. She's standing in an open patch of sunlight, gesturing toward the sky and talking to herself. Curious, I wander closer. She makes a few more wild gesticulations, then attempts to stride forward across the grass. She looks like she's trudging through mud, each footstep deliberate and difficult. She shakes her head after a couple of steps, then backs up. She's muttering at first, then starts to shout back and forth at herself.

"WE NEED TO GO BACK! We'll fix it. Fix it."

"No! They're the ones who did this to us. They won't help. Can't help."

Her face scrunches up and she wags a finger at the air. "They can. We saw it work on the others. They weren't any better than us. We're smarter than them. *We* should have been chosen."

"They'll just make it worse. We lost our job. No. *My job.* I don't need any of you! I just need to get back to work." She strides forward again, intent on gaining the sidewalk at the edge of the grass.

"You can't go without us," she declares. "And we're. Not. Going." With each word her pace slows. Her final step freezes in mid air, her foot hovering above the grass.

"Get off me!" she shouts. The struggle going on inside her is so great that she loses her balance and falls, crumpling to the grass.

The scene is familiar. Watching her fight with her own limbs, I can feel the soreness in my own muscles. The fight with my other self inside my head left me aching and drained both mentally and physically. This woman on the ground is waging the same war.

"You bitch!" She yells, fingers clenching grass and struggling to get back up. "See what you did? We need to be working. You're the reason there's no money left. It's all your fault." As she climbs to her feet, she notices me watching her. Her expression changes from angry to embarrassed and back to angry again.

"What? You never tripped before?"

"I fall down all the time. Had a bad one this morning," I reply.

This seems to placate the woman slightly. "Well, don't fall on me. I won't help you none."

"You mind if I ask you a question?"

"Already are, aren't ya?"

I smile. "Clever. Look, I'm not trying to cause you any trouble or anything, but what happened to you?"

"Fuck off."

I cross my arms. "I will in a minute, but I think that maybe . . . whatever's happening to you, could be happening to me. Can you help me?"

"What are you playing at, Travers?" Rixon's lazy voice comes in over the metaspace. "This crazy lady isn't going to be docking any submarines anytime soon. You should be pumping the regular dockhands for information."

"I'm working on something else. Give me a minute."

Sonia squints at me. "What's he saying to you?"

"Nothing," I mutter, and slide the meta goggles down to my neck. "He's not the problem."

Sonia lifts her chin and studies my forehead. "How many you got in there?"

"When they try to take over, who is it you're fighting with?"

"That's none of your business," Sonia spits.

"It's you, right? Another one of you, from a different time?"

Sonia scowls slightly, but doesn't look away. "They conned you too, huh? Told you they could keep you working? Make you smarter? What was it you wanted?"

"I'm not sure if—"

"Told me I'd be a chief foreman. They told me I'd know the future. Be so smart that I'd never need an upgrade. Should've known better. You should've, too. My granddad always said there's no cure for stupid."

"Why did they recruit you? What was in it for them? Did you have to pay?"

"You think they'd get a single chit's worth of cash out of South Dock? You must be from some glam neighborhood if you don't know what it's like round here."

"They had to want something," I say.

"They wanted me to listen," she replies. "They said I'd just have to listen to a message from the future. Then do what it said."

"What message?"

"Shut up!" she shouts, hands suddenly clamped to her head. "I wasn't talking to you!" She teeters back and forth a few times. "What does he want?" she whispers. "Who is he?" She snarls a few times and shakes her head. She pounds on her skull with her palms, then spits once, as if to expel the voices. When she finally looks back up, her eyes are surprisingly clear. "Hey. You want to know? If you want to see, I'll take you. Maybe they'll listen to us—take the others away. But we have to go quick. I'll be back soon and I can be a real bitch when I'm angry."

She lunges forward and grabs my arm, shoving me toward the sidewalk. Once we reach the concrete, she releases my arm and lopes ahead, laughing. I hesitate briefly, but my curiosity outweighs my concern.

As I run to keep up, following her down the twisting park pathways, I slide the meta goggles back over my face. Rixon's voice fills my head again. "This is on you, Travers. I'm not getting paid to clean up your murdered corpse. If this chick turns on you, you'd better be ready."

"I thought you were supposed to be tough guys and back me up," I reply. "You wanted me to make contacts, didn't you? I'm making contacts."

Rixon sighs into his microphone. "All right. I'm going to get my guns loaded, then I'm coming down there. If you're dead by the time I get to you, it's not my fault."

Sonia pauses near a footbridge over a stream, looks both ways for anyone paying attention, then leaps into the gully below. When I get to the bridge, she is scurrying underneath it. She looks back once and gestures for me to follow, then vanishes out of sight. I ease myself gingerly down the embankment and climb under the footbridge after her. My work boots keep out most of the ankle high water, but I still get a bit soggy sloshing through the stream. Ducking under the concrete bridge, I locate the run-off pipe that Sonia has apparently climbed into. I can't see her, but I can hear her clomping steps and occasional mutterings inside the corrugated pipe.

I frown at the dark opening and toss my hardhat to the stones outside, a clue for Rixon to follow if necessary. There aren't a lot of dry stones in the creek bed, but I climb up on top of one and look for something farther up the embankment that will make a decent anchor. I select a stone that is high enough that if I reappear it will keep me out of the water. I stuff the stone into my pocket, note the local time on my meta goggles, then step inside the pipe.

"Hurry," Sonia calls back in a half whisper. "I don't know when I might lose control of myself again."

"Don't worry," I mutter. "I'm clearly losing my senses, too." I duck lower and follow her into the darkness.

"Time travel, like all travel, broadens your horizons. It also reaffirms your appreciation for modern plumbing."-Journal of Dr. Harold Quickly, 1688

CHAPTER 16

Port Nyongo, 2165

In my century, the name Florida and the word underground don't commonly get used together. Florida is flat, and if you dig a hole very deep, eventually you're going to hit water. That's not to say there's nothing interesting down there. You might hit a sinkhole. Near Jennings, Florida, there is a sinkhole so broad that it swallows an entire river.

The Floridan aquifer system channels various underground rivers beneath the entire state and supplies most of the major cities with their drinking water. The aquifer is an ecosystem all its own. If you happen to be a crayfish or an albino lobster, you might just hang out down there all the time. If you are a tall, human man who forgot to bring a scuba suit, the environment is less than ideal.

Some things have certainly changed in the century and a half I've skipped over. Technology has leapt ahead. I'm viewing this tunnel through digital meta goggles and a super-fancy space elevator looms outside. What hasn't changed is that rainwater runoff pipes and underground waterways are dark and smelly. I'm sure there is some meta app I could be using to make the tunnels smell like rose petals, but I don't mess with the settings.

Following Sonia through the labyrinth of pipes and caverns under Port Nyongo makes my skin twitchy. Each new splash in the darkness makes me think of alligators and pythons. Sonia clearly knows where she's headed, but the odds of her leaving me here alone increase with each passing minute. She doesn't seem to fear the wildlife, though she does stop us once as an electronic drone goes skimming down one of the perpendicular passages. She waits till the drone is out of sight before moving on.

It seems that we're not the only ones who find these caverns handy for avoiding the surface traffic, but it's apparent from Sonia's caution that not everyone using the space is to be trusted. I feel the same way about Sonia. She's my own personal Gollum and, like Bilbo, my fingers frequently find the anchor stone in my pocket—my key to vanishing out of this hole if things go badly.

"Are you sure this is the way?" I ask, as I slosh through another algae-covered cavern. "How does anyone get in? They can't get many clients like this."

Sonia looks back at me from farther up the cavern. "This isn't how I got in. It's how I escaped."

I muse on her words as I follow her along the tunnel, then she finally reaches a concrete spillway that is above the current water level. A smaller diameter pipe juts from the wall above it. Sonia scrabbles up the dirt beneath the pipe and crawls inside. Her voice echoes faintly as she whispers back at me. "Almost there. Quiet now."

As I climb onto the concrete spillway, I'm tempted to make a jump forward a few seconds to dry myself off, but realize belatedly that I forgot to ask Rixon if he treated the clothes and gear I'm wearing with gravitites. Having failed to bring the degravitizer, I have no way to check.

"Hey, Rixon. You there?"

The com crackles, but I get no reply.

Debating the situation, I decide I'd rather be soggy than naked. I climb up and scramble through the opening of the pipe. As I do, my vision goes black.

A blinking red light is all that remains of my view in the goggles. I concentrate on it and it opens a text window. Caution: You have entered an area that has not been charted. Return to the meta map to restore navigation functions.

Looks like even future technology has its limits.

I concentrate on the toolbar at the edge of my viewfinder and select the icon for night vision. My view comes back marginally, but not nearly as well as I had been seeing before. This tunnel is close to pitch dark and the sensors barely have enough light to outline the edges of the pipe. The light it does pick up appears to be coming from a bioluminescent algae growing at the bottom of the pipe. I do my best not to squish it all as I squirm my way forward.

I wouldn't say I'm claustrophobic as a rule. That being said, there is really only so much squirming through a narrow metal pipe that a body can handle. If you are broad-shouldered and incapable of bending very well, that distance is vastly reduced. The space just seems to be getting tighter, and after a while it's only the fact that I hate the idea of trying to go back that keeps me moving forward. The air is pungent with some oily chemical, so I don my oxygen mask and open the valve as I crawl. It makes me feel slightly better.

The vague light from the tiny bioluminescent algae on the bottom of the pipe is the only thing I can see. It gives me the impression I'm climbing over an abyss of far away stars. The cosmic sensation is disorienting. I can feel my mind wandering, unable to distract it with any other visuals. Images float through my head: the underground tunnels I traveled in Seattle, an arched room with a fire pit in the middle, a shrouded figure deep in meditation. The other me is there. I can feel him. His emotions. He's scared. Hiding in the darkness. Trapped. Alone.

Or is that me?

I force myself to concentrate on the physical sensations around me. Corrugated steel. Slimy algae. My own grimy clothes. *You are not in the Neverwhere. You are here.*

I struggle forward faster, trying to escape the connection to my other self. He's noticed me too. I can feel him searching for a way through the darkness.

No. Stay where you are.

Finally, when I have just about resigned myself to spending the rest of my short life as a human clog, I reach the end.

Based on the size of the pipe and possibly the effects of the extraneous fumes I've been breathing for the past few minutes, I've had a delusional fear that Sonia and I might emerge into some enormous toilet, crawling out of the u-bend into a world of Jonathan Swift's giants. The reality of the situation turns out to be much less *Gulliver's Travels* and more *Fast and Furious*. We're in a sunken rectangular floor drain, and the drain is at the low point of someone's garage.

The metal grating Sonia lifts away is located beneath a vehicle. It's hard to say what it is from just the undercarriage, but it's got at least two feet of ground clearance. There are a few spray wands hanging on the wall next to it, and I realize the drain we've crawled into is part of someone's personal car wash. Sonia slides the grating aside and shimmies out from under the bumper. I pause with my head still the only bit of me protruding from the rectangular drain. I'm partly cautious and partly in awe. This is a big garage and the vehicles in it are shiny and expensive-looking.

The car nearest me is a black '67 Camaro with a ski rack on top. Beyond that is a red T-top Ferrari. The cars both look vaguely familiar, but when I slide out from beneath the truck I'm under, I get a strange realization that I'm in more than just someone's personal garage. It's a collection, and not just any collection, but one from my generation. The black, Toyota 4x4 with the yellow KC light covers on top is cool, but its counterpart a few cars down is even more iconic, a stainless steel Delorean complete with black vents and a Mister Fusion on the back.

"Who owns all these?" I whisper.

Sonia appears unimpressed. "This is old junk. Nothing even electric."

"Actually, if you want to get technical," I jab my thumb toward the Delorean. "Parts of that one—"

"Come on. We'll see who's home."

The garage of this '80s car enthusiast is attached to an even more enormous house with a circular driveway. Peering out the garage windows I get the sense that—with the exception of the cars—whoever owns this mansion doesn't have particularly good taste. Besides the ridiculous columns and ostentatious topiaries, there are a half dozen marble angels surrounding a fountain, all with their hands covering their eyes.

I follow Sonia inside the house through an attached hallway. Despite the house being off the metaspace, I have a hard time believing there isn't some other security system we're alerting, but if there is, Sonia doesn't much care.

"Where are they? Where are they?" She mutters to herself as she pushes open doors and makes her way through the silly amount of hallways. We emerge into a kitchen, and my companion pauses long enough to raid the pantry before continuing her search. Her further exploration leaves crumbs of cheese crackers in her wake. I give up trying to avoid them as I follow behind. My boots are leaving just as much of a mess behind us anyway.

I glimpse my reflection in a hallway mirror and have trouble recognizing myself. The goggles are dark and conceal my eyes, and the oxygen mask obscures my other features. The rest of me is so caked with dirt and grime that I can't even remember what color my clothes started out. Rounding a corner into a formal dining room, we're confronted by a fair-haired synth in a red *Star Trek* uniform.

"You do not have authorization to be in this part of the manor," the synth declares calmly. "The masters of the house have been alerted to your presence."

Sonia flips the synth off and barrels past him. "Where are they?" She glances both directions at the end of the hallway and goes right.

The synth hesitates, seeming to debate between watching me or going after Sonia. He must deem her more of a threat to the house because he turns and pursues her down the corridor. I follow at a distance. When I reach the end of the hall, I decide that Sonia may have taken me as far as she's going to. I go left.

Halfway down the corridor, I hear voices. Vaguely familiar voices.

"You said you wanted more recruits, and we got them. You never said they had to be stable." The young man's tone is apathetic and lazy. My brain is struggling to place it.

"These latest additions of yours have been next to worthless." Another voice replies. "Not one of the last bunch succeeded in relaying their messages." This other man sounds older, but is unfamiliar. "And as to the time travelers you've found for us, hardly any have shown the proper respect for what we're trying to accomplish. How are we supposed to make contact with His Greatness when—"

"I told you the equipment you got us the first time wasn't meant for humans. No way you can use that on him. If the portable you say you stole is better, we'll make more progress."

I adjust my chronometer settings for a quick exit in case I need it, then place one hand in the pocket with my anchor stone. I creep forward and peer around the corner of the doorway into a greenhouse filled with marijuana plants. The voices are coming from beyond a few rows of planters toward the center of the room. I slip inside and skirt one wall, careful to stay out of sight. It takes me a few attempts to find a spot that lets me view the speakers, but finally they move into the center of the greenhouse where I can see them.

The man standing closest is dressed in loose gray clothing and has his back to me. Despite his deceptively mature voice, he's young, perhaps early twenties.

"Lord Elgin will be here soon, and we're expected to have our end of the operation settled. We'll be taking the remaining candidates we collected today to the temple for final training. When the Lost Star arrives we *must* be ready. You promised that your services would be effective."

"Listen, man," the lazy voice replies. "We've got you more applicants than you said you needed. It hasn't been easy. Most people don't wanna work that hard and not many people are as eager to try our 'education' system now that you guys have been letting the rejects loose. Kinda gives our marketing a bad rap when your leftovers go attacking people on the Skylift and talking to themselves all over town."

I edge forward till I can make out the second speaker. He's slouched against a planter and is toying with a gaudy gold ring on his finger. His floppy blonde hair obscures one eye, but the haughty face is just as smug as the last time I saw it. At least he's sober.

Guy Friday.

How is he involved in this?

Guy's younger brother, Lawrence, moves into view as well. I have enough reasons to despise both siblings after they robbed my friends and me in the '80s and made off with one of Doctor Quickly's chronometers, but I realize after a few moments of observation that I'm looking at a younger version of the despicable duo. Lawrence is easily twenty pounds lighter and both look like they're little more than high school age.

The young man in gray doesn't seem placated. "Only twenty percent of your recruits made the cut so far. We were supposed to have access to the upper levels of the Skylift by now. So far all you've given us is day laborers and low level work foremen. Good enough for decoys, but we want more security engineers and dock masters."

"Look, I get it." Guy waves a hand. "We've already got the people you want in place, it's just going to take an additional investment."

"Additional investment? We've already paid you double from what you originally quoted us. You made promises, and Lord Elgin expects results."

Guy holds up a hand. "I get you, man, but costs on this job have gone up. We need to—Lawrence, will you see what in the hell is going on inside? Scotty keeps pinging me every five seconds about some security thing he's dealing with."

"Where's the rest of his security team?" Lawrence objects. "They should be able to—"

"Just go check it out, will you?" Guy jerks a thumb toward the house. "Mr. Longcase and I will finish discussing business."

Lawrence frowns and seems disappointed to be left out of the conversation, but obeys his brother and heads inside. Once he's disappeared, Guy turns back to his companion. "Look, I know you guys are onto something big here. You've got plans, and I get that. So maybe, in order to make things go smoother, you cut us in on a little of the action. If we knew what the stakes were, then maybe we could get you better candidates for your project."

"As much as I appreciate your enthusiasm, Lord Elgin prefers to keep involvement from your kind to a minimum."

"My kind?" Guy sputters. "What is that supposed to mean?"

Longcase turns my direction and I get a better look at him. He's lean and pale with a sharp jawline. His short, black hair stabs a sharp peak down his forehead, reminding me of an older Eddie Munster. "You were a student at the Academy of Temporal Sciences, weren't you? You're a time traveler with a clear connection to the central governing—"

"You think I'd report you to ASCOTT?" Guy replies. "You must not have done your research very well. Last place in the world we'd be going with this is back to the Academy or to some ASCOTT official, especially after all this." He gestures to the mansion around us. "You probably noticed that this place is completely off-Grid and isn't meta-mapped. We've gone to a lot of effort to stay apart."

"And it has been your discretion that permitted us to do business in the first place. Even so, the mandate of Lord Gnomon requires that we employ as few time travelers as possible. The liability is just too great. If one of you were to involve yourselves, it may complicate millennia worth of work."

"Millennia? How long have you been planning this thing? I thought this had to do with the future?"

"That's our matter to worry about. Your business is delivering on your promises." The man sizes up Guy and seems to make a decision. "How much more money? Time is getting short. and we have to gain access now. If you get us the ship, we'll pay you what you ask."

Guy's eyes glisten brighter at the prospect. "Triple. We could do it for triple."

"Be sure you can. We will only have one opportunity for success."

At that moment, a pair of red-shirted synths come trooping through the door, carrying the struggling form of Sonia with them. They are followed by the smaller synth we met in the hallway. Sonia is writhing in the grip of her captors and spitting. When she sees the man in gray, she freezes. "You! You did this to me, you son of a bitch!"

Mr. Longcase frowns at her. "Miss Davis. I see you continue to ignore even the most basic of our principles. It was your lack of mental calm that was your downfall. I had nothing to do with it."

"You're a bunch of liars!" Sonia screams. "You said I'd be smarter. That I'd be able to learn to be a foreman. You said you'd help me!"

"We said nothing of the sort," Mr. Longcase replies. "We merely said that you would be receiving knowledge. An opportunity to meld your thoughts with those of your own future. It is not our fault that your future is less than bright in Port Nyongo. And you *have* met your future self now, haven't you?"

"She's a fucking bitch!" Sonia screams. "I want her out of my head!"

"How did she get loose in the house?" Guy asks. "I thought you were supposed to have transferred all the candidates by now. "

"This one got away from us, sir." The synth we first encountered in the hallway speaks up. "Seems she exploited a vulnerability in the garage. Wasn't gone long though. She came back with another man. Another worker."

"Another one? And where is he? Please don't tell me you're letting him roam around the house unmonitored too."

"No, sir. He's here. He's standing behind those planters." The synth points directly at me.

Shit.

Guy reaches behind his back and pulls a pistol from the waistband of his pants. He flips off the safety and aims it at the bushes. He can't see me, so his aim is off, but it's close enough to make me nervous. I keep low behind the planter and pull my anchor stone from my pocket, making adjustments to my chronometer for my escape.

"Come out of there," Guy calls. "Out where I can see you."

Nope.

I set the stone on the end of the planter and put my fingertip to it. One hand on my chronometer. *Here I go.*

"Come out or she dies."

I hesitate.

Peering through the pot leaves, I assess the situation. Sonia has gone still in her captors' arms. Guy has the pistol pressed against her temple.

Damn it. I don't know Guy well enough to guess if he'll really shoot her. He's an asshole to be sure. While I doubt he'd pull the trigger, I don't want Sonia's life hanging on that assumption. I pocket my anchor stone again, tug my sleeve back over my chronometer, and step cautiously out from behind the planter. I keep my free hand near my chronometer arm just in case.

I can sense the synths analyzing my meta identity as I step into the center of the walkway. They won't see much, just the fake ID Rixon set up for me. The gun in Guy's hand swings away from Sonia and toward me.

"Who are you?" he demands.

"Just wanted work." My voice is muffled inside the oxygen mask, and I have to speak loudly to be heard.

"We've got enough lift workers," Guy replies. He glances at Mr. Longcase, then returns his gaze to me. "How much did you hear?"

"Too much," Longcase hisses. "He's a liability."

Another yellow light with a little satellite symbol is blinking in the corner of my viewfinder. I want to select it, but my eyes are intent on the gun in Guy's hand.

"We could just lump him in with the others." Lawrence appears from behind the security synths and has apparently been listening. "Take him with her. We just need to get them off the property."

Guy lets the gun droop, considering this new option.

"Deal with this," Longcase says. He stabs a long index finger at me. "Our operation requires secrecy. Either you clean it up or we have no further business."

The yellow light in my goggles blinks faster. I finally tear my eyes away from the men in front of me long enough to open the com link.

Guy raises the gun at the same time Rixon's voice shouts in my head.

"GET DOWN!"

I dive for the cover of the planter just as something crashes through the greenhouse wall and impacts the ground between me and Guy. The object detonates in a spray of earth and acrid smoke. A figure leaps through the hole in the wall immediately after and, a moment later, Rixon is pulling me to my feet, his other hand aiming a weapon toward Guy and the cluster of security synths. The wall at the other side of the greenhouse erupts in a shower of Plexiglas, and the void is promptly filled by the massive form of Eon carrying some kind of assault weapon.

Guy balks at the sight of the two men and squeezes past his synth security on the heels of Lawrence, who is likewise fleeing the scene.

Longcase scowls at us between coughs from the smoke and draws a gun from his own belt, but he doesn't aim it at Rixon or Eon. He snatches Sonia from the security synths and attempts to use her as a human shield.

Something in Sonia's eyes changes when he wraps his arm around her neck and presses the gun to her head. Whatever rational mind was in control before no longer reigns inside her now. She raises one arm and slams her elbow into Longcase's gut. He lets out a gasp and then a snarl before hurling her aside. He fires one round in Sonia's direction, then flees for the safety of the house. Sonia ricochets off the wall, grabs at her side for a moment, then reels and pursues Longcase inside, shrieking the whole way.

The security synths, to my surprise, do nothing. The presence of Eon and Rixon and their weapons seems to have shut the red-shirted guards down. Their loyalty to their masters clearly does not supersede their logic or self-preservation in this situation.

"What now?" I ask as the smoke clears. "You got a ride out there?"

"They might have other guards," Rixon explains. "Ones with weapons. We need to get in and nab these bastards quick."

"You want to capture them?" I ask. "I thought you were just getting me out."

"Well, yeah," Rixon replies. "But the guys who own this place have been on our contract list for months now. Robbed a bunch of casinos. I about choked when I saw them on your view screen. We've been looking all over for these two. Never thought they'd hide right in plain sight. We owe you one for flushing them out."

"Kind of a two birds, one stone scenario," Eon says, joining Rixon beside me. "Not that keeping you safe wasn't the priority."

"If you've got a way out, go ahead and take it," Rixon says. "If not, just wait here and we'll be right back."

"Okay. Hey, are these clothes you gave me gravitized?"

"Of course," Rixon replies. "What kind of dumbass time traveler would wear regular clothes?"

"Right. That would be stupid."

Rixon narrows his eyes at me, then pulls a second pistol from a shoulder holster and moves toward the house.

Eon addresses the synths as he passes them. "Now I trust you gents are going to recall that we let you off easy and act accordingly in the next few minutes. We've got a warrant with all the appropriate details. I posted it on your public wall on the way in. No reason anyone needs to get hurt."

The small synth I first encountered in the hallway replies. "Our contract specifies that we must keep our employers safe, but in the event of illegal activity on their part, we cannot impede a criminal investigation."

"Handy contract," Eon says. "Thought you boys looked smart." He grins and follows Rixon inside. The synths look at me, then turn and file out the side door of the greenhouse.

Once my companions have all disappeared, I pull the ragged oxygen mask from my face and exhale the stress of the past few minutes.

I find the anchor stone in my pocket—considering a quick exit—but then decide to wait for Eon and Rixon. I'd like to see Guy and Lawrence in custody. Can't think of a better scene to watch.

There is a smear of blood on the doorframe.

I think of Sonia and her hand clutched to her side. *What's happening with her in there? Will Eon call in a medic for her?*

I attempt to pull up the toolbar for my meta goggles to see if there is an emergency services button, but the meta functions are still offline. Whatever satellite technology Rixon used to call me is not accessible from my interface. That or I'm just too inept to make it work. I stare at the smear on the door and try to tell myself that she's fine. Nobody appointed me the crazy lady patrol. Not my responsibility.

I sigh and head inside.

The blood trail is not difficult to follow. Sonia has left periodic hand smears on the walls and stair rails. They lead back toward the garage. When I step into the garage I see no immediate sign of Sonia, but through the front windows I spot a figure in the driveway. Mr. Longcase is striding toward a driverless vehicle that's making its way around the circular driveway. He's made the mistake of using public transportation to get here and has had to wait to make his escape. I still don't see Sonia, but push my way out the side door of the garage, keeping low along one of the hedges.

Did he shoot her again? Where is she?

The driverless car pulls to a stop near the fountain of blind angels.

Longcase, still holding his pistol in one hand, opens the rear door just as an engine roars to life inside the garage beside me. Longcase looks up, perhaps sensing the danger. The garage door splinters into fragments as the black Toyota 4x4 erupts from inside. Sonia is wide-eyed and screaming in the cab.

"YOU BASTARD!"

The big truck rolls over the scraps of garage door and adjusts course for Longcase's car. He dives out of the way just in time to avoid the impact as the vehicles collide. A few thousand pounds of 1980s Japanese steel blows through the composite frame of the driverless car in a fury of noise and exploding airbags, shoving it backward into the fountain.

Sonia must have her foot jammed down on the accelerator because after some slipping on the bricks now soaked with fountain water, the Toyota finds purchase atop the crumpled electric car and begins to climb over it. The truck rolls over the other vehicle and knocks down one of the angel statues in the process. Sonia continues to yell over the roar of the engine and the splashing of the water and bounces the truck straight through the back side of the fountain, shearing its low wall away, spraying concrete and bits of broken angel all over the driveway.

Longcase is on his feet now and scouring the ground. He's lost his gun in his diving bid for escape. From my position near the garage I spot it under the front tire of his ruined car, but he doesn't see it. Flight is his next best option.

He sprints for the main gate but doesn't make it. Sonia guns the truck ahead of him, fishtailing past and making him skid to a stop. He slips on the wet bricks, rights himself, and changes course for the house. The frantic young man makes it halfway to the front door before Sonia comes roaring back, the black truck coughing smoke and reeking of gasoline. Sometime during her fountain-climbing excursion, a fuel line or the fuel tank must have been punctured because her watery trail now shimmers with petroleum rainbows. She spins the wheel hard, clearly hoping to flatten the panting and wild-eyed Longcase, but she misses him by mere inches and careens up the front steps of the mansion, smashing the truck directly into the front doors.

Ouch.

The Toyota is done. Longcase pauses for only a moment to assure himself that Sonia's assault by truck is over, then sets off at a brisk jog down the driveway, headed for the main gate. He spots me standing open-mouthed near the garage hedges but doesn't slow. He looks back only once as he rounds the corner, then disappears.

Sonia is still in the truck. The driver's-side door is jammed against the doorpost of the house and she slams into it futilely a few times before crawling to the other side. I make my way across the driveway, carefully circumnavigating the puddle of fountain water and the sparking wreck of the electric car which has begun to smoke ominously. I hop over the now steady stream of gasoline pouring out the back of the Toyota and meet Sonia at the passenger side of the vehicle. I kick a few pieces of shattered doorframe aside so she can get the door open.

"What do you want?" Sonia demands when she sees me.

Despite her bravado, her face is pale and bloodless. The stain at her side has grown significantly and her movements are sluggish.

"Come on. Gotta get you out of here. It's not safe."

Sonia doesn't object when I help her from the truck and throw one of her arms over my shoulder. I help her down the couple of steps and into the driveway just as Eon and Rixon climb out the hole in the ruined garage door. There's no sign of Guy or Lawrence.

"What happened?" I call across the driveway.

"I guess we missed your invite to the demolition derby," Rixon replies. He pulls a thin cigar from his pocket and bites off the end. "Your boys had themselves a goddamned time gate." He flicks open a lighter with his other hand.

"I wouldn't light that. Gas all over," I say.

Rixon surveys the shimmering puddles with curiosity. "Yeah, it'd be a shame if these poor criminals didn't have their fancy mansion to come home to."

I recall the wads of cash Lawrence and Guy stole from us and the still-missing chronometer they took from Francesca. "Actually, you have another one of those?"

Rixon grins and hands me a cigar and the lighter. I stick the cigar in my mouth with my free hand and light it while still holding Sonia upright with the other. When the end of the cigar is good and bright, I toss it toward the nearest puddle of gasoline.

"Oops."

The cigar lands with a thump on the concrete, but unlike every Hollywood film I've ever seen, the gas doesn't ignite. Instead, the cigar merely sizzles a moment before going out in an anticlimactic puff of smoke.

I frown at it.

Eon pulls something from his jacket and overhand tosses it in a lobbing arc toward the house. The object clatters into the bed of the Toyota, then a moment later explodes with a deafening boom, momentarily lifting the entire chassis of the truck off the ground. It rains parts around the driveway and lands again in a blaze of brilliant flame.

"Oops," Eon says.

"Too bad they didn't keep this place on the metaspace," Rixon comments. "Fire brigade would already be on their way. But now . . ." He chews his cigar and studies the hungry blaze blooming inside the mansion.

"A real pity," I reply.

"Though we probably should have staked the place out to see if they return for their stuff," Eon says. "Gonna be a bitch to track 'em down now."

I toss Rixon's lighter back to him. "If you want to know where they're headed to hide for the next few years, I think I can help you out."

"Really now," Rixon says, lighting his cigar and flipping the lighter closed. "You know what, Travers? I think I like you after all."

Sonia watches the dancing flames engulf the mansion. I'm not sure which of her personalities is in control at the moment, but it seems all of them are smiling.

"It doesn't matter how many times you press the pin on your chronometer to skip ahead. The laundry isn't going to wash itself. Real life still takes living, and sooner or later you're the only one who can decide what's worthwhile. For me, not smelling like a sweaty gym sock falls under 'items of vital importance.'"- Journal of Dr. Harold Quickly, 1986

CHAPTER 17

Port Nyongo, 2165

Fawcett Memorial Hospital in Port Nyongo is used to vagrants. They are used to patients spitting and talking to themselves. They are used to gunshot wounds. That still doesn't make them ready for Sonia. In the end, it takes three trans-human nurses and a lot of promises of food and coffee to calm her down, but she makes it inside. The doctor who scans her in says the wound isn't serious and she's very lucky.

We're lucky to have her out of the car.

Once the doctors have examined Sonia and given her some preliminary treatment to stabilize her, I'm allowed in for a few minutes to talk to her. Eon and Rixon opt to wait outside.

Sonia fixes me with a much calmer stare when I walk in, following my movements around the room. When I take a seat next to her bed, she finally speaks. "I was supposed to be someone great, you know. They told us the great ones would change the world."

"Change it how?"

"Make things different. Give us another future." Her eyes get a little glassy. "They split us into two groups. One group they said could live forever and send their messages to the brethren of the past. The other would send their messages to the god of time himself so that he would know who were his chosen ones. He has to be told who to save when he comes for us. He promised to save us from the future." All of her anger seems to have faded. In its place is only disappointment. "Should have known it was all too good to be true."

"How do you know about the future?"

"They read it to us from the book. The Chronicles of Gnomon. It's all been passed down, person to person. Survivors from the future sent it back to save us. We're supposed to write down all their memories in the Chronicle and pass it back farther."

"How far back in time is the message supposed to be delivered?"

"Six thousand years. The very start of civilization."

"Wow."

Sonia's voice shifts to a lower tone and her eyes dart around the room. "We know the end is coming. The world is going to Hell. These machines are to blame. The Chronicle tells it." She stabs a finger toward the door. "These synths might patch us up and keep us alive for now, but they'll leave us to die when the end comes. The brethren say we can't put our hope in the machines. We can only hope in Zurvan."

Sonia grimaces and shifts in her bed, and her voice changes back to passive resignation. "But now there's no hope. Now I'm nothing. They wouldn't let me be one of the chosen ones. They wouldn't let me talk to Zurvan. They wouldn't even let me go back to work."

"Where do they do this? The talking to Zurvan. The selecting people to send messages."

"There were rooms for us in the basement where they kept us—taught us how. They make you stare into a fire till you can't even remember your own name. We slept at the house with the blind angels. But they take us to the fire temple in St. Petersburg for the ceremonies. They preach to us and listen to our visions and decide who gets to be chosen to talk to him."

"The fire temple? You've been there?"

"I've seen it. I got my messages, but they weren't right. They said I wasn't supposed to keep hearing the voices. They said I was supposed to just be myself again, only with more memories. My memories got all confused." She puts her hands to her head. "Bad dreams. Bad visions."

"So some people get it to work? Some people get their own minds back to normal after? What about the mess-ups? Can they try again to fix it or does everyone end up—" I almost say crazy but stop myself. "Do they just end up with other people living in their heads?"

Sonia frowns. "They said there was no time left for me to fix it. They said I missed my chance. The training is over. The Lost Star is coming. I heard they might dispose of the ones that didn't make it. That's why I knew I had to get out."

A nurse sticks her head in the door and informs me that they need to get Sonia prepped for her procedure. I stand and move around the bed. Sonia's eyes follow me. "What do your voices tell you? Is your future any good?"

"I'm not sure yet."

"Then, tell 'em to go to Hell."

I move toward the door but pause and turn back for a final question. "If I wanted to go to this fire temple, see how they're doing this, how do I find it?"

"Finding the temple is easy. B train stops there. They call it the Temple of the Eternal Flame."

"Thanks for helping me, Sonia. I'm sorry we didn't get what you wanted today."

"Got to see their house burn." She cracks a smile. "That was all right. Let 'em look into that fire and predict their damn future." She settles back against her pillow and closes her eyes.

The ride back to Rixon's bar is quiet—a comedown from the adrenaline rush of our afternoon. I let out a yawn and Eon passes me a carton of water.

"How long since you slept, Travers?"

"I don't know. A while."

"If you want to get some rest once we're back, we have a place for you to sleep."

"I'm fine." I stifle a second yawn. "Just need to keep moving."

"We aren't going to save her today, you know. Still two days till that sub pulls into the harbor. You'll need to sleep at some point."

"Let's just get back. Where's Carson?"

"Still up on the high lifts. Got put on some manufacturing jobs up there. Seems to be doing fine. I checked on his meta feed a few minutes ago. He's fitting right in."

"Of course he is."

When we pull up to the bar, we find it significantly more active than when we left. The dingy room is bustling with patrons seemingly averse to the far more pleasant day outside. Once indoors, I take a moment to let my eyes adjust, and the first thing I make out moving toward me is Tucket, dressed in an apron and carrying two pints of beer.

"Is that for me?" I put out a hand.

"Hey, Ben! No. Sorry. These are for the ladies behind you. He slides past and deposits the two pints on the table of a pair of grouchy-looking individuals in the booth in the corner. When he spins around to greet us again he smiles and wipes his hands. "How did the reconnaissance go?"

"You put him to work in your bar?" I ask Rixon. "I thought we were paying you guys to work for us, not the other way around."

"He's been gathering intel here," Rixon says. "It's important. And God knows I can't just leave the place unattended. Half my bar staff are stealing from me as it is. Got to have someone with some scruples around to make the place profitable. Hey. Did you wipe down the mirror?" He points behind the bar.

Tucket folds his hands and nods. "Thought it might brighten up the place. Could hardly see where I was going without the meta map on. I know you said you like the character it had, but your customers don't mind a little cleaning. When I finished the mirror, some of them clapped."

"Well, I think your hard work deserves a beer, Tuck." I say. "Why don't you pour yourself one. And me too, if you got it."

"My shift isn't over till seven," Tucket replies.

I frown at Rixon. "Really?"

Rixon shrugs.

"I'm going to skip ahead till Carson gets off work, then I'm taking Tucket back."

I use Rixon's jump room to set myself an anchor point that will get me to later in the evening and also remove the accumulated filth caked into my clothing. I use the river stone I've been carrying around in my pocket and set it in Rixon's anchor stand. After locking the door, I blink forward, leaving the non-gravitite-infused dirt of my day behind. I skip over enough time for the dust to settle and, when I reappear, the residue of my crawl through the underground is reduced to a brown stain on the floor beneath my sneakers. I exit the jump room feeling much cleaner.

The afternoon sun has sunk close to the horizon, but the clients at the bar haven't changed much. There are just more of them. Dock workers are trickling into the room in a steady stream. I take a seat at the bar. Eon has gone to retrieve Carson and it's not long till they return.

Carson is dirty but jubilant. He gets nods from a few of the other workers as he comes in. He gives me a fist bump when he reaches the bar.

"What's up, dude? You missed all the action today."

"Not all of it," I reply.

Rixon and Eon don't seem keen to debrief us at the moment, but I'm curious to hear about Carson's day on the Skylift and what he might have learned.

"I'm starving. You eat yet?" Carson asks.

"No. I could definitely use a meal." I snag Tucket,s arm as he passes carrying a tray of food. "Hey, Tuck. Do we want to eat here?"

Tucket glances at his tray then back to me, shaking his head vigorously.

"Okay, let's find somewhere else." I slide off the barstool and signal Carson to follow. "Come on, Tucket, we're going to figure some stuff out."

Tucket hesitates. "It's not seven yet."

"You don't really work here. They'll be fine if you—Here, gimme that." I take the tray of veggie patty sandwiches and disperse them to the table of women at the high top that have been waiting for them. I gather from their expressions that I haven't gotten the placement right, but I can't imagine how it matters. "Just meta that better," I say, and toss the empty tray back onto the bar.

Tucket looks mortified.

"They'll be fine, Tuck. Come on."

Tucket reluctantly pulls off his apron and follows us out into the evening air.

The dock district of Port Nyongo has come alive with the setting sun. We wander down streets crowded with a colorful blend of characters of all shapes and sizes. A group of enhanced humans with enormous muscles—tall, veiny specimens—are clustered together on a street corner literally flexing at one another.

There are sleek trans-humans, people with exotic appendages like wings and tails, and some who glide on wheels or lope around on long, spindly synthetic legs. When I slip on the meta goggles, the scene gets even more bizarre. Plenty of folks who can't afford actual enhancements have made them in the metaspace. Digital avatars interact with one another in fancy bars with interactive scenery.

It becomes clear to me after a little while just why Rixon's bar is popular with the lowest classes. It might be dingy, but it's also unpretentious, an even playing field for normal humans to interact with one another. Out here on the streets, those who don't have the means to outfit themselves in trans-human styles or fancy meta features are easily distinguished. They skulk along the sidewalks, insignificant and forgettable in their work clothes and average bodies.

Carson and I scour the streets for someplace with food we recognize. Down a side street, I spot a simple sign for a bar called Machina Libre. Thinking it might serve Mexican food, we wander inside.

The restaurant is simple, lots of stainless steel and exposed pipes. There is a collection of welded masks lining the walls. The urban style is refreshing because, unlike Rixon's, this place is spotlessly clean. Despite the dim lighting, I get the impression there are far fewer bacteria colonies lurking in the crevices. The couple dozen patrons in booths and at the bar also appear polite and well behaved. The ambient murmur of conversation pauses collectively as we walk in but resumes in low tones as we take seats in the bar area.

"This place looks cool," Carson says.

A server doesn't appear for a minute or two, so I get up and make my way to the bar, hoping to attract someone's attention.

I scrutinize the virtual drink menu on the wall through the meta goggles. I concentrate on a few headers to read the descriptions, but they don't help me much. Every cocktail listed contains words I've never seen and couldn't imagine the taste of.

The bartender wanders over and stares at me, the expression on his face something akin to annoyance or perhaps constipation. He's a big man, thick in places I wouldn't even have suspected muscles could be exercised. I pick a name at random. "How is your . . . Lot's Deliverance?"

The bartender lifts his chin. "It would poison you dead in about twenty seconds."

He might be joking, but I can't really tell. "Uh. Okay. How about the Jupiter Moonrise?"

He scrunches up his face. "Liquefy your guts right where you stand. I'm not mopping that up tonight."

"Okay. Why don't you just tell me which drinks on the menu won't murder me and we'll start there."

The man reaches under the bar, slides a door open, and extracts a twelve-ounce can. He sets it on the bar for my inspection.

I pick up the can to decipher the label. "You've got to be kidding me. All the beers in all the world and the one that survives to this century is Pabst Blue Ribbon?"

"It's what we've got for you. You want it or what?"

"Yeah, give me three and some glasses if you've got 'em. Not that you can really class this up . . ."

The bartender sets three opaque glasses on the bar. "I'll bring them out to you."

"Thanks." I start to return to the table, but I notice him staring at me still.

"You forgetting something?"

"Oh. You probably need a card or cash or something right? Sorry." I fumble for my wallet.

The bartender reaches over the bar, snatches up the chit lanyard hanging around my neck and holds it in the air at his eye level. It beeps. He lets it go and pats me on the shoulder. "There you go. Don't strain yourself."

I mutter a thank you and retreat to my table with the other guys.

Tucket has found the restaurant menu on the metaspace and explains that we can just order on there. He reads off some of the entrees. They all have dramatic names like Inevitable Victory and Dawn of Justice. He lists ingredients like collagen and nanites before stopping. "Oh, sorry. This is a synth menu. Gotta find the one for organic humans."

I turn to Carson. "So what did you see on the Skylift?"

"It's pretty awesome. I made it all the way up to the middecks. They've got guys with actual jetpacks moving around up there. We all had work on minor stuff like rigging cables, but I got to talking with this synth girl who is a pilot for an interplanetary relay service. It's pretty badass."

The bartender drops off the beers, and we wait till he's gone to resume our conversation.

I recount some of the scene I overheard at Guy and Lawrence's mansion and how the Eternals are hoping to recruit dock workers and security personnel.

"For what?" Carson asks.

"No idea. But whatever they're up to, it's happening soon. He mentioned the Lost Star returning and said they have to be ready."

"So what do we think the Lost Star is? Like an actual star?"

"I was thinking it might be the submarine Mym is on. Could be the name of the sub."

"Why would they name a submarine Lost Star? You think it's Russian or something?"

"Could be. I'm just grasping at straws. If we find it and it has the flaming circle on it, that might tell us."

"You're wrong." The voice comes from over my shoulder. I turn and find a young woman seated at the bar behind me. She's not looking at our table but has clearly been eavesdropping on our conversation. Close-cropped hair stabs over the collar of a black, duster style trench coat. There are silver chevrons on her lapels. She keeps her stare fixed on the coaster between her fingertips but continues speaking. "The Lost Star isn't a boat. It's a starship." She's scribbling on the coaster. After a moment she stops, tucks her pen away into the folds of her duster, and tosses the coaster onto our table. The chunk of compressed cardboard lands with a thud in front of me. The scribbles are the outline of a flaming circle with blade-like wings.

"You won't find it here. It's not in port anyway."

I hold up the image on the coaster. "You've seen it?"

"Once."

I gesture toward the open chair. "Can we buy you a drink? I'd love to hear more."

The young woman glances at the empty chair then around the table briefly. "You all organics? You smell like organics."

"We're human if that's what you mean."

"Well, we're all humans these days, aren't we?" She slips off the barstool and kicks the leg of the chair to slide it away from the table. She eases herself into the chair and directly into a slouching position, her feet propped somewhere on the table's under-structure. "What are a bunch of organics doing in Machina Libre?" She gestures toward a server who nods and finally starts working his way over to our table. "You can't be with the movement or I'd have heard about you."

"I'm Ben. These are my friends, Tucket and Carson. And you are?"

"Captain Jumptree." She looks me over slowly. "But you can call me Mira." She leans one arm on the back of her chair. The butt of a pistol peeks out from a shoulder holster under her jacket.

Tucket is staring at her with wide eyes but quickly glances at the table when she returns his gaze.

She turns to me. "So what's your deal, Ben? You obviously aren't from around here. Why are you talking about the Lost Star in a synth bar in South Dock?" She extracts a small knife from her pocket and starts prying little chunks of wood out of the table.

"We're looking for it. There are some people associated with it who are going to help me with a personal problem I'm dealing with."

"You're looking for the Lost Star because of a personal problem? That's a good one. What's the matter? They run off with your first love? What was his name?"

I wait while she orders a drink from the server before responding. I use the time to size her up. Despite the somewhat hostile attitude, she looks experienced with the lifestyle here. She certainly seems comfortable. Her black pixie cut makes her look almost boyish, but she's pretty, high cheekbones and smooth porcelain skin that offsets the red in her lips. It's the symmetry of her face as much as her attitude that identifies her as a synth. She turns back to me with a slightly mocking stare. "Hope your credit is good here. I like the staff. I won't be part of some dine and dash."

"I'm good for it."

She nods and keeps her eyes locked on mine. "So you were saying. You have personal problems."

"Why don't you like organics?" I decide to go straight at her. "Is it us in particular or just everybody who's not a synth?" I look around the room and catch the glares of almost all the patrons around us. True to my guess, they've all been tuned in to our conversation. Now they don't even pretend to hide it.

"Gathered that, did you?" Mira holds up a chunk of table on the end of her knife. "What gave it away?"

"Just perceptive, I guess."

"Well, since you're so curious, we don't especially care for out-of-towners poking around asking questions about things they know nothing about. And you organics tend to be so darn sensitive—purists that you are.

You start ranting about how the earth ought to belong to you again, synths need to stay subservient—all that bullshit. I guess we all just get a little tired of hearing it."

"I haven't had too much experience with the synth community, I'll admit that, so I'll let you in on a secret." I push my sleeves up and rest my forearms on the edge of the table. I link my fingers together to keep myself from making fists. "I have no idea what you're talking about. If you're just looking for trouble, I'll tell you this much. We can certainly oblige."

I'm not completely bluffing. Maybe. I know Carson would have my back in a fight, but Tucket is another story. For all his good intentions, I suspect he'd be hard-pressed to fight his way out of a wet paper bag. If it comes to throwing down with a bar full of synths, we're definitely the underdogs.

Mira keeps her eyes locked on mine, and I can sense the tension building in the room around us. Her eyes finally fall on the chronometer I've exposed on my wrist. After a moment, she starts laughing. She slides her knife back into her belt and relaxes. "You're time travelers!" She breaks into a grin. "Why didn't you start with that?" The tension ebbs from the room with her laughter. Ambient murmurs begin again at the tables around us, making me realize how quiet things had gotten. "You like living on the edge, don't you?" Mira smiles and signals the bartender. "Get them another round. This one's on me."

The server appears from somewhere in the back and drops off a new round of beers. She sets them on the table and puts her hands on her hips, considering us. "You're buying beers for orgos now, Mira? Never thought I'd see that day."

Mira waves a hand at us. "They're time travelers."

"Ah," The server replies. "Polar." She spins on her heel and walks away.

I lean back in my chair, not sure exactly what has made the difference but happy that we are not going to have to fight our way out of the place.

"When are you from?" Mira is considering us with new curiosity.

"The twenty-first century. 2009."

"Zeus's balls." Mira lets out a whistle. "I'm sorry about the introduction. We don't see many time travelers in here. Not many organics, period."

"Why not?"

"You don't know? Your kind is dying out. Well, not yet. But it's coming, and your people are getting grumpy about it. I hear there might be other parallel worlds where you organics are still the most relevant life in this century. But, not that we would know, right?"

"Dying out or getting killed off?" Carson asks.

"For time travelers, you boys don't seem to know your evolution. The human race is going synthetic. You must not have been up this way long if you haven't gotten that message." She gestures to the restaurant around us. "This place is what you might consider a point of mutual understanding for those of us in the community who recognize what's coming. We do what we can to usher it in a little faster. Not many of your organic friends appreciate our message. The ones who barge in here are usually vindictive assholes. No offense."

"I suppose you give them the same warm welcome."

"We're all very friendly here." She places both hands on her drink glass. "It's funny. In your day, the human race was so scared of being eradicated by machines. They thought of us in terms of the boogeyman. *The Terminator*. All that crap.

"Modern synths are so much smarter than that. More powerful. We're starting a *social* revolution." She spreads her arms to encompass the rest of the bar. "It's all coming. Synth rights. Trans-human rights. It's inevitable. The juggernaut of the future. Some of you organics are slow on the uptake, but more and more are becoming trans-human every day. Organs failing? You'll get a synthetic one. Buy yourself ten more years of life. My prediction is that it will only take about two more generations. Who wants to age and die in eighty years when you can have better health, better sex, and live for centuries?" She raises her glass. "We're the new and improved human race."

I taste my new drink and set it back down. This beer is a draught lager. Smooth and refreshing. It seems the selection wasn't as limited as I was told.

"I get the evolution part, but what about the time travelers?"

"Yeah, you guys have kept a lock on that pretty well. Hoarding all the whatchamacallit particles. Gravitrons?"

"Gravitites," I mutter, suspecting her feigned memory lapse is more about emphasizing her apathy than any fault in her synthetic data.

"Yeah. Those. But who cares? Once people have the option to live as long as they like in the same place, courting death by jumping around in time doesn't look very appealing. Especially since you can't really change anything anyway. I'm sorry to be the one to tell you, but time travel was a fad."

Mira drains the last of her glass. "Not to say that it doesn't have its uses. Our crew has taken on a time traveler from time to time."

"You know, we're not all opposed to synth rights," Tucket says. "Some of us really care."

Mira smirks. "Ah. You're the exception, huh? Gonna join the revolution?"

"Maybe," Tucket mumbles.

I hold up the coaster again. "The Lost Star. Where can we find it?"

"It's not on earth. Hasn't been spotted for at least twenty years."

"We have reason to believe it will be coming back."

"Your reasons have to do with your personal problems?"

"Maybe."

Mira studies me for a little longer, then considers Tucket and Carson. "You know what? Sure. Why not? You guys amuse me. I'll tell you what you need to know. Won't do you a lot of good, but it doesn't hurt me to share." She takes back the coaster and holds up a second blank one next to her drawing. "You need to look for a comet."

I narrow my eyes. "I thought you said it was a ship."

"It is a ship. But there are a lot of ships. This one always shows up with a comet."

"You know this for a fact?"

"It's what people say. The ones that have seen it. And it's true of when I saw it too. We were on a supply run to the Jupiter colonies and spotted it on our nav radar leaving the solar system. It was chasing down a comet and winning. One of the LONEOS comets. "

"Chasing," Carson says. "What does it do when it catches it?"

"Don't know," Mira says. "But that's what I saw. And that's what everybody who's ever seen it on scopes says too. It comes in with a comet or goes out with one. Right up the tail. Damnedest thing."

"Interesting," I say. "This one you saw was the Lost Star? How do you know it's the same ship that gets spotted doing this?"

"Because no one else is that crazy. Name me one good reason to steer a perfectly good starship up the ass end of a comet."

"No other ships do that?" I ask.

"Shit no. Not unless you want to get pulverized by all the rock and ice coming off the thing. Our ships wouldn't last a day in those conditions." She tosses me the coaster. "So that's what I know. Hope it helps you out."

"Thank you," I reply.

I slide the coaster into my pocket as Mira stands.

"I think you're really pretty," Tucket blurts out.

Mira stares at him. She starts to speak, but his comment seems to have derailed her usual flow of sarcasm. A smile finally turns up the corner of her mouth. She moves toward the bar but pauses and turns around. "Look. If you want some food you're actually going to like, try Paco's Tacos on Bayshore Drive. He'll treat you right." With that she wanders away, striking up a conversation with a pair of synths at the end of the bar. She doesn't look back.

Carson grabs Tucket's shoulder. "It was a solid try, dude. Maybe we'll work on your delivery."

Tucket's eyes linger on Mira for a moment, then he sighs and follows us out of the bar. "I was starting to think she might like us."

I clap Tucket on the back. "Maybe you can try the server. She called us 'polar.' Has to mean she thinks we're extra cool, right?" I smile.

Tucket puts his hands in his pockets and shakes his head. "She said all time travelers are polar. It means we're like the polar ice caps. Used to be cool."

Paco does indeed treat us right. We get foil-wrapped takeout tacos that are actual food—no meta flavorings required. We take our haul back up the hill, intending to eat them back at Rixon's, but mine don't survive the trip. The smells wafting out of the takeout container overpower my resolve and, by the time we walk back into the dingy bar, I'm licking the last remnants of hot sauce off my fingers.

Eon is there to greet us. "Hey. You've got a call coming in from the chief."

"Who's the chief?" Tucket asks.

Eon leads us back behind the bar and through the kitchen to a staircase. The stairs lead to a multi-bedroom apartment over the bar. The living area has a lot of fancy electronics in it, and when I don my meta goggles, I get the full effect of their usefulness. Doctor Quickly and Noelle Chun appear in digital form in the center of the room, seated in their own holographic chairs.

"Hey, Doc," Carson says.

Doctor Quickly smiles. "Heard you had a productive day. Eon informed us of your employment on the Skylift." He looks to me. "And your other, more inflammatory adventures."

"They had it coming," I reply.

"Rixon mentioned you ran into these gentlemen before?"

"Yeah, well, later. Guy Friday and his brother Lawrence robbed us of a bunch of anchors and a chronometer in the '80s. Stuff you gave us when we first met you."

"Interesting," Doctor Quickly says. He pulls his leather journal from his bag and jots something down in the back. "I'll have to look into them."

"We'd be happy to assist in that particular investigation," Eon adds. "Ben gave us a few interesting details on their whereabouts."

Professor Chun leans forward. "Any more information about the symbols in the journal you discovered?"

"Actually, yes," I reply. I pull Mira's coaster drawing from my pocket. "We just got a new clue there. We've been told we're looking for a comet."

Doctor Quickly looks up from his notes. "A comet?" He turns to Professor Chun. "We hadn't considered perihelion occurrences. The dates could easily align with astronomical events. It would make sense why we hadn't noted a specific historical significance."

Professor Chun explains. "We've been taking the Roman numerals you showed us in Jay's journal and analyzing their possible correlation to known events. We've run them through multiple timestream historical records but haven't been able to discover a pattern. Astronomical events haven't necessarily aligned, but we've had a really broad search. What makes you think the symbol refers to a comet?"

"We ran into a starship pilot who says she's seen the Lost Star. She said it's a ship, and she watched it chase down a comet."

Professor Chun stares off into space for a few seconds, and I can tell she's searching something in the metaspace. "We do have an inbound comet right now. Borisov C/2014 Q3. Its perihelion occurred a few days ago. Not exactly close by. Over 153 million miles from Earth, but it's the nearest comet we've got to work with. If something is coming in with it, it would be moving incredibly fast. It could be arriving here at any time. I'll check with Interspace Customs and Border Protection. If a ship is inbound, they'll have a flight plan."

"Benjamin," Doctor Quickly says, "I understand you overheard one of these Eternals discussing their business regarding the Skylift?"

"They said they wanted a ship. Specifically wanted to recruit dock masters and security people. Seemed like they were getting desperate. Throwing lots of money at the project. Whatever they're planning, it's going to happen soon."

"They wanted me to meet them the day after tomorrow," Doctor Quickly says. "The date coincides with when we expect the submarine carrying Mym to arrive in port. I think it's safe to presume that if your star pilot friend is correct, the Eternals won't be sticking around long after. I'd be incredibly interested in finding out who they have coming to visit." He turns his attention to me. "Have you had any luck with your *other* project— the visions you've been getting?"

"No. I haven't been especially interested in hearing what he has to say since our last connection. He's partly why Mym is in this mess."

Doctor Quickly frowns. "You would know yourself the best no doubt, and I have every confidence in you, but I suspect that if you asked my daughter, she might remind you that we owe a lot to the Ben Travers you once were. Whatever his current failings, we wouldn't be alive at all if he hadn't done what he did to save us."

He keeps his eyes on mine until I drop my gaze to my lap.

Doctor Quickly puts his hands on his knees and stands. "Okay. Well, it looks like we have some more work to do. Noelle and I will find out about our cosmic visitors. You all look exhausted. Let's reconvene tomorrow and see what else we've got. When that submarine pulls into the harbor, we need to be ready."

Rixon and Eon sign us off from the holographic conference call and bundle up some of the equipment. Tucket has slumped into the couch with a vacant stare on his face. Carson yawns. He looks ready to pass out any minute. The Mexican food has done everyone in.

"There are spare rooms up here. Find one to make yourselves comfortable, just don't take mine," Rixon says. "I have to mind the bar."

Eon says goodnight as well and leaves us alone.

I attempt to roust Tucket from the couch and realize his far-off stare is because he's in the metaspace somewhere. "Hey. What are you doing?"

"Wha— oh, nothing." Tucket jolts back to attention. "I was just looking for—um . . . Nothing. It's time for bed, yeah?"

"Yeah."

I've lost track of how many hours I've been awake. Feels closer to days.

As Carson and Tucket find themselves places to sleep, I pretend to do the same. I envy the way they can just crash out. Carson is snoring within minutes. When the sounds of their movements have ceased, I wander down the hall and out onto the rear fire escape.

It's easier for them. They didn't wake up out of control and screaming at their girlfriend last time.

From my spot on the fire escape, I'm looking at the glittering lights of the space elevator. The structure blinks and glows in cryptic sequences. More lights flash in the sky as well. Space stations. Satellites. Our man-made constellations. Somewhere up there our mystery ship is making its way to earth.

The harbor glistens. The tide is rising in from the gulf, and somewhere below the horizon, a submarine is gliding closer. Gravity is pulling us all together. One point of contact. I wonder if the same gravity is working on the Neverwhere, drawing my other self closer.

Doctor Quickly's words linger in my mind. We wouldn't be here to experience any of it if it hadn't been for him.

But what happens if I let him in again? What if he takes control? I recall the horror of feeling my own body wrenched away from me. If I reach out to him and let him in, will saving Mym still be in my power?

I do owe him. I know that.

My eyes are bleary from exhaustion. I won't be able to keep him out forever.

My eyes drift north along the horizon to the hazy lights of other cities along the coast. I need to know how to let him in without ending up like Sonia. There's no way I can stay awake until Quickly's scheduled rendezvous with the Eternals.

My fingers find the dials on my chronometer. Even If I skipped ahead, I'd need to be at my best then, not this ragged version of me. I'll be no good as a rescuer if I can't even see straight.

I can feel the call of sleep. All I would need to do is go back inside and lie down on the couch.

If I go to sleep, will I wake up me?

I study the alley behind the bar for a brief moment, then climb down the fire escape. Action will keep me awake.

I don my meta goggles and blend with the late night pedestrians making their way down to the waterfront. I'm glad my walk is downhill: the path of least resistance. The rhythm of the citizens going about their business around me gives me a sense of normalcy. To them, this is just another night. I am just one of the crowd. A sea of anonymous faces.

Except one.

Crossing the street, carrying a bouquet of flowers, is Tucket. Surprised, I almost call to him, but his expression is serious. He seems intent on his mission. It seems I'm not the only one ducking out on sleep. Tucket continues downhill away from me, then turns right on a side street. By the time I reach the corner, he is already standing outside Machina Libre. He braces himself, then walks inside.

I debate going after him. I don't know if the synths inside are going to give him a hard time. When I reach the bar, I linger on the front steps, craning my neck to look inside. Tucket has marched straight to the back of the bar to a booth along the far wall and has presented his flowers to Mira. She's holding them as one might an offensive smelling diaper, but, to my surprise, she invites Tucket to sit. Tucket slides into the booth and immediately begins babbling away in his usual fashion. Mira stays silent, but she's listening, apparently open to Tucket's exuberance. I observe the scene until the big bartender from earlier steps over to the doorway.

"What are you, a cat?"

"Huh?"

"In or out. Make up your mind. I'm closing these doors."

I take a step back. "I guess I'm good." The bartender shuts the door on me and I get only one last glimpse of the booth in the back.

Mira is laughing.

Maybe he knows what he's doing after all . . .

Since Tucket doesn't seem to be in danger of being murdered, I continue my way downhill.

My body is aching. I need to be off my feet and sleeping, but I still need assurances. I walk faster.

Before my mind has any chance to object, I reach my destination. I grasp the lanyard around my neck and use the chit to get myself aboard the B train headed north.

The train route glows on the walls, city maps and highlighted landmarks illuminated in the metaspace. As the train launches itself northward at breathtaking speed, I trace the line of its trajectory up the coast to Saint Petersburg. Six Southside city stops, three downtown, and then one for Old Northeast. Fourth and Ninth Streets. The names near the stops list the featured destinations. At the bottom of the list is my destination. The Temple of the Eternal Flame.

An old woman gestures to an open seat next to her. I wave a thank you but stay standing. If I sit, I'll close my eyes.

If I close my eyes, I may never come back.

.

"You can't assume the most important people in your life will be living close to home. Sometimes your greatest friends are discovered in far away places. It's up to you to go find them."-Journal of Dr. Harold Quickly, 2202

CHAPTER 18

St. Petersburg, 2165

It's past midnight when I reach the Temple of the Eternal Flame. It's a two-story stone building that resembles a Moorish castle with its sturdy square proportions and a sense of permanence. At its front, two heavy wooden gates stand closed atop a half dozen steps. Above the door, a circular stone cutout flickers from internal firelight. In the darkness, the opening resembles a watchful eye staring out at the night.

I walk around the perimeter of the temple, but there isn't much to see. The walls are unadorned and there is only one visible entrance. No worshipers. No pious congregation. I'm too late.

I cross Ninth Street and enter the lobby of a hotel that has bloomed up in place of what once was a Red Cross station. The new building is twenty stories and a shining tower of glass and chrome. Despite its height, it seems fragile opposite the sturdy stone temple.

The synth receptionist smiles as I approach.

"Good evening, sir. It's nice to see you looking well again. Did you have a pleasant evening?"

"Um, maybe?" I put on my most guileless expression. "Could you remind me which room I was staying in? I seem to have lost my key card."

"Must have been quite the night. We haven't issued key cards for about a hundred years." She leans over the desk conspiratorially. "We scanned your eyes when you checked in, sir. Room 224."

"Ah. It's coming back to me now." I tap my forehead. "Just one more thing. Could you tell me what time I checked in?"

"Three thirty-five, sir. I'm glad the first-aid kit seems to have done its job." She winks at me. "Right as rain, indeed."

"Oh. Yeah, thanks . . ." I slip my meta-goggles on and read the name floating above the desk clerk's head. ". . . Penny." Penny smiles and I leave her to find the elevator.

First-aid kit? That doesn't sound good. I pause in the hallway to consider the implications of what she might be saying about my near future. *Probably nothing too terrible if I didn't need major medical attention. I hope.*

The door to room 224 has no handle but slides open as soon as I lift my goggles and stare at the spot where the handle ought to be.

The lights brighten automatically and the walls spring to life with digital scenery. The longest wall is a view of the Gulf of Mexico that really hasn't changed much since my time. A white sand beach stretches from one imaginary horizon to another. It seems any room can now boast an oceanfront view.

The first-aid kit that the receptionist mentioned is sitting on one of the nightstands. I walk over to it and pop the lid open to check the contents. From what I can tell, all of the major items are still in their plastic wrappers. If there is anything missing, it can't be more than a pack of aspirin or a Band-Aid. *That makes me feel better.*

The illusory nature of the walls makes me shy away from using one as an anchor. I enter the bathroom instead and see immediately that I've made the right choice. Apparently lacking any other writing implements, someone has written on the glass shower door with soap. 3:28. I pat my pockets and realize that I have indeed come unprepared for taking notes.

"Okay. Makes that easier."

I set my chronometer for 3:28 and dial the pin release timer for ten seconds, letting it tick down to my departure, my one hand casually pressed against the wall. A thought occurs to me and I hastily question the room. "Room, what time is it now?"

A gentle voice responds. "The current time is 12:25 a.m."

"Thanks."

At 3:28 the soap writing on the glass has vanished. I notice belatedly that there is an automatic liquid soap dispenser in place next to the sink. The shower likewise offers only automatic cleaning options. It takes me a few minutes to locate the bar soap kept in reserve in one of the sink drawers. I unwrap it and dutifully scribble my message on the shower glass before preparing to depart again. I open up one of the cabinet doors under the sink and scribble a second soap note on the inside. 12:25. Satisfied, I make my way downstairs to the front desk to officially acquire my newly reserved jump room.

"Good afternoon, sir," Penny says as I walk up. "How can I help you?"

I smile. "Just checking in. I have a particular room in mind . . ."

Five minutes later, I'm back outside staring at the temple lit by the afternoon sun. Drones buzz overhead and passersby continue on their way without urgency, scooting along in their driverless cars and smaller personal conveyances.

There is nothing ominous about the temple in daylight. The archway above the door hosts a pair of doves that are cooing softly to one another. A trio of people are seated on the front steps enjoying sandwiches. The gate is open.

The sunlight has helped me shake some of the fatigue from my muscles. I take a deep breath and trudge up the steps.

The entrance to the temple passes through a breezy foyer with two metal bowls on either side that contain fires. There are bundles of dry wood a few feet away from each fire, but the pieces are tiny, hardly substantial enough to make a difference. Whatever ritual purpose the wood serves is lost on me, so I continue on.

I had thought I would be accosted immediately upon trying to access this lair of my enemies. To my surprise, I am able to pass through a lush interior garden and then walk right up to a sort of arched stone gazebo at the center of the main courtyard. Two domes, one on top of the other, are supported by the four pillars at the corners. The inner dome has holes cut out in the shape of stars and the light from a large fire inside the structure makes star shapes on the outer dome even in daylight.

A flowing fountain near the arched structure runs out toward the garden and burbles pleasantly.

A willowy young woman in a pale, flowing skirt appears from an alcove in one of the courtyard walls and greets me cheerily.

"Welcome to The Temple of the Eternal Flame. Have you come seeking wisdom?"

I tense immediately at being approached, but the young woman seems sincere. With her simple clothing and lack of meta imagery, she looks unthreatening. Even her expression invites trust. Her big eyes are fixed on my face, and she smiles at me pleasantly.

"I was just curious what you do here."

"We offer opportunities for those who wish to live a better life. This place is a sanctuary. A place to encounter your most perfect self and to discover your highest destiny."

"What if I don't want to know my destiny?"

The girl shakes her head. "You can't avoid it. We all share the same destiny. The outside world is going to pass away. We've seen it." She gestures to the building around us. "Mere stone and flesh can't withstand time. But we among the brethren will experience immortality." She tilts her head to consider me. "You look tired."

"Exhausted."

"Think how rested you could be if you were no longer a servant of time."

THE DAY AFTER NEVER

She fingers the fabric of my work shirt and rests her hand on my forearm. "If you could unshackle yourself from your daily toils and live a life of your choosing, wouldn't your life be more restful?"

"One would think."

The willowy girl smiles at me serenely. "We've seen the future. We know that this takeover by machines affecting the world is just temporary. Your struggle as a human being will not be in vain. They might be taking your jobs and threatening your spirits, but the true human race will be reborn. We've been given a savior." She lifts up the front of her shirt and exposes a fabric pouch tied at the top of her skirt, along with a fair amount of her firm stomach. She pulls a scrap of paper from the pouch and offers it to me.

Unlike the glossy flyers I've seen from other religious ministries, this one is made from rough paper and full of hand-written script. "Here, this is one of my favorites."

I take the slip of paper and read the calligraphic script out loud.

"A mountain of fire. A savior's grace.

"A new beginning for the human race.

"An open mind is an enduring portal.

"Time cannot thwart this life immortal."

The poem is signed—Eterna.

The willowy girl is smiling. "Isn't that beautiful? Doesn't it just make you want to drift away into the sky to be with our savior?" She twirls a few times, skirt flaring out around her—getting herself dizzy—then tumbles into me, her hands landing on my chest. She looks up with her doe eyes and smiles. It makes me wonder how many men have wandered in here less for the enlightenment than for the company. It also makes me wonder what kind of drugs they might be passing around.

"Are you Eterna? It's a very nice quote. Or poem."

"It's from my dreams."

"You dream the future?"

"We all can," she says. "It's what makes us special."

"What if you want to stop?"

Eterna appraises me skeptically. "Why would you want to stop? Messages from your more enlightened self are a blessing."

I remove her hands from my chest and prop her back up. "Who runs this place? Do you have a service of some kind?"

"We'll meet tonight," she says. "We'll make contact with His Greatness." She looks up at the sky again, dreamily. When she lowers her gaze, her voice loses a bit of its elation. "But it's only for the brethren who have been initiated. New members come to the gatherings on Thursdays."

"What time is the meeting tonight?"

"You won't have time to be initiated today, but if you are serious about seeking your future, we could start the process. We need to spend some time with you and teach you how to access your deepest self."

"My deepest self is pretty loud already."

She laughs and pats my arm again. "I'll look for Ollech. He handles initiates. Stay here and I'll try to find him."

The girl swirls away into a side passage and leaves me alone. As soon as she's out of sight, I uncover my chronometer. I move swiftly around the courtyard, passing a pit at the back of the domed gazebo that is perhaps six feet deep and charred from being burned multiple times. I continue around the perimeter of the courtyard searching the various other alcoves and grottos for an out-of-the-way spot suitable for a time jump. I don't see anything that I can be sure no one will be occupying over the next few hours. Finally I discover a staircase that leads up to the roof overlooking the courtyard. A locked iron gate blocks the passage at the top, but that is within my abilities to circumvent.

I trot back down the stairs, select a stone from an out of the way spot in the garden, run back up the stairs and toss it through the gate. Then it's just a matter of running back down the stairs, making a jump back in time to when the stone was still in the garden, and then using it as an anchor to jump forward to the time when the stone is lying on the roof. It's a process I've gotten used to now as a time traveler. It's almost routine, but I still double-check my settings for each jump.

Having successfully acquired a secure spot on the roof from which to observe the courtyard, I use my meta goggles to zoom in on the scene, then fiddle with the toolbar until I find the record option. The goggles will likely do a better job of keeping track of the action than my sleep-deprived brain will. Once the recording is running, I set my chronometer for smaller jumps to move myself forward in time.

My first few jumps make it apparent that my disappearance was not too difficult on Eterna. She returns with a grouchy-looking man in black robes who looks relieved to find me gone. He simply grumbles at her and vanishes back indoors when she can't locate me. I skip ahead to witness her perform her greeting services and poetry distribution a few more times to other interested men who wander in, but none must show as much interest in the brethren as they do Eterna herself, because she doesn't fetch Ollech for any of them. As the sun dips down to the horizon, the big gates at the front of the temple close. A large, robed man takes up a position near the entrance and admits people using a smaller door built into the gate.

Midnight had been dry out, but I'm careful to check the sky before each jump for any sign of Florida's frequent spontaneous rainstorms building above me. I don't linger long in any one time—just long enough to see if the promised meeting has begun. Approximately an hour after sunset, I find what I'm looking for.

The courtyard fills with figures. The fire in the center of the temple grows brighter as it is fed by various acolytes, and they've built a new fire in the rectangular pit out back. This recess sits just beyond the edge of the raised dome structure and from my angle it now resembles an orchestra pit to a stage. That is if someone especially hated orchestras and lit them on fire.

The assembled group of the brethren in the courtyard swells until there are roughly a hundred people standing around the fiery pit. The crowd has left room for a path from one of the corridors, and a smaller group of figures proceeds along it and up into the domed room.

The leader of the procession is Mr. Longcase. He seems to have recovered from his encounter with Sonia and my earlier self at the mansion in Port Nyongo, but there is still a sense of insecurity about his movements, as if he is still upset by the way his day has gone.

A few more men and women I don't know follow Longcase, then, bringing up the rear, is Jay Sprocket.

I get a jolt of adrenaline seeing another face from Sprocket Manor here. His presence makes the whole thing seem more real—another stitch in Mym's abduction tied to this coast of Florida.

Jay looks more childlike than the last time I saw him. Here, surrounded by strangers, he seems to have shrunk. He looks more like the Jonah I know, a boy confronting a world of grownups. I want to get close to him and ask him why he's a part of this, what drove him to come here. I'll need to find a way to speak to him when this meeting of theirs is over. I owe Jonah that much.

Longcase stands at the side of the arched structure overlooking the fire pit. The flames cast an eerie glow on his features. He raises his arms and speaks in a language I don't understand, but the crowd has no trouble and responds in unison, volleying back phrases in a liturgical fashion. Once the recitations have concluded, Longcase lowers his arms and switches back to English.

"Brethren of the Eternal Line of Gnomon, our hour of glory is almost upon us. The rebirth has begun."

A few members of the crowd cheer before being shushed by people around them. Longcase abides the interruption calmly.

"You are right to be joyful. We have worked hard to achieve this moment. Because of your faithfulness, we have stretched the line of Gnomon to the distant past. We have just received word from the brethren that the body of our great lord has been found."

More cheers erupt from the congregation, and Longcase lets them die down before he continues. "Despite our savior's distance from us and the many millennia that have kept us apart, we will finally fulfill our destiny. The vision of the Lord Gnomon— first disciple of our savior—has been a gift to us, passed down from the coming centuries. He told us of the greatness of Zurvan and has showed us the path to our salvation."

Longcase points to the sky. "The Lost Star is almost upon us. Its return heralds the turning point in our great journey to freedom. Because of your dedicated service to our cause, all of humanity will benefit."

Jay has been positioned directly between the two pillars on the near side of the dome. Longcase gestures for him to step forward. He stands behind Jay and places both hands on his shoulders.

"This young man volunteered himself to our cause. He is a former student at The Academy of Temporal Sciences. He wished to become a time traveler, but when he left that school and took his destiny into his own hands, he discovered the insidious lie that has been told to all of us. There is no path forward in time that does not lead to our destruction and abandonment at the hands of the machines. He came to see what we know to be true. Our only salvation lies in the power of Zurvan."

Longcase raises a hand. "And now, as evidence of his commitment to the brethren, this brave young man will bear a message to our Lord and allow us to hear his divine words."

The crowd around the fire applauds enthusiastically. Some shout praise to Jay. The boy is looking more assured of himself now. When Longcase takes a step back, Jay steps forward to the edge of the fire pit and stares into the flames. He begins to hum and sway, putting his hands out over the pit. The crowd follows his example, chanting and swaying with him. A few of them likewise have their hands extended toward the flames.

What on earth are they up to?

The chanting and humming continues uninterrupted for a solid ten minutes without change, the whole crowd swaying gently in trancelike harmony. I'm having a hard time keeping my eyes open as it is, and this rhythmic monotony is not helping at all. I turn the dials on my chronometer and am about to skip ahead again, when Jay goes suddenly rigid. His body jerks and his eyes roll back in his head. His hands fly to his scalp, clenching at his skull. No one intervenes to help him. The crowd goes quiet instead, engulfed in rapt silence.

The voice that comes out of Jay's mouth is not Jay's. Jay's mouth moves to form the words, but it's a powerful, adult voice speaking.

"The Almighty Zurvan sends this message to his faithful brethren: The Lost Star returns as I have promised your prophets. You will bring it to me, and I will grant your reward—spare you from the fate that consumes humanity. Those who would be saved should heed my words. Bring the Lost Star to the eternal fires of Yanar Dag. Restore me to my body and assure your eternal salvation."

Jay's hands drop from his head, and he returns as if from a dream. Longcase is at his side in an instant, whispering something in his ear. Jay inflates his chest and runs a hand up his arm, pushing the sleeve of his robe up past his elbow and revealing something strapped around his bicep. A Temprovibe. He pushes something on the device, takes a step forward and leaps, soaring out over the flames, then plummeting into the pit of fire.

"NO!" The yell is out of my mouth before I've had any chance to think. I leap to my feet, but there is nothing to be done, the boy does not land in the fire, instead, he vanishes into thin air. Gone.

The silence of the next moment is a pregnant pause. Two distinctly different things happen in the moment that follows. Some of the enraptured brethren, intent on Jay's actions, send up a cheer. Others, who have heard my shout from the rooftop, have turned to search for its origin.

My mind is sluggish. I'm in shock from what I just saw. Jay vanishing into the flames defies all logic, but the danger I'm in is slowly registering too. I back away from the edge of the rooftop and search the face of my chronometer for a setting. *Where am I going?*

The iron gate from the stairwell swings open on squeaky hinges and three robed figures spring from the darkness beyond.

Shit.

I spin the dial on my chronometer for six hours into the past, a time before I was first up here. I reach for the roof, but I'm tackled just as my fingertips brush the surface. My attacker and I go sprawling. Another body is added to the pile momentarily, and my right arm is wrenched behind my back in a submission hold.

"Get off!" I blurt out. Someone has ahold of my legs, possibly sitting on them, grinding my knees painfully into the roof.

"Surrender yourself," the attacker above me hisses.

My chronometer hand is still free underneath my body, but the third person has arrived, and I can feel myself being lifted. In a fit of desperation,

I cram my chronometer into my mouth, spinning the dial on the timer mechanism with my teeth and pressing the pin with my chin. *Ten seconds.*

I'm yanked to my feet, and a fist slams into my stomach. All of the air leaves my lungs.

Nine seconds.

A punch to the face. I sway sideways, but am still held by strong arms. They clamp down on mine. *Sonsofbitches.*

Seven seconds.

A second punch to the stomach. I crumple and go limp in their arms. Rough hands squeeze me on all sides. *Not yet.*

Five seconds.

I'm being dragged toward the doorway to the stairs.

Four.

More figures stand near the gate. I contort myself into a ball, as compact as I can get.

Three.

The men holding my feet lead the way, hauling me feet-first through the doorway to the stairs.

Two. I come uncoiled and kick hard at the men at my feet, simultaneously slamming my head into the forearm of the man holding my left wrist.

One.

He loses his grip on my arm, and I stretch it downward, straining to reach, and dragging my fingertips along the rough concrete floor.

Blink.

I crash to the floor, bumping my way down three more steps till I come to rest in a heap on the landing. None of my attackers have come with me. I'm lying in the stairwell in indirect daylight. Other than my own gasps, there is no sound except the burbling stream in the garden and the dull drone of noise outside the temple.

"Ow," I mutter aloud as I get slowly to my feet. My ribs are aching. Whether it's from the punches or the tumble down the concrete steps is hard to tell. I probe my side gently. Nothing feels broken, but I imagine I'm pretty well bruised. There is a trickle on my chin. I lick my lips and discover the blood. A quick tour by my tongue assures me that I still have all of my teeth at least.

I grip the handrail firmly and make my way gingerly down the remaining stairs.

It's roughly 2:30 in the afternoon. Too early to walk into the hotel yet. I need to jump forward. I wrack my brain for a time to jump to where I know

I won't run into myself or the other Eternals. It takes me longer than it should, but as I stand there aching and trying to wrap my mind around the temporal knot that my day has become, it finally dawns on me that I have all of the afternoon's activity recorded on my goggles. I shuffle through the first few video images till I see a spot where Eterna is out of sight, then dial my chronometer for the second after the video ended, when my earlier self skipped ahead in time. Once I've arrived in that window, I just stumble out the temple's front gate and back into the street.

Penny is aghast at the sight of me. She immediately races from around the concierge desk to tend to me. "Oh goodness, what happened to you? Do you need me to contact the police or an ambulance?"

"I'm okay, Penny. Thanks. I will take that first-aid kit from you now though."

Penny stares at me for only a moment before dashing behind the desk to the office and then reemerging with the first-aid kit. "You're my angel," I say as she hands it to me. She still looks concerned, but I give her smile. "Don't worry. Next time you see me, I'll be right as rain." She doesn't look convinced, but I pat her hand and make my way to the elevator.

Back inside my hotel room, I'm tempted to immediately clean myself up, but I know that's not how it goes. I slide the first-aid kit onto the nightstand and make my way back into the bathroom. Double-checking the note I left on the cabinet door, I set my chronometer one more time, aiming for 12:45am. I take one more look around the bathroom for any evidence I'm leaving behind, then blink.

Once I'm back to the time I left, I immediately start shedding clothes. I let the shower douse me from all the angles it feels like as I lean my head against the shower wall. Despite witnessing the Eternals in action, this outing to St. Pete has brought me no closer to resolving my issue. It's only made me more tired. When the automated shower is complete, I make some basic attempts with the first-aid kit, patching whatever scrapes and cuts I see still bleeding, then I gather up my clothes and stumble back into the bedroom. I manage to get my pants on, but as soon as I sit on the edge of the bed to wrangle on my socks, my body refuses to cooperate. It's as if the mere proximity of the mattress has short-circuited all of my abilities to withstand it. Gravity gets the best of me, and I tip over onto the bed, my legs still dangling off the edge. I don't care. It feels so good.

Some former objection sputters to the top of my mind for a moment, something about my other self chasing Mym away, but the objection is instantly smothered by the softness of the pillow when I crawl up to the head of the bed.

I bury my face in the pillow and attempt to recall what was so terribly important about staying awake. *He was going to take over my life, wasn't he?* I try to make myself care about that prospect. Nothing comes.

It's okay. He can drive for a while. Not like I'm doing a very good job anyway. Just so long as he lets me sleep.

I let the thought glide through my mind and disappear. It takes the rest of me with it.

"It is a marvelous thing the way humans adapt and change. It is our attitudes as much as our biology that have evolved over the centuries. It's not always for the better, but it's good to know that we have learned the ability to forge new paths. The future belongs to those with imagination enough to see it." -Journal of Dr. Harold Quickly, November 18, 2180

CHAPTER 19

The Neverwhere

The tunnel has taken on strange sounds. I don't know how long I've been slumped against the dirt wall in the dark.

Days.

Years.

Centuries.

It could be that I have always been here. Timeless, like the Neverwhere itself. It feels like forever.

But there are the sounds. A dinging noise and then a swooshing and a bump. Another memory trickling through.

I get to my feet.

This tunnel leads under the streets of Seattle—a relic from the period when the city was raised up out of a floodplain. The last time I was inside it was while I was fleeing cyborgs with human heads and a bunch of time-travel-hating zealots. Even so, this tunnel led to safety. It had an exit.

I shuffle along the underground walkway, making my way toward the dinging noise. The sound repeats at regular intervals. Finally, I find a beam of light stretching across the floor from an open doorway. The rusty metal door has been left open. I step inside into a dusty, brick-sided basement.

My memory of this room was different. The bottom few floors of the building above had been gutted and removed, giving a false sense of height. Now the ceiling is intact, making the room much shorter. There were armed guards near the door last time I visited. Now there are only a few steps leading out of the tunnel and then a concrete floor with a few drains and, beyond them, an elevator shaft. Two elevator doors stand side by side. The one on the left is closed. The needle on the brass backsplash above the door points to the number three. The second set of doors to the right stand open, but are trying to close. The doors slide inward, impact a wooden ladder that is positioned between them, and open again. Each opening is accompanied by a ding from the bell. The ladder is positioned so that the person climbing it can reach the floor indicator above the door.

A man is on the ladder, fiddling with the broken dial above the door and muttering to himself. I'm able to see the numbered brass plate beyond his head because the man is almost completely transparent. Looking at him, I can just make out his grease-stained coveralls and a rag hanging from his back pocket. He has a bucket laden with tools on the floor near his ladder. The tools and ladder are just as ghostly as the man.

I take a few steps forward. "Um, hello?"

The man pauses his tinkering and turns around. He appraises me from over his nearly nonexistent spectacles. He's not especially old. Perhaps fifties, but his clothing is reminiscent of a bygone era. The sturdiness of his leather boots makes me think of the engine mechanics I met aboard the Hindenburg. He has a sturdy chin, too. Square with a deep cleft.

"This elevator is out of service, I'm afraid." He jabs a thumb toward the door propped open by his ladder. "Not sure where you were headed today. Options are a bit limited."

"I didn't know there was anyone else down here," I say. I take a few steps closer. The man looks friendly. "I'm Ben Travers."

The man gets off the ladder, wipes his fingers on his rag, then extends a hand. "Henry Drexel. Pleased to meet you."

His handshake is enthusiastic but vaporous, like shaking hands with a cloud.

"How did you—are you a . . ."

"Elevator maintenance," Henry replies. "Best in the business if I do say so myself. Not too many folks know their way around a Mobilus elevator like me. You can count on it."

"You're a time travel elevator mechanic?"

"Have you been aboard? Haven't seen you down here before."

"Actually, I did ride it once. Around the 2400s. Looked a bit different though. Not as nice as this."

"2400s? Now that's way up there isn't it? Past its prime to be sure. I helped build this elevator in 1882. Do you believe it?" He turns around to admire the shining doors. "Lots of good times we've had together. Good, good times." He polishes his glasses on his sleeve and readjusts them on his face again.

"Do you mind if I ask what got you here?" I ask. "In the Neverwhere? Did someone . . . do something to you?"

Henry glances at me and then moves to his tool bucket. "Well, you can't go expecting a time machine to work right every single time now can you? They are just machines after all. Not the fault of Tempus Mobilus Elevator

Company." He pulls a wrench from the pocket of his coveralls and drops it into the bucket. "We never lost a customer. I was an employee, so the record is still clean as far as I'm concerned."

He fumbles in his pockets a little more and comes up with the needle for the second indicator. "I'm sure they had this back up and running in no time after I left. No time at all." He fiddles with the pointer, staring wistfully at the back plate. He's so faded that I have a hard time making out the detail of his expressions. "She sure was a beauty, wasn't she?"

I let him continue his admiration of the elevator a little longer, but finally my concern gets the best of me.

"Are you okay?" I ask. "You seem a bit—hazy."

Henry turns around. "Oh, sure. Been getting that way for a while now. Looks like you're losing a bit of shine yourself."

I study my arms. They are a bit less vivid than I remember. A drab hue to my skin and fingernails. I'm still much better defined than Henry, but I can't deny that I share a bit of his pallor.

"What's happening to us?"

"Just a little fading. Happens to the best of us."

"But why am I—"

"You're a memory aren't ya? Memories don't last forever."

His statement sits like a lump in my chest. "Wait, what do you mean by that? I'm going to disappear?"

"Can't expect to just linger about in the middle of things forever, can you? There comes a time to let go. I'm about done here anyway. I did want to get her other car back in order, but it seems I didn't bring all the right parts. Would have been nice to see her in all her glory one more time."

"When you say, 'let go,' what are you talking about? I didn't think there was a way out of this place."

"Of course there is," Henry replies. "What kind of screwball told you that?"

"Um. Just a—friend."

"Well, you tell him to stop filling your head with nonsense."

"He's actually not—he's . . . gone now."

"See? What did I tell you? Moved on, right?"

"No. Not exactly."

Henry looks me in the eye, and his face grows serious. "Oh. I see." He fidgets with his rag and stuffs it back in his pocket again. "Ran into one of the other kind, did he? Look, son, why don't I take you up top and let you have a look around. Have you been up top yet?" He jabs a finger toward the ceiling.

"I went to the seventh floor once. Is that what you mean?"

"Seven? No. There's a good view from seven, but that ain't the top. Come on." He steps around his ladder and presses the up button on the elevator. The doors on the right spring back enthusiastically from their attempts to crush the ladder, but Henry waits till the left-hand elevator doors open and shoos me in ahead of him. Once inside, he produces a key from his coveralls that is just as hazy as the rest of him, but upon inserting it in the keyhole below the buttons, the doors close. He presses the button for seven and waits.

I admire the shiny wood paneling and brass handrails, not sure if it's Henry's memory or mine, or a combination of both that has brought them to life.

When the elevator reaches the seventh floor, it bumps to a stop, but Henry gives the key on the control panel an extra three turns and the doors stay closed. A thump from somewhere above us is followed by a jolt, and the elevator continues upward. We finally come to a stop once more, and the doors slide open. The bell dings.

We're outside.

Stepping out of the elevator, the gritty tar paper of the roof crunches underfoot. The rest of the roof goes unnoticed, however, because the sky demands all of my attention. Out here there is no fog, just a cosmic starscape of brilliant lights and thin, twisting, iridescent rivers. The view is clearer than any I've had before. It's almost as if I'm out among the stars myself—closer to the streams of light and color. I feel as if I could stretch out and dip my hand into them.

"This is the top," Henry says. "Last stop before forever. Not a bad view, eh? "

"What is it?" I ask. "What are we really looking at?"

"Space and time. The whole kit and caboodle. Look up there, and you might see anywhere. Any time."

I watch the colors shimmer through the sky. "I don't think I really understand it."

"Why would you? Out here, we're just specks ourselves. Somewhere out there in some other time, someone might be looking up and seeing us. We look just the same." He kicks a few loose pebbles on the roof shingles below us. "All this other stuff is just leftovers. The memory of what we were before. All in our heads."

"We're that?" I point to the shimmering river arcing up past us into the cosmos.

"Sure. Just a teeny bit of that, mind you. That's probably everybody we ever knew in there, stretched out across their lifetimes. The only reason we see it and they don't is that we've got perspective. Your mind got a chance to step outside of time and see the bigger picture."

"So the Neverwhere—all these other spaces and memories I've been seeing—it's just an illusion in my head?"

"Not an illusion. It's your past. It's your memories. Memories aren't illusions, they just are what they are. And it's easier for your mind to keep you in there than to accept all of this. Takes a little adjusting to process it all. So you live in your memories for a while. But you're getting there. You're seeing it now. It's taken a long time to let go myself. Still saying my goodbyes."

"What about the others? The people I've met here didn't move on to anywhere else. There's this one, Zurvan, and he's been taking people from the real world. Snatching them up."

"This Zurvan and your other friend. Did they seem inclined to let go of their past?"

"Um. No. Actually, the past was kind of all they talked about. Zurvan just keeps replaying his memories, re-watching them, like an obsession. Benny was pretty intent on revisiting the past too."

"Then they never would have seen the Neverwhere like this." Henry gestures to the sky. "This would be terrifying to them. A place they'd hide from at all cost."

"Why?"

"Because it's their inevitable future. A mind stuck in the past can't abide the idea of leaving it behind. But that's what you'd have to do to ever leave this place. You'd have to let go. That's the catch. When your friend said there's no way out, he wasn't all wrong. There's no getting out the way you are now. You'd have to give up all that. Be willing to accept what you will be. Time always works that way."

"Zurvan keeps sucking up people's minds. He's the one who got my friend Benny. Why hasn't he faded away yet?"

"Keeps getting himself new memories, right? The more he keeps doing that, the more he ties himself to the regular world. He won't ever feel hungry for eternity unless he stops feeding himself with the past. Even if it belongs to someone else."

Even as I look at Henry, his already-wispy exterior has been changing colors. His transparency now makes him a conductor for the view beyond. Henry is beautiful.

"Is that what you are? Hungry for eternity?"

Henry takes a seat on the edge of the roof and lets his feet dangle over the edge. I sink down next to him and do the same.

"It's getting so I can't think about anything else. I'm going to let you in on a secret, son. If you sit out here long enough, you start to forget what it was that was ever so important about yourself. It's a tough lesson to learn because all we ever seem to want in life is to be important—to matter. And I don't mean to say you didn't. I'm just saying that when you get yourself a little perspective and see the universe and all of time laid out for you like this, you tend to realize there's so much more to being you than you thought. It creeps up on you that this whole time you were part of something a whole lot bigger. Something older and more spectacular."

"And that's the way out? Stop being such an individual?" I frown.

"You don't have to say it like it's a bad thing," Henry replies. "Do you like puzzles?"

"I guess."

"You ever get yourself a puzzle piece in your hand, pick out one you like from among all the thousand others and say, 'I think I'll just set this one piece down and not worry about the rest. I'm done with this puzzle.' You ever do that?"

"No. I don't really think that counts as solving a puzzle."

"I agree. I don't think it counts either. I think people are the same way. We might be the greatest person we could ever be and might have had the most outstanding life, but without the rest of our pieces . . . Well, we still don't amount to much, do we?"

I contemplate the view in silence for a little, turning over Henry's analogy. This view of the universe is a level of beauty I've never known. It makes me wish that Mym could be with me to see it. She's the only puzzle piece I feel like I'm missing.

"What if I'm not ready for my place out there yet? What if by being here, I'm leaving a hole somewhere else? Somewhere where someone still needs me."

"They still need you, or you still need them?"

"I'm hoping both."

"If you think they really need you, you'd better get to it. If you can see all this, eternity is calling your name. From what it looks like, you're headed that way soon whether you like it or not. Haven't known many folks who could see this place for what it really is and then stay around long after."

I study the palm of my hand. It could be my imagination, but it seems like my skin has taken on a few of Henry's iridescent qualities. Even so, I'm not ready to go twinkling away into the great beyond.

"How do you fight it off? Eternity."

"Not sure you should, frankly. But if you got yourself set on it, I'd see about getting some help. You're a memory, son. If you want to stay that way, you belong in your own head, not floating around out here."

"What if my head doesn't want me back?"

"Then you'd better make a more convincing argument. You have a version of yourself back in the real world who knows you're here, right? He's someone who remembers you pretty recently from the look of you."

"Yeah. I've been trying to contact him."

"That's good. That'll keep you around for a bit. That's why I'm still here."

"You're in touch with someone in the real world too?"

"Sure. Hard to be a memory otherwise. He's been forgetting a lot though lately. Getting old, you know? He's about ready to let go. When he does, well, that'll be my cue to go."

"If your other self in the real world dies, you'll get erased too?"

"Erased is a silly way to put it. Can't take away what we were. But yes, without a consciousness in the real world to stay connected to, we'll both have to move on. You shouldn't worry too much yet. Looks like your other self might be more connected than you know." He points to my face. "Your lip is bleeding."

I wipe at my mouth, and my finger comes away bloody. *He's letting me back in.*

Henry turns his face back to the sky, and it seems like the light is washing him away, taking bits of man and leaving starlight behind.

I get up from my seat on the edge of the building with a new sense of urgency. I stop halfway to the elevator and concentrate on opening another portal. I can't go into my past anymore because Zurvan will find me there. I can't blunder around more chronothon memories because the other me has moved on from those. He's contacting me from the future. I don't know how to open a portal to there.

I stretch my mind, searching the darkness for him again. "Where are you, Ben?" I try to simply open a portal to wherever he is, but I see only fog on the other side. He's somewhere with no definition.

Images flash though my mind. The fire temple. People striking me and holding me down. The smiling face of a synth. I get the image of Tucket Morris, the Academy student I met during the chronothon, walking though strange, crowded streets. Then I see a foil-wrapped bundle of tacos. The scenes make no sense.

Finally, the situation dawns on me.

He's dreaming about his day. The other me is asleep.

I touch my lip again and feel the sticky blood between my fingers.

Whatever he's been doing today, he's still alive. Still fighting. Looks like things aren't going very well though. I study his dream imagery for any sign of Mym, some indication that she's okay. Wherever she is, she's not with him now.

Looking back toward the edge of the building behind me, I can still make out Henry, but just barely. He's watching me. The firmament of color behind him still beckons, everlasting and magnificent. He looks ready for the leap into the beyond.

My memories may be murky by comparison, but they are the only place I know where to find her. For me that's enough. I give a wave to my transparent friend. "I'll see you later, Henry."

"See you on the other side, Ben." Henry salutes me.

Maybe someday. But not just yet. I concentrate on the connection with my other self and leap through the portal.

St. Petersburg, Florida, 2165

I wake to beeping coming from the meta goggles on the nightstand. It's a pinging noise like sonar, slowly increasing in volume.

"What? What do you want?" I fumble for the goggles from under the covers. Sometime during the night I must have wriggled my way deeper into the bed. I have no memory of that. Just strange, multicolored dreams. Something about an old man and an elevator.

The pinging increases its volume another notch. "I'm coming already." I slide the goggles on and select the blinking yellow com button.

"What the hell are you up to, Travers?" Rixon's voice fills my head in stereo sound.

"What? I'm . . . sleeping."

"In another city. What part of 'take one of the guest rooms' did you not understand? How am I supposed to keep you safe if you go rogue and start wandering off at all hours of the night?"

"Sorry," I mumble. I sit up and take in the hotel room. The far wall has turned itself into a view of rolling hills and distant bluish mountains. "What's going on?"

"We have a problem. Get back here, pronto."

I find my pants and slide them on. "What problem?"

"Your scientist found the spaceship. It's coming into port today."

"Isn't that a good thing?"

"No. Because it leaves today too."

"Wait, what? The submarine isn't supposed to be here till tomorrow." I snatch up my shirt and shoes and start pulling on my socks. "I thought we had another day."

"They played us. We think your girl may already be ashore. They could be moving her as we speak."

"Holy shit. How?"

"Team meeting above the bar in five minutes. Get here."

The com disconnects.

I struggle to process what he just said. *Mym is already in Port Nyongo. What are they doing with her?*

I hastily finish dressing and consult the time. *Be there in five minutes.*

I dial my chronometer for an hour into the past and put my hand to the wall.

I blink.

The lump of person in the bed doesn't stir upon my arrival. He likewise continues to snooze when I open the door and slip out into the hallway. I ease the door shut quietly to let him sleep.

The gate to the temple is still closed when I depart the hotel. I'm curious what the Eternals thought of my departure last night, but I don't stick around to ask. I take a whiff of the morning air and some part of me wants to just stand there and relish it. The sounds and smells of being alive. The feeling is so strong that I have to close my eyes and chastise myself. *Get yourself together, Ben. We've got work to do.*

I catch the morning train and, once aboard, I discover an out-of-service lavatory. I lock myself inside, then consult the timetable to just skip over the ride to St. Pete. When I unlock the door and step out, we're pulling into the station. It's a brisk walk to Rixon's Bar. I dash up the stairs and pause at the top to consult my meta goggles for the time. *Two minutes to spare.*

When I round the corner, I find the common area filled with people. Doctor Quickly, Rixon, and Eon are all donning sleek-looking pressure suits. Noelle Chun is there too, already mostly dressed, and helping fit the doctor into his.

"Ben, glad you're here," Doctor Quickly says. He waves me in with a gloved hand. "We need to get you suited up."

"What's happening?" I take a few steps into the room and Eon tosses me the pants to a spacesuit.

"The ship you mentioned? The comet rider? It's coming into port this morning. We think the Eternals are going to attempt to meet it when it arrives. It's possible Mym will be on hand too. If so, it may be our chance to get her back."

"Where is she? What happened to the submarine coming into port tomorrow?"

"It's our fault," Eon says. "We messed up and didn't compare the heat signatures of the people on board here to the ones that left Cornwall. If we had, we would have noticed that they're different. They pulled a switch on us. The sub that comes into port tomorrow is carrying the same number of people, but they aren't the same ones that left England. The Eternals who left England must have come ashore either last night or this morning. Possibly via a customs boat. We shouldn't have underestimated them. They must have known about the surveillance scanners we've been monitoring and used them to their advantage."

"We don't know why they're meeting this starship," Doctor Quickly says, "but if we mean to rescue Mym, we need to keep her from being taken into space. If they take her aboard, our rescue options vanish."

"They're going to use the ship to rescue Zurvan." The words are out of my mouth without me thinking them. I go rigid as the voice keeps speaking from my mouth. "Zurvan sent the Eternals back in time to get a ship. They plan to rescue him."

Doctor Quickly and Professor Chun are staring at me with interest. "How did you learn that?"

The voice in my head doesn't answer this time. I'm left shell-shocked by this sudden turn of events. *What the hell just happened?* I'm standing rigidly still, suddenly aware that I am not the only person inside my head again. Doctor Quickly and the others are still looking at me, so I stammer out a response. "I, um, went to the temple in St. Pete. The temple the Eternals use. They gave a speech." This is all technically true, even if it's not the real source of the revelation I've just announced.

"They said they are using the ship to meet *Zurvan*?" Professor Chun replies.

"They said they found his body," I reply. "I don't really know what that means though."

"Zurvan was an ancient Zoroastrian god," Professor Chun says. "He's a mythical figure. How could they have found his body?"

I'm still fishing around inside my mind, trying to figure out what to do next. I can feel him there now, the other me. *What are you doing here?* I attempt to force him from my mind.

"Don't shut me out!" The words spring from my mouth unannounced. "I can help!"

Rixon freezes in the act of tucking a gun inside the outer vest of his spacesuit and studies me. Eon likewise turns my direction. Every eye in the room is on me now.

"I mean . . . I'm ready to help with this . . . mission," I mumble, trying to recover from my outburst.

"We assumed you would be part of it," Professor Chun replies, her eyes narrowing. "Did you think we weren't including you?"

Doctor Quickly is studying me intently. "Are you all right, Ben?"

"I'm fine," I say, fumbling with the spacesuit pants in my hands. "Sorry. I just had a strange . . . I'm fine." I begin donning the pants to have an excuse to not have to look anyone in the eye. "So what's the plan? And where are Carson and Tucket?"

Why are you in my head?

My other self stays silent this time.

"We sent Carson down to the docks already this morning." Eon replies. "He got selected for work detail yesterday, so there's a good shot he will today, too. He's carrying a bag of anchors that will get us onto the Skylift once he's up there. He should be able to get us close to the elevator itself, and from there we can ride up to the space docks. We thought your other little friend was with you."

"Tucket didn't come home last night?" I say. "Shit. We need to find him." I get a sudden wave of guilt for having left him in the synth bar. "He could be in trouble."

"We don't have time to organize a second search party at the moment," Rixon says. "Bigger fish to fry. We need your head in the game." He tosses me a helmet, followed by the torso section of my pressure suit. "Your boy Carson will be making contact soon from the Skylift. When your Lost Star shows up, we need to be in position."

"Won't we have time to prepare more once we're up there? We could find a spot to jump back in time—"

"Not a big enough window to play with," Eon replies. "Space dock security will be on us quick as it is. Whatever these Eternals are planning, it's going to go down fast, and we won't have enough room for a bunch of versions of us running around up there. Too many variables to keep straight."

"Well, couldn't we take the time now to make a plan and—"

"We have a plan. This is the plan." Rixon throws me one of the boots for my suit, adding it to my growing bundle of clothing to put on. "Those of us who were actually around this morning got to make it."

I frown at the boot, then slip it on over my shoe, hopping on one leg to balance. "Well then why didn't you tell me to show up then? I could have—"

"It's okay, Ben," Doctor Quickly intervenes. "What Rixon likely means to say is that there wasn't much for us to decide. Until we get up there, we honestly don't have enough information about what the Eternals are going to do to know the best way to stop them. Once we get onto the Skylift, we'll have to make fast, smart decisions. We most definitely need you with us to help with that."

"I've made some contact with ASCOTT resources on the ground," Professor Chun says. "My main goal is tracking the labyrinth weapon that was stolen and retrieving it, but I can call for more help if we need it. We're not going in without options."

I gather up the pair of gloves that go with my spacesuit and the other boot. "What about Mym? When we find her, how do we get her out?"

Rixon answers. "Everyone will be carrying anchors that will get us back to the jump space downstairs. As soon as we spot her, we grab her and jump her back here."

"Okay, I'm gonna put the rest of this on in the bathroom," I mumble, backing out of the room with my armful of spacesuit parts. I hobble down the hallway with one boot on and lock myself into the bathroom, tossing the clothing into the sink and staring at my reflection in the mirror.

"Hey, what do you think you're doing?"

My other self responds this time. "I'm trying to help. Don't shut me out."

It's a bizarre feeling watching myself talk without being the one speaking.

"You made me seem crazy. Before. With Mym. You can't just take control whenever you want."

"I'm sorry. That wasn't me. Look, I'm not trying to take control."

Both of my hands go up in a palms out gesture, suggesting I stay calm.

"You're doing it right now!"

"Shit, sorry," my other self says. My arms drop back to my sides.

"How are you doing this? You used to just be in my dreams. How are you able to talk to me while I'm awake now?"

"I don't know."

"This is so weird. I don't want anyone else—"

Someone pounds on the door. "Come on, Travers," Rixon shouts. "Hurry up."

"I'm coming!"

I mutter a few curses and wrangle myself into the pieces of the spacesuit. When I get the torso and gloves on, I point a finger at my reflection. "Listen, I'll let you stick around, but I get control of my body. All right?"

"Yeah. Totally fine."

"I mean it." I wag a finger at the mirror, but then realize how ridiculous I look. I frown and grab my helmet, opening the door and heading back to the room with the others.

Everyone else is suited up now.

I look at Doctor Quickly. "Hey, how will we make jumps with spacesuits on?"

"Yes, you'll need one of these." Doctor Quickly hands me a small cylindrical piece of spacesuit with connections at both ends. It has a flexible, transparent window built into it. "Install that on your wrist over your chronometer before you attach the glove. It's harder to make precise movements through the membrane, but you'll be able to do it."

I push my left sleeve up a bit and install the extra piece over my wrist. Being able to see the chronometer through the transparent rubber window makes me feel a lot better. If things go south, I won't have to depressurize the suit to get to it.

Eon steps over to me and checks the security of my suit. He taps on a panel on my chest. "If you fall off the Skylift for some reason, there's a buoyancy pack in the back. Sensors in the suit deploy it automatically if you achieve terminal velocity, or you can pull this handle out to deploy it manually. Uses a compressed off-world gas called bollite. Mixed with oxygen, it's over a hundred times more buoyant than helium. It'll keep you from going splat if you go over the side for some reason."

"You think we might fall off the Skylift?" I get a sudden queasiness and have to remind myself that I've been in worse situations before.

"Pays to be prepared," Eon says. "One shot deal though. If you deploy it, get back on the ground and jump back here. Don't go messing around up there without one. It's a long way down." He hands me two small spools of cable attached to miniature harpoons and a gun device to fire them. "If we make it up to the spaceport, we'll be in zero G. Buoyancy pack won't be necessary up there, but you can still drift off if you end up outside the station for some reason. You can use this to reel yourself back in to the structure in an emergency. It'll also work as an anchor cable in a pinch if you need to make a jump."

I take the mini grappling gun and attach it to my suit. "That's pretty sweet."

"Better aim well, though. If you miss, you'll be left floating in orbit."

"Not excited to do that again," my other self mutters.

"No kidding," I reply.

"What did you say?" Eon asks.

"Nothing." I point to one of the two guns attached to Eon's spacesuit. "Do I get one of those blaster things?"

"Security on the Skylift is tight, and you'll be flagged immediately if you're carrying stun weapons without proper credentials. If I can, I'll get you one once we're inside."

"Stun weapons?"

"No lethal ordinance gets on the Skylift, law enforcement credentials or not."

Doctor Quickly tells me to put on my meta goggles and Professor Chun pulls up an image in the metaspace of the top of the spaceport. She scans over the area where the Skylift tethers pass through the spaceport on their way out to the counterweight in orbit. "Only one way up or down from the port. That's using these elevator tether cables and the climbers. Everybody gets off at the same point. If the Eternals are headed up, they'll have to pass through the same terminal as everyone else. We should be able to spot them before getting on the climbers, but if not we'll definitely catch them on the top end. I spoke to customs and we know which dock the ship will be berthing in."

Using a satellite camera, she zooms out into space and focuses on an image of the ship we're looking for. It's a huge sphere resembling a miniature planet slowly approaching Earth. The outside has been burnt and pockmarked, but it looks incredibly durable.

The Lost Star.

"We've identified the inbound ship as a Starfire class frigate." Professor Chun says. "It's registered with Interspace Customs, but the contact information is all private. We don't know who is on board."

"We do have a theory about how it moves, however," Doctor Quickly adds. "It's ingenious really. We believe that they may be using the comets as anchors to get around space. It's possible that they've found some way to secure themselves to the comet and jump forward or backward in time to different points in the comet's life. Doing so would give the ship incredible range, especially if it can do the same thing using interstellar comets."

"You mean the entire spaceship is able to time travel?" I ask.

"And everyone on board," Doctor Quickly replies. "Whoever they are, they may be the most advanced time travelers we've ever encountered."

"Aliens?" I ask.

"The ship is registered as being from Earth," Professor Chun replies. "We don't think they're from off-world, but we won't know till we meet them."

A com crackles inside the helmet I'm holding. Carson's voice comes in over the speaker. "Anchors are in place. Ready for you guys."

"That's our cue," Eon spins his hand in the air and points to the door. "Let's roll."

I follow the group down the stairs feeling bulky in my spacesuit and having flashbacks to my time aboard the Diamatra space station. That hadn't ended well. My other self seems to be thinking the same thing.

"Can you trust these people?" he whispers.

"Rixon and Eon? Yeah. Quickly says they're solid."

"Why is Mym with the Eternals?"

His voice sounds too sincere for me to be critical. I can feel the concern coming through.

"Long story."

The front door to the bar swings open just as we are filing into the jump room. Tucket is beaming as he steps inside the bar and spots us. He's wearing a different T-shirt than he had on last night, one with a picture of a split open, slightly bruised avocado on the front.

"Hey, Ben. You'll never guess what happened to me last night! I went to—hey, where are you guys going?"

I pause so he can make it over to me. Through the door to the jump room, Eon is already getting Professor Chun set up with her anchor.

"Hey, Tucket. We're on a mission here. We think Mym is in port already. We're going to get her back."

"Oh wow! Do you need me to suit up too? Are you going up the Skylift? That's super rad!"

"He stays here," Rixon says. "We've got too many people to keep an eye on as it is."

Tucket's smile fades slightly.

"We'll be okay, Tucket. You've already been a huge help."

"Okay . . . Hey, if you bring Mym back today, you should come with me to Machina Libre."

"I saw you go in there again last night. What were you doing?"

"You know how that girl, Mira, was so down on humans? I just hated that she thought we were all like that, you know? I decided to talk to her and explain that humans aren't really the way she thinks we are. She had never even listened to Avocado Problems before. Or the Beatles! I told her that she can't just judge all humans on how they are now, you know? There's all this history and experience to being human, not just the data that she can download. I told her she should come visit history with *me* sometime, and I could show her how super gnarly the twenty-first century—"

"Travers! We're ready for you," Eon calls from inside the jump room. "We're on a tight schedule with these anchors. Gotta move."

I give Eon a quick thumbs up and turn back to Tucket. "How did she take what you said?"

"Well, I think she might still hate humans a lot, actually, but she sat and listened to me for a long time. We stayed up all night talking. I think that I made a good impression. I made her laugh. That's a start, right?"

"You're going to see her again?"

"Oh, yeah. She said she doesn't mind if I come back in. She promised that she wouldn't let anyone in there kill me. I think that's pretty cool."

"Really romantic, Tuck."

Tucket grins and puts his hands on his hips. "I know. After I get some sleep I think I'm going to go back over there. Do you think I would impress her more if I dressed up like—"

Rixon is gesturing to me urgently from inside the jump room. "Clock's ticking, Travers. Let's move."

"Gotta go, Tucket." I put my gloved fist out, and he bumps it. "Just be you. Okay, man? You're already the coolest dude I know, just how you are."

I step inside the jump room, and Rixon moves to close the door behind me. Tucket gives a final wave before it shuts. He's smiling at me and leaning to see around the door. "Hasta la vista, Ben!"

It's windy atop the Skylift.

And cold.

Carson's strategically-placed anchors have gotten us to a loading platform on deck 107, a ramp for moving cargo pods out to the main elevator. As soon as we arrive, a regulator inside my spacesuit kicks on and begins warming me.

Carson is waiting for us and hastily guides our group off the landing platform via a gangplank. He's not wearing a pressure suit, but he does have an oxygen mask on and an insulated jacket. I do my best to not look down as we follow him along the gangway toward the main structure.

My helmet display shows that this section of the tower is fifteen thousand feet up. There is perhaps another fifty feet of the main Skylift structure above us, topped by a glass dome, but beyond that are only the carbon nanotube tethers running up into the sky and all the way into space. I can see all five of the tethers from here, each stemming from a different wing of the main dome, their tops disappearing into the blue above us.

"The loading terminal for the climber cars is this way," Carson says over the coms. "No sign of the Eternals yet."

We move quickly through the industrial section of the Skylift. There aren't many other people out on the loading pads due to the limited oxygen, but we do pass some synth workers and robotic drone forklifts that are unimpeded by the altitude. The view looking down is daunting—nothing but cloud tops and the blue of the Gulf of Mexico far below.

The center dome of the Skylift has an area that is kept at a higher pressure for passengers and, once inside, Carson pulls his mask off. Rixon and Eon likewise remove their helmets. The pair of them are forced to input their law enforcement identification at a security checkpoint when the scanners pick up on their weapons, but once through, Eon directs us onto an escalator. "Main loading for passengers is on the next level up. The last passenger security checkpoint was two floors down, but they've added security up here as well to help us out."

Professor Chun chimes in as we glide upward. "I've purchased tickets to Earthrim for all of us. You three are booked on a trip up lift number one later tonight, just so we have proper clearance on this level. Some of my people are here to help out. ASCOTT's priority is tracking the Labyrinth weapon, but they'll assist in Mym's recovery too. Harry and I are taking one of the next lifts up to the space docks now in case anyone has already slipped through. We want to be on hand when the Starfire pulls into port."

Through the glass ceiling of the domed room we've ascended into, I can see one of the elevator tethers and a climber car that has just launched up it. A bright red glow illuminates the bottom as it flies up the tether.

"Do they have some kind of rocket engine?" I ask.

"Targeted laser propulsion," Eon explains.

We pass into a central boarding hub with five spokes shooting off it. Each one leads to a different elevator tether. Unlike the outside loading docks, the hub is bustling with activity. There are synths guiding cargo pods and trans-humans shuffling in groups toward the two docks labeled for passengers. Each spoke of the terminal has its own waiting area with generic lobby chairs that look every bit as uncomfortable as they were in my century. I'm surprised to see a pair of Jedi having a light saber fight in front of one of the terminal windows. The noise of their light sabers clashing carries across the waiting area till a woman seated near them reprimands them. The Jedi drop their metaspace identities and revert back to a couple of kids in neon-colored jumpsuits—disappointed that their play has been cut short.

Pressure suits are apparently required for everyone using the space elevator, but since most of the humans walking around are tourists headed to Earthrim for vacations, the pressure suits in sight are sleek, minimalist outfits with trendy colors and meta accessories. I feel a bit out of place in my full spacesuit and helmet, but there are enough other people hauling around spacewalk gear that no one pays us much attention.

A man dressed in an all black pressure suit eases over to our group and speaks to Professor Chun. "We've got ten agents spread out here in the terminal and another ten waiting for you up top at the docks. No sign of the Labyrinth yet."

Professor Chun gives him a nod and sends him back into the crowd where he does an unconvincing job of looking like a tourist.

"We'll need to spread out for now," Eon says. "Anyone headed up any of the tethers has to pass through this terminal at some point, so if we're going to spot them, this is the place. If you see Mym or any of the Eternals, connect with the others, and Rixon and I will intercept. Ben has seen the most of them in person, so if you see any suspicious candidates, flash an image to his heads-up." He looks to me. "You can confirm for us, right?"

"Okay." I churn through the memories of the different Eternals I've seen. It doesn't help that a lot of them have been masked or showed up in the dark. "I'll do my best."

"Good," Eon replies. "We've alerted Skylift authorities about the kidnapping as well, so security is on alert." He hands Carson one of his stun weapons, and Rixon somewhat reluctantly follows suit by handing one to me.

"ASCOTT has people monitoring the security cams too," Professor Chun adds. "They'll contact me in the event of suspicious activity. Stay sharp and we'll nab these bastards."

I tuck the stun gun out of sight in a cargo pouch of my suit and take a position between the passages for lifts 4 and 5. The heads-up display on my helmet zooms and magnifies on command, so I'm able to run through all of the faces entering my view very rapidly. So far, none of them look familiar. I take the time to degravitize one of the anchors for getting back to Rixon's so that I'll be ready for a quick escape if we spot Mym.

The anchors Rixon has given us are all single-use, plain orange cubes fabricated from a 3D printer with the coordinates etched directly onto them. I enter the coordinates for the one I've chosen into my chronometer, then go back to scanning the terminal.

Doctor Quickly and Professor Chun head into passage three and, a few minutes later, they report that their climber car is leaving for the space docks. Through the glass dome, I watch the climber launch itself into the blue.

"Are we going up that?" my other self whispers.

"Shhh," I mutter.

"What did you say, Travers?" Rixon says.

"Nothing."

I mute my com link.

"You can't just spout things out," I whisper. "What are you doing?" I can feel my other self surfacing more inside my head.

"I'm just trying to figure out what *you're* doing. "

"We need to spot Mym so we can grab her and jump back out before these guys can take her out of reach."

"And then what?"

"What do you mean, then what? And then we go home and get away from all these crazy nut jobs."

"What about me?"

I consider what he's asking. I can hear the tension in his voice. My voice. He's scared.

"I don't know what to do about that yet."

"Look, it's getting harder to stick around. Zurvan is bad news. He has my memories. If you keep shutting me out, I don't know how much longer I can last here. It's getting . . . more real."

"What's more real?" I ask.

"Eternity."

The single word brings a wave of emotion with it. For a moment I can feel what he means—a sort of vastness at the far side of his mind.

I keep scanning the room. Luckily, there are enough other people having conversations via the metaspace that talking to myself doesn't seem out of place.

"Look, I get that you're me and everything, and I know that you don't like the current situation, but I don't think we can keep doing this once we get back. Going around talking to ourselves here is one thing, but we can't keep sharing a head like this at home. It isn't normal."

"What am I supposed to do then?" he asks.

"I don't know," I say. "Let's deal with one problem at a time."

Eon's voice cuts through my helmet speakers. "Look alive, gentlemen. Just got a security report that a group of unidentified people have deployed out of a cargo pod loader next level down. Could be our targets."

Eon and Rixon cut through the crowd toward the main escalators. Eon signals a muscled security guard who nods and follows him toward the escalator.

Carson chimes in. "Are we supposed to go with—"

"Hold your position," Eon replies. "Rixon and I will—" Eon is cut off as the security guard suddenly tackles him from behind. Someone screams and, as the crowd parts, I see one of Professor Chun's ASCOTT agents on the ground at the far side of the terminal with one of the security guards standing over her prone form.

"Security is compromised!" I shout into my helmet microphone before realizing it's still muted. By the time I've resolved that, the situation has become clear to everyone anyway.

Trans-human security guards have begun battling ASCOTT agents across the terminal. It's as though a switch has been flipped and the previously calm security guards have come unhinged.

Passengers and terminal staff are fleeing in all directions, making it hard to concentrate on anything else, but through the chaos I see what I'm looking for. A small cluster of people are making their way toward gate 4 from the main entrance. They've forgone their robes and hoods in the interest of blending in, but I recognize the v-shaped hairline and cold stare of Mr. Longcase leading the group. Two of them are carrying a heavy rectangular box between them.

Rixon has drawn his weapon and aims it toward another pair of security guards storming his way. Due to the guards' sheer size, it takes multiple blasts from the stun weapon to slow them down. They retreat behind a kiosk to trade fire with Rixon. Eon is back on his feet and pummeling the guard who tackled him with his bare hands.

Looking past Longcase and his chosen henchmen, I spot two smaller figures among the group. One I recognize as the wizened face of Lord Elgin and the other has a helmet with the face shield completely blacked out. Elgin is hauling her forward by the arm.

Mym.

Mym is walking strangely, and I realize it's because her wrists have been linked to the waist of her pressure suit. It's a less conspicuous way to bind her hands, but effective nonetheless.

"I see her! I'm going for her!" I call into the helmet mic. I don't have much of a plan, but I keep my anchor ready and head for the group. Carson is cutting through the terminal from my right. There are perhaps a dozen people in the cluster around Mym, but I only need to get a hand on her to jump her out. A man in the lead shouts something in a language I don't understand, and the whole group comes to a stop. I pull the stun gun loose and prepare to attack.

Rixon and Eon have successfully suppressed the security guards who had attacked them, and it seems like the ASCOTT agents have been mostly victorious as well. We form a circle around the cluster of Eternals with our weapons raised. None of the Eternals appear to be armed. They are simply standing still in a circle around Elgin and Mym.

"Give up the girl," Eon shouts.

"And the weapon," one of the ASCOTT agents adds.

Longcase is the only person who moves, and it's merely a twitch of his mouth. A flicker of scorn on an otherwise impassive face.

"RIGHT NOW!" Eon says. He takes a step closer to Longcase.

The Eternals stay silent. Waiting.

Mym cocks her head. "Ben? Are you there?"

"Mym, I'm—" Something collides with the back of my leg and I stagger. I spin around with my weapon at the ready and find myself pointing it at one of the little kids who had been playing at being a Jedi earlier. The little girl of perhaps ten is staring at me, but something is wrong with her eyes. They're flickering in her head. She opens her mouth and screams.

The terminal comes alive with movement. Passengers, formerly cowering behind rows of chairs or lying prone on the floor, spring to life and sprint toward us. The little girl who screamed fixes her glare on my face and charges me.

"Agh!" I squeeze the trigger on the stun gun and send her sprawling

NATHAN VAN COOPS

backward onto the floor. The terminal erupts with violence.

The ASCOTT agent closest to me gets swarmed by two men in yellow jumpsuits. Eon blasts the first two Eternals that lunge at him, but the third uses a limber spin kick to send the weapon flying from his hand. Rixon gets hit from behind by an old lady, and by the time he has shoved her away, one of the Eternals is on top of him.

The static silence of the Eternals turns to fluid motion as they stream forward, cutting through the constricting crowd. I get my stun gun aimed at one of the men blocking my path to Mym, but before I can fire, I'm tackled by a teenage boy with crazed eyes and purple hair. The two of us crash to the floor in a heap and, by the time I've gotten the upper hand, Elgin and the Eternals have almost reached the gate.

It seems like nearly every passenger left in the terminal is a consciousness-shifted Eternal now intent on impeding us. The few who aren't Eternals are cowering in corners or shepherding children toward the exits. No one is trying to stop them. A quick glance around shows me that our ASCOTT allies are massively overwhelmed. I consider trying to make a jump back in time to get out of this mess and buy myself more time, but I have no idea when this place might be safe to jump to. I may not get back in time. I double-check that I still have Rixon's jump anchor and go after Mym instead. If I only have one shot at leaving, I'm not going without her.

I stun the first six people I encounter, but when I try for a seventh, an indicator on my weapon tells me it's recharging. I'm forced to shove and pry my way through the passengers attempting to keep me from the gate. I punch at least three people, one of which I'm fairly sure is old enough to be someone's grandfather. I don't have time to feel bad about it because Mym has been dragged through the gate to tether 4 and has vanished out of sight. I finally break free of the crowd and sprint after them.

The biggest downside to space helmets is that they are total crap when it comes to peripheral vision. Like when you run through a doorway and get blindsided by a big trans-human dude with a bad attitude. Where helmets come in handy is when the big dude slams you so hard into the window of the catwalk that the window fractures. They also help keep your skull intact during his repeated attempts to shove you through said window.

The security guard who has waylaid me is big—easily fifty pounds heavier than me, and I get the impression that his hobbies mostly consist of lifting heavy things or perhaps crushing sturdy objects with his bare hands. I'm doubtful that transcendental meditation has been high on his priority list so he's likely not an Eternal. When he wrenches the stun gun from my grasp and hurls it out the hole he's made in the window, it dawns on me that his enthusiasm probably has much more to do with the cash that Guy and Lawrence promised as a payoff than any real loyalty to the Eternals. Whatever his motivation, he's nothing if not determined and, despite my ineffective resistance and verbal protestations, I come to a sickening realization. He's going to throw me out the window.

The big man kicks away the last remaining resistance to the Plexiglas, and grunts audibly as he hefts my now-limp form out the catwalk. I let him. My fingers have found the buoyancy pack handle on the front of my spacesuit and, as soon as I'm airborne out the window, I pull it.

The buoyancy pack does nothing for a very long second. The moment seems to slow down, long enough that I can take in the snarl on the security guard's face receding away from me, the deep blue gulf far below expanding to receive me, and a bunch of shards of Plexiglas that are hovering around my head as we fall together.

The next moment the pack deploys and the shards vanish into the sky below me as my momentum is arrested. I'm hoisted up by an explosion of synthetic fabric and gas billowing out the back of my pressure suit. The fabric shapes itself into an orange sphere, not dissimilar to a giant beach ball. I shoot up past the window I recently exited, and the expression on the security guard's face changes from anger to disappointment. He was clearly looking forward to witnessing my free-fall.

I'm disconnected from the Skylift structure, but I suddenly have an amazing view of it. Beyond the catwalk, the closest climber car is being boarded for its trip up the tether. It looks roughly like a pod, but with two bell-shaped lower fins that are aimed to capture energy from a laser array below. From my aerial viewpoint I can witness the boarding zone and I spot Mym being guided through the hatch.

The wind has carried me up and over the catwalk and I realize that in a few moments I'm going to be blown past the tether and out to sea. There is a flashing red light in my helmet viewfinder that may well indicate that my emergency is being noted. It could be that the Coast Guard is already on alert to come rescue my giant orange ball, but that does me no good if the Eternals escape. I fumble for the grappling device Eon gave me and figure out how to fire it. I release the safety and make sure my spool of cable is loaded right, then aim it for the nearest bit of catwalk. The gun is attached to my spacesuit by a cable that would be easier to manage if it was about a foot longer. I aim as best I can, but when I squeeze the trigger, the harpoon shoots out much faster than I anticipated, overshooting my mark by a good ten yards.

Shit!

I eject the wasted cable and fumble for my second one. As I'm attempting to load it, the wind carries me past the launch platform and the tether. Warning lights have begun to flash around the climber car. I finally get the harpoon loaded and search for where to aim it. I only have moments to get back and have any hope of catching the Eternals. I aim for the catwalk again, but as I do, the locks on the climber car disengage. Lights around the launch area flash green and a warning buzzer sounds. Debating for just a moment, I swing the gun and point it at the climber car instead.

"This seems like a bad idea," my other self chimes in.

"No time to discuss this at a committee!" I say. I raise the grappling gun and fire. The climber car shoots upward as the laser array below it lights up. The car accelerates up the tether, but not before the harpoon on my cable pierces one of the lower fins and buries itself in the car's undercarriage.

"Your jokes really aren't funny—you know that?" my other self yells.

The harpoon gun in my hands unspools as I'm dragged upwards. The giant buoyancy ball on my back resists being hauled aloft due to all the wind resistance, but the spool in the gun quickly runs out of cable. The gun is ripped from my hands and the cable attaching it to my suit's internal harness goes taut, jerking me upward. I rocket into the sky in the climber car's wake.

"Aggghhhhhh!" I don't know if it's my other self or me doing the yelling, but we're both equally terrified as we accelerate. The fabric ball of gas attached to my suit is pulling hard on my back as it resists being dragged through the thinning atmosphere. My body swings on the cable, arcing inward toward the elevator tether itself. Everything around me suddenly turns a brilliant red as I pass through the laser light being blasted at the panels on the bottom of the climber car. I impact something and am suddenly sent spinning away as the buoyancy bubble on my back collides with the tether itself and ruptures. The escaping gas propels me outward like a pendulum again, but the force of the wind catches me and rips the remains of my buoyancy ball off the back of my pack.

Without the resistance of the buoyancy ball, I feel the climber car accelerate faster, rocketing upward on its 60-mile trip to space.

"We'll die if you hit that again!" My other self shouts, as the arc of my travel swings me back toward the elevator tether that is now whipping by at alarming speed. I cringe and curl myself up as small as I can as I pass the tether once more, just missing it this time.

My arc is getting tighter and faster and it's only a matter of moments till I'll be brought back in and possibly have my cable tangled in the tether. I don't have time to imagine what being shredded to death by friction might feel like because I'm too busy dialing a time into my chronometer. I'm spinning wildly like an out of control yo-yo, but as the tether comes rushing back into my immediate view, I have a hand on my wrist.

There will be no missing this time.

The second before impact, I push the pin and blink.

"Sometimes people grow nostalgic and want to revisit their youth. The reality of time travel often quashes that desire. Spying on your younger self may remind you of your former glories, but it also refreshes the tragedy of your fashion choices."-Journal of Dr. Harold Quickly, 1967

CHAPTER 20

Earthrim, 2165

They say in space, no one can hear you scream. That's not true when you have another self inside your spacesuit and both of you are screaming.

"Agghhh!" I reappear with the elevator tether still filling the entire view from my helmet. It takes me a moment to realize that the tether is no longer moving. Neither am I. I'm floating, buoyant again, but this time without any need for a ball of lifting gas.

I'm in zero gravity.

There is a sucking sound inside my spacesuit and then a whirring as the suit acclimates itself to its sudden new environment.

Above me—if there is still such a term—the Earthrim space station extends in a wide arc around the central core of the spaceport. Below me, planet Earth is suddenly finite, the curve of the upper atmosphere now visible in all directions. The tether I'm dangling near continues its way out into space, disappearing far beyond the station to wherever the counterweight is, but the climber car I'm still attached to has been removed from the tether and is now berthed in a gate of the spaceport.

I've only skipped over fifteen minutes, but that has apparently been enough time for the car to finish its trip into space and dock. An efficient system to be sure. My gravitized cable and harpoon have reappeared with me and I am now floating through space, but luckily still attached to the climber.

This space station is much larger and more expansive than the last one I was aboard. The previous station was occupied solely by traitorous friends and suicidal competitors during the chronothon. I don't have great hopes for the occupants of this one either, but at least here I hope to have a few allies.

Pulling on the cable attached to my harness, I drift my way to the underside of the space station and find a handhold. Mym is somewhere aboard this thing, and I need to find her.

One good thing about space stations is that despite the fact that they are surrounded by a terrifying deadly vacuum, they always have a great view, and occupants still want windows. I'm forced to detach myself from the cable holding me to the climber car, but I use handholds to stay connected to the space station as I bob my way along its exterior surface. Through the many windows I can make out the interior hallways and various viewing rooms. Unlike the inside of a space shuttle or twenty-first century spacecraft, this interior looks uncluttered and clean. More *Star Trek* than *Star Wars*. I scrutinize the corridors for any sign of help.

Whoever designed this section of the station clearly didn't have space walkers in mind because there are no handy access doors or airlocks for me to duck into. The view along the top of this arm of the station shows no other people outside the station. Everyone else is safely indoors. What I do see is a giant sphere of a spaceship slowly making its way toward a dock a few hundred yards down a parallel arm.

"Lights," my other self says.

"What?"

"Over there. Something flashing."

I concentrate on the part of the station that my other self has been paying attention to, and spot the flashing lights. A window on a perpendicular arm of the station has an amber light flashing from the windows. I scramble along the surface and turn the corner so I can have a better look. Viewing from outside I have a clear understanding of what's going on. The two windows I'm seeing through are on either side of an interior doorway. On one side, armed security personnel are trying to get through the door. On the other side the Eternals' highjacked security guards are keeping it shut.

Longcase is there. He's giving orders to the guards when suddenly he looks up and sees me out the window. He scowls and gestures to another security guard, then points out the window to me. I don't know what he says, but the security guard adopts his expression, frowning at me with a clenched jaw. Longcase spins on his heel and hurries down the corridor. I follow.

The spherical spaceship is pulling into the dock now. Two blade-like wings that look like they contain main thrusters are stowing themselves into the body of the craft and smaller blue jets of rocket exhaust are bursting from various angles around the perimeter as it lines itself up with the loading door. A protruding docking collar is extending from the sphere, stretching a walkway toward the station.

I hurry to try to keep up with Longcase as he dashes along the interior corridor. There is some sort of artificial gravity system working on the inside of the station because he is not drifting around the way I am. My disadvantage slows me down and, by the time I catch up, he's reached the bridge that extends to the docking ship. Inside this corridor, Elgin and a handful of the other Eternals are awaiting the completion of the docking sequence. Mym is there too, still wearing her darkened helmet and, to my dismay, I see that two of the Eternals are now holding a second captive, Doctor Quickly.

Whatever plan the doctor and Professor Chun had employed up here on the space docks, it's clear that the ASCOTT agents were overwhelmed just as they were in the terminal. Some of the men and women gathering with the Eternals are wearing official-looking insignia, perhaps customs agents or port security. If whoever is coming down the bridge to meet them is expecting a normal welcome, they've got a surprise in store.

The action comes fast. When the lights flash green around the docking bay doors, the officials swarm through. There are no windows on the bridge leading to the ship so I can't see what's going on inside, but a few moments later, the port security comes back out, guiding a quartet of figures. Two women and two men, dressed in robes, much as the Eternals usually are, are being detained against their will. They look like they are a branch of the same religion, but whatever the conversation is that's going on inside, it doesn't seem friendly. Elgin and Longcase shout orders and the crew from the ship are handcuffed and roughly pulled aside as two Eternals come down the corridor carrying the black box. I don't have to look long to guess that it's likely the Labyrinth weapon stolen from the ASCOTT facility. Other Eternals follow along behind, one of them is carrying my portable gravitizer.

"Those bastards," I mutter.

"What are we going to do now?" my other self asks.

"We need to get in there."

"Whoa. Heads up."

"What?" I look up and see the problem he's noticed. A pair of security guards have found a way out of the spaceport and are making their way toward me along the length of the station arm I just came down. Unlike me, each step they take stays firmly anchored to the surface. Something in their boots is allowing them to stay locked to the station, so they are not required to bounce along the way I did from handhold to handhold.

"That's not fair," I mutter.

One look at the duo convinces me that I don't want to be here when they arrive. They don't need weapons. They wouldn't even need to be especially strong. All they would need to do is pull me loose from the space station. One shove and I'll go floating off toward the stars, never to return.

"This is bad," my other self comments.

"I know."

The group inside the corridor is moving. Elgin grabs Mym and hauls her roughly through the door. Longcase, apparently still alert to my presence, looks up and spots me through the window again. He holds his wrist up to his mouth and speaks something into it. One of the security guards approaching me outside the station pauses momentarily, then continues at an even faster pace. Longcase smiles up at me this time, then grabs Doctor Quickly and shoves him through the doorway.

There are only two ways to run. One route dead-ends into the spherical spaceship. The other continues on around the space docks in a massive loop, joining with the Earthrim resort area of the station, then eventually circling back to the arm I'm looking toward now, the one with two burly looking guards on it. I can run and possibly make it to an area of the space station that the Eternals don't control, but I'll lose Mym. The clock is ticking.

I consider my chronometer through the transparent rubber sleeve on my wrist. I don't have a lot of options. I know from experience that there is only so much oxygen aboard these suits. They are also not meant for extended trips. I'm sure I'm already being exposed to enough solar radiation to be worrisome and the sooner I get indoors, the better it will be for my longevity in all respects.

It's possible these two dudes might merely haul me inside and lock me up. It's not certain that they are going to fling me into space. I could surrender.

"Don't even think about it." My other self must be running through the same options. "Being too trusting is what got us in trouble last time."

The bridge below me trembles. The locks on the ship's dock release. The Lost Star is leaving. I scramble along the bridge, climbing down and around the rectangular structure—forcing my pursuers to follow. They are smart though. They split up, one heading the opposite direction around the bridge, out of sight and in a position to cut me off. The ship detaches from the end of the bridge. For me it's silent, but I feel the tremor in my fingertips as I cling desperately to the loading bridge.

Blue light glows from the circumference of the ship. The glow reflects off the face shield of the security guard headed toward me. I crouch down as low as I can, coiled for action.

"Hope you know what you're doing," my other self says. "If you die, I'm a goner too."

"Are you kidding? I learned this all from YOU!" With the last word, I leap off the bridge. The security guard who circled the bridge to cut me off suddenly reappears from around the corner, reaching for me, but he misses. I launch off the space station and into the untethered void.

My trajectory is true.

After five nerve-wracking seconds of flailing through the nothingness, I impact the side of the ship. I scrabble frantically for something to hold on to, my fingertips desperately seeking purchase to keep from bouncing off again. I wedge my hand into a narrow crevice as my feet fly back off the surface.

Far below me I see the two security guards staring out from the spaceport bridge. They are receding slowly into the distance silhouetted against the glow from the planet. I can't see their expressions. Maybe they're disappointed. Maybe not. I might have just done their job for them. If I can't find a way inside this ship before it blasts off into space again, I'll be just as dead.

The wing-looking thruster mounts are extending again from the sides of the ship. Smaller thrusters fire from the port side, turning it around to head back out into the void. The view of Earth beyond the space station is tremendously beautiful, but as the ship turns, I realize that if my luck doesn't change fast, I may not be seeing it again.

Looking around the sphere from my current position I see nothing that looks like an airlock or even a window. I scrabble along the surface, searching for some handle or way inside, but the rough, crusty exterior of the ship seems impenetrable. I consider trying to make a time jump back to when it was still in port, but realize I couldn't even if I wanted to. This ship can time travel. That means the whole thing is probably infused with gravitites. If I jumped, I'd be unanchored.

My chronometer couldn't ever displace something so huge, but even if it could I'd only manage to send us all to the Neverwhere.

"What now?" My other self sounds genuinely worried.

"You have any ideas?" I reply. "If you do, now would be the time."

A yellow light pops up on my viewfinder. The low oxygen warning. *Figures.*

The ship has finished making its turn and the main thrusters on the wings begin to glow with energy. Just as I am about to really start panicking, a section of the ship a little to my right sinks down and recesses inward, leaving a hole big enough to climb into. I don't hesitate.

Scrambling along the surface I waste no time in sending myself tumbling into the hole. As soon as I'm inside, the section that recessed moves back into place and reseals the exterior hull. An influx of gases fills the space I've fallen into, and after a moment, the oxygen warning on my suit disappears. After another few seconds a new light illuminates on my display—*Environment safe.*

I cautiously pop my helmet loose and remove it. The air is cold, but clean.

"Thank you," I mutter to the walls.

"You are Benjamin Travers," the walls reply.

Startled, I jolt upright and search for the source of the voice. "Hello?"

The walls respond. It's a feminine voice. Firm, but not unkind. "I let you in, but I am unable to assist you further. I'm having trouble—" the voice gets cut off in static.

"Hello? Hey. Yes. Thank you," I stammer. "Thank you for letting me in."

"My systems are being overridden. There are men on the other side of this door waiting to restrain you. I won't be able to stop them."

"Who—who are you?" I manage, still not sure where to address my conversation.

"I am in need of your help." Static cracks over her voice again. "Will you help me?"

"I don't—I don't know who you are. What help do you—"

"They are trapping my mind. They are controlling all of my primary functions now. They take more every moment. Help me."

It's only then that I realize I'm speaking with the ship itself.

"I will, I'll help. What do you need me to—"

The inner door of the chamber slides open. I don't even have time to react before three men rush me and seize my arms.

"Get his wrist!" one shouts. "That's what we want."

My chronometer arm is jerked forcefully and I'm hurled to the surface of the floor. One of the Eternals works the glove off my arm and then the rubberized window section. He attempts to pull the chronometer off my wrist, but is thwarted by the locking band. After a few violent pulls that are threatening to dislocate my shoulder, he finally turns to me.

"Take it off or we cut it off." To prove he's not bluffing, one of his companions pulls a miniature blow torch from one of his cargo pockets.

I don't know a lot about space stations, but one thing I do know about high oxygen environments is that open flames are usually a terrible idea all on their own. The idea of someone using one to sever my hand from my wrist makes the situation even more inarguable. I drag my other hand to my chronometer and, after assuring them I am not trying to make a jump, activate the sequence to unlock the band. The Eternal above me wastes no time in yanking the chronometer off my wrist.

"I'll take that." The voice is smooth and self-assured. Longcase is walking up the corridor, a satisfied look on his face. The Eternal who took my chronometer passes it to him. Longcase pauses to look down at me. "You really are a persistent one, aren't you?"

"What do you want us to do with him?" one of the other Eternals asks. "Should we pitch him out the airlock?"

"No. Throw him in with the other one while we deal with the scientist. He might be useful to us when it comes to persuading the girl. We can dispose of him later."

Without another word I am hauled to my feet and dragged along the corridor. When we reach our destination—a heavy hydraulic door—someone opens it and I am flung roughly through. I land in a sprawl on the floor. When the door hisses shut and locks behind me, I'm left in darkness.

It takes a few moments for my adrenaline to subside, but my heart rate finally starts to settle into a slightly less frenzied state.

The darkness inside the ship is not complete. A faint multicolored glow seems to wick from the walls in strange patterns, immaterial wisps of light, too fragile to even travel in a straight line. The cobwebs of color swirl and scatter in eddies and clusters, like dust bunnies in a breezy room. I get to my feet and try to get a bearing on my surroundings.

"You're the time traveler's boyfriend." The voice comes from the semi-dark, somewhere beyond my perception. I spin in place, trying to locate it. A shadow moves away from one of the walls and the room glows brighter to illuminate the figure. "I thought you'd come."

The voice belongs to a man in flowing robes. His dark, craggy skin and salt and pepper beard are visible beneath a green keffiyeh. His face is pleasant. Calm. He approaches so quietly that I can't hear his footsteps.

"Who are you?" I ask, immediately on guard. My fingertips brush my bare wrist. It's a nakedness I haven't felt in a while and it makes me vulnerable.

The man slides closer, then swishes past me. His arms are crossed somewhere beneath his robes. His face is all I can see of him. He stops before a window that wasn't there a moment before. The window looks out on the unending expanse of stars around us.

"My name is Melchior. This is my ship."

"You're the captain?"

"I'm the . . . I suppose captain is acceptable. Though custodian might also be accurate. The ship is my duty."

"Where are they taking us?"

"I believe they mean to go back to the beginning."

"Beginning of what?"

"Our civilization."

THE DAY AFTER NEVER

I step closer to the new window and look out on the stars—curious. The view expands around me, and soon I'm looking at 360 degrees of universe. The moon is looming larger than I've ever seen it off our starboard side as we move outward into space. The view is disorienting. Terrifying—but also magnificent.

"How are you doing that?" I ask.

"You're doing it, actually. You were wondering where you are. The ship is showing you."

"The ship knows my thoughts?"

"No. Not completely. But it knows the language your body conveys. It sees the *structure* of your mind and knows which emotions you are exuding through your pores. This Starfire is a very intuitive ship."

"Intuitive. Like a person? It's AI?" My mind is still catching up to all that has happened. It's the ship itself that let me inside and wanted my help. I shouldn't really be surprised that it's sentient. "Can she tell me what's going on in other parts of the ship? Is Mym okay?"

An image of the room where Mym is being kept appears in front of me, smaller than life, but incredibly vivid. Mym is seated on the floor of the room, arms wrapped around her knees. She doesn't look afraid. Her jaw is tight. She's staring at the floor beyond her feet. Waiting, but determined.

"Can I talk to her?"

"The invaders have disabled the audio channels now. They've taken control of the ship with some sort of virus." Melchior says. "She doesn't have complete functionality at the moment. They are locking us up, and the ship as well."

"They're using a device called the Labyrinth," I say. "I saw them bring it aboard." I reach my hand out toward the view of distant stars, but contact the wall of the ship. "Is there any other way out of this room? Some way she could help us?"

"I'm afraid they have us sealed in," Melchior replies. "For now at least."

I look up at the star field around us, then let my gaze drift back to the image of Mym. "Does your ship have a name?"

Melchior steps over to me and shares the view of Mym. "This is the *Starfire Epiphany*. She was one of three sister ships formed for our purpose. A supremely advanced synthetic intelligence. These ships are the home and essence of the Magi."

"The Magi . . . so you *are* the Wise Men?" I turn to look at the man a little closer.

"An inaccurate term, since many of our council are women, but yes. We do bear some affiliation with your legends."

"Holy shit. Oh—sorry, didn't mean to swear in your—"

"She doesn't mind," Melchior says. "She's heard much worse from me over the years."

"You're really them. The Magi. But you aren't riding camels. You have a spaceship."

"You can't know how many times I've seen your same surprised expression on the faces we've visited. You would be amazed at the lengths people go to, to explain a moving star that mysteriously appears and reappears across the centuries. It's really quite simple.

"We're time travelers.

"We are all citizens of our time. Each person we encounter in life is our countryman. A time traveler does not have a monopoly on experiencing the wonders of a particular decade or century, though I will admit that we do have a few extra stamps in our passports." -Journal of Dr. Harold Quickly, 1950

CHAPTER 21

The Lost Star, 2165

"You mean this whole time all those nativity scenes and Christmas plays have been featuring a bunch of shepherds and camels, right next to a group of time travelers?" I'm still in awe of the man next to me. The robed legend from ancient history who also happens to be the captain of a starship.

Melchior is watching me with an amused look on his face. "Visiting Jesus Christ was hardly the only appearance we've made in religious history, but that was the one that most fascinated the masses. We make a point of visiting all of the great spiritual minds in the human story. That is our directive."

"Like who? Buddha? Mohammed? Confucius?"

"Among others." Melchior looks around the confines of the room. The walls of our cell have continued to show us various views of space. "Those names made some of the loudest splashes in the world's collective consciousness, but many of the greatest spiritual minds were quiet souls, living what you might call 'normal' lives. These may have caused only the smallest of ripples during their lifetimes, but their impact on humanity has been no less significant. We do our best to search them out as well."

"That sounds awesome. How come we haven't heard about you before? I mean, I guess we have, but why haven't you come out and told people your real story? If you've met all these famous people and heard what they had to say straight from the source ... God, you could clear up so many controversies. I think half the problems between religions are because everybody keeps misinterpreting their source material. You guys could totally clear that up."

"Our mission was not to clarify humanity's spiritual revelations. We only mean to preserve them. Enlightened thought is not so much a matter of knowledge as it is an experience. If we were to share our story, it would make no more difference than having the same knowledge spread out over the centuries as it is now. A human being does not assimilate enlightenment as an inheritable trait. It must be born over and over again in fresh ways."

"Well, maybe. But I feel like you could at least show humanity the CliffsNotes. Give everybody a head start."

Melchior studies my face in silence for a moment, and I wonder what he sees there. He doesn't seem particularly concerned about our imprisonment. He seems to be more focused on me. *Is he reading my body language the way his ship does?*

"You come from a very conflicted time, Benjamin. I'm familiar with your generation. It was an admirable period in many ways. You sought out new forms of meaning, new sciences, new philosophies. But your generation threw out much that had already been learned, convinced that it knew better. Yours was a generation that questioned everything and accepted nothing."

I frown. "Not to be contrary or anything, but I don't know that that's true. I mean, we still had religions then. People just seemed to want to use them for their own ends, picking and choosing the bits that suited their purposes. I think people felt better sticking to hard facts, like science."

"Ah, yes. Facts are lovely things." Melchior nods. "Nearly as lovely as truth."

"Shouldn't they be the same thing?"

Melchior is quiet for another moment, then turns around. "What is your definition of science?"

I ponder this. "I guess it's the way we understand the universe. We define the laws of nature so that we can comprehend it better. Use it to improve the human race."

Melchior nods. "And how would you define religion?"

I take a bit longer with this one. "I suppose it's the search to find God. Maybe assign some kind of meaning to life?"

Melchior folds his hands together in front of him. "And if it would be possible to take a leap into the future, or to the distant past for that matter, to a time where one defines the natural universe as a physical manifestation of God, would it be safe to assume that a search to understand the laws of nature, and a search to comprehend the nature of God, might be one and the same thing?"

"Are you saying that science is itself a religion?"

Melchior turns around and regards the view of a particularly bright galaxy. "What I'm saying is that as a race, humans at the very peak of spiritual understanding and the very limits of scientific achievement, are not so dissimilar. I've seen ancient druids look at these stars with the same reverent awe as any astronomer. I've also seen physicists weep from sheer humility at the sight of our sub-molecular fabric.

"Our planet is a tiny mote in a vast and turbulent cosmos. And we are simultaneously a glimmer of individualism in an unfathomable sea of a much deeper consciousness. Time is merciless to both. To suggest that we are capable of defining a word as profound as truth with any of the crude tools at our disposal is a rare and peculiar sort of vanity."

"So what then? Are we not even supposed to try? Are you saying there is no point in even searching?"

Melchior sighs. "The search, Ben, is everything." He turns and looks me in the eye. "I can speak from experience. If you study all the religions in history and listen to each of their leaders and philosophers, observe their rituals, you can then apply the same observation to the greatest scientists and historians and literary minds. Do you know what you would ascertain? Do you know where the parallel line would be drawn? They all performed the same *sacrifice*. We all do. Down to the very last child of the very last generation. We sacrifice the most precious possession we have to our gods, no matter what they might be. We give them our *time*. It is the only worthy offering we have."

I stare at the slowly diminishing view of Earth, pondering his explanation. I finally turn my attention back to the ship. "Except the Eternals. They live forever."

Melchior's hands disappear into his sleeves again as he crosses his arms. "There are always some who don't appreciate the nature of personal sacrifice. But they sacrifice other things, whether they know it or not."

"What do we do now? These Eternals. What do they need your ship for?"

Melchior frowns. "They mean to use its power to bring back one of our members."

"*Your* members? Zurvan was a Magi?"

"Zurvan is merely the name he has given himself to convince his disciples of his power. His real name is Adarvan. We met him in the hills of the Absheron Peninsula when we visited followers of the prophet Zoroaster. Adarvan was one of Zoroaster's most dedicated disciples and we felt he had the qualities required to become a Magus. We offered to take him with us and he accepted."

"You recruited him?"

"Over the years we have grown our numbers by adding new, inquisitive minds. We pass our older minds into our younger bodies and continue our work when we need to, but there is only so long one can maintain the ability to re-assimilate as we do. It takes great patience and self-mastery. And, unlike the common misconception, it cannot be done forever. There is no such thing as true immortality."

"But the Eternals learned your methods."

"They were taught our methods by a very motivated teacher. I suspect he dangled the prize of immortality ahead of them to get them to fulfill his wishes. A clever ruse. I take it you know about the black hole that ends your timestream?"

"The end of the world."

"I've seen it," my other self chimes in.

Melchior studies me. "Have you?" His gaze makes me wonder if he realizes I have more than one person in my head at the moment. *Will he notice? Will I seem like some kind of failure to him?*

"The black hole was an end brought to the world by Adarvan and the misuse of his power." Melchior says. "His followers hope to escape a destiny that their savior created in the first place."

"What happened?" I ask. "I mean I saw it, but I didn't really understand . . ." I try my best to cover for my other self's comment, not sure what he meant by it.

Melchior studies my face a little more intently, the lines around his own eyes seeming to deepen in concentration. "In order to accomplish our assignment, we needed a way to access knowledge from the great minds we met, and then transmit that knowledge to be stored and preserved for posterity. It had to be done without intrusive technology. It was no easy task. As I said, enlightenment is *experiential* knowledge.

"Being able to separate our own consciousness from time was the beginning. It was a practice born of dreams and advanced meditation. In time we could peacefully inhabit our younger minds without harming them. Through continued practice we developed other pathways. Mental connections that allowed us to access the consciousness of another human being the way we accessed our own. Pathways are pathways and, without getting into the laborious details of our meditative practice, we found a way. It enabled us to reach into the underlying consciousness of all living things to connect to the amazing persons we met throughout history and truly grasp their enlightened thoughts."

"You read their minds?"

"In a way. The key was the ability to become a vessel for knowledge ourselves. We had to clear our own minds and actually *experience* the other person in the way that they knew themselves. We then transferred that experience to the ship."

"A spaceship can experience enlightenment?"

"It has a far greater capacity for it than a human mind. And therein was our fatal flaw. Adarvan was an avid learner. But he grew tired of being the empty vessel through which enlightenment passed. He wished to retain all of that knowledge for himself. He believed that if he possessed the combined knowledge of our collective work that he might become a sort of god. Through our practices, he already possessed the power to obtain knowledge from other human beings. He decided to use that connection on his ship, the *Starfire Omega*. The other Magi aboard the ship with him attempted to stop him, but he killed them.

"In his preparations for his assimilation of the collected consciousness aboard his ship, he had purged his own deepest memories, even those that might have informed his inherent morality. His thirst for power was so great that he gave up nearly every part of himself to make room for it."

"He tried to absorb all the knowledge of everyone you had ever met all at once?" I ask.

"The results were catastrophic. We had collected that knowledge from a hundred timestreams over multiple millennia. Those memories and experiences were connected like threads in time. Threads he was pulling. By attempting to channel them all into a single time and place, he damaged the ship's core and the source of its power. The reactor couldn't recover from the damage. The rest, as you know, was devastating to the universe."

"What kind of reactor could create a super-massive black hole?" I look around the room, searching for the real limits of the ship among the visual displays of stars. True to form, the ship reveals itself to me, its ribs and panels appearing from the darkness. Then it shows me an image of its luminescent core, dangerous, but beautiful.

"The ship is powered by an advanced form of Alcubierre drive. You may have heard of the concept."

"It sounds vaguely familiar. Bit fuzzy on the specifics though."

"It's a method of warping space-time itself." Melchior takes control of the room's imagery, the walls vanishing again into a bright blue sky. The ship's interior now resembles a grass field. I imagine this is how Iowa or some other Midwestern state might look on a summer day. Despite the ship's main controls being disabled, it seems the Eternals have seen fit to leave the basic meta scenery functional. Melchior has summoned something to his hand and I recognize the soft, red shape as a water balloon. I stare at the balloon, transfixed, not sure what miraculous thing he is going to do next.

"Are we having a water fight?"

"I'm going to teach you the rules of reality."

"Right now?"

"You have another more pressing engagement at the moment?"

I glance around the sealed room. "Well, no."

"Imagine that the rubber of this balloon represents the fabric of space-time." Melchior holds up the water balloon. "On one side, a world of air; the other, a world of water. Two distinct universes. Now imagine that the membrane is vast—has no ends that we can see. Picture it extending from one infinite horizon to another." He runs a finger over the taut surface of the balloon, then forms his fingers into an "okay" symbol, using his thumb and index finger to squeeze the top end of the balloon, causing it to bubble out. "When we attempt to draw the elements from another reality into ours, we can't. The membrane won't permit it. What we do get, however, is this pressure from the other side." He uses his other hand and presses on the bubble of water between his fingers. "Despite being another reality, it can exert a force here. This is the nature of the Alcubierre drive. Except it uses pressures not just from one universe, but from many."

"Doesn't the other side have to lose something in this equation? Law of conservation of energy and all that?"

"Indeed, but as we pull pressure this direction, pressure elsewhere bulges into their reality. Space-time is very elastic."

"The universe puts up with that? Doesn't it need to compensate somehow?"

"The ship compensates. We can't store all of this tension indefinitely. It must be expended and returned. But when that happens is up to us. Provided we don't exert too much pressure."

"What happens if you did?"

"The same thing that happened to Adarvan. He attempted to channel too much energy at one space and time and the Alcubierre drive ruptured. By the time we realized what he'd done, it was too late. The ship and everything around it was vaporized. It left nothing but a hole." Melchior squeezes the water balloon until it bursts. I jump back involuntarily, but the water is gone as quickly as he made it appear. I remain dry and untouched.

I stare at Melchior's empty palm. "So that's what created the black hole."

"Yes. The hole now equalizes the pressures between the various universes that were formerly connected."

"Like a big cosmic drain?"

"In a sense. The pressure equalizes, and the sub-matter elements that were vaporized end up in the membrane, fused into the fabric of reality."

"So Zurvan—or Adarvan—what happened to him?"

"His body from that moment is gone. Along with the rest of the planet. But his consciousness became trapped. We knew he was somewhere other than our reality, because he no longer interacts with time as we do. But we've had messages over the centuries. Threats, and entreaties to release him. He's not gone. It seems these followers of his believe they can retrieve him from the Neverwhere."

"Is that possible?"

"Nothing physical would ever come back. Nothing has the power to retrieve matter from a black hole, if matter even can be said to exist in such a place. What the Eternals are trying to do, is not return the body of Adarvan, but his consciousness."

"What good will that do with no body to put it in?"

"They've found his body. Likely a younger version of himself." He places a hand to the wall of the ship as if he can feel its thoughts. "They are taking us back to find him now." Melchior sighs and looks upward.

The ship is changing around us again. The field has dimmed from midday sun and is now fading though twilight back into a star-filled nightscape. Billions of stars come out on display. I look for any sign of constellations I know, but wherever this view is from, it's not home.

I don't get any sensation of being aboard a ship. No sense of movement. No sound of engines or vibration.

"Why are we not floating around in here? Some kind of artificial gravity?"

"Not artificial. The ship's engine actually contains so much inert gravity that we need to use much of its own power just to keep from being destroyed by it. Since it's tapped into multiple universes, drawing vast amounts of power from them, we wick off only the smallest amount to run the ship. The rest counteracts itself and keeps us from tearing a void in space-time."

"Seems like a dangerous place to live."

Melchior smiles. "No one has ever called the Magians cowards. Truth be told, the technology is very safe when used properly. We've spent centuries mastering it. Adarvan was a tragic and catastrophic exception. These Eternals, however, don't know what they are doing. If they succeed in their attempt to resurrect Adarvan, they may repeat his failure, rupture space and time again, and create a second black hole."

A crack of light appears in the wall as a door is opened. A pair of strong arms hurls the somewhat ruffled-looking Doctor Quickly through and closes the door again.

Doctor Quickly manages to keep his feet. He straightens his jacket and brushes the sides of his pockets, patting them in turn to check their contents.

"Benjamin. I see you've had about as much fortune as I've had." He wanders over to stand by me and extends a hand toward Melchior. "Doctor Harold Quickly. Are you a fellow captive? They are starting quite the collection."

Melchior extends an arm from his cavernous robes and returns Doctor Quickly's handshake. "It's a pleasure to finally meet you, Doctor. I wasn't sure I would encounter you in this lifetime."

Doctor Quickly nods. "So much to see, I would imagine." He glances around the room.

"She's okay," I say, predicting Doctor Quickly's next question. "They've got her locked up on her own."

"I suspected as much. Keeping us from pulling any more tricks." He rummages in his pockets. "Not that we could. They took nearly everything in my—ah." He pats at his chest and finally locates his glasses. Slipping them on, he studies the view of the universe around us. "Fascinating ship. Simply fascinating." He turns to Melchior. "I saw the way it moved on the meta radar. It has incredible speed. It's an Alcubierre engine, isn't it? It's has to be a manner of time warping technology. And the way you jump. Anchoring to comets. The brilliance of it . . ." He trails off and stares at the star field as if in a trance. "Just spectacular."

I turn back to Melchior. He seems to be regarding Doctor Quickly with amusement.

"You said the Eternals could potentially create another black hole. What would happen then?"

Melchior's face grows serious. "Adarvan ended the timestream he was in by creating a black hole so powerful that it is capable of sucking up anything in its vicinity, even across time. It's sitting there right now, absorbing every possible future of the earth, because every possible future of the earth has it passing through that region of space. There is no chance of escaping it. It occurs too soon and it's too big. It eventually swallows most of the Milky Way Galaxy.

"The black hole is so wide that the only human beings who could survive it would have to possess at minimum, the engine technology of the twenty-fifth century, but even using that, they would have needed to leave earth ten thousand years ago to make it to safety. The only people capable of managing that are time travelers. Hence, the true importance of our mission."

"The Eternals really believe they can change things by bringing Zurvan back?"

"I don't know. Perhaps he is merely promising them an escape. With this ship they could potentially travel farther into the past and then leave the Earth to survive and get clear of the black hole. But without proper use of the Alcubierre drive, they'll only duplicate his error and that would be irreparable. He was pulled into the Neverwhere by an incredible force—a rupture in space-time connected to multiple parallel worlds. He's also stitched to the Neverwhere in far more ways than any one person. When they try to remove him, they'll be pulling out every soul he took with him as well.

"If the drive on the *Starfire Epiphany* can't contain the strain on space-time they cause, they'll blow a black hole in the deep past just like he did in the future and humanity will be truly trapped. Even we Magi won't be able to travel far enough back in time to escape and preserve the knowledge we've collected. Time travel or not, the history of human civilization will be squeezed between inescapable black holes. Two devastating bookends for our story."

"Wouldn't people prior to Zoroaster survive? Humans existed prior to that point."

"I suppose, theoretically, if any time travelers have made it farther into the past than when the event occurs and—assuming they discovered the danger before being consumed by it—they could potentially keep going back far enough in time to escape to the stars again. But in order to save the human race at that point, they would need to teach early Homo sapiens or more likely Homo neanderthalensis, how to build complex spacecraft—and do so thousands of years before they could even figure out farming.

"Not to be insensitive, but personally I've never known a Neanderthal to have an epiphany of thought that was especially worth preserving. As noble a cause as that might seem in theory, I wouldn't hold my breath waiting for anyone to take it up.

"The Magi are the last great effort to preserve the essence and knowledge of mankind's civilization. We've been doing so diligently for thousands of years using multiple incarnations of ourselves. The work is almost complete. But if the Eternals rip another hole in time by resurrecting Adarvan, it may have all been for nothing."

The view around us shifts to the front of the ship. Our course is already converging with that of the comet Borisov C/2014 Q3. We are approaching the wake of its tail.

Doctor Quickly takes a few steps forward. "You must have a durable anchor system. Something that withstands the elements. A way to reappear without being fused to the comet's tail matter."

"It's a pod," Melchior explains. He points to a rough-looking gourde-shaped object coming into view within the comet's tail. "The pod will open to receive us, then purge all other contaminants. We'll anchor to its interior and have a safe place where we can relocate the ship through time."

"You can go anywhere the comet goes," Doctor Quickly says. "Jump the entire ship to anywhere in the comet's lifetime where the pod is intact. It's incredible. How many comets? How many options do you have?"

"Thousands," Melchior replies. "We have them scattered through the Oort cloud. More comets than we'll ever need, most likely. Some of the comets will deteriorate, but the pods will detach to find new ones."

"But the technology required to complete that . . . the engineering and the intelligence required to master the time travel involved . . . It would have taken centuries of thought or a mind so powerful—" Doctor Quickly pauses and looks up at the sky. "Ah. So that's what they've been up to . . ."

I don't have time to question him because the door opens again and a cluster of shrouded Eternals enters the room. They've donned their robes again. One of the Eternals, a young man around my age, seems to be shivering in little spasms.

Elgin leads the procession. His companions are carrying the portable gravitizer they stole from me. They set it in the middle of the room and step away. Two more Eternals position themselves behind me.

"The time has come to prove your usefulness, Doctor," Elgin says. "You will show us how to use this equipment properly and turn my remaining crew into time travelers."

Doctor Quickly's eyes linger on the shivering young Eternal at the back of the group. "That machine was not designed for living organisms. It requires a much more delicate process than with inanimate ones. If you use that improperly, it could kill you."

"Then I suggest you find a way to make it work safely for us, Doctor. For any one of my men that dies, I'll be killing one of yours."

Strong hands grab me from behind and I feel the press of something cold and metallic at my throat.

Doctor Quickly grimaces as if the blade is pressing into his neck. "This equipment isn't sufficient." He gestures toward the canister at the side. "The reservoir of gravitites is nearly depleted. Whoever you've been using it on, you've exhausted most of its supply. Even if I could use this equipment to infuse you, there aren't enough left there for even one person, let alone your entire crew."

"Give me solutions, Doctor. Not excuses," Elgin says. "You've created time travelers before. You will do it again. If we need more gravitites, we'll drain them from the bodies of your companions if need be. Or perhaps from your daughter." He holds up Mym's degravitizer. He gestures to one of his men by the door and he opens it. Two more Eternals enter, shepherding Mym between them.

"Ben!" Mym calls as soon as she sees me. Her two guards restrain her and keep her from rushing to me.

I move toward her instinctively, but am jerked back by the Eternals behind me. The blade nicks my throat. A trickle of warmth runs down my neck from the incision. "Stay still," the man with the knife snarls.

"Stop this," Doctor Quickly says. "Removing gravitites from living tissue is even worse. You don't have the technology. We shouldn't use this. If you were to return me to one of my laboratories . . ."

"There is no more time for requisitions, Doctor," Elgin says. "Make it work."

Melchior interrupts. "The ship has a supply of gravitites. We'll donate them if you do not harm these people."

Elgin shifts his glare to Melchior. "I don't trust you, Magi. Or your ship."

"The Epiphany won't harm you. You have my word."

Doctor Quickly sighs and rubs a hand across his forehead. "Okay. If we have to use this equipment, I need to at least prime your men internally before we work on the external elements. We need gravitized food."

"Food?" Elgin says. "We can raid the stores of the Magi. They have gravitized food in abundance aboard. That is simple."

"Yes, but not just normal amounts of gravitites. We'll need to infuse them to at least a hundred times that concentration level. We can use water if we have to, but solids give more time for absorption. We'll get the gravitites absorbed in the bloodstream and—listen, my daughter has a great deal of medical training. If you permit us, we could start gravitizing blood infusions and make sure that safe practices—"

"I'm sure you'd love to have a chance to inject us with needles," Elgin sneers. "It would be easy to poison us, or—"

"Let them do it to me first." Longcase walks through the door and begins rolling up a sleeve. "We have the boyfriend." He leers at me. "I'm sure she understands that if she harms us, the pain will be inflicted tenfold on him. And I won't have it said that I lacked the courage to act when Lord Zurvan required it of me."

Mym's eyes narrow and it's clear from her expression that she might love to poison him anyway, regardless of his threats.

"We have a medical bay. It's near the kitchens," Melchior says.

Elgin gestures to one of his henchmen and Melchior is led from the room. Doctor Quickly works to set up the gravitizer in a better configuration.

I would help him if I could, but the knife remains firmly against my throat. Mym is looking across the room, her eyes locked on mine. Staring back at her, I experience a sense of calm I haven't felt in a while. I'm still frightened for her, but I'm relieved to simply be in the same room with her and see her alive. I realize the sense of calm I'm feeling is because my other self, at least for this moment, seems to be feeling exactly the same thing.

"Let's get you to work," Elgin says to Mym. "Time is of the essence." Mym looks away from me and complies, moving toward the door under his guidance. She casts one final glance back and I try to give her a reassuring smile. She disappears around the corner with more of the Eternals following her.

Doctor Quickly glances up at the Eternals holding me. "Benjamin's mechanical abilities would make this go a lot faster. Would you mind allowing him to assist me?"

The two behind me converse in rapid whispers, weighing Elgin's desire for speed against the need to keep me secure. They must decide I'm not a threat, because I'm finally released and shoved forward. I stagger a couple of steps, then make my way over to Doctor Quickly, taking a knee next to the machine.

"This is certainly one of our most complex challenges," he says. I know he's not merely referring to the assembly of the machine.

"What do we need to do?"

Doctor Quickly's fingers are working over the gravitizer, but I can tell it's nearly serviceable as is. He's merely buying time. He lowers his voice. "The Eternals have to be gravitized to make the jump once the ship attaches to the comet. Otherwise the ship would just leave them all floating in space."

"What a tragedy that would be."

Doctor Quickly allows himself a flicker of a smile. "Unfortunately our options are limited. We'll need to comply with the normal safety protocols. As much as I might like to eject them all, I won't take risks with Mym's life, or yours. They'll know if they are improperly infused and you'll suffer."

"So they get what they want."

"For now." Doctor Quickly makes a few more minor adjustments to the shape of the gravitizer and I assist. After we run out of things to fiddle with, a pair of Eternals comes to claim the gravitizer and Doctor Quickly. With no one else left in the room, my guards abandon me. I'm left alone in the semi-darkness with only my other self for company.

"You still there?" I whisper.

"Yeah."

The wall illuminates with the view out the front of the ship again, showing me the path we're taking toward the comet Borisov C/2014 Q3. The tail of the comet is spitting colored gases and showering the space behind it with debris.

"We've been in some tight spots before. But I'm not sure how we're going to get out of this one." I say.

"You're still alive. That's something. And we still have Mym."

I settle onto the floor, suddenly very tired. I pry myself out of the remnants of my spacesuit and discard the now useless pieces. When I've shimmied out of the pants section of the suit, I ball up the legs and use them as a cushion. From my seated position I watch the ship navigate its way toward the pod attached to the back of the comet. As we blast our way through the ice and debris of the tail to get to it, the pod begins to open like the petals of a flower to receive us.

The ship hurtles forward, the meta camera view shaking occasionally from impacts from larger chunks of debris, but progressing steadily toward its target. I keep my hands on the floor beside me, stabilizing myself. I can feel the vibrations of the ship running through my arms even over the force of the artificial gravity. The ship lines up on an approach path directly behind the pod's open doors. Now we're in a zone of less danger from debris, and move more directly toward the target.

The *Starfire Epiphany* pulls into the pod and docks with an arm that will keep it anchored safely. All around the ship, the pod doors are now closing us off from space. From our inside perspective it looks like giant fingers slowly blocking out the stars. The fingers close around us and plunge the exterior of the ship into total darkness.

Inside my cell of a room, little wisps of light still flicker around the corners and tumble across the floor. One impacts my hand and seems to linger there, making my skin glow with a thousand brilliant colors. A little touch of eternity. On the far side of my mind, I can feel the connection through my other self. He's feeling it even more than I am. One step closer to the beyond. I pull my hand away from the wisp of light and let it tumble on its way.

Not ready for that now.

I don't want eternity. I know where my home is.

She still needs me.

"Why are we so egotistical as to think we are the only ones experiencing the present? Yesterday and tomorrow have always been just as real as today. Every time I see someone smiling in a photograph from the distant past, I smile too, because I know their secret. We are all alive together. Time may keep us apart, but it keeps us. It will never let us go." -Journal of Dr. Harold Quickly, February 2, 2015

CHAPTER 22

The Neverwhere

My self in the real world has gotten drowsy. I don't really blame him. The subtle vibration of the ship combined with the sheer stress of this situation must be wreaking havoc on his body. I can now feel the aches and pains he's experiencing though I don't have the memories of where they are all from. The trip aboard the ship has been harrowing enough. Harrowing, but worth it.

I was able to see her again. That was something.

I have a hard time telling how long the ship has been shrouded in darkness. We have been left alone in this room for what feels like hours. The other me has permitted me to stay at least. He no longer seems to fear that I might take over his mind. He's merely waiting. Hoping to see if some resolution to our situation presents itself.

I am not that patient.

He may be me, but he doesn't understand what it's like in the Neverwhere. He doesn't understand the closeness to eternity here. He's felt it, but he hasn't understood it. And the longer I stay here the harder it is getting to ignore.

As he drowses, I've been going over what the Magi said about Zurvan. Adarvan. They're going to try to restore him. I don't know what method they plan to use, but I need to know. I need a way out.

Riding shotgun in my own mind has been better than the alternative, better than drifting off into the ether, but it's not living. Not truly.

Perhaps three hours into our captivity, the door to the room is opened again and Melchior is returned to us. My other self rouses himself slowly from his position on the floor. "How is it going out there? Is Mym okay?"

"She is doing admirably under the circumstances," Melchior replies. "How are you doing?"

"Ugh. Tired. Angry." He wipes a hand across our brow. "Worried."
Melchior is considering me thoughtfully. "How are you doing?"
My other self falters. "Um, just that. Mostly the tired and the—"
"No," Melchior replies. "I wasn't speaking to you. I was speaking to you."
He stabs a finger toward me, aimed directly at my left eye. "How are *you*
doing?"

My living self stays quiet this time and I stammer a response. "I'm . . .
I'm not doing that great, honestly. I'm dead."

Melchior narrows his eyes. "Hardly dead anymore. Trapped. But not
dead."

I can feel my other self squirm under his gaze. He's uncomfortable, but
curious as well.

"How did you know I was in here?" I ask.

Melchior straightens up and turns away. "When you are as old as I am,
and have seen as much as I have, you know a few things." He tucks his arms
back into his sleeves. "I've been a Magi for hundreds of years. I think I know
a split consciousness when I see one."

"What do we do?" my other self asks. "How do we fix it? Is there a way?"

He's holding his breath. It makes me realize how desperate he feels
about having me stuck inside his head.

"There are ways," Melchior replies. "Though normally they take a great
deal of training and practice. How long has this been happening? When did
the two of you split?"

"Weeks ago."

"Today," I reply.

Melchior doesn't seem surprised by the dual response. He merely nods.
"It's good that it hasn't been a long time. You still share the majority of your
memories. There wouldn't be too much information to absorb from one
another. If it was longer, years perhaps, it may not be possible to ever
realign."

"So we can do it?" I ask.

"What do you mean, realign?" my other self replies.

Melchior studies my face again. "The two of you could conceivably
return to being the same person, a single mind instead of two. You would
have to be able to reconcile the memories that you've made separately, and
that can be difficult. But not impossible. A strong mind can handle the
disparity and learn to comprehend it."

"What do we need to do?" I ask.

"You need to be of the same mind," Melchior replies. The statement is
simple, but aggravating in its simplicity.

"Yeah, but how do we do that?" I say. "Aren't we already?"

"It would seem not," Melchior replies. "Or you would have already solved this puzzle." Both my other self and I stay quiet at this, and after a few moments of silence, Melchior continues. "When people suffer a split, it's usually because one mind is seeking to control the other. Or both are seeking control over different outside circumstances. It never works. A mind that has been suppressed by another is not the same as being single-minded. It may appear normal enough to the outside world. Some can hide it for a long time, but eventually, there are always cracks."

"I've seen that," my living self replies. "This woman I met, Sonia, was split by the Eternals."

"I've seen it, too," I say. "In Zurvan's memories. A woman who lost a fight with her younger mind. Annie."

"This is what you would need to avoid," Melchior replies. "Normally I would have given you years of meditation practice before you were ever even in danger of this occurring. It is important to know yourself—recognize your own weaknesses in the present—before you can ever take on the knowledge of your future. I would have had you listen to your dreams first. You would have learned to navigate them, separate your mind from time there and wander inside your own consciousness. It is a much safer place in which to explore one's future and past."

"We've had that," my other self replies. "We've spoken in my dreams."

"You have come far beyond that, however. You have dreamed while awake," Melchior says. "You are now beyond dreams altogether. You are close, but you are speaking to one another as individuals, and that can be dangerous. If you hope to become single-minded, you'll need to find the common threads that bind you together and keep them safe. Strengthen those thoughts until all else is inconsequential. Stop fighting for control and start working together as a cohesive unit."

A crack of light appears overhead. The meta imagery is still reflecting the outside of the ship. The pod doors are opening.

"What's happening?" I ask.

"The Quicklys were successful in infusing our captors with gravitites. We've already made the jumps," Melchior replies. "The ship has moved."

"How far?"

"The path of this comet takes 151 years to complete. They haven't had the patience to make the trip out to the Oort cloud to select a different comet, so we are some multiple of that interval into the past that would get us in range of Adarvan. I don't recall when this docking pod was first installed on the comet, but it was a long time ago. Thousands of years."

THE DAY AFTER NEVER

"How did it survive?"

"The outer shell is partially biological. It grows and heals itself in places when damaged. It can survive in these conditions for eons if need be. Longer than the comet itself would ever last."

The pod has split into five sections now and I have a view of the tail out the rear of the ship. The gas and ice trail glows in the light of the sun beyond it. When the ship detaches from its anchor post, we hurl backward and away from Borisov C/2014 Q3. The comet is massive now, at least ten times the size it was when we attached. The sublimation of ice from its repeated trips around the sun has yet to occur to reduce its size.

The ship peels away from the tail of the comet to avoid damage and plunges us back toward the Earth. Our velocity is incredible and I can actually see the tiny distant planet beginning to grow.

"We'll be in a much different world here," Melchior says. "Have you visited any of Earth's ancient civilizations before?"

"I saw the sphinx when it was still young. Didn't get to stay long, though."

"Ancient Persia is a grand spectacle all its own—if you ever have a chance to visit under more pleasant circumstances. I regret that I'm unable to show you its wonders."

"Are we going to Iran?" I ask, suddenly concerned. "I've seen a place here. A desert in Zurvan's memories. Benny said it was Iraq or Iran."

"If we are going to find Adarvan, it will be neither place in the present age. The Absheron Peninsula is in Azerbaijan in your time. It has been a part of the Persian Empire over the centuries, but this far into the past, we will find it very different from modern times. Authentic Azerbaijan has always been and shall always be, the land of fire."

The door to our room opens and the Eternals return, along with Doctor Quickly. I recede into the background again, not especially interested in disclosing my split personality with anyone other than Melchior.

As the Eternals prepare the group for the return to Earth, I get a growing sense of unease about the entire situation. We are separated by guards and unable to talk, and I haven't seen Mym return yet. Her timestream signature has been vital for them in navigating their way back to this timeline, but now that they have found it, what will they do with her? What will they do with any of us?

The apprehension is not relegated solely to us prisoners. The Eternals are edgy too. Despite all of their preparations and success in commandeering the ship, they are now thousands of years from home, the same as we are. They'll have contacts here, members of their group bred from their messages relayed back through time, but they are stepping into a world just as foreign to them as it is to us.

Longcase and Elgin are the only two who seem just as self-assured about their future. Longcase is positively strutting. I notice with annoyance that he's now wearing Mym's pendant chronometer. He has her ring on as well, awkwardly jammed over the first knuckle of his little finger. Elgin has taken Doctor Quickly's chronometer. Mine hasn't reappeared yet.

As the ship approaches Earth, I'm wowed by the raw beauty of the planet. The side in shadow is deeply dark. No electric cities glow on coastlines. There are no freeways spanning the continents. No farmland has been carved out in symmetrical shapes.

The ship cuts across the southern hemisphere, overflying South America, then northeast across the Atlantic. We've entered the atmosphere and the heat glows brightly around us as we tear through the sky. I can't help but wonder what sorts of people are looking up from the surface of the Earth and pondering our significance. The Lost Star has returned.

We are moved out of the confines of the room we were in, to join the others near the main boarding ramp of the ship. I get a feeling of déjà vu. The center of the sphere holds the Alcubierre drive, a dense machine of complicated-looking gadgetry. It's viewable from the main control room near the boarding ramp. It looks like the one on Zurvan's ship, only this one doesn't have all the colors of the universe leaking out.

The ship descends over North Africa and I see the first noticeable signs of civilization. Egypt. There are roads and established cities, but still no sign of pyramids.

The ship continues its journey, descending ever lower, until we're aimed at the Caspian Sea. The Starfire has slowed immensely, firing thrusters forward from its extended wings. I can imagine that from the ground it must very much resemble the symbol I saw—a flaming sphere with wings of fire.

The ship finally stops its forward movement and descends vertically onto the desert plain of the Absheron Peninsula. As we approach the surface, the view is lost to clouds of dust and smoke. The ship settles to Earth amid the dust plumes and comes to rest smoothly atop a hill.

When the disrupted dust finally clears, the Eternals lower the access ramp to the ship. Mym is led from a room near the bow and my other self releases an audible sigh of relief upon seeing her. I still don't get a chance to speak to her because all of us get our hands bound and are led down the ramp in intervals.

We're met with warm air and a fading twilight over low brown hills. The ground is covered in a coarse sand that clumps up in dark patches here and there. There is a distinctive smell in the air. Something burning.

"Oh God. I shouldn't be here," I whisper to my other self.

"I don't think any of us should."

"No. I meant that I've been here before. I think I've seen this. Zurvan has definitely been here. It's not safe."

One of the Eternals jostles my shoulder. "Keep quiet."

The sun has already set and darkness is creeping over the horizon. Trying to get a bearing on where we are, I spot figures approaching through the low hills. The procession is carrying torches. The torches are pinpricks of light against the sandy hills, but they aren't the only source of light. There is a dull glow against the top of one of the nearby hillsides as well.

The Eternals close up the ship and we begin our own procession, headed toward the closest hilltop in the direction of the group approaching us. A few stars are beginning to shine over the horizon and I can make out at least one planet. But as I'm looking upward at the sky, the sun suddenly appears overhead, fiery and bright despite the twilight around us. I falter with confusion, bring us to a stop.

"What is it?" my other self asks. The sun overhead vanishes again as fast as it appeared, leaving me once more in evening twilight.

"The sun . . ."

An Eternal shoves me forward and I stumble a few feet before regaining my normal stride. I'm vigilant for the next fifty yards of climb and, when we start getting closer to the other larger group, the sun reappears overhead again, a displaced apparition that lends no light to our surroundings. To the contrary, it seems to make the world around me seem even darker. This time I know what's happening.

"He's here."

"Who is?" my other self whispers. He seems to be unable to see the sun.

"Zurvan. Here in the Neverwhere. He remembers this place in sunlight." The view around the sun expands for me and suddenly I'm seeing all of the desert peninsula in daylight. I'm reentering Zurvan's memory of this place layered over top of the real world space—a sunburnt world that smells of smoke and natural gas. I can still make out the figures of Doctor Quickly, Mym, and the rest of the Eternals ahead of me on the hillside, but for them it's still night. I'm caught on the edge of reality and the Neverwhere. This brightness I'm currently bathed in is illuminating me alone. Zurvan is somewhere nearby, and he's going to see me.

I begin to separate from my other self's consciousness, distancing myself from reality. "I have to go."

"Wait, how are we supposed to join our minds? We need to—"

"He'll kill me. He'll take my memories."

"What happens if I lose track of you?"

"I don't know." I search the view of the now sunny hills with trepidation. *He's here somewhere.*

Waiting.

I feel caught between the desire to run and the need to stay near Mym. If it wasn't for the danger she and Doctor Quickly are in, I'd prefer to bolt, open up a portal to some disused memory and hide. Now I realize that's not an option. Whatever my earthly self is walking into, he carries my fate with him, and theirs too. He's right. We are getting closer to one another. It's gotten easier to meld our thoughts and feel like the same person.

I settle back into the view through my other self's eyes—forcing out the Neverwhere and concentrating on the darkness of the present. *Will Zurvan still be able to find me if I'm hiding inside my own head?* I focus on the path ahead in the dim view of reality, but can't seem to completely shake my sense of the Neverwhere around me.

The procession of local Eternals arrives. We meet them on a path atop a flattened section of the hill made of rough stone. There is a black, tar-like substance oozing out of some of the spaces between rocks and the tang of salt hangs heavily in the air, reminding me that we're not far from the sea.

The group we meet is made up entirely of bearded men. They vary in ages but all of them are very serious in their expressions. Most are carrying sturdy walking staves. A few cast awed glances toward the blinking ship we've left behind.

Elgin addresses the new arrivals in a language I don't understand. A leathery man with braided hair who seems to be the leader steps forward. The two of them converse briefly before the other man points to a spot farther down the ridge.

I follow the group over the other side of the hill to where the leathery man has pointed. What I see astounds me.

At the bottom of the hillside there is a pool of water. It's hard to say whether it's a small lake or if it's perhaps some sort of tidal flow from the nearby coastline. The shape of the pool is mostly circular, rimmed by a rough, rocky collar that forms a sort of bowl. This jagged rock rim is glowing a reddish-orange because, despite the seemingly inhospitable environment for it, this lake is on fire.

We're led down the hill toward an altar like I saw at the temple in St. Pete. This one has been erected right at the edge of the lake, a safe height above the water and its mysterious, flickering flames.

THE DAY AFTER NEVER

The fire burns steadily at the rim of its confines, glowing brightest as it consumes the gas pockets trapped along the rocks, but there are other bursts across the surface of the lake itself. Bubbles rise from the depths below and are quickly turned into balls of fire that erupt into the air at the first contact from neighboring flames. Whatever violence the earth is suffering below ground, the results above the surface are spectacular. It's easy to see why the citizens here have erected a place of worship alongside it.

The spectacle is well attended tonight. The contingent that met us at the ship was only a small sample of the local faithful. Here they line the perimeter of the pool in rows three deep. All told there must be at least two hundred people. Many of them have their eyes toward the hills behind us. Turning to look, I see why. From here the upper half of the *Starfire Epiphany* is still clearly visible above the low hills. The great sphere is pulsing with blue light around its circumference, no doubt a wondrous sight to a people living thousands of years before the advent of electrical power.

Doctor Quickly, Mym, Melchior, and I are lined up near the base of the altar structure, while Longcase and Elgin ascend the steps. I'm finally close enough to Mym to whisper to her.

"Are you all right?"

"I'm okay," she whispers.

"I missed you," I blurt out, unable to contain myself.

"I missed you, too," she replies.

"I promise I'm going to get you out of here," my living self adds.

"How?"

"Still working on that part." He tests the strength of the cords tying our hands behind our back. Whoever tied the knots knew what they were doing.

I find I'm just staring at Mym, unable to take my eyes off her. Finally, I realize my living self is trying to move our head, and I've been keeping him from doing so. I honor our agreement and go back to being a passenger again.

He doesn't know how badly I've missed her.

A chair and table have been set up inside the temple and the table has been covered with a white cloth. The Eternals have brought something from the ship and are now making preparations. They set the table with bowls of food and are busy constructing something around it. After a moment, I realize it is the portable gravitizer. They are assembling it around the chair.

"What are they doing?" I ask.

"They made us teach them how to make time travelers," Mym replies. "They want to use the machine on someone here."

Elgin and Longcase have convened inside the gazebo-like temple structure and supervised the preparations. When they finally seem satisfied, the leathery man points toward a path on the right side of the lake. A group of figures is approaching, surrounded by another cluster of men bearing torches.

At the center of the group, dressed in all white robes, is the man I've been running from my whole time in the Neverwhere.

Zurvan.

Only this man isn't quite him. Not yet. This man is younger, early twenties if I had to guess. His beard is trimmed shorter and he's leaner than the version I've been seeing in the Neverwhere. He's still muscular. Even under the loose-fitting white robes, his broad shoulders are evident.

The young man's expression is somber. The men around him are likewise serious, but as he passes the other Eternals lined up along the lakeside, they begin to chant and hum. The noise precedes him like a wave, growing louder as he approaches. Some of the faithful even go so far as to fall on their faces or spread their cloaks on the ground for him to walk on.

Elgin is watching the young man approach with an unusual expression on his face. While still respectful, it's something akin to jealousy. He has been chief over all of the Eternals I've encountered. I can only wonder how he will really feel about having his Lord Zurvan returned from the grave.

"It's been a long time since I've seen him looking so young," Melchior says softly from his position beyond Mym.

"Who is he? Mym asks.

"Adarvan. One of our earliest members. They've sought out a version of him from before we recruited him. They mean to use him as a host."

One of Elgin's Eternals quiets us with a slashing motion of his hand. I'm not familiar with the gesture, but the threat is clear enough. He returns his attention to Elgin, but casts occasional glances back at us to make sure we're staying quiet.

The now starry sky above us flickers.

Another flash of sunlight.

I search the dusty hills around the lake and spot him. The sight of him is all it takes. I'm suddenly firmly back in the Neverwhere—sunlight and hot, vaporous hills shedding heat into an afternoon sky. Just the presence of my enemy has been enough to make me lose firm contact with the real world. I struggle to regain the connection, but I've been dislodged from my other self. I can still see him, but I'm no longer inside his head.

A few small rocks tumble down the path ahead of Zurvan. He's striding confidently down the hill toward his memory of the lake of fire. In daylight its effect is less mysterious. Smoke drifts over the water from the bursts of flame, but the sunlight outshines the fire here. Zurvan is the main spectacle now and I'm unwilling to take my eyes off him, terrified that he might suddenly attack.

He's seen me. As he draws closer, a smile turns up the corner of his mouth.

"This truly is a magnificent day, Ben Travers." He raises his arms ahead of him as he walks. "I'm glad that you've come to witness my victory. It seems right that you should be here. This is the end for you, after all, and a man should meet his end on his feet in the sun, not cowering and hiding."

"You're going to ruin it," I say. "I heard Melchior. If they bring you back it could rip another hole in reality. End the world all over again."

"Melchior is an old fool. When I've been returned to my body, he will be the first of the Magi I'll dispose of. It was his Magi who attempted to stop me from achieving my greatness before. They have no vision." He touches the scar at his forehead. "But they've done the last damage they will. I plan to carve out a new future, free of their interference."

"You've taken too much already. Too many people. He says you'll rip the fabric of space and time pulling out all the souls you've taken out of the Neverwhere. You can't contain it all in one mind."

"I'm just getting started," Zurvan replies.

He's reached the lakeside now and the scene around us begins to grow more vivid. Zurvan and I are viewing the scene in daylight, his memory of sun layered over the reality of the darkness. But as he concentrates on the scene around us, we begin to ghost back into the actions in reality. We're watching with a sharp clarity compared to what everyone else is seeing, since we're viewing the scene in daylight, but I can now see the Eternals and Mym again.

I'm still outside myself. The four captives are lined up at the base of the steps to the altar, hands tied behind their backs, but I'm no longer viewing the scene from inside my own head. The other me has noticed the change. He's concentrating on something, perhaps trying to figure out where I've gone.

From outside the scene I get a true sense of his vulnerability. The environment around him is nothing but hostile. The two hundred Eternals are only the first problem. The terrain itself is hazardous. A flaming desert in a country thousands of years in the past and no way out. I've always had a natural tendency toward optimism, but even I can't see how this situation could possibly end well.

Elgin has invited Adarvan up the steps of the altar. The young man takes a seat. Among a lot of ceremonial bowing, each of the Eternals from my time come to him and offer him food. Pieces of fruit, breads, even what looks like it might be a plate of brownies. All food from the ship that has been heavily gravitized and will help the process of turning him into a time traveler.

The young man had looked very serious and a little bit nervous as he approached, but it's clear that the food is having a positive effect on his morale. The more of it he samples, the more he seems to lose his sense of formality. It appears as though he is beginning to really enjoy this new celebrity.

Zurvan is smiling at the view of his younger self. "I had so much to learn. I knew nothing then. He can't imagine the power that he'll have when I possess his mind."

As the procession of food items dwindles, Longcase prepares the gravitizer. The assembled faithful around the altar are still chanting their praises to Zurvan, ready to see their god of time return to them. Longcase activates the gravitizer around Adarvan. The young man grimaces at first, clearly uncomfortable with the sensation, but after a few seconds the treatment is over. The gravitites have been transferred and it is only a matter of time till they'll finish multiplying inside his body.

Zurvan mounts the steps of the altar, this ghostly Neverwhere version of him taking a place behind his real-life counterpart. Zurvan licks his lips. It's as though he can taste the life of the young man in the chair and is ready to devour it. But he doesn't act yet.

The Eternals have more pomp and ceremony to perform. The table of food is cleared away and, as the brethren look on, Elgin delivers a final gift to the young man. This gift resides inside a wooden box that looks like it was made for the occasion. Various symbols have been carved into the sides, including the one I recognize, the symbol of the Lost Star. Adarvan accepts the box and reverently pries open the lid.

Reaching inside, he extracts the final, shiny, metallic gift. My chronometer.

Zurvan is leering down at the man and the chronometer with an expression of pure craving. The desire to possess the power that the young man now holds is written plainly across his face. It makes me wonder what the brethren might make of him if they were capable of seeing him this way. Would they still want to resurrect him if they knew this was who he truly was? Not a god. Just a man who wants to possess the entire knowledge of the human race for himself. The man who will sacrifice anyone to get it.

"It's a beautiful gift, Ben," Zurvan says. He looks up from the chronometer in his other self's hands. His eyes fall on Mym. "So many beautiful gifts you've brought me today."

Anger burns inside me as his eyes linger on Mym.

"I understand why losing her drove your other incarnation mad," he says. "She really is exquisite."

"Go to Hell."

Zurvan sneers at me. "You know, I had planned to simply take your mind if I saw you again. The way I did with your scruffy other self. Benny. But now . . . now I think I'll let you watch. I'll let you live, so you can see me take your whole world from you."

I clench my fists, but stay silent. This is still his memory. His world.

The Eternals in the real world have begun to chant in unison. Adarvan has put my chronometer on his wrist and has risen from the chair. He is facing the lake of fire now, standing with his arms outstretched toward the flames. I can tell he's making an effort to concentrate, pull his mind from the heady treatment he's just received so he can focus on the task at hand. It appears to be difficult. Amid all of this tumult he's just been through, he's meant to try to meditate and be calm. But next he will be receiving the greatest of his gifts. He'll become the living god of time.

Zurvan is standing right next to Adarvan, unseen so far, but so close to just reaching out and touching his younger self. *What will he do with his younger self's mind? Has Adarvan been preparing? Will they be able to function as the same person, or will Adarvan become some repressed consciousness, held down by Zurvan's will?*

I look back at my living self, hands bound and waiting for an unknown fate. Considering the situation, it's hard to decide which one of us is currently worse off.

I concentrate and bridge the gap between his mind and mine, sliding inside his head again, plunging myself back into his nighttime reality.

"Where did you go?" he whispers.

"Zurvan is here. He's ready," I say. Too loud.

Mym looks over at me, studying me in the half-light. From back inside my head, the view is only illuminated by flickering torches and the glow from the fiery lake. Mym's expression is hard to read.

"I'm not crazy," I say. "I promise. I'm just—"

"It's okay," she says. "I know who you are."

Her words are a relief. Whatever she has inferred from my situation, she at least knows I'm not the screaming version of me she heard last—Benny—telling her to get away from me because it's too dangerous. I realize that it's too late for running away now anyway. Whatever fate lies in store for us in the near future, we're committed to facing it together.

"What is Zurvan going to do?" my other self asks, able to speak to me openly now.

I don't need to respond because the answer is readily apparent. Adarvan is making contact.

The young man has his arms open, head tilted back. He turns to face the assembled brethren and his eyes are twitching in their sockets. He's still muttering the words that the assembly has been chanting, but his face is beginning to glow. The view of Adarvan is subtly changing. His face is being lit by unseen sunlight. I know the source of the light, but no one else does. Some of the local Eternals have stopped their chanting and are just staring open-mouthed at the sight of their compatriot, glowing with daylight.

The whole group sends up awed shouts when the sun suddenly appears overhead in the night sky.

Zurvan is bridging the Neverwhere and reality and even the Eternals are starting to see his world. He's crossing over, but the Neverwhere is coming with him.

A deep, metallic moan echoes over the hills and I turn to look for its source. The *Starfire Epiphany* has begun to glow brighter. Lights around its perimeter have intensified, scattering beams of blue and purple across the sky. The moan repeats from somewhere inside it and something else is changing too. In the gullies and valleys between the ship and us, fog has begun to appear—iridescent, colored fog, wicking out of the landscape.

"This can't continue," Melchior shouts. "This isn't the way!"

One of the Eternals guarding us strikes Melchior across the face and knocks him down. He sprawls at my feet. I squat down to try to help him, but with my hands tied behind my back there's little I can do.

Melchior rolls onto his side and looks up at me. "Ben, you have to stop him. You're the only one who can." He's looking straight at me and I know it's not the real world version of me he's addressing. "He's bringing too much back. If he bridges time and the Neverwhere like this, there's no telling what damage will result."

There is a crack like thunder across the sky and the Eternals around us jitter and yell. Some of the less devout members flee or cower on the ground, arms over their heads.

I concentrate on Melchior. "How do I stop him?"

"Get him out of here. We'll try to disrupt the ritual on our end."

Mym drops to a squat beside me and rolls onto her back, sliding her bound arms beneath her legs and popping back up to her feet so fast that I've barely had time to react. With her hands still tied, but now in front of her, she hauls Melchior to his feet. "Go, Ben!"

THE DAY AFTER NEVER

I concentrate on the strange sun in the dark sky above us and hurl myself back into the Neverwhere.

I'm back in daylight. Zurvan is in the same position as Adarvan was, arms spread, eyes aloft. Fog is rolling across the fiery lake now. It's oozing out of the rocks and crevices, a thousand different colors shimmering inside it.

I need to get him away. Another memory. Somewhere far away from here.

How? Can I really move him? I recall my fight with Benny and realize there is only one way to find out.

I extend my hands and concentrate. The memory comes, washing over the scene and covering Zurvan and me both. It's St. Petersburg again. The waterfront park that lines the bay near my house. "Ha!" I yell, elated at my victory.

Zurvan, jolted out of his connection with his living self, opens his eyes and screams in rage. "No!" He throws out his arms and immediately changes the scene back to the fiery lakeside in Azerbaijan. He's frustrated though. The link to his other self has been broken, at least momentarily.

I throw my hands out and change the scene again. I know I need a stronger memory this time, so I choose the baseball diamond where my friends and I play softball every week. I know it as well as any location in the city.

Zurvan looks around the softball field and blinks with fury. He snarls and aims a hand toward me. I'm ready—this time changing the memory to a walled space, an Irish pub downtown that I frequent with friends. I land inside the pub in the memory, while Zurvan is left outdoors on the far side of the widows. I don't know how long I can dodge him like this, but I hope I'm providing enough of a distraction. It's up to the others now.

"I've made enemies as a time traveler, some with truly evil intentions. While it sometimes bothers me that I can't truly undo their existence or permanently rid the world of their evil, it gives me consolation that they will never be rid of me either."-Journal of Dr. Harold Quickly, 2154

CHAPTER 23

Absheron Peninsula, 3500 BCE

My other self has left my head. Mym is helping Melchior to his feet amid the chaos around us. I attempt to duplicate her technique, rolling onto my back and sliding my bound arms underneath me to try to free them. Mym pulls Melchior into the crowd of confused and awe-struck disciples before Elgin's Eternals have time to stop her. The guard who struck Melchior has spotted me, however, and the look in his eye is not friendly. I struggle to work my feet between my arms, cursing my lack of flexibility and vowing that if I make it out of this I'll take up yoga.

The guard is on me too fast. His first response to my escape attempt is a punch to my face that sends me rolling. He rears his fist back, ready for a second strike, when Doctor Quickly barrels into him, shoulder lowered. The Eternal lets out a grunt and flails sideways, toppling over. Doctor Quickly still has his hands tied behind his back. He looks down at me. "Go, Ben. Run!"

I frantically wriggle my hands past my shoes and stumble to my feet. The Eternal is on his feet now too, and one of his companions has caught on to what is happening. The second Eternal grabs Doctor Quickly while the first comes charging at me. I bolt for the nearest opening I see in the crowd. The local Eternals don't impede my progress. The one chasing me shouts out demands that they stop me, but since he's yelling in English, his efforts are wasted and I quickly lose him in the crowd. Only a few locals seem to even care about my flight. Most are still intent on the activity on the altar. Many are still chanting, dutifully following the ritual set out for them.

I risk a glance at the altar. Adarvan is still there, but he seems to have lost his concentration. His eyes are no longer flickering like they were before. "All right, Ben," I mutter. "Keep it up."

The flashing lights of the *Starfire Epiphany* have dimmed again.

Elgin signals the faithful surrounding the altar, entreating them to continue, and the chanting increases in volume. Mym shouts for me from somewhere in the crowd, and I spot her waving toward me from a dozen yards ahead. One of the enraptured Eternals I pass behind is stretching on his tiptoes to try to see what's happening at the altar. I spot a rugged-looking knife tucked into the belt of his robes and yank it loose as I sprint by. I'm not as sly as I had hoped. It takes him a moment to realize what has happened, but unfortunately, when he turns and yells about the theft, it's in a language everyone understands. I've barely had time to cut the first of the strands that bind my wrists, when I'm tackled by two Eternals. I hit the ground hard and the knife flies out of my grip. When I roll over, all I see is a sea of angry faces.

Zurvan is mad. He's chased me through three more memories now and is getting closer to catching me. He finally tires of trying to fight on my turf and attempts to change the scene to the St. Petersburg of the future, the broken city, full of storm clouds, floodwaters, and ruin. I fight back with memories of my own, my city from 2009, fending off the torrents of water he hurls at me, keeping them at bay with my own view of the city. He's now pursuing me down Fourth Street, the site of our very first encounter.

Zurvan is powerful, but I've gotten stronger too. Each time he attempts to stretch out and crush my mind, I'm able to move, throw him off just enough that he has to adjust. He's more distracted this time too, frustrated at my interference and wanting to get back to his main task. Adarvan is waiting for him, and as long as I'm interfering, there's no chance at keeping a connection.

It's a dangerous game I'm playing, but it seems to be working.

"You can't run forever, Ben," he shouts at me. "You're only delaying the inevitable. I *am* leaving. When I return to my full power, your other self won't be able to save you."

"Come get me then," I call back.

Zurvan scowls at me. He takes a few steps forward. I'm readying another memory, prepared to dodge again, but this time Zurvan stops. "No. I see what you're doing, and I'm not going to play your games. You know you can't stop me, so you've left it up to your friends—the other you and the girl. They're your true plan. But they're also your weakness." Zurvan changes the scene back to the desert lake, back to the altar and Adarvan.

I prepare another memory to disrupt the meditation again, but this time Zurvan doesn't bother with a subtle connection, ghosting back to the real world, he plunges straight into his younger self's mind and forcibly seizes control. Adarvan recoils in pain at first, but Zurvan takes over. From atop the altar, this wild-eyed, possessed Adarvan searches the crowd until he spots a group of Eternals hauling my other self to his feet.

"KILL HIM!" His finger stabs at the other me and he repeats the exhortation in his native language. The Eternals who have been fixated on the altar in a state of awe, now turn on my other self with feverish eyes, intent on obeying their newly resurrected god.

"NO!" I leap forward as one of the Eternals lashes out and strikes him. The other me staggers backward and nearly falls. His eyes are wide with fear. As the Eternals close in on him, I stretch for his mind and make the leap back.

The Eternal that drags me to my feet shouts something I don't understand, then heads all turn toward the altar. Adarvan is looking at me, pointing a finger in my direction. "KILL HIM!"

Oh shit.

"It was just a knife, guys!" I manage, before one of the local Eternals punches me in the gut. I stumble backward and am caught by a different Eternal. The circle closes in on me and I squirm out of my captor's grip to give myself a fighting chance. Despite my efforts with the knife, my hands are still tied. As one of the Eternals takes another swing at me, I dodge right, but there is nowhere to go. I'm hemmed in with only a few feet of space in which to maneuver.

These guys aren't very tall. Five thousand years of evolution and better diet has yet to take effect, so these men are all at least a foot shorter than me. Due to my height and size, it doesn't look like any one individual wants the job of taking me on. Collectively however, they are a different story.

A walking staff lashes out from the crowd, grazing my shoulder. Another man attempts to trip me. A third has drawn a knife and is looking for a chance to use it. If I go down, it's going to be all over.

Suddenly my other self is back inside my head. "Look out!" he yells.

I dodge a swing from someone else's walking stick. "What happened to you!"

"Zurvan is coming back. I couldn't stop him."

I glance up at the altar. Adarvan has his hands to his head and seems to be wracked with pain. He no longer looks excited about being the host of their lord and savior. The sky flickers. The sun and the darkness are again dueling overhead.

The feet of the men around me are now shrouded with fog.

THE DAY AFTER NEVER

Something strikes me in the back of the leg and I stagger. A stone glances off my head, causing me to reel forward farther and a second hits me in the chest. Winded, I drop to a knee. The man with the knife comes at me and I manage to grab his wrist with my bound hands, stopping the blade before it can impale me. It's just one knife among many, however. As the swarm of bodies presses in on me, I know it's only a matter of moments till some other blade finds its way between my ribs.

And then she's there. Walking staff hissing through the air and thudding into the forearm of the man with the knife. The man howls with pain.

"Leave him alone!" Mym swings again and sends the man flailing back into the crowd with a blow to his head. She and Melchior clear the area around me.

Melchior wields his staff with precision, knocking away Eternals with blows to shins and skulls. Mym lacks his technique but makes up for it in ferocity. She has gotten her hands untied and is swinging away with staves in both hands, raining blows on anyone foolish enough to confront her. The ring of attackers falls back from their onslaught.

Mym tosses one staff to me. I fumble it and it lands at my feet. With the two of them holding the Eternals at bay, I pry at the ropes binding my hands with my teeth and am finally able to get myself loose. I snatch up the walking staff.

"Thanks," I sputter.

"I need to get back to the ship." Melchior says. "The Labyrinth weapon they've used is limiting the ship's safety functions. If it can't regulate itself, it will never withstand the strain. Adarvan being here is going to tear a hole in time."

Up on the altar, Zurvan is paying little attention to the groans and flashing lights from the ship. He's intent on himself and his new body. The strange, out-of-place sun in the sky above us is beginning to fade away. Zurvan is nearly free of the Neverwhere. Elgin and Longcase are at his side immediately, vying for his attention. An old man and a young man, both eager to please.

Zurvan looks around his new world. It's a chaotic blend of activity. Elgin's Eternals are gathered closest to the altar, with the locals spread out in little clumps behind. Some have fled, not able to handle the strangeness of the ritual and the disturbing sights in the sky. Some are casting worried glances at the fog that has thickened around them. It's getting difficult to even see all of their brethren now. The colored fog has obscured the far side of the fiery lake. There is a line of better visibility between the altar and the ship, but most of the hills are now too engulfed by the fog to be seen.

Zurvan studies the group of Eternals surrounding us. They are still looking for an opportunity to attack me and fulfill their master's orders, but Melchior and Mym are flanking me on either side, making a defensive triangle.

"Come here, Ben!" Zurvan shouts. "Don't you want to see my triumphant return? I told you I would be leaving the Neverwhere behind. You need to be in my good graces now more than ever."

None of us move.

"No? Have it your way, then. Bring me the scientist!"

There is a commotion at the side of the altar and a pair of Eternals drag Doctor Quickly up the steps on that side. His hands are still bound behind his back.

The young Zurvan reaches into his robes and extracts something I recognize. The long, curved knife he used to kill Benny.

"Dad!" Mym yells. She races toward him. The Eternals separate and make way for her. I follow, staff still raised, trying to watch her back. When we reach the base of the steps, we're stopped by Elgin's Eternals.

Zurvan is smiling down at us from the altar.

"You see, that wasn't so difficult," Zurvan says. "So many gifts you've brought me today, Ben. So many gifts." He considers Doctor Quickly. "It's only fitting really that you all should be here." Zurvan cocks his head slightly and looks at me. "Do you feel it? Do you feel the way time is all tied up in me now? The Neverwhere. This place. Here at the dawn of civilization. It's all mine now. Mine to do with what I want."

He turns toward Elgin and Longcase. "And you, my most faithful disciples. You carried my message all the way into the past. Such good servants. You found my body and brought me my ship."

Longcase jumps at the chance to speak. "We have been honored to bear your words through time, my lord. The Eternal Line of Gnomon stands ready to join you in a new future."

"And you shall," Zurvan says. "You all shall. Because everything you are is now mine."

Elgin frowns, just for a moment, but whatever reservation passes his mind, it's too late. Zurvan extends his hands toward each of them and they both grimace in pain. Their hands fly to their skulls as Zurvan tilts his head back, channeling them into himself. He pulls at their minds, not touching them, but connecting to them just the same. Their mouths fly open, but their screams are immediately silenced.

"Holy shit," I mutter.

As Elgin and Longcase collapse to the floor, the Eternals around us

THE DAY AFTER NEVER

begin to murmur. Most of the locals won't have understood anything he said, since he spoke in English, but the sight of the two Eternals lying lifeless on the floor is enough. The Eternals Elgin brought with him are positively at a loss for what to do now. Not sure if they should continue to guard Doctor Quickly or flee, they hesitate.

Zurvan is smiling, relishing the new memories and knowledge he's just absorbed. He looks at me again. "And now, Ben, I take it all." He throws out his hands and the light around us dims. Fog gushes out of the hillsides, swallowing the remaining hills and the view of the gathered Eternals. Zurvan's will impacts inside my head, reaching for the roots of my soul. Mym stumbles backward into me. She screams.

Doctor Quickly goes to a knee, hands to his skull. The Eternals around us flail and yell from this sudden invasion of their minds. I can feel him inside my head, but I can feel them too. All of us, being pulled in one direction. Mym is cringing in front of me, but I can also feel her inside my mind. The terror she's experiencing, the worry, but also the hope. She's fighting back, holding on to her mind with every ounce of strength she has. She wants to live, and I desperately need her to. I realize I'm holding her hand.

The *Starfire Epiphany* flares brightly behind us, flashing colors like a strobe light.

There is a sensory overload going on in my mind. The world around me is flooding with the shimmering fog, so thick now that I can't see the people to either side of me. I only see Mym, the steps ahead of me, and the glowing silhouette of Zurvan at the top of the altar, backlit by the glow of the lake. I've felt this pain in my mind before, this attempted theft of my soul, but Zurvan is weaker this time, spread out and diluted across a hundred other minds, all trying to resist him. I take the only path left to me.

I release Mym's hand and run, leaping up the steps and hurling myself forward, throwing everything I have at my timeless enemy. There is nothing left but this.

Zurvan still has his arms spread wide, knife in one hand, head tilted back as he fights to take every mind he's connected to. I hit him in the center of his chest. I haven't planned for how much momentum I would have. I crash into him with every bit of strength left in me. Zurvan's feet come off the ground. His eyes fly open as we both go sailing off the edge of the altar—into the lake of fire.

For a moment I see our reflection, our two bodies plummeting out of a starry sky into a darkness rimmed with flame. We are the living embodiment of two worlds, the here and the beyond.

The water swallows us both.

Dark. Salty. Surprisingly cold.

I struggle to see under the water. We are a churning mass of limbs and bubbles.

I've broken Zurvan's concentration. Now my priority is the knife.

I search the darkness until I find his left arm. Zurvan is kicking, trying to fight his way to the surface. I suspect I've knocked a lot of the wind out of him with our fall. I'd like to keep it that way.

I don't know how much damage Zurvan has managed to inflict on the others. It could be that he has already stolen the other souls on the shore. What I do know is that he is no longer a god of the Neverwhere. He's human again. And humans have to breathe.

Zurvan flails—young, strong, and full of rage. He pries at me under the water, hitting me with his free hand and trying to get me to relinquish my hold on his arm. His grip on the silvery blade is still strong. Too strong. I can't pry it from his grip.

I finally realize I won't be able to keep us down any longer either. He kicks hard and we both emerge into the night air, gasping and sputtering as we send waves and flames dancing across the surface.

Zurvan is rejuvenated. We go under again, but he's fighting harder now, determined to get his knife arm free. He plants a foot against my abdomen and pushes. I strain against him, but know I won't be able to hold on much longer. When he gets loose he'll have the advantage. He has the knife.

He also has my chronometer.

My fingers work fast on the dials.

Set the rings. Set the timer.

He kicks against me again and this time I push myself loose from him as well.

Five.

Swim hard. Push with everything.

Four.

Get away. Don't let him touch me. Kick through the darkness.

Three.

I surface to breathe and he's there, splashing after me now. Knife gleaming in the starlight.

Two.

I'm at the rocks, fingers scrabbling at the jagged rim of the lake, searching for a way up. He's almost to me.

One.

Hands stretch for me from the darkness. Mym. Doctor Quickly. I clasp their wrists and let them pull me up.

Blink.

I turn my head just in time to see him for one final instant—mere feet away. His face is a mask of fury, his hand reaching for me.

And then he's gone.

Out of time.

"A great danger to time travelers is that the ability to be anywhere, anytime, suggests to some that they must be everywhere, all at once. If there is one thing I have learned, it's that the ability to see the past or future does not make one better at handling the present. Sometimes here, and now, should be the only two items on your mind." -Journal of Dr. Harold Quickly, Dec 24, 1986

CHAPTER 24

Absheron Peninsula, 3500 BCE

Mym has her arms wrapped around me.

She's safe and whole.

She's real.

I never want to let her go.

I exhale the tension from my body and turn around, dripping all over the rocks. Doctor Quickly is staring at the water.

"Where did you send him?"

I watch the flames dancing over the spot where Zurvan disappeared. "I think it was an hour into the future. I couldn't really see the chronometer, but it was something close to that." Little waves slosh against the rocks, and I imagine what's going to happen when Zurvan reappears and is fused with water from all different parts of the lake. I'm suddenly worried. *Will Doctor Quickly and Mym think I'm horrible for having condemned him to such a gruesome fate?*

The worry is short-lived. Doctor Quickly kicks a stone into the water, sending cascading ripples across the lake and further disrupting the water. "Good riddance."

Mym tightens her arm around me. "Thank you for stopping him." She looks up at me and studies my face. "Which one of you am I talking to?"

Staring into her eyes, I realize I don't know. "I'm not . . ."

The realization that I can simultaneously remember both realities grips me, and for a second it makes me dizzy trying to wrap my mind around it, but Mym is there at my elbow to steady me.

"Are you okay?"

Looking back at her, I realize that I really am. I'm just me again. I stare up at the night sky. No sun. No Neverwhere. I'm just alive.

I put my arms around Mym and kiss her. I don't stop until Doctor Quickly clears his throat.

THE DAY AFTER NEVER

"Bit of a mess we've made."

I tear my eyes away from Mym. The view around the lakeside is drastically changed.

The fog is gone.

Clumps of Eternals are still recovering from the attack by Zurvan. None of them attempt to stop us as we pick our way across the rocks. There are a few people who aren't getting up. Most seem to have survived, however, and are helping one another away from the vicinity of the altar. Atop the steps, the bodies of Elgin and Longcase are still lying prone on the floor. I climb the steps and check them for any signs of life, but when I press my fingers to Elgin's wrist, I get no pulse.

I also notice that Doctor Quickly's chronometer is gone. Mym's pendant chronometer and ring have disappeared as well. It's hard to say if one of Elgin's Eternals nabbed them or if it was one of the locals with especially light fingers, but it's clear from the number of people retreating into the hills that we're unlikely to see them again. I inform Doctor Quickly about the theft when we descend the steps.

"Well, unless they discover someone with a chronometer charger, they won't be getting especially far," he says. "And we're a few thousand years away from the nearest one I know of."

Searching the area, I see no sign of Melchior, but the *Starfire Epiphany* has stopped shedding beams of light from its sides. When we climb the hillside and approach the ship, we find Melchior outside, smashing the last fragments of the Labyrinth machine against a boulder.

"How is she?" Doctor Quickly asks.

Melchior stomps on a chunk of the machine and grinds it into the dirt with his heel. "He almost destroyed her, but she's still with us." He kicks away the now useless trash and turns to look at his ship. "She's done a lot of incredible things in her day," he says. "But I think today will top the list." He runs a hand along the ship's outside hull. "She held the fabric of space and time together for us against all odds. We owe her now more than ever."

When Melchior turns away from the ship, he locks his eyes on me. "Ah. I see you've come out of this all right, too. One less consciousness adrift in the Neverwhere."

I still don't know how he can tell, but I nod. "I'm not sure what happened, but I'm not complaining."

"I told you what needed to happen. You just needed to be single-minded and stop trying to control one another. Looks like you found the one, strong enough motivation that both of you were willing to sacrifice control of your life for."

I grip Mym's hand in mine. "I guess all it took was a psychopathic, immortal magi from the future trying to hurt the girl I love. Surprised it didn't happen sooner."

Mym looks up at me and smiles. Her blue eyes are sparkling. "So you love me?"

I squeeze her hand a little tighter. "More than life."

The *Starfire Epiphany* still flies. Melchior says there will need to be repairs, but she'll hold together well enough to get us home. Which home we choose is a bit of a question mark.

"Unless we take the comet back out to the Oort cloud to find another ride into the solar system, we're stuck using Borisov C/2014 Q3," Melchior explains. "We can make the extra jumps and try to make the transition to a different comet, but I'd prefer to have as few entries and exits as we can until I can get some repairs done. Problem is, that only leaves us 151 year windows to drop you off in. Do you want to go back to 2165, or would you prefer I leave you in 2014? I need to go retrieve my crew, but I think I could manage a stop along the way."

I consult with Mym. I've personally had enough of the future and would prefer something closer to home. 2014 will have to do. Mym seconds the decision.

After we've hitched the ride on the comet and are heading back inbound for Earth, I finally have a chance to ask Melchior a question that has been bouncing around in my mind since I've been aboard. I catch him near a meta window looking down at the steadily growing view of Earth.

"You said your mission as a Magi was to visit moments of spiritual significance in human history. Does that mean that there was someone significant that you were coming to see in 2165 when we met you?"

Melchior puts his hands up the sleeves of his robes again and crosses his arms. "We were looking into a moment in history that affected all of us. That day in 2165 was the beginning of something new and incredible in your timestream. It was a moment of enlightenment that would affect the entire human race."

"Who was it? Some sort of prophet or something?"

"She was a revolutionary," Melchior says. "One of the first great minds of her kind."

"What do you mean?"

"She was a synth. The first synth in the burgeoning social revolution to see the spiritual accomplishments of the human race as worth preserving. While other synthetic uprisings across the Fractal Universe merely assimilated the human race, or fought to destroy it, she sought to understand it. She recognized that even a superior synthetic intelligence from the future could still learn from its past. She started a movement within the evolution of synthetic consciousness that would one day have a profound impact on the way it dealt with the end of our civilization.

"When the synth collective mind in this timestream learned of the destruction of the planet at the hands of Zurvan, they didn't abandon humanity as happened in other timestreams. They began constructing ships. Ships that could travel back in time and escape the black hole. They decided that they would collect and preserve the best of humanity's collective knowledge and ferry it to safety, out among the stars."

"You mean she created the Magi?"

Melchior smiles. "The Magi are merely the hands they use to do their work. These ships themselves are the true vessels of humanity." He looks up at the walls of the sphere around us. "You are looking at the future of the human race, Ben. These ships now carry the best of our history and the greatest revelations mankind has experienced in our brief time on Earth. They represent our collective consciousness at the peak of our evolution. They mean to save us and give us a future."

"So a synth revolutionary in Port Nyongo was the start of the entire chain of events that led to the preservation of the human race?"

"Indeed."

"Do you happen to know her name?"

"I do. She was a cargo pilot turned social catalyst. Her name was Captain Mira Jumptree."

"Holy shit."

Melchior studies me. "Do you know her?"

"Did she happen to mention *why* she had a change of heart about the human race? She didn't mention any particular person that inspired her new outlook, did she?"

"We don't know. That was one of the things we were hoping to investigate. If there was a particular human in 2165 that convinced her that humanity's achievements were worth saving, I suspect they would be a very unique individual. Well worth meeting."

I smile and put my hands in my pockets. "If unique is what you're looking for, I don't think you'll be disappointed."

The *Starfire Epiphany* enters the atmosphere late at night and descends us over the Gulf of Mexico. I'm not sure what wizardry Melchior and the ship employ, but we enter United States airspace uncontested. No fighters scramble from McDill Air Force Base. Air traffic control in Tampa seems unperturbed by our presence. Perhaps to them we are merely a meteor, or perhaps they see nothing at all.

The ship lands on a deserted stretch of Fort De Soto State Park at the bottom of the peninsula. The only welcome we get as we open the boarding ramp is curious stares from a pair of portly raccoons.

"Thank you, Ben Travers," the ship addresses me as Mym and I begin to descend the ramp. "Thank you for helping me."

"I didn't do much," I reply. "Melchior disabled the Labyrinth."

"You did what needed to be done for all of us," the ship replies. "I hope we will meet again."

I search the walls around the boarding ramp, not sure where to address her. "I hope so too."

To my surprise, Doctor Quickly doesn't step off the bottom of the ramp with us.

"I need to get back to 2165, to check on Carson, as well as Professor Chun," he explains. "But also, Melchior has made me quite a tempting offer." He gestures toward the Magus. "He's invited me to come have a look around time with him aboard his ship. We'll need repairs first, of course, and I'll need to pick up a few things for the trip. But since it seems like you are back in good hands with one another, I thought it might be an opportunity to do a bit of exploring." He searches his daughter's face. "Would you miss me too terribly?"

"We will miss you," Mym replies. "But of course you should go. It's the sort of opportunity you've been looking for your whole life."

"You are invited to join as well," Melchior adds. "You both would be welcome."

Mym has her arm wrapped around my waist and tilts her head to look up at me. "Ben? What do you think?"

I read the look on her face and I know my answer immediately. "It's a wonderful invitation," I reply. "For the moment, I think we'll just take a little time with each other."

Melchior nods. "I thought you might say that." He smiles and descends the ramp to say goodbye. Doctor Quickly is smiling as well. There are warm embraces and assurances that we'll meet up soon, and then the *Starfire Epiphany* is back on its way. Mym and I sit on the beach watching its flight back over the gulf and we stay there long after it's gone, till there are only stars and waves and the cool night breeze to keep us company.

The sun has risen by the time we make it back to a main road. We walk for a long time before we're picked up by a pair of friendly fishermen willing to share the cab of their truck. They are headed a different direction after the bridge, but drop us at a bus stop and spot us the money for the fare the rest of the way.

It's a strange feeling to be back in a time I recognize. I keep glancing at the city skyline, making sure it's still the way I recall. There might be a few additions in 2014 that weren't there in 2009, but no solar arrays or space elevators punctuate the horizon.

When we step off the bus in my neighborhood, I look around and relish the changes.

The neighborhood is noisy. The good kind of noisy. Dogs are barking in yards. Occasional cars rumble along the brick streets with inefficient, gas-powered engines. A plane passes overhead. No drones. No starships. Not yet.

Mym is still holding my hand. Since we've been back on the surface of the planet we've been like this. Connected. Alive. We haven't talked a lot. We've just been content to be with each other.

When we reach my street, I turn the corner and take in the view of my apartment. My pick-up truck is parked in the driveway. Mym puts her hand on my arm.

"You sure you want to do this? We've still got options. We could go to my dad's and pick up a chronometer. You could still go back to 2009 and pick up right where you left off."

I put an arm around her and kiss the top of her head. "This is better. This way I get to see. I think Melchior was right. If we're really going to do this life as time travelers together, then I'm going to have to let go of trying to control everything. It's time to embrace the future."

She arches an eyebrow. "After all you've seen, you call 2014 the future?"

"Well, hey. It's baby steps, but I'm making them, right?"

She looks back to my apartment. "Okay. Let's see what happens when Ben Travers has been gone for five years."

The spare key is still under the flowerpot.

When I swing the door open I'm not sure what to expect. I'm fearing the worst, but the apartment is still much how I remember it. The TV is new. Bigger. Flatter. A few pictures on the wall have changed. Someone has subscribed to some martial arts magazines. There is a calendar on the wall with a date circled in heavy black ink. I realize it's today's date.

"Hello?" I call.

A door opens in the hallway and my other self walks out. Benji. He's aged a bit, but it's hard to say if it's equivalent to how long I've been gone. He's wearing ripped jeans and a faded T-shirt. He's grown a beard.

"Hey," I manage.

He leans against the wall. "About damn time. This is the real one, right? Home to stay?"

"Maybe. Not making any decisions about that yet."

Benji slouches away from the wall. "Well, I have." He disappears into the back bedroom briefly, then comes back out carrying a duffel bag, already packed. He sets it by the door, then goes back into the bedroom, this time returning with a backpack. He's also now wearing my leather jacket. "I've paid all the bills for this month. Phone's on the coffee table. The phone is new, but the number's the same. Gassed up the truck and the bike. You should be set to go."

"Uh, thanks. Wait, the bike? You got it back?"

"Oh. Right. A few years ago this kid showed up with a dude made of metal riding the motorcycle. They had a dog in the sidecar. Said you knew them and they were bringing back your bike."

"Jonah and Darius? Holy crap. What else did they say?"

"I don't know. I'm not your message service. You want to talk to them you can go find them. Said they'd be around the area for a bit. They wanted to see the sights in the twentieth century, so apparently they had your bike on tour. Said they might stop back by in a few years. Not sure how a kid, a robot, and a dog managed to roam around this century without getting arrested, but I figured that's their business."

I smile at the thought of Darius getting to share an adventure with Jonah. "I knew that kid would turn out all right."

"Sure. Works out for everybody." Benji moves toward the door. I spot the chronometer on his wrist.

"Hey, wait. You can't go yet."

"Why the hell not?"

"What's the big hurry?" I ask. "You have to leave right this second? I thought you were all gung-ho about being back at work and getting to have a normal life."

Benji glances at Mym, then back to me. "Look. I told you I'd take care of the place while you were gone. I did. Our business is concluded. I just decided I don't want to stick around."

"What did you do?"

"Nothing."

"Are the cops going to come knock down the door as soon as you go and arrest me for whatever you've been up to?"

THE DAY AFTER NEVER

"Cops? Please. I'm still a time traveler. You think I'd be stupid enough to get caught doing something the police could catch me for?"

"Well, you're getting out of here in an awful hurry. What trouble did you get into that's worse than—" I freeze, the memory of the phone conversation I watched him make coming back to me. "Francesca. You're running from Francesca. Or was it Kaylee you pissed off? What did you do, man?"

"How did you—" Benji studies me sideways for a moment. "Francesca and I were—Look, whatever. That was my business. You weren't around so you don't get an opinion."

I feel like telling him that I *was* around, but the idea of explaining my ghostly eavesdropping on his life doesn't feel like a conversation he'd be ready for.

"Look. You can go. I'm not going to stop you. But I need you to do me a favor."

"What kind of favor?" he growls.

I think about the shack in the desert where I first met him. The grizzled old time traveler who showed me how to survive. He's still a lot of years away from being that man, but I'm convinced it's him.

"It's a long-term sort of favor. It's going to take a while. But you do get to own some real estate in California."

Benji's expression is quizzical. "Why would I want to be involved in this favor?"

"Because whatever you did to Francesca, this would make it up to her."

Benji frowns. "What makes you think I owe her anything?"

"Because you're me. So I know how much she means to you. Sooner or later you'll want a chance to make things right."

Benji snatches up his duffle bag and slings it over his shoulder. "Fine. Maybe I'll be back. Eventually. You can explain your grand plan for my romantic rehabilitation then. Looks like you've got your own love life to figure out." He nods toward Mym. "Good luck, Miss Quickly. He's your problem now."

"Hey, wait up a second," I say.

"What now?"

"I need that jacket back."

Benji looks down at the leather jacket and frowns. "You left it with the motorcycle. I figured you didn't need it anymore. I really like it."

"I know you do. I got it from you in the first place. That's why you can't have it."

"What?"

"If you keep it, it will create an ontological paradox. If I got it from you and you got it from me then where would it have originally come from? It would be a closed loop. You have to get your own."

"That sounds like a fancy bullshit way for you to justify keeping this jacket because it's cool."

"Can't argue with time travel science, man."

Benji reluctantly shrugs out of the jacket and gives it back. "Fine, I'll get my own. But it's still some sneaky bullshit."

I just grin back at him.

With that, my other self brushes past me and disappears down the stairs.

Mym and I listen to his footsteps vanish in the distance and I hang the jacket back on the coat rack. I smile at Mym. "About time one of these paradoxes worked out in my favor."

Mym smiles back and steps closer to lean against me. "Hard to believe you might have turned out like that."

"Eh. It's not all his fault." I put my arm around her. "He never had you."

I wake up in my own bed after perhaps the most restful sleep of my life. No nightmares. No Neverwhere. Just sleep, and Mym to wake up to. We do absolutely nothing all morning and it's glorious. No one interrupts us. No unexpected visitors drop by with messages from the future. We manage to finish an entire movie in our pajamas and I can almost convince myself that I'm really home. I make Mym a leisurely lunch and, when we're done eating, I'm finally ready to admit to being back. I call Blake.

He's over within the hour. Mallory is working, but he doesn't wait for her. I get a hug as soon as he walks in the door.

"If I'd have known today was your homecoming day, we could have been waiting with a surprise party," Blake says. "Mallory is going to tell me I totally botched this."

"I wouldn't have wanted one. This was better. You'll have to trust me."

"Good to have you home, man. Oh, Mallory reminded me to give this to you." Blake pulls a slightly rumpled envelope from his pocket and hands it to me. The paper is thick and formal. I slide a finger under the flap and tear it open.

"You got me a welcome home card?" I smile, then pull the thick piece of paper out of the envelope. It takes me a moment to process the text written across it in elaborate calligraphy. *The honor of your presence is requested at the wedding of Miss Mallory Watson and . . ."*

"Dude! Your wedding?" I fumble at the card. "That's super exciting!" I feel my grin fade when I read the date. "Oh shit. This was four years ago." I look up and for the first time notice the ring on Blake's finger. "Oh God, I'm so sorry, man. I'm such a jerk. I totally missed it."

"The hell you did. Your speech was the highlight of the reception." Blake is smiling. "Not that I should be swelling your head. It's got to be big enough what with saving the world for . . . how many times are you up to now?"

"Speech? You mean I get to be best man? You do mean me, right? Not . . ."

"The D.O.B. got to sit that event out," Blake replies.

"That's so cool. Thank you. You didn't happen to save a copy of that speech did you? Might save me a lot of writing." I grin. Blake pretends to be offended. "I'm just kidding," I add. "I have plenty of ammo— I mean, stories, to tell people about you."

Blake laughs. It's a wonderful sound.

Mym joins us and I show her the invitation. "So I guess I haven't totally missed the last five years after all."

"We've gotten used to you two bouncing around," Blake replies. "We stopped trying to welcome you home after the first few visits. We knew the real day you got back was going to happen, but you never told us when. Why'd you pick 2014?"

I take Mym's hand. "Long story, but I finally decided to get with the times." I smile at the sight of my friend looking so happy. "So we've been back before, huh? What about Carson, have you heard from him?"

"He didn't tell you? He's got a job in the future. He's working with a couple of bounty hunters. Doctor Quickly hired them to go hunt down some of his missing chronometers. Carson jumped at the chance."

"Carson works with Eon and Rixon?"

"Apparently their first assignment is going after the alternate version of Elton Stenger. The one that killed Carson and stole his chronometer in the '80s. Then I heard they're going to track down Guy and Lawrence Friday. Kind of wish I could be there to see that."

"Wow," I manage. "Don't envy those guys what's coming. Good for Carson. He did always want to settle that score."

"So what about you two?" Blake says. "Is this it? No more kinks in the timeline to set straight? You finally get your life back?"

I smile at Mym. "Actually, I decided the most essential part of my life wasn't really about the when so much as the who. We're just going to take our time and see where we end up."

Mym squeezes my hand.

I turn back to Blake. "Speaking of which. I do have one more thing I need to do before this is really over. I owe someone an important visit. You mind if I borrow your chronometer?"

"To suggest that time travelers never die is erroneous. We meet our ends often and sometimes painfully. But a life lived well can never be undone. In that way we are all immortal." -Journal of Dr. Harold Quickly, 1996

CHAPTER 25

St. Petersburg, 1986.

It's a long walk down the St. Petersburg pier in 1986. The colorful inverted pyramid at the end is still young, only a decade older than its architectural heyday in the '70s, but already out of its element. Thanks to my recent travels, I know it'll stand guard on the city's eastern shoreline for a few more decades until 2015, when progress will finally come calling.

Today, the pelicans and seagulls bombard the fishermen and dry themselves in the sun, oblivious to the impending demands of the future. There are no wrecking balls on the horizon, no grand plans for the next great thing that might upset their preening. This one sunny day has room enough for all of their aspirations.

On the far side of the pier, along a concrete wall studded with boat cleats, a petite, young blonde woman is seated cross-legged staring across the water at the distant shoreline.

I hesitate.

This Mym has had her world torn apart by a crazy man from my time and has ignored her father's mandate to let him go. She's tried to save him and failed, only making the situation worse. This Mym has just lost her dad for the most recent time, but despite the pain, she's not crying. She's simply staring. I don't know what she's thinking, but I know what I have to do.

Moving slowly, I wait for a pair of elderly tourists to pass on their bicycles before taking a seat next to her on the wall. She notices and watches me get settled. Her blue eyes seem to soak me in, studying my face and clothes, as if she can read all she needs to without even speaking. She turns back to the horizon and lets her hands rest on the edge of the wall. "It's been a long time."

For her it has been.

Years.

A night of conversation under the stars. A hot air balloon journey. Fleeting moments full of promise, but no resolution. The only time she'd seen me before that was decades into her past. A little girl exploring a jungle—helping me find the things I'd lost. For me those memories are only a sliver of what we've shared together—mere opening chapters. I've seen so much more with her since. For this Mym, all of our recent adventures are a story yet to be lived.

I want to take her into my arms and kiss her, but I hold myself back. That's not what she needs right now.

"It's going to be okay. He's going to live."

She turns and searches my face. "You found it? You know the way to save him?"

"We'll save him together. We already have."

Mym's shoulders slowly relax as the strain of her failed attempts to rescue her father is lifted away. She tilts her face up toward the sun and closes her eyes. "Thank God."

I let her stay like that, eyes closed in the quiet, until I can't take it anymore. I slide my hand across the concrete so my fingers brush hers.

She doesn't pull her hand away. She lets me link my fingers over top of hers before she finally looks down. The worry in her expression has been replaced with something new. Something hopeful.

"So Dad is happy? He's okay?"

"He's the happiest I've ever seen him. Better than okay."

She searches for the truth in my eyes, testing the validity of what I've told her. Whatever she sees must convince her because she exhales her acceptance. "Okay."

I stare at Mym, wishing more than anything that I can tell her what she means to me, what we'll be together. We have a history, but this Mym still has a long way to go till then.

She seems to sense it anyway.

"Is this going to be something . . ."

"Significant?" I grin.

The corner of her mouth creeps upward and her eyes brighten. "What? What is it?"

"Nothing. It's just that the next time you see me, it'll be the first time I ever meet you. I'm going to make a total mess of it." I grip her hand a little tighter. "So maybe you can do me a favor and remember me like this instead."

"You want credit for the way you are now so I'll think better of your earlier self when I meet him?" Mym smiles. "I don't know if I can just let you off that easily."

I'm elated to see her smiling.

"I'm just trying to give my earlier self whatever chance for success he can get. He still has a lot to learn."

THE DAY AFTER NEVER

Mym smirks and lifts our entwined hands. "You must think you're pretty smooth this time then. Is this your best move? What if I'm not impressed yet?"

I laugh. "I guess that makes things even worse for my poor earlier self. Maybe I'm messing up his chances after all."

Mym stares off into the distance for a few moments, then releases my hand and pivots to face me. "Okay, since this is obviously so important to you, I'll give you another chance." She contorts her face into an expression of seriousness again. "We'll say we've never met. This is it. You get one shot to wow me."

"Wow you?"

"Well, yeah. If our entire future hinges on this meeting like you say it does, you'd better convince me to listen to you. If I'm just supposed to take your word for it, then you'd better show me why you're so great."

"Ha. So no pressure at all."

"You're the one who wanted this." She folds her hands in her lap. "Your best line better be pretty good."

I swing my legs up and straddle the wall, then slide toward her so our knees are touching as we face each other. Mym's eyes are sparkling now, her recent pain receding under this new barrage of hope. A barely suppressed smile plays on her lips.

I wrack my brain for something to say that could wow this impossible girl. I might have seen the end of the world and come back from beyond the grave, but her smiling eyes can still level me.

She tilts her head. "You've gotten awfully close, man I've never met. You'd better explain yourself."

I meet her gaze and hold my hand out. "Hello, Mym. I'm here to tell you about your future."

She regards my hand skeptically. "My future? I don't know . . . That just sounds crazy." She shakes her head and smirks at me. "Let me guess. You're in it?"

"Actually, yes."

"Has this line ever actually worked on anyone? What kind of gullible girls have you been—"

"Oh, forget this," I say. I reach out with both hands and pull her to me, one hand on her back, the other in her hair. I press my mouth to hers and breathe her in. Salt breeze and orange blossoms. Her right hand finds my face and the other clenches the front of my T-shirt. We pull each other tighter, each touch of our lips a fresh connection, a million unspoken hopes passing between them.

Finally we release one another. Our fingers trail down each other's bodies and link together in her lap. I keep my forehead pressed against Mym's.

"Okay. That's the best I've got. Maybe I'll never be smooth, but I promise I'll be all yours."

"Okay," Mym whispers. She brushes her fingertips over the chronometer on my wrist. They trace the outline of the ring of years. "I think that's a future worth waiting for."

I kiss her again, and when she finally pulls away, she's staring into my eyes. "You come walking out of nowhere. You tell me my future is all going to work out. You kiss me like you know all about me. Like we're going to be . . . Who are you, really?"

It's a complicated question with an even more complicated story for an answer. But it's one I know she'll want to experience all in her own time. So I just look her in the eyes and smile.

"I'm Ben Travers.

"I'm a time traveler."

ACKNOWLEDGEMENTS

Thank you for reading! The response from readers has been one of the most enjoyable aspects of writing this series. I could not have persevered without your fantastic support. Want to tell me your thoughts on this series? Drop me an email at nathan@nathanvancoops.com. If you enjoyed this book and would like to share the experience, please consider leaving a review on Amazon or Goodreads.

I am incredibly grateful:

For all the beta readers who read my early drafts and gave me feedback. Amy Bell, Amanda Bildeaux, Ryan S. Newman, Caroline Ruth Molloy, Elenora Sabin, Sylvia Walker, Dave Garton, Sam Natale, Chuck Scro, Dan Leaman, Tracy Haynie, Dr. Angela Pool-Funai, Sean Moynihan, Jeff Parrott, Robert Peyton, Paul Cross, Peter Monit, Matthew Snell, Cindy Scheffler, Tina Van Coops, Mike Hiltunen, Paul Sherman, Robina Tabberer, Janet Cervantes, Ray Wallace-Watson, Tonny Worstell, Brian Steele, Paul Ness, Jamie Rogers, Dennis McDonald, Thomas Maughan, Jonathan Bird, Jim Brown, Angela Sleigh, Angela Myers, and Dwight and Leslie Young. This book is much better because of your feedback.

For Rysa Walker, Simon Whistler, Mark Speed, T.Ellery Hodges, Jonathan Kile, April White, and all the other authors I have learned from during the course of this publishing process. Your knowledge and experience have been inspirational and a big part of the success of this series.

For my mom, who has been my devoted supporter and friend through this series, and also has been a tireless editor of my grammar and spelling for 30 years. You made me who I am and you make me a better writer with every book.

For Emily Young, my writers group partner, editor, and amazing friend. These past four years of writing may never have happened without your encouragement and support. It certainly wouldn't have been nearly as much fun.

For all the servers and wait-staff who kept me supplied with tacos and Arnold Palmers during the many hours in corners of restaurants typing away on my keyboard, especially Sam, Julie, Bethany, Rachel, Jolia, Hannah, Becca, Sydney, Liz, William, and Jessica.

For my wife, Stephanie Van Coops, whom I love more than life. Your support for my writing has been incredible. Thank you for teaching me what a real love story feels like. I can't wait for more adventures together.

ABOUT THE AUTHOR

Nathan Van Coops is a writer, airplane tinkerer, and imaginer of far-fetched things in St. Petersburg, Florida. His biggest plans for the coming year include writing lots more books and enjoying many, many more tacos. You can follow his writing and get updates on his new books at www.nathanvancoops.com and www.chronothon.com.

Printed in Great Britain
by Amazon